Frida's Cook

Frida's Cook

A Novel

FLORENCIA
ETCHEVES

PRIMERO
SUEÑO PRESS

ATRIA

New York Amsterdam/Antwerp London
Toronto Sydney/Melbourne New Delhi

PRIMERO
SUEÑO PRESS

ATRIA
An Imprint of Simon & Schuster, LLC
1230 Avenue of the Americas
New York, NY 10020

Originally published in Spain in 2022 by Editorial Planeta, S.A. as *La cocinera de Frida*

Published by arrangement with Editorial Planeta Mexicana S.A. de C.V.

Book & Film Rights Latin America

First Primero Sueño Press/Atria Books hardcover edition March 2026
PRIMERO SUEÑO PRESS / ATRIA BOOKS and colophon are registered trademarks of Simon & Schuster, LLC.

Interior design by Jill Putorti

Manufactured in the United States of America

1 3 5 7 9 10 8 6 4 2

Library of Congress Control Number has been applied for.

ISBN 978-1-6680-7615-6
ISBN 978-1-6680-7617-0 (ebook)

Preface

This book was born from a proposal from the editors at my Mexican publisher, Planeta México, who wanted me to write a novel with Frida Kahlo as a main character. As an Argentinian journalist who built her author career writing detective novels, this seemed like a wild proposal. As a fiction writer you can make up characters and stretch reality; that all changes when you insert real figures, especially ones as interesting and iconic as Frida Kahlo and Diego Rivera. Ultimately, I decided that writing about a distant time and a faraway country is a journey into the unknown. But if the traveling companions are Frida Kahlo and Diego Rivera, and the destination is Mexico, the challenge turns into an adventure.

FIRST PART

1

Buenos Aires, August 2018

My grandmother was an expert on other people's deaths. Mexicans have an intimate, almost carnal relationship with the art of dying, and that made her something of an authority on the subject. As though hoping to offend it or drive it away, she gave death mocking nicknames that turned it into a skeletal, hairless old crone: La Huesuda, La Parca, La Chingada, La Pelona. But no amount of defiance could hold off the inevitable.

"The party's going on without me, mi niña," she murmured as I rested my hand on hers. The powerful torrent of her voice had weakened to barely a trickle. "La Huesuda is close by; I've seen her. Can't you smell her?"

On the nightstand, a glass jar with water and slices of orange and ginger filled the room with the smell of citrus, an aroma that took me back to childhood afternoons, those hours sitting at my grandmother's kitchen table following her precise instructions: cut limes and grapefruits into nice thin slices, combine rosemary, bay, thyme, and mint in piles no bigger than my palm, and crush vanilla pods and cinnamon sticks in the stone mortar until you have a powder like fine sand. The alchemist who had taught me to make natural room fragrances was lying in bed, slumped back against the white pillowcases, swaddled up to her chest in one of those dark purple woolen blankets that make every geriatric bed look the same.

"I hope the exit is joyful, and I hope never to return," she declared.

I didn't know how to reply, so I made do with squeezing that bony hand, which time had worn down to the size of a child's, and eyed a pot of cream sitting next to the orange aromatizer. Opening it carefully, I sank my fingers into the gloopy white concoction; with my free hand, I pulled off the purple blanket and slowly slid back her nightdress.

My grandmother's legs still held their shape and tone. She had always claimed to have a ballerina's legs, and no one had ever dared refute it. The years had discolored her brown skin; any veins that were once hidden had started to show themselves, forming a pattern resembling a map scored by thin rivers that stretched from her ankles to her thighs, crossing her knees at either side. I followed those blue lines, depositing small dabs of moisturizing cream as I went. When her legs were covered in white dots, I used my palms to massage them, slowly but firmly. Every muscle, every pore, every inch. I paused at the birthmark on the side of her right thigh, just above the knee: a complete oval the size of a coin. My grandmother tended to wear skirts long enough to cover the spot but short enough to show off the perfect curves of her calves. But on hot summer nights, her thin muslin nightdresses allowed me a glimpse of that mark that, to my child's eyes, made her special.

As I stroked the dark chocolate-colored outline with my index finger, I remembered her reaction when I asked how she got the mark. She had swiftly smoothed down her dress, as though I had caught her doing something wrong. Staring at the floor, she told me in a whisper that many years ago, in her native Oaxaca, a group of hunters had stopped to rest by a huge rock on a hill. On that rock, they found a silhouette drawing of a naked woman with long, long braids and a mark on her thigh. Nearby, they found vast amounts of lead ore. Without hesitation, thinking of all the bullets they could make, the hunters filled their bags. Most of those men were never seen again. The locals swore that at night they could hear their terrified cries. Only one returned and, with a panicked look in his eyes, claimed repeatedly that the naked woman with the braids and the mark on her leg had the demon in her. My grandmother swore that she was a direct descendant of that Indigenous woman. And I was so convinced that for a long time I used to draw the birthmark on my own leg with a brown pen. It was the only way I could feel like I truly belonged to my grandmother's lineage. A rather ineffectual way that vanished every night with soap and water.

"That's it, Paloma. It's time to let her go. She has to follow her path," said one of the nurses, placing a warm hand on my shoulder.

Nayeli Cruz, my grandmother, the magical Mexican, died at the age of ninety-two, before I could finish rubbing cream into her ballerina legs.

2

Tehuantepec, December 1939

As she did every morning, just before opening her eyes, in those fleeting seconds between sleep and wakefulness, Nayeli stretched out and searched the other side of the bed with her fingertips. She couldn't imagine starting the day without placing a gentle hand on her older sister's warm cheek. Despite there being three years between them, they were often mistaken for twins: they had the same slim legs and rounded thighs; broad hips; full lips with upturned corners that made them seem to be constantly smiling, although they did not in fact smile often; and masses of smooth, shiny black hair that hung to their narrow waists like silk curtains. It was their eyes that marked the difference. Rosa's were almond-shaped, the same brown color as the Tehuantepec, the river where the girls used to swim naked, as though the water might filter through their pores to blend with their Tehuana blood. Nayeli's eyes were round and green, like two paddles of a prickly cactus. "We Tehuanas have all the races of the world flowing in our veins" was the response that Ana, their mother, used to give if anyone raised an eyebrow at the idea of an Indigenous girl with such light eyes.

They had shared a room since they were little, the largest, most spacious bedroom in the adobe house built and patched up over the years on the Cruz family plot. Miguel, the father, never had to raise his voice for his word to be respected; he was energetic but measured, a man of eloquent silences, and when he made the decision that the sisters would sleep together, after a terrible fever had almost taken Nayeli's life as a baby, no one even contemplated defying him.

They had tried everything to save her. Her body had become a tiny bundle of hot embers. In the end, it was Rosa, just six at the time, who provided the solution.

"A white-haired woman gave me this to help my little sister," she'd announced, holding out a small basket containing a mixture of copal resin. "She told me we should burn the copal and bring Nayeli close to the smoke."

The certainty with which the girl delivered these instructions left no room for doubt.

In an instant, the spirals of white smoke joined to form a cloud that enveloped the baby like a blanket dropped from the sky.

When a full-throated cry burst from Nayeli's lungs, it made them jump.

"You've saved your sister, Rosa," said Miguel. "From now on, you will be her guardian, her protector. You'll sleep in the big room, so you can defend her from demons, and from the jaguars that sometimes prowl around the house at night."

The elder sister followed his orders to the letter. Over the years, she became a talisman: she was the last thing Nayeli needed to touch before she went to sleep and the first when she awoke. But that morning, her fingertips couldn't find the heat of Rosa's body. Nayeli stretched out a little farther but found nothing. She had no choice but to open her eyes to confirm her suspicion: her sister wasn't there by her side. A coconut cocooned in a white cloth with blue and red stripes had taken her place.

"Mamá, Mamá!" she shouted as she ran down the long hallway. She was barefoot, wearing only a white cotton nightdress and clasping the coconut and cloth to her chest. "Why did Rosa leave me this present when it isn't my saint's day?"

Ana barely looked up as her younger daughter burst into the room. She remained still, sitting in a wicker rocking chair, her lips tight and her arms folded across her belly. Nayeli couldn't remember the last time she had seen her mother sitting down, her hands not busy cooking, embroidering huipils for herself and others, or weaving baskets in infinite shapes and sizes. The woman reacted only when the coconut hit the floor with a clatter and cracked open, the gelatinous pulp of the fruit seeping between Nayeli's toes.

It had slipped from her grip when she noticed her mother was wearing her gala outfit, her Tehuana finery, which she only ever wore to the patron's party, for the village festival or a special mass, and to pay her respects to the dead: a short, muslin huipil embroidered with flower and leaf motifs in purple, bright red, and deep crimson; a swinging velvet skirt with a starched lace flounce. Hanging from her neck was a doubloon of gold coins and, to crown the majestic ensemble, a huipil headdress, its multiple lace folds framing her face and giving her the look of a warrior.

"Mamá," Nayeli persisted, this time without shouting. Only a thin warble left her throat. "Where's Rosa? Why are you dressed up?"

"Pedro has stolen her, mi hijita," whispered Ana.

Miguel approached his younger daughter and tenderly stroked the black tresses that fell down her back.

"It's the tradition, Nayeli," he explained. "Your sister is of an age to start a family. Your godmother Juana, your cousins, and aunts are all at Pedro Galván's house vouching that Rosa has honored this house and this family."

Nayeli could have started to yell, to tell them that her sister wasn't in love with Pedro, that they should be stopping this wedding, that Rosa was still too young to be thinking about starting a home and having children; instead, she stamped her bare feet on the shards of coconut, slammed the door, and ran the few blocks to Pedro's house.

The Galván family home was spacious, with exposed brick walls and roofs that were part adobe, part tiled. They had migrated to the isthmus of Tehuantepec in 1931, days after the Oaxaca earthquake had turned their considerable assets to dust. The horrific shifting of the earth had razed not only the city but also the social status the Galváns had enjoyed:

they went from rich merchants to humble market traders selling fruit and vegetables. They could never forget the tragedy, nor the cries of their neighbors, punctuated by the sickening creaks of the ground beneath them and the thundering of the bell plummeting from the tower of the San Francisco temple. Having managed to stumble to the street, father, mother, and children knelt there, swearing to the Almighty that, if they survived, they would never complain about anything ever again. The Galván family survived, and they kept their word. All except Pedro, who didn't recall having made any such promise.

Nayeli didn't need stealth to be able to see or hear what was happening inside the house, as all the windows and the green-framed door stood wide open. Peering through what seemed to be the main window, she saw her sister lying on a small bed made with brilliant white sheets; her body, draped in a cotton blanket, was equally white.

Their godmother Juana was guiding the ceremony. Behind her sturdy form, her sisters Josefa and Leticia were assisting by scattering red petals and confetti over Rosa, who watched them with a sad smile from her place of repose. Someone had tied a vermillion bandana around her head.

"Are you here of your own free will, hija?" Juana asked her.

Rosa sat up in the bed, back against the wall and arms crossed over her chest. From outside the window, Nayeli attempted to decode her sister's delay in answering the question.

"Yes, Madrina," Rosa said finally, in a firm voice. Her dark cheeks lit up and her brown eyes filled with tiny lakes held back by her lashes, as though stemmed by a dam. Her bare shoulders trembled and, for a second, the shine of her hair seemed to dull. Rosa was lying, and Nayeli could tell immediately.

It didn't take long for the women to start issuing endless marriage advice that seemed to bounce off the walls: "From now on, you'll have a new family to love and obey"; "You mustn't be disrespectful to your husband or your new elders"; "Don't take too long to bring children into the family, that's the gift we women can give." Words and more words that refused to penetrate Rosa's ears.

Nayeli knew she had to rescue her sister, to save her life. She owed her that much. She moved away from the window and tiptoed around the house, pausing for a few seconds at a small door that led into the Galváns' kitchen; the aroma of freshly baked bread and tamales made her stomach rumble—in her haste to save Rosa, Nayeli had forgotten all about breakfast.

When she reached the front door, with its bright green frame, she strode in with such confidence that none of the women sitting in the room paid the slightest bit of attention. Some were busy peeling fruit; others, constructing crowns of red roses. Nayeli made her way down a dark hallway, a passageway between damp adobe walls that the sunlight didn't reach. She recognized the room she had seen through the window, crept in slowly, and stood quietly in a corner.

She had arrived just in time to witness her sister, still on the bed, hand her godmother Juana a white cloth stained with red. Godmother, aunts, and cousins all cried out, clapping with excitement. They took barely two minutes to leave the room in a procession, with Juana at the head; in her arms, as though it were a newborn baby, she carried the cloth soiled with Rosa's virginal blood.

"What are you doing here, niña?" asked the elder sister when she was sure they had been left alone.

"What are *you* doing here? Get dressed, we're going straight home!" ordered Nayeli. She picked up Rosa's Tehuana skirt and huipil, which had been left scrunched up on the floor, and tossed them on the bed. "Come on, get dressed!"

"Come here, little sister," said Rosa in a maternal voice.

At that moment, Nayeli understood that she had lost her. Nevertheless, she did as she was told and sat down on the edge of Rosa's bed, as though visiting a patient.

Rosa took both her hands, kissed her, and issued a warning: "You have to leave." Nayeli opened her mouth to interrupt, but Rosa placed an index finger on her lips and continued, "I'm already Pedro Galván's wife—I've given him my body in exchange for yours. But you aren't safe; it won't be long before his brother Daniel comes for you."

"What are you talking about? I don't understand."

"You're a Tehuana with green eyes, niña. That counts for a lot in the Galván family. They're certain it would give them back the status they lost in the earthquake."

"Our family won't allow it. Let's go, right now."

"I'm staying," declared Rosa. "I'll have my children and my family with Pedro."

"But you don't love him," said Nayeli, on the verge of tears.

Rosa stood. She was stark naked. A scattering of bruises on her thighs made it obvious that consent had not formed part of her night with Pedro. Despite her anxiety and resignation, her movements were gentle, dancer-like, as though her body were caressing the air. In silence, she stepped into the long skirt and pulled the huipil over her shoulders. As she braided her hair around her head with a violet ribbon, she noticed that Nayeli, her cherished treasure, was watching with her customary fascination. She couldn't help but smile, then knelt down in front of her sister, who was still perched on the edge of the bed.

"You're right, mi niñita. I don't love Pedro, but do *you* know what love is?" she asked.

Nayeli shook her head, biting her lower lip in her attempt not to cry.

"Love is a tragedy. Some people embark on it of their own free will, and others have it thrust upon them. But it's never happy. Happy love has no story, and I want you to be happy and make your own story. Run away, my precious little sister, far, far away from here."

"How far, Rosa? And what should I say to our parents? Where will I find the money to run away? I've never been farther than the hill before." The questions gushed from Nayeli's mouth like waterfalls. She knew her sister was never wrong, and she trusted no one else.

Rosa squeezed her sister's hands firmly and held her gaze more intently than she had ever done before. She carefully removed the necklace she was wearing and, as she passed it over her sister's head, declared, "This amulet will always protect you. You're the daughter of the moment, Nayeli. And I won't allow you to get lost."

And so it was.

3

Buenos Aires, August 2018

Minutes after my grandmother took her last breath, I shut myself in her bathroom to look in the mirror. I needed a moment of solitude to confirm whether or not I appeared to have aged. Nayeli had always said that, when our ancestors die, those they leave behind on this earth start to look older.

Before I began my scrutiny, I washed my face, the cold water merging with my warm tears. I dried myself on the pink hand towel, which still held the familiar violet scent of the talc Nayeli used all over her body.

I raised my eyes to the mirror, and my grandmother's theory evaporated: I didn't look any older just because she was gone. Nevertheless, I was starting to feel rather alone.

"Paloma, dear, are you okay?" Gloria said, rounding off the question with three firm knocks on the door.

Her voice brought me back to reality, the reality in which my grandmother's corpse lay on the other side of the door, waiting for me to organize a farewell I wasn't ready for.

At the age of ninety, Gloria Morán had adopted the role of guardian of Casa Solanas, the care home where my grandmother spent her final years. She oversaw everything from her spot at the edge of the courtyard, where the nurses had set her up with a small white wooden table and a wicker armchair. When they realized that Gloria was intent on spending her every waking hour there, they added a sunshade so that the strong summer rays wouldn't land directly on her head. Gloria herself had provided the finishing touch with a stack of magazines from which she very carefully tore the back pages so she could cut out the grid of a lottery game that drove her crazy.

When I emerged from the bathroom, Gloria had been joined in the bedroom by Don Eusebio Miranda, the manager of Casa Solanas. He was sheathed in a brown linen suit and wore a somber expression to complete the look: lips pursed, eyes watery, and chin raised, as if he would be able to make sense of death from up there.

"Señorita Paloma Cruz, my condolences; it's a terrible loss for us, too. We will all miss Nayeli very much," he said, reciting by rote the phrase that he churned out with some frequency, given that he ran a care home.

I only listened to the start of his little speech. My mind wandered for a moment as I thought about my name: Paloma Cruz. Cruz meaning cross, Cruz like my mother, like my grandmother. The surname that had come to me from the isthmus of Tehuantepec, Mexico. Four letters that marked the destiny of three women without men. "The three crosses," Nayeli used to say and laugh, making light of the pride she felt at raising a daughter on her own and bequeathing her, my mother, that same cross: to live without a man tainting with his surname a lineage that could do perfectly well without any protection.

I had to call my mother. She was one of those people whose empathy surfaces when they see a corpse laid out on the table. That's when she would put on her show: dark glasses; a fitted black dress to prove that, despite her age, she still had a slim waist; hair tied back neatly; and a whole range of faces and gestures as vigorous as they were studied. Felipa Cruz knew how to say goodbye as though she was suffering. She was a highly skilled artisan of farewells.

"Bye, love," she had said with tear-filled eyes the morning she left me at my grandmother's house, intending to return only for birthdays and

Christmases. I didn't wash my face for three days, not wanting to erase the red kiss her lipstick had stamped on my forehead.

"Señorita Cruz, I'm at your disposal, whatever you need," said Eusebio Miranda, with that mixture of kindness and anxiety people tend to show when they're eager to be rid of something. That "something" was my grandmother's body.

I gave him the details of the funeral home that had organized the service for a woman from our neighborhood a few months earlier. Back then, I had the foresight to note down the number, knowing that sooner or later I would need it.

The room suddenly felt suffocating. The combination of the citrus aromatizer, the violet talc, and the moisturizing cream that death had prevented me from fully rubbing into my grandmother's legs made me feel nauseous.

As though she could sense what was happening to me, Gloria came to my rescue. "Let's go into the courtyard, dear. There's nothing we can do in here. We'll wait outside until they come to take her away." She placed a hand on my shoulder, squeezed firmly, and lowered her voice. "Your grandmother Nayeli isn't here anymore. She must be in some paradise cooking up one of her heavenly feasts for the gods."

I couldn't help but imagine her there, surrounded by vegetables, fruit, pots and pans, clouds, and angel wings, and I smiled.

"Or playing the exquisite corpse game," I murmured.

"Or insisting on one of her irrefutable truths," added Gloria, mirroring my smile.

She was right: my grandmother was hard to argue with; she never doubted a thing. She imparted assertions with scientific rigor, despite her lack of science. The many blanks in her knowledge she filled with a formidable imagination. She was an expert at weaving conspiracies and macabre plots and twisting the ends of stories. To her, reality and facts were minor circumstances that could be modified at whim. Perhaps that's why my childhood navigated the hazy boundary between reality and fantasy, a boundary that my grandmother did her best to erase on a daily basis.

"Let's play exquisite corpse," she would say every night, as she set the table for two. She wasn't interested in how I got on at school or the geography or math homework that was usually awaiting my attention. Her ears only pricked up when I described the boys I liked. "Love is a good reason for everything else to fail," she would repeat, inserting that phrase into any gaps in my story, so that I would never forget that love and failure go hand in hand.

She would start off with a nugget of an invented tale, I would continue with the second part, and then she would pick up with the third. We could spend hours elaborating on our stories, and in the end, we were never quite sure how much of it was real and how much was a product of our imaginations.

The courtyard at Casa Solanas could be used in winter as well as summer, thanks to a sliding metal roof that adapted to all weather conditions. Moving like an arthritic tightrope walker—a hand on each knee and rocking at the hips—Gloria settled herself on one of the chairs. Her pink cotton dress gathered midway up her plump thighs, and I could see the little chains of veins decorating her milky white skin.

"I'm going to miss those Mexican dishes she used to make me. I never could learn the names, but your grandmother's food was delicious," Gloria reminisced as she smoothed down each wrinkle in her dress. "All she needed was a bit of flour and milk, a few eggs, and some sugar, and she would fill the whole place with the wonderful smell of her fluffy sponges. I'll tell you what, there must be a scrapbook full of her recipes somewhere. She wrote them all out by hand."

"My grandmother wrote out her recipes?" I blurted.

Although she had learned to read and write as a teenager in her native Mexico, it wasn't something she enjoyed; she said the letters all came out in a jumble, like newborn kittens, curled up on the lines. The only thing she read were the signs showing prices in the supermarket, and that took her long enough.

"She certainly did. She used to sit right here with a pen, in this very courtyard, and she would write and write," Gloria replied.

"Where is this scrapbook? I'd like to keep it as a memento."

Gloria shrugged, feigning indifference. "No idea. I can only assume it will be with her things."

I gave a slight nod. Of the few belongings my grandmother kept at Casa Solanas, the scrapbook wasn't one, and I was only too aware of that. I was the one who put away her clothes, her toiletries, her sewing kit.

"The people from the funeral home have arrived," Señor Miranda interrupted.

I nodded again. The hours that followed that announcement are still a blur in my mind, although a few images stand out clearly: the outfit I chose for Nayeli to wear at the send-off—a white muslin blouse with tiny flowers embroidered on the chest—and the arrival of my mother.

Felipa Cruz made her entrance with astonishing prowess: without causing any disturbance, she managed to capture the attention of everyone in the room. Black linen pants that draped perfectly, a cream silk blouse buttoned to the neck, a small satin purse with wooden handles, hair tied at the nape of her neck with a silver butterfly-shaped clasp, and subtle makeup that accentuated her exotic features and gave a depth to those green eyes she inherited from Nayeli.

She crossed the foyer without taking her eyes off the polished cedar casket, which was visible through the double door connecting to the main room. The clacking of her high-heeled footsteps began to lose momentum, until it stopped just inches from where my grandmother, her mother, lay at rest.

"Why did you go for a closed casket?" she asked me. There were no hugs or kisses, no greeting of any kind.

"Abuela always said she didn't like seeing women with no life in them," I replied. "She wouldn't have wanted to be seen in these circumstances."

My mother raised an eyebrow, that characteristic but indecipherable gesture of hers that she employed frequently.

"What a pity. I would have liked to have seen her one last time." She sighed.

You could have visited her at Casa Solanas, given her a quick call every day, or even taken her for a walk in the park—she loved doing that . . . A flurry of words surged from the depths of my stomach, climbed my chest and throat, but seemed to stall at the tip of my tongue. I decided to do what I always did in my mother's presence: hold my silence. As a child, it was the simplest option, faced with the fear of her no longer loving me. When I understood that she didn't love me anyway, those unspoken words turned into a voluntary reservoir of peace. A space in which I could choose to expel her disquieting presence.

"A pity, yes," was all I said, as I watched her pull a small dark green velvet pouch from her purse.

I moved close enough to smell her cloying perfume and see what those perfectly manicured fingertips were taking out of the bag. Very slowly, she unrolled a long, braided leather cord, knotted in the middle to hold a lump of shiny black stone.

"What's that?" I asked, drawing even closer.

My mother startled. I tried to remember the last time our bodies had been so close. I couldn't.

"An amulet. It belonged to your abuela," she answered as she circled the casket, her brows knitting together as she assessed the best place to deposit the stone.

After a few minutes that seemed an eternity, she decided to coil the leather strap into an arrangement of white flowers that Gloria had positioned on the metal cross that adorned the lid of the casket.

"This black stone is obsidian," she continued, even though I hadn't asked for an explanation, "a volcanic glass that forms when lava cools very quickly before it can crystallize. Perhaps because it comes from the center of the earth, we Mexicans believe it has protective powers. We use it like a shield against all evil."

I stared at the black stone, which stood out against the white petals of the floral arrangement. My mother took great pleasure in excluding me in order to wound: Mexicans on one side, and me, alone, on the other.

"You grew up in Argentina, Mom. You're more a feature of Buenos Aires than the Obelisk," I said before I could stop myself.

I stood waiting for her cunning riposte. My mother had a dagger for a tongue; on this occasion, however, she was the one who chose silence.

She folded the empty velvet pouch into her purse and smoothed down hair that didn't need smoothing.

"I'm going to get a coffee," she said.

"I'll come with you."

Felipa Cruz raised her right hand and regarded me with an icy glare. "I'm going to have it at home. You stay here."

Her straight back was the last thing I saw of her. She withdrew like the Queen of Hearts in *Alice's Adventures in Wonderland*, chopping off my head.

4

Tehuantepec, December 1939

Nayeli clutched the obsidian amulet her sister had given her so tightly that its hard glassy edges started to split the skin of her palm. She didn't care. All her attention was focused on running as quickly as her skinny legs allowed. She stopped to catch her breath when she reached the main square, narrowing her eyes to avoid being dazzled by the sun's reflection on the water.

To the west, the river spread out before her in an open vista. Behind her, the activity in the market seemed different somehow: neither the women who set up just before daybreak nor those who came along later in the day to sell, buy, and show off their clothes were at their customary places.

That space where women reigned as queens without crowns had been taken over by men, laboring tirelessly and against the clock, setting up for a celebration.

In the midst of the clamor, she spotted her father, in his dress pants and dark shirt, straw hat, and a red bandana around his neck. Miguel Cruz could tolerate the heat like no one else: he didn't sweat, he didn't suffer from hot flashes, and when the irrepressible temperatures of the isthmus left everyone with their heads in a muddle and dragging their feet, he walked erect, his clothing fresh and uncrumpled, without a sweat stain in sight.

"Papá, what's going on?" shouted Nayeli, knowing that her father would recognize her voice over the many others echoing through the square.

Miguel crossed over to her, the noise of his firm steps on the wooden boards of the temporary dance floor drowned out by the beating of drums, the whistle of clay ocarinas, and the jingling of bells: the musicians were rehearsing. When he reached his daughter, he placed a hand on her shoulder.

"What are you doing here? You should be at home helping your mother prepare for tonight."

It suddenly dawned on Nayeli that it was the end of December, the time of year when all of Tehuantepec comes out to honor the saints.

"Noche de vela is tonight?" she asked.

Her father nodded. "Go and get your Tehuana clothes on, and then you can help with the crowns and candles."

Noche de vela was Nayeli's favorite night of the year. A fiesta night, when Tehuana women became the center of the universe, parading their splendor in dresses they fabricated with whatever they managed to scrimp and save over the year. Those worn by her own family were particularly special: the skirts that covered their petticoats were dyed in vivid shades obtained from the secretions of the murex, a mollusk harvested for that very purpose in the lagoons of Tehuantepec.

Nayeli made for home, thinking about the festivities she loved so much.

The Cruz household was a hive of activity. The women of the family were getting ready for one of the high points of the year. All together. Some were singing; others were shouting instructions to the younger girls, telling them the rules of the vela, as if they didn't already know; and a few were putting the finishing touches to the complex but delicious dishes they planned to show off to the neighborhood.

Ana Cruz was dazzling. Every time she saw her mother dressed for a party, Nayeli's eyes and mouth opened wide, as though she needed to expel her amazement from her body. This time the outfit was a petrol blue velvet; the skirt and huipil featured brocaded bands of geometric motifs, scattered with flowers embroidered in brightly colored threads; the flounces at the foot of the skirt were made from a lace she had spent months sewing by hand. On her chest, a necklace of golden coins tinkled with every movement, making her body seem like a musical instrument played by angels. The folds of lace in the large huipil formed a headdress that framed the delicate features of her face.

"Nayeli, hija!" she exclaimed when she saw her. "What are you doing still in your nightdress and with mud all over your feet? Your outfit is laid out on your bed. There's water in a tub out back. Clean yourself up and get changed. It's noche de vela!"

Nayeli rushed to do as she was told, and as her mother had said, she found her outfit on the bed. For an instant, the sight of those garments, laid out with such care, made her forget her sister's absence and her own plans to flee. This year her mother had chosen red for her. Nayeli stroked the embroidery decorating the lower edge of the skirt and closed her eyes. She felt the way each cotton thread came together in a perfect geometric figure and couldn't help but smile.

Her huipil was simple, as was proper for a girl of fourteen; in addition, however, Ana had draped over her pillow a necklace, dangling with a cascade of small coins. Nayeli was excited: this was her first fiesta jewelry.

She slipped it over her head, and, as it fell on her chest, the coins clashed against the obsidian amulet Rosa had given her. That jangle brought her back to reality, to her reality: that night she would take advantage of the merriment and distraction of the vela to make her escape.

5

Buenos Aires, October 2018

One Sunday at midday, two months after her death, my grandmother finally left me for good. From her care home, Nayeli had always made sure that my refrigerator was never empty: hand-crumbed escalopes; endless variations of vegetable tarts; all kinds of sauces, broths, corn tortillas, and bread she kneaded for hours.

When her bones started to fail her and living at home alone became an uphill struggle, she was the one who'd decided to move into the care home. She didn't want to hear my arguments against it, nor did she consider the possibility of my moving back in with her. I insisted, I implored, I wept, I invoked a whole range of scenarios, I even got angry. It was no good. My grandmother was digging in her heels: she wanted to spend her final years at Casa Solanas. She assured me that lots of her old friends from the Boedo neighborhood lived there now, and she wanted to share what time she had left with them.

In the kitchen at Casa Solanas, my grandmother kept on being my grandmother. She always said that the person who raises you isn't necessarily the one who teaches you good manners or reads you stories. Her argument was that a person is raised by whoever cooks the food in their belly. My grandmother kept on raising me even after her death, until that Sunday when I ate the last thing in my freezer. That farewell tasted of black bean stew.

My bereavement was already well underway by that point. On several occasions I had to contain the urge to catch the bus that would drop me near the care home; countless times I dialed the first few digits of her phone number in the certainty that at the other end of the line I would hear that voice so gravelly it could have belonged to Chavela Vargas, saying, "Hola, mi niña, how nice to hear from you," and I even bought the same violet-scented talc in the drugstore, despite the fact it set off my allergies. The dead take some time to leave the bodies of their loved ones, and they seem intent on messing with our plans.

After a period that was more for the benefit of the others than for me, I made my return to the stage. My three colleagues in FemProject, the band we had formed as a hobby, welcomed me eagerly with joy, kisses, hugs, and a bottle of whiskey.

"We have five performances before Christmas, and I'm considering the possibility of opening for a feminist festival in San Isidro," announced Natalí, who, aside from being our guitarist, was also our manager. "And I think we should spend the summer writing some more songs. We can't keep on churning out 'Diluvio.' I don't think we should sing it anymore . . . "

"Now wait a minute," exclaimed Sabrina. "Listen to me, all of you. 'Diluvio' isn't just any old song that we can toss into the trash. 'Diluvio' is the spirit of our band, a spirit that identifies us and strengthens with every show. And we have to nurture that spirit, because if there's anything worse than not taking good care of a spirit, it's not taking care of it at all."

Sabrina's tirade froze my smile.

"What did you say, Sabri?"

"What I said was that 'Diluvio' isn't some piece of trash—"

"No, no. What did you say about spirits?" I cut in.

"Oh, that 'Diluvio' is a spirit we have to nurture," she replied, oblivious to how much her words had affected me.

The argument went on, but, although my body remained seated there, propped upright at the bar table, my mind had traveled far away, to the patio of my grandmother's house. The patio of my childhood. I could almost smell the jasmine growing in huge cement pots. I even thought I heard the song of the little birds that flew down every morning to devour the breadcrumbs I left for them behind my grandmother's back. My friends' voices were fading, and the lullaby of Nayeli's soothing tone flooded my memory.

I remembered her, and I remembered myself: both of us sitting in wicker chairs, one summer afternoon, drinking lemonade. She used to tell me stories that seemed like fairy tales; as I grew up, I began to realize that many of them evoked her native land. One of those stories had prompted me to ask questions for days. It was the tale of a woman who sent her son out to look for wood and flowers to make an offering to the dead of their family. The boy decided to spend the afternoon napping by the river instead. On his way home, he came across a procession. In it, he recognized his father and his grandmother, both of whom had died when he was very young. He saw that they looked unwell, hungry, and cold. At that moment, it dawned on the boy that when the dead arrived at his house, there would be no offering to relieve their suffering, but it was too late. The spirits were angered and decided to leave the boy tied to a tree for the whole night. Suffering souls can be very mischievous.

"We're taking a vote, Paloma. Come on, it's your turn," said Sabrina, shaking my arm.

I looked around the group as though I had just woken from a long dream. I struggled to remember the reason for the argument. "Diluvio," that was it. I took a deep breath, exhaled slowly, and said, "'Diluvio' is a spirit. We have to honor it."

No one realized that my decision had little to do with the song itself and much more to do with my origins.

I smiled in satisfaction.

6

Tehuantepec, December 1939

Over time, the Galván family had managed to carve out a prominent place for itself within the community. The fact that they had survived the earthquake that devastated Oaxaca assisted their welcome considerably. They were a model of resistance, and resistance always makes a good impression.

Dolores Galván called for Pedro, her eldest son. The family revolved around that sturdy woman who always made sure she stood out from her peers, cultivating and perfecting a position until she made it her own, and giving orders was what she did best.

"What is it, Mother, what do you need?" the young man replied in a loud voice as he hurried toward her. No one kept Dolores waiting.

"I need your future wife to be ready as soon as possible; we can't be late. And tell her to pack up the paper flowers I have to deliver tonight."

Although she had been the one to convince the whole family that Rosa Cruz was the perfect match for Pedro and had ordered her son to seduce her by fair means or force, she struggled to say the girl's name. For Dolores Galván, to utter the name of her future daughter-in-law would be to give her an identity, and for the moment, she wanted her to remain invisible. That's why she took matters into her own hands and gifted Rosa the Tehuana dress for the festival. Controlling Rosa's attire was a good start for Dolores's purposes.

Meanwhile, the Cruz household was no less of a hustle and bustle. Miguel and Ana Cruz were the mayordomos of the village, fulfilling the role of religious officiators. They left the house with the women leading the procession, Ana at the head. Anyone who happened upon this rhythmical march couldn't help but be dazzled. The Cruz women excelled at the codes of merrymaking and flirtation. One by one, the onlookers were infected, joining in the choreography devised by their ancestors. The men in white shirts, dark pants, sombreros, and red bandanas; the women like queen bees, sovereigns of paradise. Nayeli followed the rhythm of the march and, in a low voice, sang along to a verse of "La Sandunga."

In the main square, the tables were set. Dozens of pairs of hands had helped get the banquet out on time: chicken with carrots and jalapeños, de-veined chiles, tacos filled with shredded beef, pickled mango, chocolate, bread, and milk atole to drink, all served in fired earthenware or baskets decorated with flowers.

Dolores Galván had arrived early. Holding court from a chair brought from the house, she made sure everything was in order.

As Ana approached, the two women looked one another up and down, each openly assessing the other's outfit. This was the inevitable yardstick that everyone else used, too. Days later, many commented that Dolores's embroidery didn't show much skill; others, that they had never seen anything so original as the petrol blue velvet of Ana's dress.

Minutes later, the band launched into a leisurely tune, which lent itself to slow, elegant movements, effectively starting the party. The men started their courtship ritual, even while knowing they were small and practically invisible next to the spectacle of silks, cottons, lace, and pleats that enveloped the voluminous bodies of their Tehuanas. Nayeli took advantage of the distraction.

"Rosa, Rosa," she whispered at her sister's back.

Rosa wasn't eating, she wasn't dancing, she wasn't smiling. With the excuse of a stomachache, she had persuaded her future mother-in-law to let her sit on a chair under one of the arches in the square. Nayeli was about to make a snide comment about the Tehuana dress she was wearing, but she swallowed her words when she realized her sister had been crying. Her red, swollen eyes couldn't lie.

"Nayelita, my precious," she said with a smile, "I've got everything ready. Come with me."

The two girls crossed the square in silence. Although she was tense, Rosa walked with poise; it wasn't just blood that ran through her veins: her every step was imbued with Zapotec sounds, making her humble full-bodied skirt ripple like silk of the finest quality.

They slipped around the edge of the market to a secluded spot at the rear, which the party seemed not to have reached. They swatted away the large green flies and shook their feet, clad in leather huaraches, to scare off any snakes that might be lurking nearby.

Rosa placed her basket on the ground. "Here you go," she said, and handed her sister a bundle of clothing. "I found it in Daniel's room; I think it will fit."

Without hesitating, Nayeli took off her dress and pulled on a pair of black pants, a white shirt, and a sombrero. She wrinkled her nose at the stench of impregnated sweat.

"You really think no one will notice I'm a girl?" she asked anxiously.

Rosa laughed and pointed at her sister's head.

"If you don't lose those ribbons in your hair, they'll struggle to believe you're a boy."

Although the straw sombrero was large, Nayeli's braids refused to fit under it, a few colored ribbons escaping rebelliously. Between the two of them, they tried to fix her hair, but their efforts were in vain. Their eyes met; both knew what had to be done.

"Stay here, I'll be right back," ordered Rosa.

Still swaying her hips, partly because she liked to, partly as a bluff, Rosa crossed the square once again. The festivities were in full swing. The musicians had split up and were playing different songs at either end of the party, making it hard to identify a specific tune, but no one seemed to mind.

She couldn't waste any time: her sister was the priority. Striding confidently around the back of one of the tables, she found the wooden box holding the implements that had been used to dish out the food. She took out a sharp knife and swiftly concealed it in her waistband, between the skirt and huipil.

Without excusing herself, she used hands and shoulders to barge through the men and Tehuanas packed onto the dance floor and returned to where her younger sister was waiting for her.

Nayeli was sitting cross-legged on the ground, her back against one of the columns that held up the roof of the market. Her hair fell loose like a waterfall down her back; her green eyes were closed.

"Get up, niña, there's no time!" Rosa exclaimed. She took her sister by the arm and turned her around. Gently but firmly, she separated Nayeli's hair into sections and, using the pilfered knife, began to cut. A cushiony pile of wavy hair started to form around Nayeli's body.

"Done, turn around," commanded the impromptu hairdresser when she had finished her task.

Without her brown mane, the girl's features stood out even more: the perfect oval of her face; the prominent cheekbones; the long, slim neck; the smooth dark skin; the wide, heart-shaped mouth, and the eyes, above all the eyes.

"That's more like it," Rosa said in satisfaction, as she tucked what remained of her sister's hair behind her ears and pulled the hat down to her eyebrows.

"How do I look? Like a boy?" asked Nayeli.

Rosa hugged her and, with a smile, whispered, "You really do, mi muchacho."

7

Buenos Aires, November 2018

He croaked"; "She bit the dust"; "He checked out"; "She left with la Huesuda"; "The devil took him": for years, initially with amazement and later with amusement, I had listened to my grandmother's infinite euphemisms for the act of dying. I witnessed her heated discussions with the neighbors at the house where we lived:

"Don't you mock my brother's death!"

"You don't even cry for your dead."

"I don't cry, because the dead visit me."

"You're crazy!"

"You're the crazy one!"

And so on, for hours and hours, until night fell and they left the battlefield of the sidewalk, each woman withdrawing to the peace of her home, muttering curses.

Returning to my grandmother's house, my childhood home, was easier than I thought it would be; it isn't always such a bad idea to return to the places where we were happy. The little house in Boedo, with its long hallway and wooden shutters at the windows; the patio with geraniums planted in old cans of candied sweet potato and the wooden floors polished with perfumed wax; the huge oak closets and beds with creaky springs; the high ceilings, blue tiles, and frontage that always needed a lick of paint; that little house where I was happy was still there, being looked after by Cándida from next door. She refused to accept any money in exchange for her loving care of Nayeli's things. Once a week, though, I liked to send her a large order from the supermarket. "Maybe you could add a bottle of wine, dear, or even a bit of fizz; we old ladies are much improved by alcohol," she suggested once. And how could I have refused such a request?

I opened the screen door, then the wooden door behind it, and ventured down the hall. The mosaic tiles were damp, and everything smelled of pine disinfectant. I smiled, thinking of Cándida. Inside Nayeli's house, the sun was streaming through the window, highlighting the dust on the furniture, the tattered cushions on the red canvas armchair, and Cándida's fingerprints on the glass. I didn't dwell on the details nor did I let myself be swayed by the inevitable emotion of the situation. I did what I needed to do as quickly as possible.

I crossed the geranium-filled patio—at the back was the little room we used for storage, the only part of the house that hadn't been ventilated. When I nudged open the metal door, a blast of stale air made me recoil. The shelves held a row of cardboard boxes labeled with my teenage handwriting. Still sneezing from the dust in the air, I went through the boxes one by one: *Christmas decorations*, *Tools*, *Books & Magazines*, *Winter blankets*, *Old sheets*, *Wooden BBQ plates*, and *Vinyl*. Then, finally, I found what I was looking for: the brown leather suitcase.

I dragged it outside, holding my breath, and paused for a moment in the middle of the patio, taking in the small, glass-topped iron table with its two matching chairs. The green-and-white-striped canvas cushions looked grimy and stained. I could almost taste the toast with butter and dulce de leche of my childhood snacks, the fruit cut into thin slices that accompanied every breakfast. Tears dampened my cheeks—and not because of the dust this time. It was because it reminded me of those little things that make a person a habit, and that habit, for me, had been my grandmother Nayeli.

"Who's there? Is that you, Paloma?" Cándida's voice reached me from the other side of the fence separating the two properties.

"Yes, Cándida, it's me. Rest easy. I came to look for some things," I called as I lugged the suitcase to the door.

In response, the vigilant neighbor turned up the volume on her radio. Roberto Goyeneche singing the tango "Desencuentro" provided the soundtrack for my goodbye.

Everyone was waiting for me at Casa Solanas the next day. Eusebio Miranda had agreed when I called to say that I wanted to pay tribute to Nayeli and that there was no better place to do it than the care home where her friends lived.

As I passed through the iron gate, it struck me that this would probably be the last time. Keeping that in mind, I moved slowly, one step at a time, like someone deliberately savoring the last spoonful of chocolate ice cream, or dancing to the last song at a party that's drawing to a close. The blue paint on the gate was flaking badly. The years, the sun, the rain, the extremes of winter and summer had all left their mark. I touched one of the bars with my fingertips and slid my hand down it. My nail varnish was chipped, and I was relieved to think that my grandmother wouldn't see such unkemptness. She believed that our hands say a lot about us, women's hands in particular. And she was right: I felt broken, as chipped as the color on my nails.

I studied the old tiles paving the courtyard: each square had a brown fleur-de-lis in the center and a pale pink background that made each petal stand out. Some of the tiles were cracked, with thin, subtle black crevices that changed the appearance of that well-trodden floor. The first time we went there together, arm in arm, my grandmother had stopped dead and scrutinized the meadow of fleur-de-lis welcoming her. "They look like dead rats," she'd declared in that throaty voice that added intensity to her every word.

Gloria Morán was waiting for me, as usual, in her wicker armchair. It was immediately obvious that she had risen early. Her white mane was swept into an elegant do, her cheeks and lips subtly made up; she wore carefully selected earrings, a short necklace and bracelet, and an impeccably ironed navy linen suit that were not the outcome of mere minutes: she had spent hours achieving this sophisticated effect. But she wasn't alone. Next to her, Lourdes also sat waiting. She had gone for the simplicity of her flowery quilted housecoat, accessorized only by a gold ring with a giant stone. The welcome committee was completed by Rebeca, my grandmother's first roommate, wearing black—skirt and cotton blouse—and the twins Emita and Esther Rodríguez, who were dressed identically, as always, in cream pants and matching blouses.

I had made an effort for the occasion as well. Although my grandmother had never said anything about my tattoos or ever-changing hair color, limiting herself to pursing her lips at my leather skirts and lace corsets, I wanted her to see me, if her soul happened to show up, in the outfit she gave me the day I graduated from the music conservatory: a fitted pink linen dress, with two pockets at hip height, and leather shoes with a modest heel. My hair was combed back and held at my nape with a golden clasp.

"Good morning, Señorita Cruz," Eusebio Miranda greeted me, wearing his brown linen suit, the one reserved for funerals. "We'll leave it to you to decide where you would like to hold the homage to our dear friend Nayeli."

At that moment, I decided the courtyard was the best place for what I had in mind. Lina, the cleaner, had just finished hosing it down. Everything smelled of chlorine and lemon disinfectant. My grandmother was fond of courtyards; she always said they were small spots of freedom for those who lived caged in cities. She hated cities.

"What's that big old suitcase?" Gloria asked.

"I've brought a few things for Nayeli's tribute," I replied.

I spent a few minutes chatting with Gloria and the other women, until Lina appeared.

"Señorita, I've set up a table where Señor Miranda told me to." She pointed at a medium-sized white plastic table standing against one of the courtyard walls.

"Perfect, Lina," I said with a smile.

Not wasting a moment, I knelt on the damp tiles and opened Nayeli's brown leather suitcase to reveal a white tablecloth embroidered with flowers, starched and folded in four. I unfolded it and spread it out over the plastic table. Using the two rolls of thick but flexible wire, I fashioned an arch and attached each end to the edges of the table. Next, I wound purple satin ribbon around the wire and, at the top, tied four muslin bows in different colors. On the table, I arranged two stoneware bowls filled with sticks of palo santo. At the bottom of the suitcase were the Mexican marigolds crafted from crepe paper.

"Can you do me a favor?" I asked Lina, as I arranged some straw baskets on the ground in front of the altar. "Mark out a path with these paper flowers from the main door to here."

"Yes, señorita." Lina nodded, looking slightly disconcerted.

Finally, I unwrapped a package I had prepared the night before. I smiled in satisfaction when I uncovered what was hidden on my metal tray.

"What's that?" asked Gloria.

"A pan de muerto. Bread of the dead," I replied.

"Who's dead?" cried out Lourdes, looking frightened.

We couldn't help laughing. Lourdes's deafness was sometimes rather endearing.

Adopting the role of a master baker, I recited the recipe: "Eight cups of flour, eight eggs, one cup of softened butter, one and a half of sugar, a spoonful of orange-flower water, an ounce of yeast dissolved in half a cup of warm water, and a teaspoon of salt."

"That's quite the list of ingredients, Paloma!" exclaimed Gloria, and waved her hand for me to continue my description.

"You tip the flour onto the counter and make a well in the middle. That's where you add all the other ingredients, and the eggs one by one. Then you knead until the dough stops sticking to your hands. Then you have to leave it to rest for an hour, knead it again, and let it rest for another hour. Then it goes in the oven at four hundred degrees for about thirty minutes."

I placed the tray on the table. The guests drew closer, unable to tear their eyes from the huge golden loaf.

"What's that strange decoration?" asked Eusebio Miranda.

Seeing their surprise, I decided to explain further: "These strips of dough resemble the bones of the dead and the ball at the top is the skull. In Mexico, where Nayeli was born . . . "

I couldn't finish my explanation. I was struck dumb by the presence of a woman emerging from the door and crossing the courtyard. She was clutching one of the crepe flowers Lina had used to create the path to the improvised altar. Wearing a light blue cotton dress, she looked elegant, despite the simplicity of her outfit. One foot after another, the basic choreography of walking cost her considerable effort. We moved aside to let her pass as she made straight for the altar, without taking her eyes off it for a second. Eva Garmendia had always been like this: secretive. When she placed the flower on the white tablecloth, I could see her hands riddled with marks and veins, yet her nails were long and varnished red. She coughed quietly to clear her throat. I thought she was going to speak, but, instead, she sang.

Her voice was hoarse and faltering, a voice that had remained hidden for a long time. She had chosen to dust it off with the song with which Nayeli had brought music to my childhood.

I drew closer on tiptoes, not wanting to break the spell. As Garmendia sang "La Llorona," I placed a photo of my grandmother in a golden metal frame in the middle of the altar. For many years, that photo had stood on my nightstand. I liked to see it before I went to sleep, and when I woke, to have Nayeli's image before my eyes. She looked young; the photo had been taken before my mother was born. Her green eyes were slanted, her cheekbones pronounced, her mouth highlighted with pink lipstick, and her mane of black hair framing the perfect oval of her face. Beneath, only her rounded shoulders and the thin straps of what appeared to be a red dress could be seen.

"How wonderful that you've left your room, Eva!" said Miranda, gently placing his hand on her bony shoulder.

The woman stopped singing.

Eva Garmendia was ninety-six. Out of all the Casa Solanas residents, she had seen the most springs, but she meant much more to me than that: she had been Nayeli's close friend, and, at the same time, she'd been the only person my grandmother had kept at arm's length from me. When I was a girl and Eva used to visit us in the little house in Boedo, my grandmother couldn't get rid of me quickly enough, using clumsy, nervous excuses, like sending me to the most distant bakery for bread. In a box under her nightstand, she kept the boxes of chocolates, candy, pantyhoses with little pictures on them, hair ribbons, and other gifts that Eva had brought me but which Nayeli refused to hand over. I never knew why my grandmother kept me apart from Eva, but in my child's mind, that woman who always smelled of roses seemed so beautiful to me that being close to her even just for a few moments became my priority. Then one day I never heard of her again; my grandmother erased her from my childhood without explanation. Years later, I bumped into her at Casa Solanas and understood why Nayeli had been so insistent on moving to that particular care home.

"I came to say goodbye to my friend," announced Eva.

"That's lovely, Eva. I know my grandmother wanted to spend her final years near you," I said, feeling the urge to question rather than welcome her, but I restrained myself. This wasn't the time.

Eva turned to face me and placed a bony hand on my cheek.

"Paloma," she murmured.

I nodded and placed my hand on hers. I closed my eyes, and Eva brought her mouth toward my ear.

"As time goes by, the love drains out of an old person's past."

I opened my eyes at this. Eva Garmendia stopped whispering and started to spit out her words as though they were burning her tongue.

"Our pasts are full of sins. That goes for your grandmother Nayeli Cruz, and for me, too."

8

Tehuantepec, Tehuantepec Railroad, Coatzacoalcos line, December 1939

Nayeli walked through the middle of the vela celebrations without anyone recognizing her. Initially, she was terrified that some beady eye might break the illusion, but by the time she was a few steps in, she started to feel powerful. Rosa's instructions had been clear: go to Tehuantepec railroad station, find a secluded corner to spend the night and, as soon as it starts to get light, make for the platform and find Amalia.

The station was empty when Nayeli arrived, so she skirted the building and looked for a place to settle down.

A few feet from the station, she reached a leafy tabachín, the only tree she found, and slid her back against the rough trunk until she was sitting on the soft, cool grass that grew at its foot. She placed the basket under her head for a pillow and covered her face with the straw sombrero. As her heavy eyes began to close, she could hear her sister's melodious voice, issuing her final order. "*Don't take off your men's clothes until you're with Amalia. Being a man is what's going to protect you.*" She gripped the obsidian stone that was still hanging around her neck and drifted off under the tree.

* * *

It wasn't the heat that woke Nayeli, or the discomfort of sleeping on the ground. It was a woman's cry. She snatched the sombrero off her face and jumped to her feet, then made her way to the station and onto the platform.

"I won't give you a thing! My goods are Mexican made! Go look for some real smugglers!" shouted a plump woman with very long braids, her voice growing louder and louder. She was wearing a Tehuana dress, a simple huipil and skirt without embroidery, and was tugging at a bundle wrapped in a knitted blanket folded widthways, defying the uniformed man who was trying to take it off her.

"You don't fool me. You've got contraband in there," argued the man who, although physically stronger, was no match for her.

Nayeli stood frozen in the doorway, trying to get a handle on the situation, until another two women, intent on getting to the platform to help the alleged smuggler, shoved her against a wooden bench. Shouting and whacking the man with branches, they managed to rescue the bundle.

The security guard, embarrassed, said threateningly, "You haven't seen the last of me, señoras. This journey has only just begun. You won't find it easy to get to Coatzacoalcos—"

The woman with the bundle cut in, still shouting, "Don't you try cursing us, I'm the witch here. Don't mess with me or my sisters. We're descended from Didjazá."

"That's enough, Amalia," said the second woman. "Let him go. We've won this round."

Nayeli's eyes widened, and her heart leaped. The one who claimed to be a witch was Amalia.

"Señora Amalia," she said, pulling off her hat as she approached the woman. "I'm Nayeli, Rosa's sister; I'm dressed as a man, but I'm actually a Tehuana . . . "

Amalia placed a hand on either side of her broad waist, and her face lost the anger that had been stamped on it since her fight with the train guard.

"Yes, yes, of course. Rosa told me about you. She asked me to look out for you until you get well away from Tehuantepec. The train should be arriving soon. We have a long journey ahead of us, so you'd better hurry and take off those boy clothes."

Rosalía, the third woman, wasn't happy about Nayeli joining them, but she held her tongue. No one wanted to argue with Amalia. Instead, she helped the other women unfold huge blankets and create a private space around the Tehuanita's body so she could change her clothes.

"A little Tehuana with short hair!" exclaimed Lupina, laughing.

"Leave the girl in peace, Lupina," Amalia scolded her, and she handed Nayeli a large basket, brimming with crunchy totopos. "You go in front of us, selling the totopos. Don't get sucked in by the mothers asking for freebies for their children. If they want some, they have to pay, got it?"

Nayeli nodded, gazing at the gargantuan mound of tiny corn tortilla triangles she had been instructed to sell, her trance broken only by the noise of the train arriving at the Tehuantepec station.

Nayeli's first few hours as a traveling saleswoman were a success, even though she'd never traveled by train and had spent more than a few minutes being fascinated by the wooden bench seats at the large windows. Even then, the basket emptied quickly, and she amassed a pile of coins that barely fit into her cupped hands.

"Very good, niña. You've done brilliantly. You've got the gift and enough class to make it in this game," Amalia congratulated her.

As the evening wound down, all four women found themselves in the last carriage, the only one with no seats and only a single tiny window up high. Amalia had ushered Nayeli, Lupina, and Rosalía there so they could spend the night lying on the wooden floor or leaning against the luggage of the wealthy travelers. Lupina had put together a light meal of bread rolls, mole, and shrimp. As they ate in an amiable, almost sisterly silence, Nayeli felt like she was going home. To a new home.

After dinner, the rhythmic sound of the train rolling along the tracks lulled Nayeli into a deep sleep. Neither the hardness of the suitcase she had chosen at random to lean on nor Amalia's snores interrupted her rest. When she opened her eyes, it was still night. Standing on tiptoes, she peeked through the tiny window to find a sky riven in two: above, a deep blue, almost black; below, a vivid orange. Dawn was breaking. Another day of work was about to begin.

All those miles, all those hours, all the passengers buying their wares and all those left wanting to buy, made Nayeli almost forget about her village and her family.

But shortly before they reached the Limones station, one stop before their final destination, the atmosphere in the train suddenly turned hostile. The guards were getting short-tempered, and more than once they pushed the women out of the carriages; another group of women who had gotten on in Jáltipan were moving from one wagon to the next with more original and cheaper merchandise that competed with theirs. For the first time, Amalia ordered Nayeli, Lupina, and Rosalía not to leave their things lying around; a new fear had arisen: theft.

"Get everything ready—we'll be getting off soon," ordered Amalia so seriously that none of the three girls had the courage to contradict her.

While Rosalía and Amalia went to the first carriage to try to sell the last silks from the bottom of the basket, Lupina and Nayeli bundled all their belongings into knitted blankets. Carrying the weight on their shoulders, the two Tehuanas walked down the entire length of the train to the meeting point.

They found Amalia deep in conversation with a woman as plump as her, but much older and with a scarred face that was missing the right eye.

"Things have gotten ugly in here," murmured Rosalía, leaning on a handrail. "Amalia is arranging the passes with One Eye."

"We'll be getting off early, in Limones, to help with the confiscated items," added Lupina confidently.

Nayeli had no time to ask about passes or confiscated items: Lupina was right; the group got off the train in Limones, One Eye in front. As they moved away from the station, the urban features disappeared; the stone streets became narrow dirt tracks flanked by bushes and cacti. The houses were different from those in Tehuantepec. They had no colors or flowers at the windows, no dyed net awnings. Everything in Limones was the same ochre tone as the earth.

They walked in single file for a half hour, until they reached a large house of clay brick with a wooden roof neatly covered in straw—a picturesque scene. The door stood open to reveal a room crammed with merchandise, with a narrow space left in the middle to walk through.

"Come in, come in. It's cooler in here," One Eye encouraged them. "Welcome to my little kingdom."

Huge baskets were overflowing with all kinds of cotton, plain and embroidered; silk with subtle textures; lace and ribbons in all colors. Carved wooden chests held necklaces and earrings of fake gold coins. Fired earthenware pots filled with cold water were chilling Tonalá dairy products. Dried fish, bottles of mezcal, and tobacco leaves completed a scene that left Nayeli open-mouthed. Amalia, Lupina, and Rosalía were also inspecting the merchandise, but without the same astonishment: they were well used to trawling storehouses. They moved slowly, calculating the value of each of the items on display.

One Eye stood in the center of the room and, as though it were the most natural thing in the world, started to remove the lengths of silk and rolls of lace she had hidden beneath her petticoats.

"Ah, so that's where you keep the good stuff, you old trickster!" exclaimed Amalia, laughing.

The women knelt on the hard earth floor and started to assess the fabrics, which still held the warmth of One Eye's body.

"It's all imported," she announced proudly. "Some traveler friends of mine from San Gerónimo brought them. It's the finest silk from El Salvador, only for Tehuanas with a lot of money. Not just anyone can sew a huipil or a skirt with this material."

"This is very good," said Amalia. "Beautiful, and original, too. I can get good money for it. I know Tehuanas who would pay anything to stand out on noche de vela."

One Eye smiled, and the scars on her face darkened. Nayeli stared at the floor. The woman terrified her.

They hadn't quite launched into the usual negotiations over money, when they were interrupted by shouts from the street outside.

"Get back! Get behind those pots right now!" shouted One Eye as she hid the fabrics beneath her petticoats again.

Rosalía grabbed Nayeli by the arm and dragged her to the corner where the large pots stood. They threw themselves to the ground, stomachs pressed against the earth. The smell of the water cooling the dairy products was nauseating, and both had to cover their mouths to contain their retching as large green flies buzzed near their ears.

Two girls ran into the house. One of them, the younger of the two, was crying; the other didn't stop shouting.

"We need help, sisters, please! The police found our stockpile, and they're confiscating our merchandise. They've arrested my mother," she said, panting through her tears.

Amalia, One Eye, and Lupina had no time to answer. Three uniformed men burst in and pointed their weapons at them.

"Stay still, all of you! If anyone moves, I'll put a bullet in them right here, right now," one said.

"Let's stay calm, señores, please," said Amalia, taking charge of the situation. "There's nothing illegal going on here. Everything you see is good Mexican merchandise."

Nayeli and Rosalía, spying on the scene through the gap between two huge pots, exchanged a look of panic and tacitly agreed to remain silent. The policemen hadn't seen them.

"That's of no concern to us, señora. These two smugglers," said another man, gesturing at the girls, "have come here to seek refuge. That makes you accomplices. Come on, you're all under arrest."

There was no point resisting. Four more policemen arrived, agitated and sweaty, to help their colleagues, forcing the women to put their hands on their heads.

"This is an outrage, señores!" shouted Amalia. "Saint Eulalia will deal you the worst kind of punishment, have no doubt."

That was the last thing Nayeli and Rosalía heard before one of the uniformed officers closed the door and left them alone, their presence still unnoticed.

9

Buenos Aires, November 2018

Eva Garmendia's room had always been on the second floor, but when her legs ran out of strength to keep marching up and down the stairs, Don Eusebio decided to move her somewhere that wouldn't be a problem: right at the back of the first floor. Gloria told me Eva's move had caused one of the biggest uproars she could recall at Casa Solanas. Nibbling on pan de muerto dipped in milky coffee, she launched into what she loved doing best: gossiping about other people to avoid talking about herself. Her tactlessness had always struck me as part of her charm.

"She went crazy. That old woman doesn't talk much and won't share her things with anyone. She's really quite selfish and fussy. Because she comes from a wealthy family, she thinks she can manipulate everything to suit her. She's a very difficult old woman," she said mercilessly.

I found it funny that Gloria called Eva an "old woman"; there couldn't have been much of an age gap between the two of them. I didn't laugh, although I wanted to.

"Why was she so mad?" I asked as I repacked all the elements of my grandmother's altar into the brown suitcase.

"She said that people would steal her things during the move and that they were actually changing her room to make her die quicker. All shouts and insults. There was no calming her."

"But they moved her all the same . . . "

"Of course they did! She couldn't climb the stairs. One night she slept on the sofa in the lounge for fear that Eusebio would realize she was too much of an invalid to get to her room." Gloria paused briefly to cut another slice of pan de muerto, then immediately resumed her tale. "When she saw the new room, she settled down a bit. It's positioned well away from the everyday commotion of the place. We oldies tend to be a bit deaf; we can be quite noisy and we laugh a lot, loudly. Laughter is all we have left. And besides, the new room is bigger and brighter, and there's space for some small armchairs and a little table, to makeshift a small private living room. The old woman enjoys receiving visitors as if she were the lady of Casa Solanas, but the only one who ever spent whole afternoons there was Nayeli."

Hearing my grandmother's name in someone else's mouth still felt like a thorn jabbing into me.

"Yes, they were friends for years," I said, without offering any further explanation.

Gloria rolled her eyes; she wanted to make it very clear that she disapproved of anything related to the "old woman."

"I know. They were joined at the hip. Your grandmother was very good, and that woman . . . well, she's a horrible thing. Nayeli spent hours and hours in the kitchen. She said she was cooking for everyone, but that was a lie; she just wanted to flatter Eva."

"Well, she was fond of her," I said, wanting to make excuses for her.

"No one could love Eva. No one."

After my conversation with Gloria, I felt a sudden urge to visit Eva Garmendia, this time without feeling guilty for betraying my grandmother's furtive desire to keep me away from her. Mulling over the few details Gloria had divulged, I walked to the end of the long corridor. She was right: the farther I went, the deeper the silence. It was like entering a bubble. I could barely hear the murmur of a tango playing on a radio somewhere.

The door I found at the end of the corridor was different from all the other doors at Casa Solanas. The sturdy wood had been left bare rather than being painted white. Just like the metal entrance gate and the women of Casa Solanas themselves, the worn parts marked the passage of time. With a tight fist, I knocked twice timidly and leaned my ear against the wood. I could hear the approach of shuffling footsteps. I waited for a few seconds but nothing. I repeated my two knocks with a bit more energy. More dragging of feet. And nothing.

"Eva, it's Paloma. I've come to say hello," I said in a friendly tone.

"We've already said hello. There's no reason to do it again," she replied.

Her voice made me jump. She was close, only the door stood between us.

"Yeah, you're right. I want to talk to you."

"Lies don't make for a good introduction. They're undignified and vulgar," she said.

I took a deep breath and released the air all at once. I felt exposed and confused.

"Okay, okay. You're right, I shouldn't have lied. The truth is that I'd like you to explain what you said to me during Nayeli's tribute."

"I don't remember what I said. At my age, words disappear like dust."

"You mentioned my grandmother's sins," I said, playing my final card.

Eva fell silent. I took her silence to be a good sign. Perhaps I had gotten it right: the only card worth playing is the truth. The door jerked open. The woman in front of me, just inches away, seemed to be someone else. She was enveloped in a long dress that fell to her ankles, dark blue with little white moon shapes, and a brown leather belt fastened with a golden buckle defined her tiny waist. Her white hair was combed to one side, giving her an aristocratic air that combined perfectly with the pearl necklace wrapped twice around her long neck.

"You look lovely, Eva," I said clumsily. I couldn't think of any other way to break the ice.

With devastating elegance, she fluttered her hand like someone well used to compliments.

"Don't talk nonsense, Paloma," she replied, and moved away from the door. "Come in, if you like. It might not seem like it, but I was expecting you."

As Gloria had said, the room was spacious, and the light pouring through the window gave it a natural warmth. Eva invited me to the area she reserved for guests: two small leather armchairs next to a round table with a polished glass top. I sat down, unable to keep myself from thinking how much Nayeli must have enjoyed this place, so different from all the others she had inhabited. Before I could change my mind, I shared my thought with Eva.

"It's true," she replied as she settled herself in the other chair. "Your grandmother liked coming to chat with me. It was the only good thing about moving to this floor. She didn't like climbing the stairs."

"And what did you talk about?"

Eva stared at the floor.

"Life. Her things, my things," she replied.

"And sins," I ventured.

"And sins, yes."

My usual strategy of staying silent so the other person would keep talking wasn't working here. Eva didn't feel the need to fill the gaps with words. On the contrary, the blank spaces were her refuge.

"I'd like to know more about my grandmother. Gloria told me—"

"Gloria's nothing but a windbag," interrupted Eva. "Don't waste your time with her."

"But that's why I came to see you, Eva," I said, feeling slightly guilty. I had no option but to pick a side of the gulf between them. "You mentioned sins . . . What were my grandmother's sins? There are aspects of her life I never knew about. She never told me very much."

"She did right. Nayeli was a very intelligent woman."

"But I want to know," I insisted.

"Your grandmother always said you were a curious little thing, that you couldn't keep secrets, and when you got something into your head, you wouldn't let it go. I can see that was no exaggeration."

Eva stood up. She walked to the window, gazing out for a while. I stayed quiet, struck dumb; I was afraid that the slightest gesture or comment might interrupt whatever was going through her mind at this moment. Eva was making a decision.

"You're going to have to help me with a mission that my dear Nayeli entrusted me with," she said, her back to me, and then added, "Because I do know how to keep secrets."

"Yes," I murmured.

"On the top shelf of the closet, behind my hatboxes, you'll find some answers."

I leaped up from my chair as though I had been electrocuted. The magnificent closet occupied an entire wall, carved on the sides and on each wooden door, with polished bronze handles. I opened it with the fascination of a child. My grandmother's Narnia was behind those doors.

"Use this stepladder," said Eva. "The top shelf is very high."

I did as she said, the aluminum steps creaking beneath my feet.

"I'll just slide the hatboxes to one side," I said, containing a sneeze. The smell of mothballs was overwhelming, but it was the only way Eva had found to keep the pests at bay. "There's a lot of dust up here. If you like, I'll ask Lina to come with a duster."

"Certainly not. Don't even think about meddling with my things," she retorted sharply. "Don't be nosy. That was something else your grandmother used to say: 'Paloma is a nosy person.'"

"Okay, okay, don't get mad," I said.

There was nothing behind the hatboxes. All I could see was the back of the closet.

"Eva, there's nothing of Nayeli's here."

"Look harder," she ordered.

I took my phone out of my dress pocket and used the flashlight to illuminate the back, when a tiny reflection caught my eye. I stretched out my other hand, and my fingertips just managed to reach the find: a golden key. I clambered down the steps and showed Eva.

"The key," she said.

"Yes, I can see that. What's it for?" I asked impatiently.

"I haven't a clue, my dear. One day before she died, your grandmother called for me and gave me this key," she said, her eyes glued to mine. "She hadn't been able to get up for a while—she was in bed all day. She told me to keep it, that it was very important to her. She also told me that when she died, it had to be passed on to you, but not before. And that's what I've done: fulfilled my mission."

I felt like I had reached the end of a tunnel with no way out.

"Did she say anything else, something that might help me find out what this key opens?" I asked hopefully.

"No, not a thing," she replied rather unconvincingly.

I slipped the key into my purse and thanked Eva for her time: a courtesy that was far from heartfelt. It hadn't been much of an exchange: I had come to her room with a question and was leaving with a mystery.

When I was halfway down the corridor, retracing my steps to the exit, I heard a voice behind me: "The story is worth more than the painting. The story is the true work of art."

I spun around and stared at her. She was leaning against the doorframe. Smiling.

"That's what your grandmother said to me when she entrusted me with the key."

I didn't even have time to open my mouth. Eva Garmendia turned on her heels and disappeared into her room. I could hear her singing "La Llorona" on the other side of the door.

10

Buenos Aires, November 2018

I left Casa Solanas and wandered aimlessly. My mind was racing at the thought of the key Eva Garmendia had given me. In a pocket at the bottom of my purse, that tiny piece of bronze hid my grandmother's secrets.

I dived into the first subway entrance I came across; after having to switch twice, I finally reached my neighborhood.

I didn't want to shut myself away in my apartment, and, more to the point, I needed a beer; the last bottle in my refrigerator was almost empty. The bar on the corner was my best option. I headed straight for my favorite table, next to the window. Along with the beer, I ordered a plate of salami and cheese to nibble on. Don Plácido, the owner, added some olives, on the house. They looked rather dubious, but I thanked him anyway.

I occupied myself for a while scrolling on Instagram. Glancing around, I looked for something nice or interesting to photograph; I hadn't posted all day, and I was feeling ludicrously guilty. Nothing caught my eye.

I slipped my hand into my purse and drew out the key that opened something belonging to my grandmother, if only I knew what. I inspected it carefully on both sides. It was shiny and fairly new. I compared it with the keys for my apartment, and the difference was vast: the bronze was opaquer, with some barely visible marks. I laid it down on the table. The red Formica looked pretty good against the gold of the key, so I took a photo and applied a filter to intensify the color contrast.

I spent a few seconds mulling over a caption to go with the post. I never was very good with words; music was my thing. I went for something brief and a bit corny: *The key to my heart.*

I downed my beer in two gulps. The bubbly freshness in my throat raised a smile. I thought about Ramiro, the guy I'd had three dinner dates with at La Costanera, a night bowling, and an ice cream at Puerto Madero.

I returned to my phone and looked up Rama's Instagram account. He used it a lot, one photo per day at least. He never uploaded images of himself; it seemed a rather impersonal account, but it wasn't. His drawings said so much about his personality—anything else would be a waste of information.

Before messaging him, I liked his most recent post: a sketch of small, delicate feminine feet, with a ring on the big toe. They weren't my feet, and I felt a prickle of jealousy in my guts.

As I waited for him to respond, I browsed the notifications I had received beneath the photo of Nayeli's key. My bandmates, who seemed to be online at all hours, had sent heart emojis; a former classmate from the conservatory hoped that, no matter who unlocked my heart, I would always be happy; my neighbor from the third floor added flame emojis. But it was a message from Liliana, the receptionist at the school where I taught music, that caught my attention: *Lovely key, nice and new. I don't know if it will open your heart, but I'm sure it will open a brass filing cabinet. I know one just like it, ha-ha.*

I automatically slid my fingers down my phone screen and sent Liliana a WhatsApp. I needed to see with my own eyes what kind of filing cabinet she was talking about. In less than two minutes, the answer was in my inbox: a hasty snap that got me thinking. I couldn't recall having ever seen a piece of furniture like that in my grandmother's house.

Do you think the key is from something similar? I asked hopefully.

No doubt, she replied triumphantly. *Where did you get it?*

It turned up under my bed. It's very strange, I lied.

I was about to ask Liliana to send me a photo of her key when Rama replied. He wanted to see me, too. I smiled and ordered another beer to celebrate.

Nayeli's house was halfway between the school and my apartment. As I did every Wednesday, I had dropped by the supermarket to buy some nice things for Cándida, not forgetting the bottle of wine she always requested. I rang the bell, and she came out instantly, as ever. Sometime ago, I realized that she had placed a wicker chair by the door; she would sit for hours waiting for one of her children or grandchildren to call in to see her, an increasingly sporadic occurrence.

"I've brought you a few things," I said as I entered.

Cándida's house was the mirror image of Nayeli's: a long hallway, spacious living room, extensive kitchen, two bedrooms with high ceilings, and a patio filled with plants and empty birdcages that at some point had held canaries.

"Thank you, Paloma, dear. I see you brought me some wine . . . How lovely! I'll have a little glass tonight while I read a book of poems the baker gave me."

"Great," I said. "Poetry and wine, I can't think of a better plan."

Once I had put away her food in the refrigerator, I took out my phone and showed her the photo of the filing cabinet from the school library.

"Did you ever see anything like this in my grandmother's house? I don't remember it," I said.

Cándida went to the living room and grabbed a magnifying glass that was sitting on the poetry book.

"I'll have to use this to see it; my glasses aren't up to the job." She laughed, then studied the photo for a while, frowning as she did. "Something rings a bell . . . It'll come to me, Paloma," she murmured, and thought for a few more minutes.

"It doesn't matter, Cándida. If you can't remember, it's no problem. Maybe Nayeli never had a piece of furniture like that."

"Yes, she did!" she announced suddenly. "I gave her something very similar. She stored some knickknacks in it and left it here. I'll show you, if you like."

I accepted her offer, sensing a lie behind the story: my grandmother's house was just as big as Cándida's; there was no reason for her to have left it here.

"Come this way," she said, heading for the patio. "I stowed it away in the shed where I keep my old junk." Cándida continued, "A few years ago, I asked the boy from the grocery store to push it to the back."

As I followed her, I realized, with some annoyance, that Nayeli had hidden several things from me.

"There it is," she said, pointing.

The little room where she kept her old junk was just like the one on my grandmother's side of the fence. Although Cándida's was less full and somewhat cleaner.

I took out the key and hesitated. A kind of lethargy sparked by uncertainty overpowered me for a moment. Playing for time, I prowled around the filing cabinet, key in hand. Then I took a deep breath and plunged the key into the lock. It gave a metallic click. I eased it to the right and then to the left to soften the mechanism that had hardened over the years. I didn't have to do much more. The lock suddenly yielded.

"Oh! See, Paloma! It's full of junk. It all belongs to your grandmother, dear. Take what you want; it's yours."

The first thing I found was a cylindrical box made of bright pink corduroy. Printed in golden letters were the words: *Shocking de Schiaparelli. Parfum.* Inside, an empty perfume bottle shaped like a nude female torso—the most beautiful perfume bottle. At the top, concealing the lid, a bouquet of white and pink glass flowers lent the tiny sculpture a touching delicacy. I held it to my nose to see if it had retained any kind of scent that would lead me to Nayeli, but nothing. It had no smell at all. I placed the box and bottle on the floor, out of the way. Then, carefully, I took out a light package wrapped in white silk paper.

"Clothes, perhaps, do you think?" murmured Cándida.

She was right: it was clothes. But not any old, everyday clothes. I laid out in front of me a red blouse, made from a cotton so fine it was almost transparent. It had short sleeves and geometric embroidery around the neck. I folded it gingerly, afraid it might disintegrate.

"This one's a skirt, is it?" asked Cándida.

I nodded silently. The skirt was red, too. Sewn inside it was a white petticoat with a lace flounce that hung below the lower edge of the skirt. Both garments were quite small; they seemed to be made for a girl. Inside the package, between the folds of the skirt, were two pencils: one yellow and the other blue. I noticed their tips: they looked as though they had been freshly sharpened. When I smoothed out the silk paper to wrap up the clothes, I heard a jingling sound. It was a necklace in a gold so dull, it was almost black. From the chain dangled a cascade of tiny coins in different sizes.

The filing cabinet seemed empty, as though it had decided enough was enough and was refusing to give me anything else of my grandmother's. I took one final look before I closed it, just in case, and plunged my hand right inside, as I had done when I found the key in Eva Garmendia's closet. My fingers closed around a rough tube. It was wedged in diagonally, between the top and bottom of the cabinet.

"There's something else here," I said as I tried to yank the object from the depths of the drawer.

"Shall I bring you a flashlight, dear?" asked Cándida.

"No, no, thanks. I've got it now."

I sat on the floor with my legs crossed, cradling in both hands a roll of tough, creased, yellowed canvas. I unrolled it bit by bit. Inside was hidden another smaller canvas, no more than sixteen by twelve inches, or so I estimated.

The storeroom was quite dark; the bulb dangling from a corner of the ceiling emitted a very dim light that couldn't quite reach the whole room.

"Let's gather up these things and take them to the patio," I said to Cándida. Although the day was getting on, there was still enough natural light.

I smoothed out the two canvases on the tiled patio table. For a while, Cándida and I stood there, mute, unable to tear our eyes from the smaller piece.

"It's a painting . . . and rather risqué, that's for sure," she declared.

I had to sit down. The butterflies in my stomach and weakness in my knees all but knocked me off my feet. Cándida was right: it was a rather risqué painting. The only subject was a naked woman, painted side-on, bending over with one hand on her knee and the other on her thigh. The curve of her back, the roundness of her buttocks, and her left arm strategically hiding her breasts were hypnotic. The dark skin conveyed a wild, animal beauty. Even though her head was tilted over, allowing the long, thick hair to tumble down in pronounced waves, the left profile of her face and her long neck were perfectly visible. She wore nothing but a slick of bright red lipstick, which made her half-open mouth more of a provocation than her nudity.

The background revealed little, or perhaps it revealed everything. At first glance, the figure appeared to be set against a deep yellow, but a few greenish brushstrokes circling the calves gave the sensation that the woman was bathing in a river. Only one part of the painting was indecipherable: on the lower right-hand corner, a patch of red paint almost entirely obscured the water.

"Look at that lovely little ballerina," said Cándida, pointing at the red patch.

I glanced at her in astonishment and also with a touch of tenderness. No one with half a brain could have seen the figure of a ballerina in a stain that clearly ruined a precious painting.

"I think someone spilled red paint on that bit," I said confidently, and looked closer at the work. From the corner of my eye, I could see Cándida emphatically shaking her head.

"Oh, my dear . . . I know my eyes aren't what they used to be, but that red bit is a ballerina."

Cándida's insistence aroused my curiosity. I dragged the table up against one of the patio walls and propped the painting upright. Someone once told me you have to look at paintings from a certain distance to appreciate them in their entirety. I took a couple of steps back. Within seconds I had changed my mind. Before my eyes, that red splotch had turned into a deep red ballerina against a lighter red background. Arms raised, head back, slim legs with pointed toes. It was all perfectly clear.

I went up to Cándida and planted a noisy kiss on her cheek. "You're right, I can see it perfectly now. It's a ballerina, and you know what else I think . . . ?"

I had to stop speaking. The words stuck in my throat. How could I have missed something so obvious? I moved closer again. On the woman's thigh, in ochre, round and the size of a coin, was a mark just like my grandmother's birthmark.

As I tried to compose myself, Cándida went back into the living room to get the magnifying glass again. When she returned, she leaned her forearms on the little table where the canvas that had been protecting the painting was still spread out.

"*I don't want anyone to see what's inside me when my body breaks. I want to return to the blue paradise. That's all I want,*" she read aloud.

I leaned on my elbows beside her. On one side of the canvas, I recognized Nayeli's handwriting, that timid and insecure lettering of someone who learned to write late in life and not particularly well.

"My grandmother wrote that," I said.

"What do you think she meant?" Cándida asked loudly. "Your grandmother always was a bit odd."

I smiled sadly, eyes glued to the painting. I couldn't stop staring at that naked, voluptuous woman; that outrageously erotic image. That woman who I had just discovered was Nayeli Cruz. There was no doubt about it: the nude bather was my grandmother.

11

Limones, Isthmus of Tehuantepec, January 1940

Saying goodbye to Rosalía had been easy. Just days before, Nayeli had learned to leave behind everything she knew. The bar was already set high when it came to goodbyes.

That night she slept beneath the stars. Nayeli was curled into a dry hollow in the earth, on the side of a flat-topped hill. Her body barely fit inside what must have served as a hideaway for some wild animal. She thought of jaguars and started to tremble. Her mouth was dry; her swollen, furry tongue made it hard to swallow.

A few branches and dried leaves were scattered carelessly across the entrance to her little cave. She couldn't remember actually arranging this effective hiding place, nor did she have any sense of how much time had passed since her decision to leave the traveling saleswomen to their endeavors. What she did know was that she was alone now and had to work things out for herself. Going back to Tehuantepec, to her house and family, was no longer an option. Rosa had been very clear, and Nayeli took her older sister's word as gospel.

She crawled out of the hollow. The night sky over Limones was such an intense blue it seemed almost black, but the stars had the same glimmering potency as the stars under which she was born. Her eyelids felt heavy and swollen, and her skin was hot and prickling.

She took advantage of the solitude of the night to do one of her favorite things: she slipped out of her clothes and let the warm breeze fill her pores. Leaving her skirt, huipil, and petticoat to one side, she lay back, gazing at the sky, on a mattress of damp grass, the only bit of green she had seen in Limones. She took this detail to be a blessing. Weakened by fever, fatigue, and adrenaline, each muscle in her body seemed incapable of reacting. With the little strength she had left, she lifted her hand to her chest and squeezed the obsidian pendant firmly.

Once again, Rosa's voice filtered through the stench of dried sweat and the buzzing of mosquitos. "*Someday we'll go to Mexico City, mi Nayelita. A traveling salesman came to the market today; he told me all about it. I know, I know, you don't need to tell me he was a charlatan, of course he was. All travelers are, but Mexico City exists, it's real, and one day we'll go together . . .*"

Nayeli opened her eyes abruptly. She squeezed the amulet even tighter; she felt certain that the piece of obsidian was a direct channel of communication with her sister. From somewhere, she received a surge of energy. Groping around her, she found the basket, stuck her hand right to the bottom, and took out the banana leaf folded in four. She stroked the coins with her fingertips: Rosa's entire savings were there. Suddenly, her head felt as clear as the stars lighting up the sky. She knew what she had to do.

12

Buenos Aires, November 2018

The Museo Pictórico de Buenos Aires had many tricks hidden within its walls, some so obvious they were invisible. Even the marble staircase between the sidewalk and the main door, the building's grand entrance, was fake. No websites or catalog entries certified that the stairs were made of original ivory-cream marble. But there was no need to take the lies too far or to document the fairy tale for it to be effective. The devil lies in the detail: next to the entrance, on a wall, an acrylic sign with black lettering stated: *Visitors are permitted to take photographs of the staircase.* That simple phrase was enough for each visitor to produce a certificate of authenticity in their mind's eye, and the first thing they did was whip out their camera phones to amass a series of shots of the famous stairs from various angles and distances. It would never have occurred to any normal person to take a bottle of vinegar and spray it on a small section of the marble to see whether it produced the bubbles that form only with genuine ivory-cream marble. The only person who ever did was not who you might call a normal person. Emilio Pallares, curator and director of the museum, took seconds to corroborate this sneaky deception and ordered the removal of the acrylic sign that manipulated gullible visitors.

"There's no one more vulnerable than the ignorant. Ignorant people want to hide their ignorance, but they're too lazy to take precautions. That's why this world also has room for those of us who know, who study, who stockpile knowledge: to look after the ignorant as though they were children. Because deep down, that's what the ignorant are: children," Pallares used to say.

His second order, issued just hours after being appointed to his post, was rather more complicated than removing a simple sign. That day, he arrived very early, an hour before the museum opened. He took advantage of the extra time to enjoy a peaceful breakfast in the bar on the corner.

"Grapefruits and oranges have an inner and outer rind, juice sacs, membranes, a central axis, multiple seeds," he'd explained to the waitress as he indicated each part of the fruit with his knife. "There's far too much going on. These fruits lack modesty, they have no elegance. Take them out of my sight, please."

This fit of ill humor distracted him from reading the newspaper headlines. He grudgingly forced down a few peach segments, emptied his cup in three gulps, and strode across the short distance separating him from the museum. The security guard hastily opened the door with his pass. The entrance hall still held its nighttime freshness.

"Good morning, Señor Pallares," said the man.

"This is ridiculous," replied Pallares. He had come to a halt in front of one of the doorways on the back wall, leading off the hall. He cast his eyes over the arches on one side; then he swiveled his head to look at the other. "How could something like this have been allowed to happen?"

"I'm sorry, boss. I don't know what you're talking about," the security guard said finally.

Pallares sighed and adjusted the knot of his silk tie.

The guard removed his hat and held it under his arm.

"Where does the door on the right lead?"

"To the sculpture room," the guard replied confidently.

"Excellent! Perfect!" exclaimed Pallares. "Now, allow me to ask you another question: Where, then, does the door on the left lead?"

"To the sculpture room," replied the guard.

Pallares nodded. He stopped halfway between both doors, under the signpost, and raised his arms.

"How can a museum of this caliber have two doors that lead to the same place? Have you ever seen such nonsense?" he asked, as the guard scratched his head, unsure how to respond. "I need one single route. A nice wide one that leads to the sculpture room. Is that clear?"

"Yes, señor."

Emilio Pallares had been nicknamed "the Lord." His bearing; the way he dressed, spoke, and walked; everything he did made him look like he had been born in the bosom of the British crown. Nevertheless, Pallares couldn't demonstrate any kind of noble title, or even a passport that wasn't one hundred percent Argentinean. His father had worked all his life as a driver for an upper-class Buenos Aires family; his mother, as the housekeeper. Thanks to the generosity of their patrons, he had access to scholarships at the best schools in the city. His parents' humility and the lack of inheritance had not infringed on his choices or desires.

Confident that by having issued an order it would reach the ears not just of the museum staff, but also of many others in the Argentinean art world, he crossed the sculpture room and went down the corridor to his office. He closed the door and stood for some time looking out of the window. The vivid pink blossom of the lapacho trees surrounding the park opposite seemed to him to be the height of vulgarity, but he could do nothing about that. With age, he had grudgingly accepted the fact that he couldn't make the world aesthetically perfect.

His desk held no more than was absolutely necessary: a laptop, a notebook bound in black leather, a Montblanc Classic pen with red gold detailing, and a rotary phone. Emilio Pallares didn't like communicating with a cell phone, he only used one when there was no other option. He didn't like leaving a record of his calls; for him, privacy was one of the few remaining bastions in a world where exhibitionism vampirized people every day, every minute, every second.

He lifted the receiver and, from memory, swiveled the dial number by number, eight digits in all. Finally, after two rings, the call was answered by a deep male voice, which grunted a hello.

"How's *La Martita* coming along?" asked the Lord. "It has to be hanging in the room again by tomorrow."

"It won't be dry by tomorrow."

"Cristóbal, I will say this one last time: the painting has to be hanging in the room again by tomorrow."

From the other end of the line, Cristóbal knew this was a serious ultimatum. It wasn't often that Emilio Pallares called him by his name. To everyone else, he was Cristo, a nickname he liked for its holy connotations. Giving Cristo no time to reply, the Lord hung up, as he usually did after giving an order.

La Martita, as it was known by those in the art world, was an oil painting on a canvas eighteen inches wide by twenty long. Against a background of green leaves, it depicted a black horse with a luxuriantly long mane, painted with a technique so perfect that the viewer could feel the breeze fluttering through the animal's hair just by standing in front of the painting. But its value had nothing to do with the pigments or brushstrokes; it had to do with its history, a detail that is often decisive when it comes to a valuation.

The artist, Marta Limpour, had painted the horse in 1870, when she was just sixteen. She was regarded as rather scandalous at the time: when she worked, she would eschew her dress in favor of men's pants and, thus attired, scour the stables in search of equine models for her paintings. Despite her parents' fury, the mocking of her rural French neighbors, and the punishments issued by her teachers, the girl continued for years to wear men's clothes when she painted. Over time she became a renowned artist, with works in the best museums in Europe, but the painting of the horse languished for a hundred and fifty years in the reserves of a museum in Madrid. It came to light after feminist movements in various countries launched a social media campaign to demand that exhibition curators feature women artists more prominently. And so *La Martita* started to circulate around other continents.

Before accepting the commission, Cristo had spent the best part of a spring afternoon in the Museo Pictórico. Visiting museums always got his pulse racing. As a child, he never hung out in squares or amusement parks, there were no ice cream parlors or bicycle rides along tree-lined avenues. His childhood took place in museum galleries, in the workshops of artists—some renowned, others less so—and in classes for drawing, painting, and mixed techniques. His father always said he had been born with a gift, and that gifts have to be nurtured. His brother was also a competent visual artist, but in the competitions they both entered, Cristo always prevailed, thanks to his talent and perseverance. He didn't like to lose, even less so if he was competing against his brother. He had suffered enough from the fact that his mother did little to conceal her obvious preference for his younger sibling. Good thing the cancer had taken her quickly, Cristo often thought.

The first thing he did when *La Martita* arrived in his workshop, shrouded in nylon and fully adhering to security protocols, was to admire it for an unspecifiable period of time, following a ritual that allowed him to truly immerse himself in the work. He propped the painting up on the stand, opened a bottle of red wine, and, savoring each mouthful, ran his eyes over every stroke, every mark, every intention the artist had expressed on the canvas. Then he placed the glass on the floor and rested his hands on his belly. He could stay for hours and hours in that position, until his fingertips started to burn. At first, he felt just a light tingling, then he needed to rub each extremity. The prickling became extreme, and eventually he was overcome by heat, too much heat. At the precise moment when the unpleasant sensation started to creep toward his palms, Cristo would stand up, mix his oil paints, his walnut oil pigments, select his brushes, and, on a virgin linen canvas cured with tea, start to copy the work like a man possessed.

After his eight years in prison, time was no longer a unit of measurement for Cristo. He didn't care whether a piece took days. This was the main source of conflict with Emilio Pallares. The Lord constantly had one eye on the clock, causing an anxiety that undermined Cristo's work as an artist—because he regarded himself as an artist. The best.

La Martita was almost ready. As the oven came up to temperature, he rinsed his mouth out with mineral water and plunged his hand into a jar of Colombian coffee beans; he arranged a small pile in his palm and sank his nose into them. He needed to have a clean sense of smell for when the painting was inside the oven. The oils in the paint would dry out and, very gradually, start to crackle; from the smell, Cristo knew the exact moment to remove it from the heat.

He gently placed the stretched canvas on a metal plate and, as though it were a steak with potatoes, placed it carefully on the oven shelf and closed the door. As the heat worked its magic, he devoted himself to the final detail: the back of the painting.

The real horse, painted by Marta Limpour more than a century ago, was still on the stand, a silent witness to the infinitely talented Cristo cloning each of its details with a mastery possessed by few in the world. With the same delicacy he would use to undress a woman, he eased the painting from its wooden frame and turned it over. A piece of tape, a wax seal, some kind of annotation or inventory number: the kind of important information that all artworks have on their verso and which is just as important as the front. Collectors, museums, dealers, auctioneers all leave their mark to document a painting's journey over the years.

La Martita had followed a simple path before and after being abandoned in the museum basement. There were only two marks on the wooden frame that held the canvas: a strip of yellow adhesive tape with the inventory number of the Spanish museum and, farther down, seemingly written in India ink, the words: *Salle à manger*. It wasn't the first time Cristo had come across a painting on which the artist had specified where the work should be hung. Martita had painted the portrait of the horse with the intention of seeing it hanging in her own dining room.

Finding a nib and some calligraphy paper, Cristo wrote out the three words several times. His final attempt raised a smile. It was perfect. He unstuck the tape using a scalpel, then removed the painting from the oven. He poured himself another glass of wine and, as though watching a tennis match, flicked his eyes from one to the other. Fake to genuine. Genuine to fake. He smiled again. He hadn't lost his magic touch.

13

Mexico City, January 1940

She was down to her last few coins. The train wouldn't take her all the way to Mexico City, the station guard explained, but if she got off at the final stop, she would be able to find other means of transport. Nayeli didn't dare ask what other means of transport he meant, or the name of the last station; she didn't know whether, with the little money she had, she would be able to afford the final leg of her journey. The fear of revealing her tender age and country roots dissuaded her from opening her mouth again.

Although she was only fourteen, her appearance allowed her to trick most unsuspecting folk. She was quite tall, and her Tehuana dress made her look like a young woman. But on the platform, she felt like everyone was staring at her—such short hair wasn't usual for a girl. Every few minutes, she took a deep breath, holding the air in her chest, pulling her shoulders back, and lifting her chin. It was a posture she had often seen in women who had just arrived in her village in Tehuantepec. They faced their first days as market vendors with a noble bearing; the only way to carve out a place for themselves was to show a confidence they didn't possess.

The sound of the train filled absolutely everything. The air, the sky, the clouds, the sun, and even the earth trembled when the machine finally pulled into the station, like an exhausted bull.

"Don't just stand there, get on!" said a woman, gently pushing Nayeli toward the carriage.

Instinctively, she hugged her basket to her chest as though it contained a whole world. Her world did in fact fit into that limited space, and she would have defended it with her life if necessary. She stood still, just inside the door. She didn't know what to do. Men, women, and children were flooding in all at once, trying to get the best seats next to the windows. While some took their places, others stretched up to put their luggage on the high rack.

Nayeli couldn't tear her eyes away from the woman who had addressed her moments earlier. She was hypnotized by her voice, the way her black pencil skirt hugged her hips, the fair hair held in a ponytail with a bow clip, and the slim hands with pink polished nails. She had never seen a woman like this. She, too, was traveling alone, but with an air of experience that made the train seem like her home. She sat down next to a window and took a white handkerchief from a small purse to clean the glass, leaving a large, round, shining space to peer through. Then she raised her head, and her eyes met Nayeli's.

"Hey, niña!" she said with a smile and a wave. A gold ring caught the sunlight. "Don't stand there by the door; it's dangerous."

Nayeli's heart jumped. She looked to either side and behind her: there was no other girl. The blond woman was talking to her.

"Come here, sit next to me," said the woman, patting the seat with her hand, before adding in a lower, confessional tone, "It's where my husband was going to sit, but at the last moment he canceled the trip. It's better this way; I could do with a single girl's vacation."

Still clutching her world to her chest, Nayeli shuffled over to her.

"Thank you," she whispered as she sat down.

"What's your name?"

"Nayeli. Nayeli Cruz," she replied automatically. All her attention was focused on trying to identify the flower that had been used to produce the perfume that floated around the woman.

"What a lovely name! I'm Marivé. Where are you traveling to?"

"Mexico City," replied Nayeli with conviction. Given all that had happened over the last few hours, her destination felt like the only thing she was certain of.

Marivé opened her mouth and eyes wide at the same time, like a little girl who's just received some good news.

"That's perfect!" she exclaimed. "I'm on my way to Mexico City, too. We can go together. If you want to, of course. Unless someone is waiting for you at the last station . . . "

"No, no one's waiting for me," confessed Nayeli. "I'm traveling alone."

"Ah, intriguing! So young . . . "

"I'm not young. I haven't been young for a long time."

"Sure, sure. My apologies. So what do you say? Shall we go together?" insisted Marivé.

There was no need to reply, Nayeli's face lit up in a dark-skinned, white-toothed smile.

Marivé de los Santos had the ability to talk almost without breathing and to tell stories, about herself and others, without interruption. They chatted and munched on bread rolls as though they had known each other their entire lives, until sleep overtook them both. An hour later, the sun started streaming through the windows.

"Come on, wake up! We're arriving," whispered Marivé as she shook the Tehuana's arm.

When Nayeli opened her eyes, she saw a woman who looked very different from the one she had eaten and chatted with hours before. Her long eyelashes were painted with black mascara; blue shadow covered her eyelids; her cheekbones seemed much pinker, and her mouth looked like a shiny red flower. She had also let down her hair in a mane of golden waves that reached her shoulders. It was the first time Nayeli had ever seen someone so blond and white.

"You look like an angel," she said, her eyes glued to Marivé.

"Or a devil," replied the woman archly.

They got to their feet. Most of the passengers had formed a line at the closed carriage door. When the train stopped, the glass and steel panels juddered open, and a blast of cool air burst in.

"Oh, it's cold!" exclaimed Marivé. "I hope you have a shawl to wrap around you."

Nayeli didn't reply. The only garments she had in the basket were those that Rosa had pinched from the brother of her new husband, but that didn't matter. Nerves and anxiety were running through her Tehuana blood at such a rate that she didn't feel cold. Arm in arm, they left the train.

The station was crammed with people, all very different from those Nayeli was used to seeing around her. They looked much more like Marivé than her family and neighbors. No one was barefoot, and very few wore huaraches. She had never seen so many leather shoes in different colors on the feet of both men and women. She could count on one hand the few Tehuana skirts; the rest were dark garments in a coarse fabric that sheathed the legs and hips, leaving the calves on show. There were no braids or flowers to decorate the hair, and certainly no ribbons with coins. The hairstyles tended to be more modest, held at the nape of the neck with invisible clasps. Everyone walked erect, eyes forward, fixed on a certain point; there was no dallying or distraction in their movements. No one looked at anyone else. They strode ahead, with no time for greetings or smiles.

"Nayeli, this bus will take us to Mexico City," said Marivé, gesturing at the long vehicle with small windows. "We're about an hour away."

"I only have a few coins . . . " the Tehuana confessed.

Marivé burst out laughing and took her by the hand.

The seats were hard. With every mile, the wooden bars dug into their backs and thighs a little more. Despite the discomfort, Marivé and Nayeli settled in as best they could and drifted off.

When the bus reached Mexico City, the driver shouted, "Arriving in Coyoacán in five minutes!"

Nayeli frowned and gently woke her traveling companion.

"There's a problem, Marivé. It seems we aren't in Mexico City after all. The man said we're going to Coyoacán," said Nayeli worriedly.

The laughter echoed loud and clear.

"Oh, but, honey, one of the neighborhoods of the great Mexico City is called Coyoacán, the place of the coyotes!" she explained.

"There are coyotes here?" asked Nayeli, eyes popping out of her head.

"No coyotes, don't fret," replied Marivé, still laughing. "There's a lovely big market and some very grand houses. Churches and parks, too. I'm going a bit farther; I need to get to the Zócalo square."

Nayeli listened closely to her traveling companion's every word. A glimmer of hope warmed her chest.

"Tell me about the market in the city of coyotes," she said.

"It's big. It takes up a whole block, and it's always full of people coming and going. They sell fruit, vegetables, cheeses. Clothes and jewelry, too. Lots of women set up a little chair, light a fire, and cook tortillas and mole. It's a wonderful place!"

"I'm going to get out in Coyoacán," declared Nayeli. Ever since she was a child, she had been taken every day to the market in Tehuantepec. She knew what to do and how to get work. She felt at home in markets. Marivé agreed, but before Nayeli alighted in Coyoacán, she slipped some banknotes and a red lipstick into her basket as a parting gift. They embraced like two old friends and planted loud kisses on each cheek.

"Coyoacán, Coyoacán!" called the driver.

Nayeli stepped down from the bus still hugging her basket. She stood in the middle of a park, until the bus became a tiny speck in the distance. The few people who had gotten off with her moved away on foot along narrow paths that led to paved streets. The trees were regularly spaced and leafy. She picked a path to follow and rested her palm on each trunk as she went by—touching trees calmed her.

She sat down under one that stood a good distance from the busy street. The roar of the trolley cars and green buses terrified her. She tried to decode the letters on the posters plastered over the façades of the shops around the park, but it was hopeless: Nayeli couldn't read. She squeezed the obsidian around her neck tightly and concentrated on trying to hear Rosa's voice. Would her loving advice reach this far?

Shortly after, a woman's cries caught her attention. She was robust like the women in Nayeli's Zapotec family, but she wasn't wearing a Tehuana dress. Nor was she in one of those tight skirts like Marivé wore; she was entirely shrouded in an ochre tunic. She was walking briskly, two small children hanging from the back of her dress trying to keep up with their mother.

"Come on, come on! Hurry up, I have to get to Mondragón on time!" the woman kept shouting.

The obsidian stone suddenly grew hot, so hot that Nayeli had to release it. She took the change in temperature to be a message from Rosa.

She stood up and swiftly followed the woman.

They left the park and walked straight down a street with narrow, paved sidewalks, and firm, flattened earth in the center where the cars passed. Two eyes weren't enough for Nayeli to drink in all that was going on around her: stores with people entering as quickly as they exited; mothers with children on their backs; men hurrying along with leather briefcases. On every corner, the aromas of the street food stalls made her stomach rumble.

She tried to catch sight of the woman in the ochre tunic but couldn't find her. Desperately, she looked all around. The mother and her children had disappeared. Perhaps she should return to the park, where she had felt safe.

In the end, curiosity got the better of her, and she decided to press on. On a corner, to her right, a large house caught her eye. It was at the intersection of two quieter streets. Four rectangular windows looked out over one street; over the other, four more windows and a double door. Except for a red border, the walls were all painted a vivid blue.

She crossed the street, feeling more inquisitive than afraid. All but one of the windows were covered by white lace curtains. Nayeli Cruz wanted to peer in, and, without attempting to hide, she stopped just a few feet away from the uncovered glass. On the other side stood a woman. Her face seemed to hold all the sadness in the world.

14

Buenos Aires, November 2018

After my shower, I inspected myself in the mirror. I still liked my naked body, although my waist wasn't as narrow as it used to be. Luckily, I made up for that with my long, toned legs, which I inherited from my mother's side. I never knew much about my father's side of the family. Or my father, for that matter.

I chose black lace lingerie and a short, loose dress. It was hot, and, what's more, Rama didn't have much time for the art of undressing. I decided I wouldn't dry my hair, my platinum locks always looked sexy without much grooming.

Rama arrived late, as always. And as always, I let it go. Perhaps because since I was a child, my father had gotten me used to the idea of waiting for men, although sometimes he didn't even have the decency to show up at all; or maybe it was just because I really liked Rama.

He was wearing blue jeans and a white T-shirt, a simple look that nevertheless seemed premeditated. His naughty boy's smile and a good bottle of wine got the best of me, and the tray I had prepared with two wineglasses slipped from my hands, falling in a shower of glass on the floor. We laughed.

One of the things I liked about Rama was that he had an original and unexpected reaction to everything.

"Hold it!" he exclaimed as he opened his brown canvas backpack. "Don't pick anything up; don't clear it. Let's get something good out of this disaster."

I stood still, broom in hand, expectant. Rama sat on the floor, crossed his legs, and rested a sketchbook on his knees. My eyes were transfixed by the fingers of his right hand: I couldn't help but be aroused by the way he held the black pencil.

The concentration he gave each stroke, each bit of shading, each line, was hypnotic. The graphite caressed the rough paper, spawning perturbing images. I put the broom in a corner and, like an interrupted Cinderella, sat next to him to watch the creative process more closely.

"What is it, Rama?" I asked in a very low voice so as not to break the spell.

"The shards of glass," he replied mechanically.

"But I see human body parts," I corrected him.

"Yeah, sure. They do look like that," he answered with a capricious half smile.

Feet, hands, heads, eyes out of their sockets, mouths open in screams. All broken, messed up, in pieces. Anyone else in my place would have found them disturbing, but to me, that kind of perversion was gratifying. I shuffled back so that I could appreciate the full perspective of the drawing Rama seemed about to finish. A lock of hair tumbling down the side of a face reminded me of the painting I had found a few days earlier in Cándida's house. The painting of Nayeli.

"Rama, when you're done, I want to show you something you're really going to like," I said, eager at the possibility of surprising him.

"I'm never done drawing. Art has no end and no beginning," he said, looking at me intensely. After a couple of seconds, seeing my confusion, he relented. "But show me now. I'm curious."

I hadn't looked at the painting of my grandmother again since the day of its discovery, partly because anything that reminded me of her caused a stabbing pain in the middle of my chest, and partly out of annoyance. Nayeli had lived a life she had never told me about; seeing her depicted like that, naked in front of unknown eyes and sharing an intimacy that was foreign to me, was rather discomfiting.

When I returned to the room, clutching the roll of canvas, Rama's eyes lit up. His nose was finely attuned to anything that smelled of art. And, whether I liked it or not, Nayeli's painting was art. He took the roll in his hands, with the delicacy of someone picking up a newborn baby, and raised one end toward his nose.

"Wonderful!" he murmured as the smell of old canvas filled his lungs.

"You can unroll it wherever you like," I suggested, trying to divert his attention back to me.

First I had to compete with the shards of glass, now with the painting. I felt like an unwanted guest in my own home, on my own romantic date. He didn't seem to pick up on the unspoken message in my words, because he immediately cleared the table and smoothed out the white cotton tablecloth with both hands. Very carefully, he unrolled the larger canvas; the smaller roll, with the picture, stayed coiled in the middle.

"Do you have a pin or a needle?" he asked.

I ran like an obedient lapdog to the box where I kept a few sewing things and handed him a little box containing pins of various sizes. Rama chose the longest pin and ran the tip around the edges of the canvas. He had to force it a bit; the metal didn't penetrate it easily.

"It's a period piece," he declared.

"I don't know what you mean," I said, confused and by now rather fed up with hovering outside the range of someone whose attention I wanted.

"It's a vintage linen canvas—it isn't new," he explained. "If it was new, the pin would have passed through without difficulty. This canvas is tough."

I shrugged at his obvious comment.

"I know it isn't new. It belonged to my grandmother," I said sarcastically.

Rama ignored me and skillfully unrolled the picture. Not just his face but his entire body seemed to tense all of a sudden, as though he had received an electric shock. His brows knitted together so much that his forehead filled with wrinkles and his eyes narrowed.

"Paloma, I need you to take this painting and hold it up at chest height," he instructed me, and it was almost an exhortation.

I did as he asked.

Rama stood in front of me, a couple of feet away. Although the air conditioning was on, I noticed he was sweating.

"Where did you get it?" he asked without lifting his eyes.

"From an old filing cabinet. It was my grandmother's," I said. Then I corrected myself, "Actually, it *is* my grandmother."

For the first time that evening, something I said had caught his attention.

"What an unusual color palette, and such crude lines! What else do you know about it?"

"That's it, not much more. The naked woman is my grandmother, in her youth."

I can't remember how long I stood there holding up the painting for Rama, but after a while my arms started to ache.

"Okay, Ramiro. I'm getting bored now," I said with a forced smile, and placed the painting down on the table.

He sighed like a child whose toy has been taken away, and he apologized. Then we ordered a pizza and had sex.

We drifted off afterward, intertwined and barely covered with the fresh sheets I had put on the bed that morning.

I'm not sure why, but I awoke with a jolt. Getting out of bed slowly, I tiptoed to the living room. The broken wineglasses were on the floor where we had left them, the sketchbook, too. I took it into the kitchen and started flipping through the pages.

There were drawings on almost every page. One in particular caught my eye: the portrait of a woman. Only half her face was visible, the other side obscured by charcoal shading. Short, wavy hair that sat above the ear; a pendant earring with a small crucifix dangling from the lobe; and a lock of hair falling over her straight nose. At the foot, written in capitals in ink, a name: *GINA.*

"What are you looking at?"

Rama was completely naked, leaning against the half-open kitchen door.

"I was looking at Gina."

He didn't say a word. He just emptied the bottle of water I had left on the kitchen counter.

"I don't like you looking through my things," he reproached me, calmly, not upset. "It's my sketchbook, they're my drawings. And when I draw, I show the hidden things inside my head . . . "

"From what I can see, the inside of your head is filled with broken women, screams, loose parts, and . . . Gina," I said ironically.

"Gina doesn't exist."

And with that, Rama brought the conversation to a close.

The short time it took me to prepare breakfast was long enough for Rama to dress. When he came into the living room, he stood by the table, hypnotized once again by the painting of my grandmother. He seemed to be moving his lips, as though he was talking to that bathing naked woman.

"Can I take a photo of it? The more I look at it, the more I like it. It's a strange effect."

"Yeah, sure. I'm thinking about taking it somewhere to get it framed . . ."

He reacted abruptly, saying firmly, "No, Paloma. Don't even think about it. This type of work must be handled with care; you can't just take it anywhere."

"It's a memento that I want to be able to look at every day on the walls of this apartment," I explained.

Ramiro sighed and ran his hands through the hair falling over his forehead. He seemed troubled. Not a trace remained of the man who had covered me with kisses and caresses just a few hours earlier.

I left the tray on the coffee table and went to my bedroom to put on one of my cotton robes. I couldn't figure out why I felt the need to cover myself. Perhaps it was a combination of fear, insecurity, and shattered confidence. No one wants to have to make their escape naked. On some level, I felt that that wasn't such a ridiculous possibility.

"Okay, Ramiro, I've got stuff to do," I lied as I tied the belt of the robe. For the first time since he crossed the threshold with a bottle of wine, I wanted him to leave. "I want to be alone."

"Yeah, sure. I'll be off," he said, and took a couple of shots of my grandmother's painting on his phone.

Although I had just authorized him to take those photos, I was annoyed when he did. I seemed to have crossed that clear line where you go from wanting everything to wanting nothing at all from a person. In silence, I went to the door and opened it without taking my eyes off his. In silence, Rama packed the sketchbook into his bag, and, still in silence, he left.

I slammed the door behind him, leaving no doubt as to my dissatisfaction. I peeked at him through the spyhole. He was standing by the elevator, still close enough for me to see his fingers nervously tapping at the screen of his phone.

15

Coyoacán, January 1940

She was fed up with being told that those papers sitting on the yellow table were her passport to happiness. What did they know, those who spouted such nonsense over and over, about what happiness meant? How dare they even attempt to explain, to her of all people, what was best for her? She, who had transformed herself alone, without anyone's help, into a work of art. She, who had reinvented herself to save her life; who had become an Indigenous maiden; who had just spent forty-five minutes suspended from the ceiling by a harness, a twenty-pound bag of sand hanging from each thin ankle. No one had suffered enough to talk of happiness to a woman who bore this calvary for the exclusive purpose of stretching out her failed spine.

Before signing the papers, she emptied a bottle of brandy. By force of habit, she managed to get to the bottom in just four long gulps. Using the back of her hand as a napkin, she wiped her mouth. Her favorite orange lipstick left a smear of color. She had spent the early hours of the morning mulling over a box of pencils, choosing which she would use to print her signature on the divorce papers. She decided to go for black; to her, black amounted to nothing, absolutely nothing. The last page had a dotted line. She couldn't help continuing the dots to the edge of the sheet, and right at the end, adding a little drawing of a skull. She was good at skulls.

She turned the page over. It was blank and smooth. What sort of person could leave such a virginal white unblemished? Not her. In her neat, rounded cursive, she composed her own divorce maxim:

Diego—the beginning
Diego—the builder
Diego—my boy
Diego—my boyfriend
Diego—the painter
Diego—my lover
Diego—"my husband"
Diego—my friend
Diego—my mother
Diego—my father
Diego—my son
Diego = me
Diego—Universe, Diversity in unity.

She took a moment to reread the words that had come from her heart. Then, she flipped over the page and, on the dotted line, signed: *Magdalena Carmen Frida Kahlo Calderón.*

She peered over at the wheelchair languishing in the corner. Although her doctor had repeatedly told her to use it, she refused to sit in it in her house. Over the years, she had learned to ration her rebellions in front of an audience. But inside and alone, anything was allowed, even opening another bottle of brandy. She deserved it. It had been a difficult day.

She did try to exert some control, though: instead of long and full swigs, she decided to fill only half her mouth and hold the amber liquid between her tongue and palate for as long as possible.

After a few minutes, she went to the window overlooking Calle Allende, remembering how that same window had captivated her when she was just six, when this room wasn't her living room but her bedroom. Whenever she felt alone, really alone, filled with the most abject solitude, she had found a game that brought the blood thundering back into her veins: she would breathe hard on the glass to fog it up and draw a door with her finger. Through that door, her luxuriant imagination had escaped with joy, with urgency. She would cross a vast plain, until she reached a dairy called Pinzón. The *o* in the name on the sign was open, and on the other side an imaginary friend would wait for her. A cheerful, agile girl, who was always laughing soundlessly and dancing like a feather.

Frida remembered how she used to tell the little ballerina all her sick-girl problems, her secret problems, and that she would run with all her hidden secrets around the courtyard of Casa Azul and hide them under a lemon verbena bush. How happy she had been with her imaginary friend! Every time she thought of her, her world grew a little more.

She filled her lungs with air and emptied them slowly. Then, with both hands, she adjusted the shiny metal buckles of the corset that held her back straight—a seasoned leather corset, waxed and shaped by hand—and immediately felt her organs being squeezed against her ribs. It didn't bother her; she was used to it by now.

Driven by impulse, she parted the lace curtains at the window and misted the glass with her brandy breath. In the cloud of vapor, she drew a door with a finger, and inside the door, the magic *o*. Then, she caught sight of something that made her step back. She closed and opened her eyes several times to see if the vision disappeared. It didn't. The daydream was still there.

Frida placed her hands on the glass and peered through the *o* she had just drawn. On the other side stood a girl with short, wavy hair, wearing a red Tehuana dress. Tall, thin, rather awkward-looking. They gazed at each other for some time, one's green eyes merging into the other's brown eyes. The Tehuana smiled. Frida smiled. The imaginary friend had returned.

16

Buenos Aires, November 2018

Cristo had delivered his fake *La Martita* on time and to spec. The painting crafted by his own brushstrokes and pigments, complete with the log of the work's journey on the verso, was hanging on one of the main walls of the Museo Pictórico de Buenos Aires, in exactly the same place and under the same lights as the original *La Martita* had been displayed for so long. The fate of the real painting was of no great concern to Cristo.

He had always understood that for his job to exist there had to be an artist and plenty of ignorant people with deep pockets. And he was convinced of the value of his work; he wasn't merely making copies: what Cristo did was pure art. He liked to define himself as a "creator of authentic fakes." The terms *con man* or *fraudster* offended him. He put heart and soul into painting works without deceit, works that said what they were. And besides, what was the value of a falsity? What was the value of the truth?

Whenever he had finished and delivered a piece, Cristo would visit his best friend in the San Roque Open Prison, where elderly convicts went to serve their sentences, men who no longer knew how to live in freedom and had no interest in doing so. "El Abuelo," the grandfather, was one of the most respected inmates, not just among the prison population but also among the guards. A man of few words and a friendly demeanor. But he hadn't always gotten on so well behind bars. The early days had been hell.

Back then, everyone knew him as Arjona, "The Murderer." He had been given a life sentence for killing a woman and her four-year-old son. Arjona always claimed to be repentant. He wasn't a murderer. But all his regrets couldn't change what had happened that Christmas night.

It hadn't occurred to anyone that the metal scaffolding that had been erected to allow for repairs to the rear façade of the museum might turn out to be a perfect launchpad for thieves to sneak inside. But that is precisely what Miguel Arjona and the cousins Danilo and Esteban Páez did. They navigated the broad and breathtaking galleries of the museum to the exact place they had been directed. The instructions had been very precise: collect twenty jade pieces and the work *Muerte Amarilla* by the Argentinian painter Leopoldo Blates.

In less than two hours, the three thieves had packaged up the loot, stashed it in the trunk of the car, and started celebrating their own Christmas by uncorking a bottle of Veuve Clicquot.

A woman who'd happened to be leaving her mother's house at that moment alerted the local police. "Get down to the museum. There's something funny going on—there's a metallic blue car parked there and three men drinking very expensive champagne on the sidewalk. Go and see what's happening; that's what we pay your wages for."

Miguel Arjona had been the first to see the flashing blue lights of a patrol car whizzing along Avenida Libertador. A single shout was enough for the three men to jump into the car, Arjona at the wheel and the Páez cousins in the back seat.

The chase went on for more than fifty blocks. Just before Retiro station, a mother and her young son were crossing the road. The woman held one of the boy's hands while he used the other to hug the teddy bear Santa had brought him. Arjona had no time to swerve. The bumper hit them full-on. Mother and child were left sprawled in the middle of the street. Arjona didn't brake; he just concentrated on getting away. He was carrying twenty million dollars in the trunk.

Cristo showed his ID at the security entrance. He endured the body search and watched as the guards destroyed the lemon pudding he had brought, looking for drugs or blades. He wasn't fazed; he was used to eating cakes, breads, and cookies broken into a thousand pieces. His eight years behind bars had prepared him for anything.

El Abuelo was waiting for him, as usual, sitting under the vine in the little yard where the inmates had set up a community garden. He had prepared some yerba maté that, as usual, had gone cold.

"Hey, what's up, muchacho? Good to see you!" he greeted him. "It's been a while. . . I guess you've been busy painting?"

Cristo smiled and nodded.

"I did a Martita that turned out perfectly."

"You don't say! *La Martita*'s a beautiful work!" exclaimed El Abuelo thoughtfully. "They should be able to shift it quickly. It's a low-profile work, calm, and worth a fair whack. And I don't suppose it was too much of a bitch to paint . . . "

"No, it wasn't. I must admit, it was kind of a cinch, boring even."

El Abuelo burst out laughing and slapped Cristo on the back. "Well, my friend. You can't always screw the hottest women or drink the finest wines, much less fake the best paintings. But we've all gotta make a living."

"True enough. Not everything in life is a Blates."

The painting *Muerte Amarilla* by Leopoldo Blates had made a mark on both their lives. After the hit and run, not knowing whether or not the woman and her son had survived, Arjona stuck to the plan and drove to a warehouse on Calle Suárez in the La Boca neighborhood, where he was expected. Two men he had never seen before checked over the jade pieces and pulled the cotton cover off the Blates painting.

That was the first time Arjona saw Cristo, a boy who seemed hypnotized by the perfect brushstrokes.

"Yes, I can do it," Cristo had said with astonishing confidence.

The following day an unknown man had left the canvas at the boy's door.

"And how are things with you, son?" asked El Abuelo with genuine interest.

"I feel like I want to travel to Europe, to study painting."

"What the hell for? You're the best—you were born with all that studying already inside you," said El Abuelo.

Cristo always liked to hear his art being praised, but his desire to perfect his technique was stronger.

"And how's your brother?" the old man asked to change the subject. He noticed that Cristo didn't like the question, and added, "Is the asshole still painting?"

Whenever anyone mentioned his brother, Cristo feigned a fraternal love he had never felt. When he saw him, Cristo had a terrible urge to punch him, but usually tried to restrain himself. There had been only one occasion when he couldn't control his rage and landed such a thump that it had left the boy, eleven at the time, flat on the floor with a split lip. That was the night he had started to copy the Blates.

He had folded away the cover, placed the stolen painting on one of his easels in his bedroom, and lost himself again studying its details. Just as he was about to start setting out the palette of colors he would need, his brother burst into the room without knocking and called him by his full name.

"Cristóbal, did you hear what they're saying on TV?" he'd asked in that infuriating high-pitched voice.

"No, and I couldn't care less. Close the door and get lost," replied Cristo, without lifting his gaze from the colors he was mixing.

"Come and see! Come on, I mean it!" insisted the boy. "Some thieves robbed the museum and killed a woman and her son. On the news—they're showing a painting just like the one you've got there. It's exactly the same!"

Cristo felt his hands start to cramp up. Had his brother mentioned deaths? He thundered out of his room and stood right in front of the television in the living room. When he saw the photo of the woman and her son filling the screen, he thought he might faint.

"Cristo, are you one of the art thieves?" asked the boy.

The thump hit the intended mark, right in the middle of his face. The boy dropped right there, next to the telephone table, the blood gushing down his neck, staining his T-shirt.

At that moment, at the tender age of eleven, Rama swore to get revenge on his brother.

17

Coyoacán, January 1940

Frida opened her front door. It was unlocked, as usual; she simply couldn't imagine anyone having the nerve to enter a sanctuary without permission, and Casa Azul was her sanctuary. She crossed Calle Londres diagonally, toward Allende, without looking both ways, seemingly unconcerned about an oncoming car or bus. She wasn't what you would call a cautious woman. Her talent lay in dealing with the consequences. The heels of her red boots sank into the cracks in the damp earth that outlined the paving stones on the sidewalk. She couldn't tear her eyes from her imaginary friend. She was almost scared to blink in case the girl disappeared.

The young Tehuana was still standing in the same place, in her red skirt and huipil, gripping the basket that hung from her scrawny shoulder. Frida felt the urge to embrace her and confess just how much she had missed her.

"Señora, why are you crying? Has something happened?" Nayeli asked.

She, too, was reluctant to avert her eyes from the woman approaching her. Everything about her seemed extravagant. The long, deep green skirt, with the lace petticoat hanging to cover her feet, and the white huipil embroidered with leaves made her feel for a moment like she was back in Tehuantepec. But the leather straps with silver-plated buckles girdling the woman's torso, and her rickety gait, sparked Nayeli's curiosity.

"You've happened," replied the woman with a smile, followed immediately by a question. "Are you real?"

"Yes, of course. Well, I think so anyway," she said, shrugging her free shoulder. "My name is Nayeli Cruz."

The woman repeated the name several times under her breath, as though wanting to imprint the letters on her brain, and she answered the question Nayeli hadn't asked.

"My name is Frida. Frida Kahlo. Would you like to come to my house to play with my dolls?"

Nayeli had to stop herself from clapping with excitement. She had never had a doll of her own; at home there had been only one, which she shared with Rosa.

"Thank you, Señora Frida, but I don't want to be any bother," she replied. The politeness her mother had instilled in her ran deep.

The woman burst out laughing and took her by the arm. That was Nayeli's first encounter with one of Frida's dominant character traits: she always got her own way.

That first time she set foot in Casa Azul, she had no notion of what was to come, but she would never forget the sensations taking hold in her chest. The wooden door, painted a livid green, led to a short corridor with walls in the same blue as the façade. Hanging up high to one side, huge Judas figures fashioned from colorful papier-mâché welcomed them.

"They're good, aren't they?" commented Frida, obviously accustomed to everyone stopping to admire them. "They were made by Carmencita; she's a wonderful artist, my chief Judas maker. No one crafts such wonderful figures as she does."

She gently pressed the small of Nayeli's back, inviting her to continue along the path. The corridor came out in a courtyard that at first glance seemed unkempt: bushes outgrowing their pots, cacti blocking the way, and countless pieces of iron and sheet metal daubed with different colors of paint. Once the eye got used to the chaos, however, the beauty emerged.

Nayeli extracted her hand from Frida's and hurried to the stone fountain. The gushing of the crystal-clear water attracted her like a magnet. It sounded just like her river, the River Tehuantepec. When she saw the bottom of the fountain, she gave the first of many belly laughs that would surge from her body at Casa Azul: two spread-eagled toads, painted on broken mosaic tiles, struck her as the funniest, most original thing she had ever seen. Frida, who was a fine companion in drunkenness, tears, and laughter, had no hesitation in joining in.

"I made those toads in honor of Diego, who is also a fat, ugly toad," she said, and adeptly changed the subject. "Let's go to the kitchen for a drink, and you can tell me all about yourself."

The joy transmitted by the garden contrasted with the dark living room. The closed windows and curtains allowed only minimal light to enter; the smell of enclosure and tobacco was suffocating. The table was strewn with empty bottles, papers, dirty plates, and glasses. In the middle of the room, between one of the windows and an archway that led to the dining room, stood a wheelchair.

"Whose wheelchair is that?" asked Nayeli.

"It's mine. Everything here is mine," replied Frida, thumping her chest.

"But I don't understand . . . You can walk."

"Not as well as I used to." She raised her skirt and stuck out her right leg. "See how skinny this leg is? I had polio as a child, and it stayed like this: my peg leg."

Nayeli examined it with interest; she could see the defect clearly.

"Is that why you wear that corset with braces?" she asked, gesturing at Frida's torso.

"No, of course not. That's a whole different story. Misfortune has always been pitiless with me. I was in a collision that broke my spine and neck into a million pieces. That accident knocked me off course and left me all broken."

"You don't look broken to me," said Nayeli, to whom the woman seemed more of a drama queen than her godmother, Juana.

Frida hid her legs beneath her skirt again and placed a rough but tender hand on the girl's cheek.

"Of course I am. You might not see it, but inside I'm in pieces, like broken glass. The accident happened when I was more or less your age. It was a strange kind of collision. Not violent, but oddly quiet, slow, and everyone involved was hurt. Me more than anyone," she added pensively.

"Tell me more about it," asked Nayeli, who was always reminded of her grandmother when someone told a story.

Frida sat down in the wheelchair. Nayeli sat beside her on the floor, legs crossed, ready to listen to Frida talk about her favorite subject: herself.

"In those days I had a boyfriend, Alejandro. He was a good guy, handsome. We had been at the Zócalo, and we were taking the bus back to Coyoacán. We had caught an earlier one but had to get off because I had lost a lovely little paper parasol. Do you like paper parasols?" asked Frida, interrupting herself. Nayeli gave a slight nod, eager to get on with the story. "Well, right at the corner of the San Juan market, we crashed. A trolley car was coming the other way, very slowly, and our driver was impatient. When the trolley turned the corner, it rammed the bus against a wall." Frida fell silent and gestured at a bottle of brandy on a yellow cabinet. Nayeli jumped up and reached for the bottle. After two long glugs from the neck, Frida continued: "When we collided, all I could think about was the lovely balero toy I had in my hand, which went flying with the impact. I couldn't gauge how bad my injuries were because I felt no pain, nothing. It's not true that you're aware of what's happening in a crash, or that you cry. I didn't shed a tear, even when the handrail pierced right through my body like a sword. A man picked me up and put me on a billiard table in a bar nearby, until the Red Cross medics arrived."

"Rail and all?" asked Nayeli, eyes wide.

"Rail and all. All I remember is voices shouting: 'The ballerina! The ballerina!' Sometime later, Alejandro told me that one of the other passengers on the bus was a painter who had a bag of gold dust and that, with the impact, the dust showered my body and I was all gilded, like a ballerina. Isn't that a lovely image? Blood and gold make a nice combination."

Although Nayeli nodded her agreement, in reality, she was shocked. As the brandy disappeared, one swig at a time, Frida told her about the months in the hospital—the operations, the treatments, and her efforts to get her boyfriend, Alejandro, to visit her.

"I didn't know that my prince had gone to study abroad, and I spent hours writing him love letters, while death danced around my bed every night. I sealed my letters with kisses in a red lipstick that my sister Cristina had brought me, and I would take pink feathers from a pillow I burst out of sheer fury one afternoon, and slip them into the envelopes. At that point I still hadn't gotten used to suffering. Later, when they brought me back here, they left me lying in bed with my entire body in a cast, like a mummy. You have no idea how funny it was trying to draw beautiful pictures on the cast."

"I don't find it funny, Señora Frida. It must have been very painful," said Nayeli.

Frida placed the empty bottle on the floor next to her wheelchair and looked at her. "Nothing is more valuable than laughter: that's something you must learn. It takes strength to laugh and to let yourself go, to be lighthearted. Tragedy is the most ridiculous thing."

That was one of the first lessons Nayeli learned from Frida. She swore to herself that, from that moment on, laughter would be a companion for life.

"Well then," said the woman, standing up with some difficulty. "Shall we go and meet my dolls?"

She tottered sideways, like a tower about to collapse. With effort, she managed to regain her balance, defying the law of gravity. With every abrupt movement, she adjusted the leather straps of her corset. She looked so thin, so fragile, and so ephemeral, as though she might disappear at any moment.

Frida's bedroom was small. The white walls and the polished wooden floor and baseboards gave it a sober, monastic feel, very different from the rest of the house and indeed its owner. A few small frames holding old photographs and a bookshelf were the only decorations.

It was the bed that really caught Nayeli's eye; she had never seen anything like it. The single mattress was deep and covered in a white cotton bedspread with a delicate embroidery of orangey flowers and leaves in different shades of green, done in cross-stitch, a stitch achieved only by skilled embroiderers, like those of her family in Tehuantepec. She herself had never been meticulous enough to be good at embroidery, nor did she have the required patience. On the pillow was a linen cover with more embroidery, this time depicting Christmas mistletoe and, in the center, in red thread, a short word that Nayeli was unable to read.

"What does the pillowcase say?" she asked.

"It says 'Cariño,'" replied Frida. "Don't you know how to read?" she added with concern.

Nayeli didn't reply, but her eyes dropped to her toes, head bowed.

"That's terrible! This can't happen!" Frida exclaimed furiously. "The true revolution will come when all Mexicans, men and women, know how to read, when they all have access to education. Lift your head, Nayeli. The people who should be hanging their heads in shame are the ones who haven't yet brought the revolution to you. I will be your revolution, you'll see."

The young woman raised her head and smiled. She took a deep breath and held back her tears.

"Come here, help me lie back in bed. My spine hurts like the devil," said Frida. "And lie down beside me."

Frida's arms were thin as sticks. As soon as Nayeli took hold of them, she had to lessen her grip for fear of breaking them. She followed the woman's body down and adjusted the pillow beneath her head. Nayeli's nose filled with the scent of the flowers that adorned the dark braids wrapped around the crown of Frida's head. They lay side by side, on their backs, looking up at the canopy of the wooden bed, supported by four columns. A mirror reflected their bodies from waist to head.

"Why does your bed have a wooden ceiling and a mirror?" asked the Tehuana.

"To look at myself, so that I don't lose myself," replied Frida. "This is the bed I lay in for all those months when I was convalescing after the accident. My face was the first thing I saw when I opened my eyes and the last thing before I closed them. No one has looked at me as much as I've looked at myself. The accident deprived me of many things. But I never lost myself. There I am in the mirror; there you have me."

Nayeli, who had grown up seeing her sister Rosa's face first thing every morning and last thing every night, now fixed her eyes on the mirror and concentrated on Frida's face. She felt the same peace, the same soothing sensation as they fell asleep.

Nayeli wasn't sure how many minutes or hours had passed when a deep, hoarse voice woke them from the other end of the house.

"Frisita, Frisita! My little dove, where are you?"

Frida struggled to sit up, resting her back against the wooden headboard.

"Here comes that sapo gordo, shouting like a crazy man," she said with barely concealed annoyance. "He must be hungry, for sure. Those little brats he chases around can't even cook up a tortilla."

Nayeli helped her stand up. The man was still calling.

"Why does he call you Frisita?" she asked. "Isn't your name Frida?"

"Because children play with words, and that fat toad is a child," she replied as she left the room and headed toward the voice.

Nayeli was surprised: Frida now seemed much frailer than she had a moment ago. Not only was her walk twisted, but she had to support herself on the walls as though they were a crutch. Her tender, lively expression had become a painful, deathly grimace. Even the color of her skin seemed to have dulled from a gleaming tan to a pale yellow.

They went out into another part of the garden and up some wide stone steps. Mysteriously, Frida seemed quite agile again as she climbed. They entered a room more spacious than the living room. The walls were windows of spotless glass from floor to ceiling. Everything was bathed in sun and light. In the middle sat an enormous polished wood table, the biggest Nayeli had seen in her life. And the person on the other side of that table was no child.

Standing with hands on hips, a giant of a man was watching them both with surprise and curiosity. He was wearing a black suit with a white shirt and starched collar, and a wide leather belt with a metal buckle. His felt hat made him seem taller than he was, and his miners' shoes had left a muddy trail on the floor. Two features of this colossal body stood out: the taut, rounded stomach and the bulging green eyes. *Frida's right*, thought Nayeli, *he does have a toad face.*

"Frisita, my love, look at you! You can barely stand!" he exclaimed, coming around the table and, with a firm, almost effortless movement, lifting Frida in his arms as though she were a baby. "You must use your wheelchair until you're better, or stay resting, my dove. Like the gringo doctors told you."

Frida sank her head into the man's chest and took a deep breath, as though she could fill her nose, her lungs, her blood, and even her brain with the strong scent of sweat and laundry soap.

"Put me in that little chair," instructed Frida, "the one next to my painting."

When Nayeli tried to cover her legs with the knitted blanket she found on the arm of the chair, Frida stopped her.

"Leave it, leave it. I'm not cold. Take a good look at this man, Nayeli. Don't ever forget a single detail," she said ceremoniously. "He's the greatest muralist you'll ever meet in your life. Or rather, the only one. He is Diego Rivera."

Diego and Frida applauded as though they had just listened to a show being performed.

"Go easy, my dove. You always exaggerate. I'm not the only one," said Diego, laughing. "Don't forget Siqueiros and Orozco . . . "

"Don't utter their names in this house!" shouted Frida from the very depths of her being, causing Nayeli to jump. "We don't name traitors here, or those who have done you harm, mi niño. Anyway, look at this pretty little green-eyed girl. Her name is Nayeli Cruz, and she's my imaginary friend."

Diego approached Nayeli with one hand outstretched. With the other, he took off his hat and held it against his chest as a mark of respect. "Welcome, Nayeli Cruz. It's a pleasure to have you here. Any friend of Frida's is a friend of mine," he said, squeezing her hand firmly.

"Thank you, señor. But I'm not imaginary, I'm real."

Frida and Diego burst out laughing at the same time. They seemed remarkably coordinated in the way they reacted to jokes and stimuli that only they understood. They possessed an amazing ability to create a world of their own in a matter of seconds, leaving everyone else on the outside.

"Naturally, I can see that you're real," replied Diego, replacing his hat on his head. "But you are very honored to have entered the imaginary world of my dove Frisita. Not everyone is so lucky."

Frida took advantage of the greetings between Diego and Nayeli to open some cognac she had hidden under her chair. The second gulp, straight from the bottle, gave her the impetus to say something she didn't want to say.

"What are you doing here, Diego? I've signed the divorce papers. I've got the message loud and clear; you want to abandon me—"

"Don't say that, Frisita," interrupted Diego in distress, his shoulders slumping and head dropping to one side. "You know it's not for lack of affection. I love you too much to cause you any future suffering and torment."

"And you've won, mi niño. I'm letting you go. Although you've always been free. You've always wooed any goddamn woman you wanted to woo, and I've allowed it. My problem is when you sleep with women who are unworthy or inferior to me. That's what you don't understand."

Diego turned around and stood with his back to Frida and Nayeli. Looking out at the garden always helped him think.

"But Frida . . . if I let you draw that line, I allow you to delimit my freedom . . . "

"Ayy, sapo gordo. Ayy, mi Dieguito!" she exclaimed. "You're the depraved victim of your own sexual appetites. The divorce is a lie you're telling me and the worst thing you're doing to yourself."

They fell silent. Nayeli had the uncomfortable feeling of being an extra, listening to a private conversation between adults. But Diego and Frida were accustomed to airing their dirty laundry in public, as though their issues had to be evaluated by everyone.

"You can leave now, mi Diego," said Frida, breaking the silence with a luminous smile. "I'll stay here with Nayeli, my imaginary friend, my Tehuana doll."

She asked Nayeli to see Rivera out, as though he didn't know the way; it was her attempt to make him feel like an outsider in his own home.

"Where did you spring from, then?" Rivera asked her as they crossed the main room to the door onto Calle Londres.

Nayeli didn't know what to say. For the first time, she felt as though this place where she longed to stay was under threat. Diego Rivera was no longer using the contemplative tone he had deployed with Frida.

"I'm the new cook, Señor Rivera," she lied. "I'm Frida's cook."

18

Buenos Aires, December 2018

Following our failed date, Rama left me several messages. I didn't reply to any of them. Sometimes women need to be in control; we have to take the reins for ourselves. Rama had told me not to get the painting framed, so that was precisely what I was going to do: frame it.

I rolled up the canvas with my grandmother's picture and slipped it into a garbage bag. After a quick internet search, I decided to take it to a place the Google reviews claimed was "friendly and reliable," as well as being one block away from Cándida's house—a not insignificant detail—which meant that I could drop by to say hello. She was the closest thing I had to a grandmother now, and I felt the need to redress the absence of that deep bond.

As I took the subway toward disobedience, I thought of my mother. Since my grandmother's death, we had exchanged only a couple of messages out of courtesy: *How are things? Are you feeling better? Lovely day.* In the last one, she told me she had noticed at the funeral that I was looking "a teensy bit chubby." I don't know what annoyed me more: how quickly my mother's manners disappeared, or the cutesy words she deployed when she aimed to wound, as though she wanted to do it gradually, stabbing with a blunt knife. Was she even aware that her own mother had posed nude in front of some unknown painter?

The image of the necklace with the obsidian stone she had placed on Nayeli's casket was nagging at my mind more and more. Occasionally, I regretted not having plucked it off the bouquet of flowers where she had left it, but at the same time, I thought it was good for mother and daughter to share a secret; it was almost touching.

I always knew my mother hadn't wanted to be one. She never said as much, but she made sure I knew, and that revelation comforted me. The problem wasn't me. The problem was her complete inability to give of herself. Anything that demanded her attention or presence got broken; I didn't break, thanks to my grandmother, but I did pay a lot of attention to my mother—everyone does.

Nayeli always said she had been brilliant and engaged as a child, and an extremely intelligent and independent teenager. The woman I knew was eccentric, able to cut through the atmosphere wherever she went. With the same elegance she employed to empty champagne bottles with no apparent effects, she would stop someplace random, stick her hand into her purse, and start to hand out money as though the bills were advertising flyers. Or she would take off her shoes and majestically perform some ballet steps on tiptoes. Then she would return to her stern, conservative persona with such speed that her silliness was forgotten and no one would dare think of her as crazy. Felipa could still terrorize with her gaze or with her words, whichever came first; she handled her lethal weapons with the same skill.

As a child, I often wondered if I had been adopted. Sometimes, I still do. She only ever told me about my father once. She described him as a one-night stand she never saw again and whose name she didn't even catch. In secret, I invented names for him, nicknames and physical features. By now, he was nothing but a shadow, as vague as he was unnecessary. All I needed was the memory of my grandmother and—just a tiny bit—my mother's presence.

I got off at Boedo station and walked to the picture-framing store. It was tiny. The window display was covered in dust, crammed with mirrors and frames of different materials, piled up carelessly. In one corner, a striped cat napped peacefully. I smiled. But my smile faded when I saw the little white notice with blue lettering announcing that the store would be closed until the following week.

I was about to walk away when I noticed a movement behind the counter. I drew closer to the glass and cupped my hands around my eyes. A thin man wearing dark blue overalls was rifling through some drawers at the side of the room. I knocked gently on the door. The man raised his head. Looking rather annoyed, he walked over and opened the door a couple of inches.

"Señorita, can't you read?" he asked. Although the question was hostile, his tone was friendly enough.

"Yes, I saw the notice, but I took the liberty of knocking because I need to frame a painting, and everyone in the neighborhood tells me you're the best man for the job," I lied.

The man deliberated for a few seconds, then finally opened the door properly and grudgingly ushered me in. The smell of canvas and wood glue was intense but not unpleasant.

"The store is closed. I came for some invoices that need to be paid. The smell is quite strong for the unaccustomed, but, well, don't complain," said the man.

"I'm not complaining," I said, my irritated eyes filling with tears.

Taking pity on me, the man started up a small electric fan on the counter and pushed it toward me.

"A bit of air will soothe it," he said. "Let's do this quickly. What do you need framed?"

Without delay, I took the roll with Nayeli's picture from my nylon bag. The man cleared the counter and stretched it out over the Formica.

"Very nice painting, señorita. How would you like to frame it?" he asked.

"I thought maybe a thin, gold frame might bring out the colors."

"I wouldn't go for gold. Black would be better. Thin and black," he replied, decision already made.

I smiled and held up both hands in defeat. "All right, you know best. When will it be ready?"

The man took down my name and phone number in a notebook. "I'll be in touch next week. You can pay when the work is done."

I thanked him and checked the time. If I hurried, I might make it to Cándida's house in time for lunch. At the bottom of my purse, the missed calls from Rama were starting to add up. I didn't hear them.

19

Coyoacán, January 1940

The sun streaming through the high rectangular window, its green-painted wooden frame splitting the glass into perfect squares, highlighted all the yellow around the kitchen: table, chairs, shelves, cupboards, dressers, and huge vases.

"Why so much yellow?" asked Nayeli as she wandered around the kitchen, a spacious room that she knew would become her haven.

"Because it's the color of fertility. Although by this stage, I think we can assume that the spell didn't work for me," replied Frida in that tone of pained resignation she did so well.

Nayeli didn't pick up on Frida's shameless attempt to elicit pity from her; her attention was caught by the row of earthenware pots on a cement counter clad in blue and yellow tiles. She couldn't help smiling. Since she was a child, in her humble house in Tehuantepec, those pots had been part of almost every instruction she was ever given. No one in their right mind would cook beans in steel, iron, or copper pans. "True Mexicans are nourished by the flavors that build up in the ancestral clay of the pots we use to cook," her mother would reiterate every time she lugged the heavy pan to the fireplace.

Frida's cooking pots were new; they looked like museum pieces.

"Does no one eat frijoles in this house?" asked Nayeli, astounded by the pans' unblemished bases.

"Of course we do! We're Mexican!" exclaimed Frida, with an abrupt laugh. "We have frijoles running through our veins. Black beans are my favorite. I could eat an entire bag."

"But where do you cook them? Not in these pots . . . " insisted Nayeli.

"No, that's true. My Diego is a gluttonous toad. I told him to take everything he needed to his new house so that Irene can cook his broths, his tamales, his enchiladas, or whatever other treat he takes a fancy to," she replied, hands on her waist, the movements of her head making her earrings jingle around her. "You know how to make frijoles?"

"I know all the secrets of cooking," replied Nayeli. "So is Irene Don Diego's cook?"

Frida flicked both hands contemptuously. "Not at all. Irene is a dreadful painter, and she's that gordo sapo Diego's latest squeeze. But I don't want to talk about that woman—she's just another one of them. I want you to cook for me. See how skinny I am? I'm practically a skeleton! I need to nourish my body and soul. Are you up to the job?"

Nayeli nodded enthusiastically, never imagining that the soul of the woman in front of her could devour much more than plates and plates of beans. Since Diego had moved out of Casa Azul into his workshop in San Ángel, Frida had been living off brandy and tequila; occasionally, she would chew unenthusiastically on a lump of bread with butter, or sip a glass of milk she kept cool in a bucket of cold water.

"Do you like milk?" she asked suddenly. Throwing out statements and questions at random was another of Frida's personal trademarks.

"Yes, of course," answered Nayeli. "I love it."

Frida started to spin around. Her green silk skirt floated around her legs with such ease and lightness that it managed to hide the clumsiness of that rusty body. But a couple of spins were all she could manage. She groped for one of the wooden chairs and dropped heavily into it, like a sack of potatoes, smiling with the satisfaction of a single woman in constant search of camaraderie.

"You've made me so happy, Nayeli! I'm so full of joy I even feel like dancing. Milk is my favorite; I'm convinced it's a taste we develop from birth. That warm, thick, white liquid was my first pleasure, the most intense of my whole life. Not long after I was born, my mother got sick. It was an Indigenous wet nurse who fed me. She was meticulous: she would always wash her breasts before offering them to me. I remember it perfectly; she used a white cloth," she said, gazing up at the window.

Nayeli listened to her doubtfully. It would have been impossible for Frida to remember that kind of detail when she was just a baby, but she held her tongue. She loved hearing stories; their plausibility wasn't really the point.

Frida plowed on with an activity at which she excelled: talking about herself. "My mother had nervous episodes and couldn't take care of me. It was my sisters, Matilde and Adriana, who raised me and pampered me, and my wet nurse's milk, of course."

"What was wrong with your mother?" asked Nayeli, sitting cross-legged on the floor.

"Misfortunes befell her, one after another. And my father, too. Everyone in my family is ill-fated. My mother witnessed her first boyfriend take his own life right in front of her eyes. And my father had to see his first wife die in childbirth. So much tragedy and so young!" she exclaimed pensively. "But the Virgen of Guadalupe did her thing and made them fall in love with each other, although tragedy was already part of their DNA, and it was all passed down to me. My mother couldn't read or write; all she could do was count money. And she was good at that. And my father is an artist, a photographer who has taken pictures of everyone, even poor people. It's not just the rich who deserve to have a face. That's why I'll paint anyone. Although most of the time I paint myself because it's the subject I know best."

As the words were leaving her lips, Frida's voice thickened. The momentum with which she embarked on each story diminished bit by bit, as though her body were a deflating balloon. Her smile became a barely disguised grimace of pain; her black eyes gradually lost their shine, becoming a pair of glass marbles that seemed to float in a small pool of water, formed of teardrops that eventually rolled down her cheeks.

"I'll make you something to eat, if you like," said Nayeli, standing up. She knew when a story had reached its end, even though this story didn't have a clear ending. "I'm very good in the kitchen, honestly . . ."

Frida smiled and got out of her chair through sheer willpower. Her vertebrae crunched with every movement. Her skinny legs could barely support her battered body, which leaned to one side like a reed in a hurricane. Nayeli darted forward to catch her, but Frida held up a hand to stop her. A pride that rose from the very depths of her being prevented her from accepting help.

"I can do it alone, Nayeli. I want to feel alive. And I don't want to ignore that feeling, because since you arrived, I have felt it more than ever."

Nayeli didn't need to remember the torrent of instructions Frida had issued as she wrapped herself in her cotton shawl and pulled the basket onto her shoulder to go shopping. By the time she had walked the first block along Calle Allende, all her senses were telling her what to do: the market was close.

Women of all kinds appeared in her line of vision. Her ears were flooded with sounds that were so familiar, they made her emotional. *All markets sound and smell the same*, thought Nayeli. At the tip of her nose was the picante fragrance emanating from the mountains of tomatoes that vendors were piling on blankets; the sweet perfume of cinnamon, clove, and anise. All those aromas mixed in her blood.

"Hey, Tehuanita. Want to try a slice of pineapple?" called a scrawny boy wearing a straw sombrero so large it completely hid his face.

Nayeli didn't know what gave her greater pleasure, the possibility of savoring that fresh, juicy fruit, or the knowledge that she was still recognizably a Tehuana. She decided to enjoy both sensations, and soon her sense of taste overpowered all the others. Markets were her favorite places, and the Coyoacán market reminded her so much of home that she couldn't help but shed a few tears.

As she retraced her steps to Casa Azul, Nayeli made a decision: requesón empanadas. She was sure Frida would love them. Crunchy on the outside, contrasting with the surprise of the hot cheese filling.

The Tehuana went straight to the kitchen and, without opening her mouth, as though in a trance, she let her hands evoke the skill of the ancient cooks of Oaxaca. It was no mean feat to get the tortilla dough so perfectly round, large, and delicately thin, but Nayeli achieved it in just minutes. She was concentrating so hard that she didn't even notice the creaking of Frida's poorly oiled wheels as she watched the proceedings from the sidelines with fascination.

Having rolled out each of her ten tortillas on the yellow table, she used all her strength to lift over a huge basin filled to the brim with pumpkin flowers, requesón, chopped epazote, and crumbled dried chiles. With a large wooden spoon, she filled each tortilla, forming perfect little balls inside each one.

"Wonderful!" murmured Frida.

"I hope you're hungry. They need to be eaten as soon as I fry them, nice and hot," said Nayeli with a confidence that made it seem like an order.

"Well, of course, my belly's growling at me. It must have been ten days since I gave it a single bite. Ten days and ten nights," said Frida, exaggerating as usual.

They devoured the requesón empanadas in silence, the moment the young woman lifted them out of the pan of simmering oil. For the first time since Diego had abandoned Casa Azul, Frida didn't feel the need to resort to alcohol; she replaced her tequila and cognac with a large glass of warm milk.

The smell of frying hung in the air long after they had finished eating. Frida wouldn't let Nayeli open the windows to ventilate the kitchen; she wanted the air to retain the memory of their first lunch together.

"What's the matter? Why are you looking at me like that?" asked Nayeli, after washing the dishes and pans.

From her wheelchair, parked in the middle of the kitchen, Frida hadn't taken her eyes off the girl, as though she were a new discovery. For a second, Nayeli thought she could sense a glimmer of hatred.

"You're a true Tehuana," declared Frida.

"Yes, I am," she agreed with a smile. Nothing in the world gave her greater pride. That was the only thing that identified her: being a Tehuana.

"Are the red skirt and huipil the only ones you have?" asked the painter. Although she knew the answer, this was the way she approached any subject: never directly, always circling around it.

"Yes, the only ones," replied Nayeli, embarrassed. "I left another two back at home in Tehuantepec. This is my fiesta outfit."

Frida used both hands to launch her wheelchair forward to move closer to the girl.

"Come with me—I have some clothes you can wear. I'm a Tehuana, too."

To reach the studio where the painter spent almost all her days, they had to leave the wheelchair at the foot of a stone staircase and climb the steps, one by one, which took great effort. As always, Frida refused any help. Through willpower and stubbornness alone, she reached the top with barely a gasp of air left in her lungs. Her every movement made the corset holding her spine straight dig into her ribs. But she endured it, stoic and proud.

At the back of the room, a huge wooden armoire held her treasures, those garments that had turned her into something she wasn't.

"I'm eccentric enough that I don't have to justify myself," she said, leaning her back against one of the doors. "Come on, let's open this one. You'll see what I mean."

Nayeli turned the bronze handle, and the wooden door yielded as if by magic. A penetrating aroma flooded the studio; suddenly, everything smelled of Frida. Nayeli's eyes became greener, shinier, and larger than ever. Her voracious gaze could barely take in the contents of the closet.

On the top shelf, several piles of perfectly folded huipils formed a rainbow of silk, gauze, and cotton—embroidered, hand-painted, or decorated with tiny sparkling gems. On the second shelf were the shawls. Most were soft and woolly, but some were adorned with fuchsia feathers, which Frida adored. Next to them, hanging from metal rings, the skirts were the stars of the show: gala skirts, in deep, elegant shades of velvet, their lace flounces grazing the base of the closet; everyday pieces in light linen scattered with little flowers or stars embroidered in silk thread; and some more unusual pieces decorated with iridescent geometric figures that turned violet depending on the angle of the light.

"Shut that mouth, Nayeli, unless you're catching flies," exclaimed Frida, laughing. "I have some beautiful things, don't I?"

The girl closed her mouth, although her surprise didn't go anywhere.

"I've never seen anything so, so, so . . . "

"Sew, sew, sew—are you a seamstress?" Frida was still laughing. "Go on, choose what you like. A true Tehuana like you can't go around wearing the same thing all the time. It's an offense to your ancestors."

Nayeli couldn't choose. It was impossible. All she could do was run her fingertips slowly over a petrol blue velvet skirt. She was so captivated that she didn't notice that Frida had slid down the armoire doors until she was sitting on the floor with her back against the wall. The pain had overwhelmed her, like it had so many times before, but the spasms didn't stop her talking.

"What you see here are the devices of my biggest lie. I invented a personality for myself so that I could hide behind it. To be desirable, sometimes you need to be someone else. That's something you have to know from the start," she said in the tone of a mother talking to her daughter. "I'm a Tehuana to please Diego."

That huge, fat, arrogant man she had seen only once in her life was starting to become the focus of Nayeli's hatred. Every time Frida uttered the name Diego, she seemed to suddenly fade.

"Being a Tehuana is something we carry in our blood. We aren't trying to please anyone, Frida. We are what fate has made us," murmured Nayeli, wanting only to console her.

"Well, I'm not. You are. I was born in this house in Mexico City. For a long time, I thought this big old place, with its airy rooms and huge windows, the garden full of cacti and water fountains, was a paradise for my gordo sapo Diego. But it isn't. He told me so, years ago, loud and clear: the Isthmus of Tehuantepec is paradise, and Tehuanas are the queens."

She fell silent for a moment and gazed tenderly at the young queen in front of her. "And you know what I think? I think a Tehuana could carry the whole of Mexico inside her."

"You are one!" insisted Nayeli, almost shouting.

"No, I just try to be. For me, the Tehuana dress is much the same as a portrait in the absence of a person."

"What person?"

"Me," replied Frida, without hesitating.

Finally, at Frida's insistence, Nayeli selected two Tehuana outfits: one with a pink skirt and yellow huipil, trimmed with green ribbon, and the other with a violet skirt and matching huipil. She also borrowed two shawls with a pattern of leaves, branches, and flowers.

"I like your hairstyle," commented Frida.

"I don't have a hairstyle," replied Nayeli, "just a hurried crop. I used to have long braids like yours, and my mother used to tie them with ribbons and flowers, like you do."

Using her hands and the wall for support, Frida stood up. She didn't flinch, having learned to hide the pain when necessary. She went to the big wooden table and found what she was looking for: a pair of scissors.

"Come here, Nayeli," she said with the enthusiasm of someone who has just made an important decision. Without hesitation, she stretched out her hand, a ring on each finger, and gave the scissors to Nayeli. "Cut off my braids and make my hair just like yours."

The girl shook her head as she searched the painter's eyes for a trace of insanity. Only a madwoman would make such a request.

"I mean it, Tehuanita," she insisted. "Do it. Nothing would make me happier than seeing how my mane of hair drops to the floor. Do you think it will form a mountain or a meadow?"

"No, your hair is . . . "

Frida raised her free hand, and Nayeli understood that she had no choice but to obey.

"Fine, as you like, but sit down at least."

Frida took a few difficult steps and settled into the small chair she used for painting.

Very carefully, Nayeli removed the flowers and unwound the two braids that crowned Frida's head. Her hair fell down her entire back, stopping just above her waist. And once again, that scent, that perfume that evoked one single body: Frida Kahlo's. The locks fell around both their feet and formed neither a mountain nor a meadow.

"A labyrinth! Look!" exclaimed Frida. "A labyrinth made from the only bits of sensuality I had left."

Nayeli smiled. For a second, she felt like they had a lot in common.

"You look lovely," she said confidently. "You're very beautiful."

With the toes of the red boots she always wore, Frida started to play with the remains of what had been attached to her head seconds earlier.

"That's not true. I only have a body. And it's one thing to have a body and another thing altogether to be beautiful. That's something else you need to learn."

20

Buenos Aires, December 2018

Lorena Funes's job consisted of making friends for the purpose of ferreting out their secrets. It was a skill she had possessed since childhood, but as she grew up, she decided to professionalize her gift in order to make money. She liked money as much as she did other people's mysteries, and neither was in short supply.

Her father, Belisario Funes, had worked since he was a teenager in a jewelry store in Bogotá, Colombia. He started out cleaning the floors and display cabinets, but his quick mind and intelligence soon made him the jeweler's right-hand man. He came of age cataloging pre-Columbian pieces that smugglers had found in the jungle.

Lorena had never gone without, never had a need that wasn't met. Belisario had amassed a fortune that allowed his Argentinean wife and his daughter to live like queens. The girl went to the best schools in Bogotá, majored in art history in the United States, and attended workshops in Europe with top-level museologists. But it was a chance encounter that really opened the door to the art world for her.

One night, over flutes of expensive champagne, a Swiss art dealer confided in her that he was in possession of the original Gospel of Judas, which had surfaced in Egypt in the seventies. Months after that conversation in a bar in the ski resort of Gstaad, the newspapers started to show photographs of the document, which, as far as could be established, was written in the second century and revealed that it was not in fact Judas Iscariot who betrayed Jesus. Its owner had no other option than to negotiate the handover in exchange for his name being kept out of any legal proceedings.

In secret, someone started the rumor that Lorena Funes had been the woman who had plotted to recover one of the most controversial documents in the history of Christianity. She took great delight in denying her involvement in the find, although she used to say, smiling enigmatically, that what gave her life meaning was being able to negotiate with the bad guys to recover stolen works. Her fame grew in art circles, particularly in the world of forgery. Overnight, she became the go-to consultant on the subject.

She never stayed for more than three months in the same city or more than six on the same continent. She liked boarding planes almost as much as visiting museums and galleries in every capital city. She was convinced that the world was too big to root yourself deeply in one single place. Having said that, Buenos Aires and Bogotá were her favorite cities, the only ones where she felt a direct bond with her father and mother.

"How lovely to see you, Ramiro. I didn't think you would want to have anything more to do with me," she exclaimed as she opened the door of her apartment in Puerto Madero. "Things didn't end too well between us last time."

Rama ignored Lorena's words. He was familiar with the woman's emotional manipulation and preferred to ignore it. The work they often did together as a team was more important than the many nights of passion they had enjoyed, which, it was fair to say, both of them planned to repeat.

"I have some information from the Museo Pictórico," said Rama, dispensing with any form of greeting as he settled into one of Lorena's leather armchairs. "I thought you ought to be aware."

Lorena sauntered over to the bar she had installed in a corner of her living room. The glass shelves displayed a collection of whiskey bottles, purchased in each of the countries she visited. She selected a Nikka single malt and poured two measures into tempered glasses, at the same time surreptitiously checking her appearance in the wall mirror. Her smooth, shiny bobbed hair framed a face with prominent cheekbones and highlighted her green eyes. Her aristocratic bearing was a default setting that made any clothes she wore look elegant; the simple black gabardine pants and cotton blouse in the same color made her seem dressed for any occasion.

"I'm always aware, Ramiro, and I can see that your obsession with certain subjects hasn't lessened. Not everything that happens in the museums of Buenos Aires is connected to your brother. Cristóbal is just a grain of sand on the huge beaches of forgery in this world." With a gentle sway of her generous hips, she sat next to Ramiro and handed him his whiskey. "It's Japanese. Try it, you'll like it. So who gave you this information that brought you back here again?" she asked flirtatiously.

"One of the cleaners."

Lorena's laugh rang out loud and clear, using every particle of her body.

Ramiro placed the glass on the coffee table and frowned at her. "I don't know why you're laughing. I've seen you slip dollar bills into the pockets of janitors, waitstaff, and even VIP prostitutes just to get a nugget of information, a clue, a thread to pull until it leads you to some lost artwork. You've taught me a lot of things"—he smiled—"including this. Your words are imprinted on my brain . . . "

Lorena rested a hand on Rama's knee. "Information flows from bottom to top? Yes, yes. But I didn't say that; it was my father."

"Well, in this case, the bottom is one of the cleaners," insisted Rama.

"Okay, okay, you've persuaded me," said Lorena. "Give me the title."

Ramiro stood and went to stare out of the large window. Heavy rain clouds were approaching the city.

"*La Martita,*" he said.

"Nice work. Marta Limpour, 1870," added Lorena.

"Precisely. A few days ago, it was taken from the museum for maintenance work."

Lorena gulped down the dregs of her whiskey and became silent, pensive. Very few museums nowadays carried out the task of cleaning or restoring artworks. Although it had been the routine for years, a way for a painting to recover its original shine, the experts had protested, arguing that the treatment alters the top layers of pigments and sacrifices the most important aspect of the work: its originality.

"You surprise me, Rama. I didn't think Emilio Pallares would allow such brutality against a masterpiece. I thought he was more refined than that. Is he still in charge of the museum?"

"Yes, and no one dares question him. But I disagree with you, Lorena. I see neither innocence nor brutality in his decision . . . "

Lorena returned to the glass shelf and ran an electric blue fingernail down the side of a bottle.

"Has *La Martita* gone back to the museum, or is it still in the workshop?"

"It's back," replied Rama, still gazing at the clouds. "And it's the type of painting my brother excels at. I have a feeling he's back to his old tricks."

"Very well. I'll take care of it. Would you like another glass of any of these delights?"

"No, thanks. I need another favor."

"Oh, darling! This is going to cost you! I'm not the kind of woman who likes to do so many favors at once," she exclaimed jokily.

Ramiro walked up to her and showed her his phone. "Look at these photos. What do you see?" he asked anxiously.

With a bored expression, Lorena took the phone and slipped her glasses on. She glanced at it uninterestedly, then again with curiosity.

"What is it?" she asked, now unable to tear her eyes from the screen.

"What do you see?" insisted Ramiro.

"Well, I see a naked woman who seems to be bathing in a lake or river. I see a stain covering part of the original painting."

As she described the photo of Nayeli's painting, Lorena's voice changed; little by little, she was starting to see far beyond anything she could express in words. Falling silent, she zoomed in on the image and examined the hair that hid the naked woman's face, the ripples on the water in which she bathed, the curve of her back and the dark brushwork that gave volume to each thigh.

"Where did you take this photo?" she asked.

"A friend inherited it from her grandmother," Ramiro replied, careful not to give away too many details.

"And what made you show it to me?"

Neither of the two wanted to share their suspicions. Both were adept at holding their cards close to their chest.

"I'll tell you one thing: Paloma's grandmother was Mexican."

"Paloma who?" asked Lorena.

"Paloma Cruz," replied Ramiro.

Lorena gave a slight nod. Her lower lip began to tremble, as it did every time she sensed a mystery on the horizon.

"Let me see the photo in natural light," she said, going over to the window and using her fingers to zoom in. "What kind of animal is responsible for the red stain? If it was your friend, I want to see her in person, to give her a good slap."

Rama went to join Lorena at the window.

"It wasn't Paloma. It's an original stain, but not entirely original—I'm not sure. But what I do know is that the stain is from the same period, and the canvas—"

"So you saw it up close?" asked Lorena, still gazing at the red patch.

"Of course. And the photo doesn't do it justice—it's a beautiful work. It has a strength in its calm, an intensity . . . "

"A passion," finished Lorena. "In the stain, I mean. I'd like to see it up close. There are some things that—"

"What?" interrupted Rama, covering the phone screen with his hand. He wanted Lorena to look at him. "What is it that grabs your attention?"

The woman handed the phone back to him and remained silent, her eyes fixed on the clouds gathering outside the window. Caution had always been one of her greatest tools, and she wasn't about to throw it to the wind right now. She tucked her hair behind her ears. She could sense Rama's anxiety, an energy that oozed from his every pore.

"If you can arrange for me to see this work in person, I'll help you with *La Martita*," she said, using the tone she always used in negotiations.

"Done," agreed Rama, and smiled.

21

Coyoacán, April 1940

The final drag of her cigarette was so deep it made her cough. A dry, labored cough. Frida liked the sensation, an uncomfortable and fleeting pleasure. With a gulp of liquor, she brought an end to the cough and to the fantasy of being left without air, emptied of oxygen until her skin turned blue and the whites of her eyes became flecked with red or purple veins. As she imagined the colors of her body if she died of asphyxiation, she plunged her thickest paintbrush into the pots of acrylic paint. Her mind dictated the blends, the pigments, the color combinations and results. Bright blue. Mexican flag green. Carriage red. Royal yellow. Darkness gray. Void black. The most intense part of her work was at eye level, right in front of her. She looked at it, and she looked at herself. One Frida, two Fridas, three Fridas. Which of them was her? Perhaps all of them. Or none.

She finished the spare bottle she kept under the blankets that covered her legs when she sat in the wheelchair—both the use of the wheelchair and the empty bottles were becoming increasingly frequent. Painting in the metal and leather corset that squeezed her ribs and forced together the jigsaw pieces of her spine was a torture that grew with each brushstroke, with each line. But Frida found a degree of self-flagellation in her pain, which she enjoyed at times. She was adamant that she had worked out how to cultivate an idyllic relationship with pain. Her body hurt. Diego hurt. And there was no doubt about it, Diego and her body were one and the same.

She used her hands to push her chair back to gain a bit of distance and assess the final path of the work she had been painting for months. She twisted her head to one side, then the other. She closed one eye, opened it; closed the other, opened it. She clamped the brush between her teeth in the corner of her mouth and folded her arms across her chest. She liked what she saw. Sadness always shone through every part of her paintings. Even if she used the brightest colors and the most luminous washes, or traveled right around the color circle, the anguish was still there. It was her trademark, her destiny.

Nayeli's laughter drifted in from the garden. The sun still held enough warmth for all the windows at Casa Azul to be wide open. Frida wheeled herself to the glass door leading onto a stone staircase. Only ten steps separated her from the water fountain, the cacti, the iron and wood benches that her father had given her years earlier, and her beloved pets. Those innocent creatures who would never harm or abandon her.

She carefully lifted herself out of the chair and perched on the top step. The cold of the stone penetrated her long cotton skirt and made the hair on her calves and thighs stand on end. Frida felt like the princess in the tower. One of her favorite puppies was chasing the young woman all around the garden. Dark-skinned and completely hairless, the Xoloitzcuintle had become Nayeli's shadow, and she spoiled him with scraps of food from plates and pans; the two cats, meanwhile, stalked the party walls, watching the street, awaiting Diego's return.

"Hey, Nayeli! Look! Don't get sidetracked!" shouted Frida, laughing fit to burst. "See how beautiful the macaws are."

Nayeli placed her armful of roses on the ground, raised her head, and saw Frida at the top of the stairs. The artist's beringed fingers were pointing at the branches of the lime tree that filled one corner of the garden; her metal and acrylic bangles clinked with each movement of her thin arm, and with each clink the macaws' intrigue grew: male and female unfolded their wings like fans.

"You see how beautiful they are, Nayeli?" she called. "The red and yellow, with the white beak—that's the male. He's called Dieguito, like the sapo gordo. The orange with turquoise wings is the female."

Nayeli ran over to the stairs and climbed them side-on so that she could keep watching the dance the macaws were performing for Frida. It wasn't just birds; other animals seemed to sense that she was one of their flock. Her colors, her laughter, her scent; the way she got annoyed, got tired, cried; the cool caress of her hands, the warm embrace of her chest. Everything about her made Frida a magnet for anything with a beating heart, and pets were no exception.

"I've fed the puppies and I gave some spinach to Bonito," said Nayeli, as she helped the painter back into her wheelchair.

"Ah, very good! That parakeet is so spoiled! I'm glad you've taken a liking to him. Take me to the studio—I have to finish a large piece for some people who think they're very important. I need money, gringo or Mexican, it's all the same to me," she said loudly. Although she was looking at her, Frida wasn't talking to Nayeli. Frida was talking to herself. "I don't want Diego to give me so much as a centavo. I don't want anything from that sapo gordo. You have to learn that, too. Don't ever take money from a man in your life. You have to be able to make a living for yourself. What are you doing with the pesos I pay you for cooking for me?"

"I save them all, every week. I keep my money in a cloth bag, in the bottom of my basket," replied Nayeli with pride.

Frida smiled in satisfaction. Through these small acts, Nayeli was unwittingly starting to wreak revenge in the name of all the oppressed women Frida had known in her life, herself included.

The painter returned her attention to the giant painting she had to finish. She took the black cotton ribbon that was always hanging from one side of the wheelchair and tied it around her head. Her clean face, without a trace of makeup, framed by her short black hair, made her look like a young girl.

"Nayeli, what do you think of this painting?" she asked with genuine interest, without lifting her eyes from the painting.

The question caught Nayeli off guard. Her lower lip started to tremble, as it did whenever she got nervous. What could she possibly know about works of art? Why should her opinion matter to a woman as decisive as Frida?

She took a deep breath and released the air slowly. She gazed at the painting as she untied the black ribbon that decorated the waistline of her skirt. Absentmindedly, she did what she had watched Frida do seconds earlier: she tied the ribbon around her head, achieving an identical hairstyle.

Inside and outside the painting there were two Fridas. Some had been fabricated with oils and pigments; the others were of flesh and bone, with pain and black ribbons around their heads.

"Tell me, Tehuanita, what do you see? And don't lie to me, eh, you have such transparent green eyes I can read your thoughts."

She was as nervous as Nayeli. The girl's impressions mattered to her much more than the torrents of words that would undoubtedly pour from the snooty, soulless art critics.

The painting was huge. Frida had made a self-portrait, as usual, but this time it was a double.

"I see two of you. One Frida is wearing a Tehuana skirt and huipil and is holding the hand of the other Frida, who is dressed a bit oddly," said Nayeli, almost in a whisper.

"Of course, the other Frida is wearing a white dress with lace and trims and ruffles, in the European style," said Frida. "One is the Mexican who Diego loved; the other is the Frida who seeks refuge in her European ancestry, far removed from this vogue for all things Mexican—"

"Both have their hearts on display, two naked hearts," interrupted the girl. "They're strange, I never imagined them looking like that."

"They're suffering hearts. And that's what they look like: red, swollen, about to explode. And see how I've joined them with a bright red artery; it's almost as though the snubbed Frida is bleeding out. I don't have a name for it yet, and we need to find one. It's bad luck for something not to have a name. Can you think of anything?"

Nayeli moved forward a few paces and stopped inches from the canvas. She could feel the sting of the solvent prickling her nose, but she didn't mind. She moved her ear close to the image of Tehuana Frida and waited for the secret to be revealed.

"The Two Fridas," she said a minute later. "That's the name the painting wants."

Frida used her teeth to yank the stopper out of a metal hip flask, warmed her throat with a long swig, and repeated in a very low voice the name the Fridas had dictated to Nayeli.

"Very well, *The Two Fridas* it is."

Artistic decision made, Frida and Nayeli left the studio and crossed Casa Azul, on foot, at the painter's insistence.

The kitchen smelled of fresh fruit, stews, spices, and freshly baked bread. Ever since the Tehuanita had appropriated the short stretch of counter loaded with pans, baskets, and utensils, a new world had reigned in that corner of Casa Azul.

"It makes me sad that Diego can't enjoy these flavors you magic up with your hands. He's a gluttonous beast; I've rarely seen anyone eat as many beans, not to mention tortillas and enchiladas. Diego is an elephant child," said Frida as she dropped into a chair and leaned her elbows on the kitchen table. "I think you should go to his house in San Ángel to cook him something or take him some of your Oaxacan tortillas. Although I'm pretty sure he's involved with Irene, and we all know you eat less when you're in love . . . "

"I'm not entirely sure who Irene is," said Nayeli.

Frida's face clouded over. There was no sadness, distress, or tears; just a shadow that turned her dark mane even darker, the hollows of her eyes into small black pits, and her lips, always painted red or orange, into thin, tight lines. She stuck an index finger in her mouth and with the saliva wrote *IRENE* on the yellow table.

"No one important," she said emphatically. "She's just a woman whose turn it is to suffer."

Nayeli sat next to her and took her hand.

"Why is it this Irene's turn to suffer, Frida?"

"Because it is. All women suffer with Diego. It's the price they have to pay. Anyway, I want you to go to San Ángel and take him some of your tortillas."

Nayeli accepted readily. She was eager to see the houses at San Ángel. Frida had told her one was blue and the other red, and that they were linked by a walkway.

"All right, my pretty Tehuana girl," said Frida. She stood up and tightened the first two leather straps of her corset. She smiled triumphantly; she had managed to straighten her back. "Get everything ready to visit Dieguito. I'll ask the driver, Benancio, to take you. And remember one thing: my weakness isn't my spine or my broken neck, nor my peg leg or my shattered health. Weakness doesn't lie inside us; it's always in something on the outside. And I have Diego on the outside. That's another thing you have to learn."

22

Buenos Aires, December 2018

Boedo is a quiet neighborhood. Except in February, when the streets flood with carnival bands rehearsing their colorful processions.

Along its main avenues, the squat old houses form a geography that sets it apart from the rest of the city. I always liked the fact that my staunchly Mexican grandmother Nayeli lived in one of the most quintessential Buenos Aires neighborhoods, famous for the tango.

"Have another slice of this pascualina I bought in the Clara deli," insisted Cándida.

I wasn't hungry but accepted a generous wedge of pie regardless.

My visits to my grandmother's neighbor were becoming more frequent, but that day I had joined her for lunch with the singular intention of informing her of a decision I had made, even if it was still poorly formulated.

"Cándida, I want to leave my apartment and come live in my grandmother's house again."

The woman stared pensively at the savory pie as she wiped her wrinkled hands on a blue dish towel.

"I think that's a good idea," she said. "You know, Palomita, my love, it's an old house—it needs a human presence."

"Yes, I know. I did think about selling it. My grandmother put the house in my name some years ago," I said. "But I'd prefer to just come and live here myself. My grandmother would have liked that."

With a tenderness that was unusual in her, Cándida rested her callused hand on mine and squeezed it tightly.

"I'm delighted, dear. When will you move in?"

"I don't know yet. I suppose I'll start bringing some things over this weekend."

The conversation was brief, and we sealed the deal with a slice of dulce de leche flan.

Before accepting Cándida's offer of a coffee to round off the meal, I popped out to fetch Nayeli's painting. The man in the framing store had sent me a message that morning to let me know that it was ready. I walked the few blocks to the store. As I approached, my attention was caught by a group of people congregating on a corner, trying to see what was happening up ahead. A man with a dog on a leash was standing next to me, seemingly oblivious to the animal's sharp barking; I was about to ask him what was going on when I saw the police cordon across the sidewalk and street. Neither cars nor pedestrians could pass.

I retraced my steps and tried to get to the store the other way around the block. I wasn't the only one; several other people, looking rather ill-humored, were doing the same to avoid the closed-off street. When I turned the corner, I almost walked into a police officer. Before I could continue on my way, she held out her hand to stop me.

"No access this way," she said firmly.

I sighed wearily. "I need to get to a place right on this block," I explained, equally firmly.

I looked over the woman's shoulder and realized that all the police activity was taking place just outside the door of the frame store. My heart beat faster. My desire to know became a need.

"What happened?" I asked.

"A robbery at one of the premises on this block," replied the officer, unwilling to share any more details.

"The place with the paintings and mirrors?" I said, praying for a negative answer, which wasn't what I got.

"Yes. The owner was killed," she replied.

I took a couple of steps back on hearing this. Sometimes words have the power of a punch or a shove. And that's what I felt: a punch and a shove. Both at the same time.

"It can't be . . . " I babbled. "He messaged me this morning . . . "

"Who messaged you?" For the first time I was something more than a nuisance, and she didn't hide the fact.

"The owner of the frame store," I replied mechanically.

The woman fiddled with her radio, and, before I could work out what she said into it, a man wearing a suit and skewed tie approached us. He was young, although his movements, speech, and dress suggested someone older.

"Good morning, I'm the detective in charge of this investigation," he said, holding out his hand. I returned his greeting, gripping his cold, thin fingers tightly. "Officer Arana tells me you were in contact with Señor Dalmiro Mayorga."

As I opened my mouth to reply, he took me gently by the elbow and asked me to go with him to the entrance of the store. I had no time to refuse. My objections on the basis of freedom of citizen movement lasted as long as it took to reach the door a few yards away. What I saw on the other side of the glass made me retch and my blood ran cold.

In the middle of the store, stretched out on the floor, was the man who had served me the week before. He was dressed exactly the same, in workers' overalls and black shoes, but his fluffy white hair had become a sticky, bloody mess. His mouth and eyes were open, as though he had seen death coming and was unable to prevent it; the shards of glass from a broken mirror were scattered around him; the desk was untidy, and, tossed into a corner, I saw the yellow plastic bag in which I had brought the roll with my grandmother's painting.

"What time did you receive the message, señorita? I'd like to see it, if you don't mind."

The detective's voice dragged me out of my stupor, and I gazed at him with the bewilderment of someone waking from a bad dream. It took me a few seconds to remember the message.

“Oh yes, sure. I’ll show you,” I said, tapping at my phone screen with cold, trembling fingers.

I hadn’t saved Dalmiro Mayorga’s number, but the text was clear and simple: *Señorita Cruz, the painting is ready. Please collect it at your convenience.* The detective wasn’t interested in the content, only the time. He glanced at his watch and asked the officer when the crime had been reported. According to the records, the 911 call had been made at eleven forty in the morning.

“Make a note that the victim was alive at ten oh six and sent a work-related message,” the detective instructed the officer. He turned around and took hold of my elbow again. “Señorita, could you describe the painting Señor Mayorga was referring to?”

“Yes, of course. It was a family portrait,” I replied.

I spent some time explaining, and even offered to enter the store to find it. I wasn’t allowed. The detective was under pressure to decide whether they were investigating an inadvertent casualty of the robbery or a targeted murder. As they waited for someone from the morgue to come for the body, I overheard the crime scene investigators discussing certain points that caught my attention: there was still money inside the cash register; they hadn’t taken Dalmiro Mayorga’s gold ring from his pinky; and his high-end smartphone was still sitting on the desk.

After nearly an hour, the detective took my details. He told me the district attorney’s office would contact me to take my statement because I had been the last person to have contact with the victim. Before I left, I asked about the only thing that mattered to me: my grandmother’s painting.

“Detective, I’d like to get the painting back. It’s a family memento, and it’s important to me,” I said, feeling slightly guilty for thinking about my own interests just a few feet away from a still-warm corpse.

The detective fixed his eyes on me and gave one of those noncommittal answers people tend to give to random questions. “Don’t worry. We’ll keep in touch.”

We shook hands. The officer accompanied me to the cordon and saw me off with a timid “Thanks for your help.”

I returned to Cándida's house. I felt such an overpowering urge to tell her what had happened that I almost ran those few blocks. Since my grandmother's death, I hadn't felt the need to share my everyday issues with anyone. But a grandmother is always a place of welcome, and Cándida was starting to fill that role: a place to go back to.

She opened the door with surprise. She had changed into one of her many floral robes with pockets and mother-of-pearl buttons.

"Cándida, I came back because I have to give you some sad news," I announced.

Perhaps the years had tempered her curiosity or capacity for surprise; she ushered me in with her usual unhurried calm. She told me to sit at the dining table and offered me the coffee I had skipped earlier. When I told her the owner of the frame store had been killed in a robbery, she clamped a hand over her mouth.

"How awful! I've taken several mirrors to Dalmiro to be polished over the years, what a great pity. I liked the man—he was rather poor, a man of few words, not the brightest spark . . . a simple soul," she said in a rather unconventional attempt at an obituary.

"I only saw him once, and he was kind of curt. What worries me is that I don't have my grandmother's painting. The detective told me—"

Cándida's eyes widened, and she covered her mouth again, with the other hand this time, and interrupted me. "But Palomita, that's terrible! Strange things seem to happen around that painting. First it turns up in that old cabinet, then people come asking questions about it, and now . . . it's disappeared again."

"I don't understand," I said, surprised and confused. "Who came to ask you about the painting?"

"A lady came yesterday. Didn't I mention it?"

"No, you didn't mention a thing."

"Oh, my memory's all over the place. A lady came yesterday, very courteous she was, and rang the bell at your grandmother's house. I was just in the patio—that's how I heard. I opened my door and asked what she wanted," she said as she poured the coffee. "She asked about you . . . "

"About me?"

"Yes, yes. She said she was looking for Paloma Cruz. I told her this was your late grandmother's house and that you didn't live here. And that was that." She dropped a spoonful of sugar into the coffee and held it out to me, smiling.

"Cándida, what did she say about the painting? You just said she asked about the painting," I insisted.

"Oh yes. My memory is so unreliable! When I told her it was your late grandmother's house, she asked me if your grandmother was the owner of a painting of a nude woman . . ." She paused, trying to recall the conversation. I waited for a few seconds that seemed to last centuries, then she continued: "And I told her yes, that painting was of your grandmother. I think she asked me whether you had it at home, and I told her you had taken it to be framed by Dalmiro, God rest his soul. And that's it, nothing else. The truth, that's what I told her. You told me you were going to get it framed at Dalmiro's, and I never lie."

I hid the trembling of my hands so that Cándida wouldn't worry, and drank the coffee in tiny sips. It was the only way I could loosen the knot tightening halfway down my throat.

Later that day, I left the house with a devastating certainty: someone had been killed because of my grandmother's painting.

23

Buenos Aires, December 2018

The slap rang out clearly, like an explosion. Lorena's palm was burning red, her body trembling. For a few seconds, she waited for the counterattack; she knew Cristo was a violent, impetuous man. But the retaliation didn't come. The man merely straightened his head, which had been forced to one side by the blow, and stared at her, his eyes swimming with tears. Lorena knew he wasn't about to cry; it wasn't sadness or anguish. It was the strongest kind of hatred: contained hatred. She considered apologizing for her outburst but decided against it.

She tucked her hair behind her ears and straightened the lapels of her silk jacket. Then she cleared her throat, not wanting her voice to wobble. Every fiber of her being was focused on putting on a performance.

"Why did you have to kill him? A dead body was never part of the plan," she said, carefully measuring each word.

Cristo opened and closed his fists several times, releasing the fury that had tightened every finger.

"The only plan was to recover the painting," he replied as he drew the framed picture out of a large bag. "And here it is. All yours."

Cristo didn't understand boundaries. He had a tendency to get carried away, to defend himself against the wrong people, against anyone, for that matter, using one single tactic: violence. In one of his recurring dreams, he found himself digging a deep, perfectly formed pit, shovelful by shovelful, his only aim to turn it into a grave for that woman he loved, hated, and desired with equal intensity. She had been his savior; but over the years she had become his jailer, a hard drug that he couldn't and didn't want to quit.

He had always known that the moment when he first laid eyes on her had paved the way for what came next. But it was inevitable: he was young, afraid, full of hate, and in prison. At that time, five years had passed since the Christmas-night robbery at the Museo Nacional de Bellas Artes. A few months after the theft, the Blates painting *Muerte Amarilla*, skillfully forged by Cristo, appeared as if by magic in a storeroom in the south of Buenos Aires province. An anonymous 911 call had given the tip-off. Police officers, a judge, a district attorney, art experts, and even the media flocked to the scene, never suspecting that they were a necessary part of a setup that, within hours, would have international repercussions.

No one paid enough attention to the forged work. The act of returning it to the museum, amid cheers and congratulations from the most eminent names on the Buenos Aires art scene, was an event the authorities wouldn't have missed for the world. Hanging on the museum wall, the fake work attracted hundreds of visitors; meanwhile, the genuine article, each original brushstroke by the hand of Leopoldo Blates, decorated the living room of a European collector.

That painting had benefited a lot of people. Some made money from it; others, prestige and heroism. But as always, the thread broke at the weakest point, and the thieves who had stolen it fell into disgrace. Miguel Arjona, the man who had killed a woman and her four-year-old son during the getaway, was arrested one week later. The mechanic who had taken in the car, complete with bloodstains and signs of impact, had turned him in.

Arjona's arrest brought down Danilo and Esteban Páez. One of the cousins' neighbors swore to the police that the man she had seen on television had visited them several times. That man was Arjona. Cristo, however, had better luck: another five years of grace, which ended one rainy afternoon after the burial of his mother, Elvira.

His memories of the period around his mother's death contained a lot of blanks, which, being blank, became all the more significant.

The day of the burial, he woke up angry—that much he remembered. He had felt sufficiently brave, or desperate, to disobey the orders of his father, who had given him a handwritten list of all the people he had to invite to Elvira's send-off. It wasn't enough for Cristo to fail to call a single one; he needed to pretend that none of it had ever happened. Using his lighter, he burned the piece of paper. In doing so, he erased his mother and his mother's contacts. All he had left of Elvira was a small pendant in the shape of a crucifix.

The funeral was desolate. Black clouds glowering in the sky; icy rain; a polished wooden casket decorated with a bronze cross; the anodyne words of a shabby-looking priest; and Cristo, Rama, and their father, wearing suits and ties.

"Why is no one here, Cristo?" Rama had asked in a low voice, so as not to interrupt the chain of solitary prayer that their father was murmuring, his gaze lost somewhere beyond the clouds.

"No one cared about Mother," Cristo replied with the malice of someone both adept at and desirous of wounding.

Rama raised his voice. His brother had managed to shake him out of his usual composure. "That's a lie! Where is our aunt, her friends from the embroidery workshop, her painting teacher? It can't be—"

Cristo cut him off before he could list any more. "Don't be a pussy." He punched him lightly on the back of the neck. Then he lied: "I forgot to call them. Now shut up and don't even think about telling Dad. If you squeal, I'll beat you to death. Got that?"

Rama bit his lower lip until the metallic taste of his own blood flooded his mouth. He nodded as he made the most important decision of his short life: he was going to talk; he wouldn't stay quiet. He could be disobedient, too. And when he did talk, years after having discovered his brother producing a forgery of the stolen painting they were talking about on the television, the earthquake of his words devastated what little remained standing in his family.

All families are a system, and, if that system stays strong, it's only because it benefits each member. And so it was with the Pallares family. For years, Emilio Pallares had been the one pulling the strings of this scheme with a cutthroat technique: he pitted his sons against each other. Small challenges that wore away at the fraternal bond until it became a living hell.

Elvira had been the victim of her own decision. From her first years of marriage, she knew that if she wanted a family with Emilio Pallares, being a defenseless woman wasn't going to be a valid option. And she found a form of strength that allowed for all kinds of emotional abuse: silence. Elvira said nothing, reproached nothing, questioned nothing, saw nothing, heard nothing. Nothing. Elvira wrote. Every day she would fill a page in her personal diary. Years of notebooks with orange covers, filled with her perfect, sharp, almost calligraphic handwriting. And she hid. She wrote and hid. And burned. She wrote, hid, and burned.

Cristóbal Pallares had gotten used to being the winner. His talent for drawing and painting, not to mention his physical strength, had turned him into a source of noise within the family. Ramiro Pallares, the perfect blend between mother and father, didn't express his discontent. Cristóbal was the terrible child. And terrible children turn to evil, not to revolution. Ramiro was the revolution. The one who said "Enough." The one who understood that you can never win against someone so depraved; that, at best, you can learn something about yourself. And learn he did.

Ramiro Pallares's revolution threw everything up into the air. The shards of the Pallares family landed differently for each of its members.

"It was my brother who turned me in. That was my mistake: I underestimated his fear," Cristo had told Lorena the first time they saw each other in the visiting room at San Gregorio penitentiary. "I pulled the rope too tight. I created a devil in me, but the devil was him."

Lorena couldn't have been less interested in the Pallares family saga, which she saw as a mediocre version of Cain and Abel. But the Cain in this story had a gift that very few possess: an infinite capacity for forgery.

After Ramiro Pallares appeared before the authorities, identity withheld, to denounce his brother, the pieces of the game changed. The boy provided proof that exposed much more than the affairs of a young man who invested his talent in forging stolen works. Unwittingly, Ramiro revealed that the painting that had been on display at the Museo Nacional de Bellas Artes for five years, supposedly recovered after a robbery, was a fake.

Initially, the investigators didn't pay him much attention and sent him home. But Ramiro Pallares didn't just sit on his hands; he got to work on a plan that he carried out masterfully.

"When I say that my brother is the devil, it's no exaggeration," Cristo had insisted. "You know what he did? He contacted the husband of the woman who was killed in the crash. The guy had found peace because he thought the killers were behind bars, but no, the putrid ulcer that is my little brother got into his head. He told him there was one who got away and that was me—"

"Well, that was true," interrupted Lorena.

"No, it's not true. I didn't kill anyone." He stood up from the wooden chair and shouted: "The law took the widower's side—that's different. I didn't kill anyone, and now I'm here, in prison as an accomplice to something I didn't do."

A security guard approached and took Cristo by the arm, but Lorena told him to leave, that everything was fine.

"Sit down, Cristo. Do me a favor and stop making a fuss. I have an offer that might be good for you." She then finished with a key phrase: "Your father sent me. He was always on your side."

Cristo liked feeling needed. That's why he didn't think twice when his father had asked him to forge *La Martita*, nor when Lorena showed up at his house in the early hours and, with a kitten-like demeanor and a little-girl voice, kissing and caressing, asked him to steal a painting from a frame store in Boedo. He had done as Lorena asked, so what was the problem? What plans had he ruined? He had envisaged gratitude—silk sheets, champagne, lust—but all he got in return was a slap.

"I asked for a painting, and you brought me a painting and a corpse. Do you genuinely not realize how serious this is?" insisted Lorena.

In the end, the woman lost her composure and her confidence. Questions scurried through her head all at once. Were there any witnesses to the framer's murder? Would the city's security cameras have captured Cristo arriving at or leaving the location? And did he leave fingerprints or any other traces that could lead the investigators to him or, even worse, to her?

Lorena fell silent, frozen. Her body seemed to have run out of adrenaline. She stretched her neck to ease a tight spot and picked up the framed painting. After all, this was what mattered. The framer had done a simple job, of dubious quality. The picture had been given an enameled black molding and ordinary cheap glass, as though it were no more than a page ripped from a magazine. Lorena couldn't help bemoaning the lack of care.

Her annoyance turned to anger, anger that made her blood boil: Cristo had killed the owner of the store for no reason, and the painting had been handled by the most inexpert hands she had ever encountered. She felt the same moral exhaustion she felt every time she attended art classes around Europe, that feeling of solitude caused by knowing you are unique and professional in a world of ineptitude. The only person who matched her level was Ramiro Pallares, but that secret could take her to the grave. She was sure—that's why she remained silent.

She returned to the painting and once again felt her instinct kick in: that little bell that rang in her ears whenever she was in front of a work of art; that clanging that deafened her when Rama showed her the photos of the picture belonging to his friend Paloma Cruz. That name was seared with fire in her mind.

She had entered the name Paloma Cruz into a search engine that she often used to assess her clients' financial situation, but she found nothing out of the ordinary. Paloma's only asset was a small house in the Boedo neighborhood of the federal capital. She had also searched for her on social media and Google; she checked her profile pictures, her posts, and her sketchy work history. She lingered repeatedly on the photos of Paloma striking sexy poses while singing onstage. It distressed Lorena to think that this was the kind of woman Ramiro liked. And she berated herself for getting distracted. She was a businesswoman, and this Paloma was just a small player in what she assumed could be a monumental deal.

The back of the work had been left open. Lorena closed her eyes and ran her fingertips over the original canvas. She couldn't help but smile. Experts needed technical and scientific tests, ultraviolet light and chemicals to tell whether a canvas was old or new. She didn't need any of that. Her pores were attuned to the differences; her sense of smell was that of a bloodhound who could tell the acidity of any product and detect with astounding accuracy the year in which the materials had been fabricated.

Using a pair of tweezers, she tried to remove the painting from the frame. As she did, Lorena prayed that the murdered man hadn't used strong glue to attach the canvas to the cardboard mount. She released one end, then the other. She was nervous, droplets of sweat trickling down her back.

Cristo's curiosity had gotten the better of him, and he wandered over. He wanted to know what Lorena was trying to do.

"Are you going to tell me why the hell this painting is so important?" he asked.

Lorena jumped. She had been so focused on her task that she had forgotten about Cristóbal's menacing presence. She didn't know how to answer, so she let him keep talking.

"Before I brought that piece of crap here," continued Cristo, "I took a good look at it. I'm not as knowledgeable as you, but I'm not completely ignorant either, and to be honest, I didn't see anything that particularly caught my eye. It's a pretty mediocre painting, no technique, no charm. It lacks depth, heart . . . I don't know. There's nothing special about it, and that red stain is a disaster. It looks like something a child would make in art class."

Lorena couldn't help but smile. Without saying a word, she picked up the tweezers again and managed to separate the original canvas from the frame. Thankfully, the framer had done such a shoddy job that he hadn't even glued the edges. She closed her eyes and brought the painting up to her nose, slowly filling her lungs with the acidic smell of the paint.

"Are you going to answer me, Lorena? Or do you want me to grab that piece of trash from your hands and rip it into a thousand pieces?"

The woman fixed her eyes on his in surprise, as though she had just seen him for the first time.

"While I take care of the disaster you created in Boedo, I'm going to ask you to study the lines and brushstrokes of an artist who is anything but a scholar," she said as she rolled up the painting. "I'll lend you some books that might come in handy."

Cristóbal felt his anger and confusion dissipate as if by magic. In their place, the feeling of being important and needed relaxed the tensed muscles of his body. Even the tone of his voice changed.

"Very well, princess. And who is the artist to whom I must offer my talent?"

"The one and only, the best of all. You're going to forge an authentic Diego Rivera."

24

Coyoacán, August 1940

Her back stopped aching. Her hip, the bad leg jabbing into it like a knife, suddenly became less swollen. The mycosis that had spread to her hands overnight seemed to have disappeared: her fingers no longer burned and the imaginary red ants that scurried across her palms had gone quiet. This state of grace had not been achieved by doctors, medicine, or liquor. It was fury, resentment, and desperation that turned Frida's battered body into a light, torment-free feather.

It took three attempts to get through to Diego on the telephone. Calling the United States from Mexico was no easy task.

"Why the hell did you bring him to Mexico? It's your fault. You play the big hero, and now he's dead. Everything always has to be about you, always, always, always," shouted Frida, her tears and distress barely allowing her to think straight, to catch her breath.

"What are you talking about, mi Friducha hermosa? What has gotten you so worked up?" Diego Rivera replied with more questions, accustomed to placating the outbursts of his now ex-wife.

"They killed old Trotsky. Are you listening? They killed him. Dead. Done for. And you're sitting pretty there in Gringolandia with those little heroines of yours, oblivious to what's going on down here. Tell Irene and Paulette it was entirely your fault."

Leon Trotsky was dead, this time for sure. It had been only three months since the last failed attempt to shoot him at his house on Calle Viena, but fate had changed the rules of the game. And that fate had a forename and a surname. The name of a murderer. And Frida was suddenly filled by a fury, which belonged entirely to her and not to Diego, like a wave in a stormy sea, like lava spewing from a volcano. Leon Trotsky was dead. They had finally done it.

A pickax, a plain old pickax plunged into his skull had ended the life of the Old Man. And instead of crying, she exploded. That was her nature. Frida Kahlo suffered like a volcano.

The telephone conversation with Diego was brief. Just a few insults, some clashes of opinion, reproaches, and an order: it was imperative that they rescue his belongings from San Ángel. Although Rivera had been able to flee to the United States a few days after the first murder attempt, the rumor mill had made sure that all eyes were on him.

No one cared about the inner workings of the Mexican Communist Party nor the ups and downs with the muralist Siqueiros, even less the fabricated tales Diego had allowed to circulate before hopping on the plane to San Francisco. Everyone knew that Rivera loved both danger and personal attention and if to achieve both he had to lie, he would do so without so much as a blush.

"Nayeli, this is very serious. We must go to San Ángel to rescue Diego's belongings. He has some very valuable things. Years ago, he spent all his money on his pre-Columbian figurines. We can't allow them to fall into enemy hands. . . "

The Tehuana looked at Frida curiously, several questions on her lips. While Frida listed the items she felt were in danger, the tears continued to flood down her cheeks. She wasn't crying for the objects or for Diego. Frida never got attached to anything with no blood or beating heart, and her tears for Diego tended to be accompanied by shouts and insults. These tears were different.

"I don't understand what's happening. Whose are the enemy hands? Is Señor Diego in danger?" asked Nayeli in a wavering voice.

"No, no, mi amor. Don't upset yourself; we have quite enough of that with my nerves," she replied, and stroked Nayeli's cheek. "The sapo gordo Diego is fine in the States—he's safe, thanks to you. It would take me more than my lifetime to repay you for all you've done."

Frida was referring to the moment, three months earlier, when Nayeli had been the one to help Rivera flee from the police, when a group of men had shot at Leon Trotsky's house just hours before. At the time, the authorities believed that the internal disputes of the Mexican Communist Party had been directly related to the attack, and they went looking for Diego Rivera at his studio house in San Ángel.

Nayeli, who happened to be there taking him some candied fruits, became not only the unwitting witness but also the protagonist of a historic event. In the days that followed, Frida was like a child who needed to hear the same story over and over again. She followed the girl all around Casa Azul, asking her to tell her the tale at all hours of the day, even in the middle of the night.

"Tell me again how you rescued my Dieguito from the police, Nayeli. Don't miss out a single detail, go on, tell me . . . "

"That morning when I went to San Ángel, I did everything you told me: I took the candied fruits to Señor Diego with the letter you wrote him. Everything was calm until a telephone call made Señor Diego's face go pale. He went white, completely white, as if it was the devil on the line."

Frida would interrupt the story at certain points to ask the same questions, over and over. "Who ate your sweets?" she asked, anxious, as though she didn't already know the answer.

"Señor Diego, Señorita Irene, and me."

"And do you think Señorita Irene is pretty?"

"No, she isn't pretty," lied Nayeli.

"Less pretty than me?"

"Much less! You're beautiful. She isn't."

Frida smiled, pacified, and gestured for Nayeli to keep talking. The part where Nayeli managed to distract the police so that Diego and Irene could escape through the back door wasn't Frida's favorite part. What happened afterward, however, was of particular interest to her: the disconcerting presence of a third woman in the story.

"Tell me everything about this Paulette," insisted Frida. Although she knew the actress Paulette Goddard, she feigned ignorance.

"When the police left, I was alone in San Ángel," Nayeli resumed her tale. "I was pleased—I felt like I did what needed to be done. I didn't get nervous, and they believed me when I lied and said that Señor Diego wasn't in his studio. I can't remember how much time passed, but when I decided to go out to find my way back here, something very strange happened . . . "

"Oh, Nayeli, my heart, my eternal friend! I can never thank you enough for saving my Dieguito. Carry on, carry on . . . "

Although Frida had heard the details of that day dozens of times, she oohed and aahed as though this were the first telling.

"A lady came up and took me by the arm and told me to go with her; she said she knew where Diego was."

"What was the lady like? Was she pretty?"

"Yes." Nayeli had decided not to lie about Paulette. She couldn't have disguised the fact that the woman had made quite an impression on her. "She looks like an angel or a goddess. She has white skin, very white, and her eyes are turquoise, the kind of color you use in your paintings. And red hair that comes down to her neck. I followed her; I couldn't refuse. It was very odd, because I couldn't understand what she said. She spoke in a strange language, like some kind of secret code."

"English, mi amor. Paulette is a gringa, a gringa actress. My Dieguito and I met her in Gringolandia. She's no fun, like all gringa women. She has neither soul nor heart. So where did she take you?"

Nayeli had to describe in detail all the fittings and fixtures of the San Ángel Inn, the luxurious building across the road from Diego's house. Paulette happened to have been looking out of the window in her room, saw the police cars surrounding the painter's house, and phoned to warn him. It had been the actress's succinct words that tipped off Diego.

"The room was huge, really huge. I've never seen anything like it. But everything was in the one place: the bed, the table, the chairs, even a little kitchen with a coffeepot and two cups," described Nayeli. "Señor

Diego was stretched out across the bed; he hadn't taken off his boots, and the actress was shouting at him and pointing at the white sheets all dirty with mud. I couldn't understand what she was saying, but Señor Diego was laughing a lot."

At this part of the story, Frida would give a full-bellied laugh. Even when they were apart, she laughed at the same things Diego laughed at, she suffered for the same things that made him suffer, and, when she had no news of her giant's mood, she felt empty inside. Nothing at all. But now, three months after Diego's escape, Leon Trotsky was dead. Those who had wanted him six feet under had achieved their goal.

Frida wrapped herself in the yellow shawl that was always draped over the back of one of the living room chairs. A deathly cold had swept through her body. The painter's every movement was accompanied by calm but heartfelt weeping. She tried to conceal her sadness with words, instructions, and orders. Gazing at her, Nayeli realized what was happening: Frida was crying for Trotsky.

The days following the attack at the little house on Calle Viena were still fresh in Nayeli's memory. One afternoon, her curiosity even led her to walk those few blocks to see what everyone at the market was talking about: the bullets embedded in the wall. Nayeli remembered the days and nights when Frida's Old Man would appear, as if he were a ghost. The first time she saw him, it frightened the life out of her.

He didn't knock to announce his presence or make a noise with the cans Frida had hung at the entrance for tradesmen to rattle when they delivered food. With the painter's complicity, the Old Man had found a way to sneak in silently. His clothes were like a disguise: woolen pants, checked vest, and a thick jacket that reached his ankles; a broad hat always covered his face, and he wore dark mirrored glasses that he switched for a round, gold-framed pair when he entered Casa Azul.

His greeting, when he crossed the threshold, was always the same: "Is my time up, my dear Frida?" And Frida would laugh her head off, with the pleasure of knowing her own power. No one has more power than those who dictate the time and term of others, and that's what Frida was for the Old Man: an oracle.

Nayeli often lurked behind a door, listening to the pair's conversations. Most of the time, she couldn't understand a word, as they spoke another language. But she could tell that the tone of Frida's voice changed; she became another woman in front of this mysterious old man. A more complete, less pained woman. Only once did she pluck up the courage to ask about the nocturnal visitor, and she could see a flash of terror in Frida's eyes, the same glint that appeared in the eyes of the goats in Tehuantepec seconds before they were slaughtered. A glint of death. And she didn't ask again. Frida hid everything related to her nighttime visitor. In the end, she even concealed the goodbye.

25

Buenos Aires, December 2018

I left the police station clutching the canvas that had been wrapped around my grandmother's picture, but as for the painting itself, no news. Those were the precise words the detective used to tell me that my precious possession had disappeared: "*No news.*" Nor was there any news of the person who had killed the store owner; either through laziness or apathy, they seemed to have decided that the painting wasn't connected to the murder. I disagreed. I was convinced the crime was related to Nayeli's painting. Admittedly, I was raised by my grandmother in a world that revolved around me, built by her alone for me to live in, but in this case, my egocentricity had nothing to do with it. I could sense it; I could imagine it. That painting was cursed.

I walked several blocks, needing to organize my thoughts. I couldn't settle; I had that feeling you get when you have a big decision to make and you try to avoid it, as though you're in a playground pretending to be chased by a dog. A decision is always made in the meantime, while you're busy dodging it. Not before, not after. It happens in a split second. And in that split second the power of the impulse, when it comes, is impossible to stop. There's no going back.

I paused at the street corner, folded the protective canvas in four, and slipped it down the side of my bag before stretching out my arm to hail a taxi. The impulse had arrived.

It took less than forty minutes to reach Rama's house. Although it was a perfect evening to be out and about, the traffic was quiet, which was unusual for Buenos Aires. The decision to call on Rama without warning had more to do with the urgency of my suspicions than any curiosity about what he got up to when I wasn't in his life. Although I considered the possibility that he might be with another woman, I didn't care.

Before I rang the bell of his apartment, I couldn't help checking my appearance in the glass of the entrance door. I had chosen my outfit well that morning, even though I didn't know I would end up here. My leather pants accentuated all the right places, and the long-sleeved black cotton blouse emphasized my narrow waist. My hair wasn't looking its best, but with the emergency hairband I always have around my wrist, I made up for that minor inconvenience. I touched up my lips with a salmon pink gloss and dabbed a couple of drops of perfume behind my ears.

"It's Paloma," I said when his voice came through the intercom.

After a few seconds of silence, which I put down to surprise, he told me to come up. When I stepped out of the elevator, he was waiting for me with his door open. Smiling.

"I'm really happy to see you," he greeted me.

At that moment, I forgot about my grandmother's painting and the murdered merchant. My feeling that the world was coming to an end dissipated in an instant. And I felt like crying just for being near him again.

With the door still open, he kissed me. A calm kiss of welcome. He closed the door and kissed me again. Then he asked if I wanted a drink.

"Wine," I answered.

I waited for him in the living room. A three-seater sofa, a coffee table, and some shelves crammed with art books were the only decorations.

In one corner, near the door into the hall, there was an object I hadn't noticed the only other time I had been in his apartment: an old-looking wooden easel with bronze fittings. On the frame, a half-finished picture piqued my interest: it was a portrait of a woman. I moved closer and couldn't help touching the drawing with my fingertips. I needed to make sure it wasn't a photo. The level of detail was astounding.

"I've held that image in my memory for years," said Rama behind me. "The oval face, the shape of the eyes, the curve of the nose. That's what they taught me at the art classes I went to my whole life: you draw from the largest to the smallest. And I got used to memorizing in the same way."

"Who is it?" I asked, almost whispering.

"My mother. She died years ago, and painting is my way of evoking her. I've been trying for the perfect portrait for ages. Dozens of discarded sketches. Pencil tests, for intensity, shading. But nothing is enough . . . It's missing something."

I turned to face him, emotional. Although we had shared a bed on several occasions, this was the first time we had shared any kind of intimacy. And there's nothing more intimate than unburying your dead in front of another person, not even undressing . . .

"It's a beautiful portrait," I said, resting my hand on his cheek. "It looks like a photo. It's perfect."

He handed me the glass of wine. "Okay, Paloma. I'm delighted you came, but surprises aren't really your specialty," he said, regaining the upper hand. This was the Rama I felt more comfortable with. The Cruz women sailed better in stormy waters. "What's happened?"

We settled onto the sofa, and I started my tale. The Mexican blood running through my veins meant that I had always known how to tell a story, and stories have a beginning, a middle, and an end. This time, however, my talents as a Scheherazade were wasted. I had just reached the part where the police officer was preventing me from getting to the frame store when Rama interrupted me with a question.

"Where's your grandmother's painting?" he asked, his voice filled with such urgency that I didn't have time to be offended at my story being cut short.

"I don't know. It's disappeared, and that's why I came." I finished my story of the dead merchant as I rummaged in my bag. "Look, the only thing the police managed to recover was the protective canvas. They called me today for me to go and identify it, and they returned it to me."

Rama unfolded it carefully. It was the first time he had seen it. It had never struck me as important, and, what's more, the message written in Nayeli's handwriting felt like something private, a family matter.

"*I don't want anyone to see what's inside me when my body breaks. I want to return to the blue paradise. That's all I want,*" read Rama.

"My grandmother wrote that. It's her writing, her final wish," I explained.

We sat in silence for a moment. I was trying to find the words to express my suspicions, which, as time went on, were starting to seem childish and unfounded.

"Rama, ever since I saw that dead man on the floor, I've had the feeling that he was killed because of the painting. I know it sounds crazy, but the day before, a woman came to my grandmother's house asking about me—"

"Well, that doesn't mean anything," he interrupted, trying to calm me. He had noticed my trembling hands.

"It wasn't just that. Cándida, my grandmother's neighbor, went to speak to her. The woman asked if my grandmother was the owner of a painting of a naked lady."

For the first time, Rama seemed to take an interest in my story. I realized the attention he had given me thus far had been purely out of politeness.

"Now, that is strange. Who else knows about your inheritance?"

I couldn't help but smile. Describing an old painting as an inheritance seemed rather presumptuous.

"No one. That is, you, the neighbor, and me . . . well, the dead merchant, too. And it seems as though this foreign woman knows as well."

"Foreign?"

"Yes, Cándida said she had a Venezuelan or Peruvian accent—she wasn't entirely sure."

"Colombian?" asked Rama anxiously.

"I suppose it could have been. Certainly not Argentinean or Mexican."

Rama took a deep breath and exhaled quickly through his nose. He seemed almost furious. He jumped up from the sofa and stood staring at his mother's portrait, arms folded across his chest.

"Her name was Elvira. My mother's name was Elvira. Whenever the fights with my brother escalated, she would say the same phrase, loudly, almost shouting it. She said that in a survival situation, staying still is a death sentence. If you don't move, you die."

I stood up, went over to him, and placed my hand on his back. I gazed at Elvira's eyes. Her wavy, neck-length hair; the straight nose; the wrinkles around the eyes that didn't diminish the sparkle of her gaze one iota; the long, bare neck; and the small crucifix earrings. Rama's voice broke through my thoughts.

"We're going to move, Paloma. My mother was always right about everything."

26

Coyoacán, August 1940

The syrup gradually turned a deep golden color. The magic of water, sugar, and anise swirling slowly in the base of a hot iron pan was a wondrous sight to Nayeli's eyes. The moment it turned dark brown, she took it off the heat and left it to rest. That's what her mother had taught her: "Food needs time to rest to restore its energy." In another pan, she heated more water and added anise and a good knob of butter, then waited for it to come to a boil. The bubbles crowding to the surface told her it was time to sprinkle the sieved flour over the mixture like rain. And the magic happened again. The liquid thickened to form a soft, white, fragrant dough. Closing her eyes, she filled her lungs with air and let the scent of anise permeate her body. She smiled.

She didn't have the patience to let the dough cool; an overwhelming urge to plunge her fingers into the sticky, cotton-like dough made her lift it out as tenderly as a mother caressing her newborn baby. She wasn't bothered by the heat of the dough or the thought of her fingertips melting until they merged with the burning mixture; that almost seemed like a good idea. With a wooden pin, she stretched the dough over a board. She formed a perfect circle, and then, with a swift, sure movement, kneaded in two beaten eggs. The yellow foam turned the mixture into a soft, ivory-colored ball. She covered it with a cotton cloth; the dough needed its rest as well. The last part of the recipe was the hardest. The huge bottle of olive oil held nearly two gallons and the greasy glass almost slipped from her hands. Finally, she managed to pour a generous amount into the frying pan.

The shrill sound of Frida's wheelchair arrived seconds before her voice. Nayeli had gotten used to the painter's presence being announced by that metallic creak as a kind of prelude.

"What a wonderful smell! What are you making?" asked Frida.

Her deep voice was subdued, and she looked exhausted.

"Buñuelos del cielo," replied Nayeli as she cut the dough into pieces and skillfully rolled each one into a little ball. "It's a long way to San Ángel, and I'm sure we'll be hungry by the time we get there."

Frida fell silent. Various things were flitting through her head, one after another, converging, confused. Then she managed to get her thoughts in order and remembered that she had asked the girl to accompany her to Diego's home studio to rescue his collection of pre-Columbian statuettes.

The dough yielded more than Nayeli could have imagined. She counted the buñuelos as she fried them. Twenty-three delicious, warm confections, drizzled with a golden syrup. She arranged the little balls on a large ceramic platter decorated with geometric shapes and covered it with a pink cotton cloth. In the back of one of the cupboard drawers, Frida kept dozens of ribbons in a variety of colors, which she often braided into her hair. Nayeli selected a deep purple one to wrap around the cloth and the plate, then tied a bow in the middle.

Leaving the plate on the kitchen table, she went through the house to look for Frida, who was no longer in the kitchen. Not finding her in her bedroom or the studio, a small knot of worry formed at the top of Nayeli's stomach. Before going out to look in the street, she peered through a window overlooking the garden. Among the dense vegetation of shrubs, cacti, and flowers, she could just make out the yellow shawl, discarded in the greenery.

Running down the stairs to the garden, Nayeli plunged between the plant pots and retrieved the shawl from the ground.

"Here I am, here I am, my little ballerina!" called Frida.

Clutching the shawl to her chest, Nayeli followed the sound of the painter's voice. She found her a few feet away, sitting on the ground with her back against a tree. Her face was awash with tears, her black eyes swollen, and her makeup running. Her loose hair hung down over her torso, her gaze fixed on nothing.

"You know, I can smell the blood, Frida; you don't need to hide. The wound is there, even if no one can see it. I see it."

"Nothing is more valuable than laughter," replied Frida. "Tragedy is the most ridiculous thing we humans have. Animals suffer, of course, but they hide it. When they suffer, they don't go showing their pain on a stage. I like to think their pain is more real. And that's why, my beautiful ballerina, I want to suffer like the animals. I'm tired of pain being a performance. It's time to feel pain like the animals, with truth and decorum."

Nayeli didn't know what Frida was talking about. She hardly ever understood the painter's ramblings, often fueled by liquor, opiates, or delirium; but she could always sense what lay behind them. And she never got it wrong. This time, however, everything was different. This time Diego wasn't the cause of her tears.

The thought of Diego, the sapo gordo, boiled in her head as it had many times before. The man seemed to have been born with the gift of making sure others were constantly thinking of him, imposing his presence even from afar. She felt a stone growing in the middle of her chest, but the knowledge that he was still safe in the United States turned the stone into butterfly wings, their tickly fluttering filling her whole body.

She helped Frida to her feet. The trip to San Ángel was a long one, and it would be best if they could get back to Casa Azul before nightfall.

As they passed through the kitchen to pick up the buñuelos, a thunderous knocking made them jump. Four police officers, with the same detective who had visited three months earlier when Trotsky had been shot at, walked straight into Casa Azul without waiting for permission. Two of the men hung back, mesmerized by the papier-mâché Judas figures hanging inside the entrance. They had heard that Rivera's wife was a bit of a witch, but they had never imagined this level of eccentricity.

Nayeli and Frida had no time to react. They were still making their way across the hall into the living room when the men reached the kitchen. This time their faces were less than friendly. Good manners were clearly a thing of the past.

"We've come to ask you some questions," said the detective, without preamble, addressing Frida. "Your answers will determine where you sleep tonight."

Frida understood the threat but showed no fear. She raised her hand, with all its rings and bracelets, by way of authorization.

"Do you know Señor Ramón Mercader?"

"No," replied the painter. She had never heard that name.

The detective glanced at the scribbles in the notebook he was clutching and continued: "Do you know Jacques Monard?"

"Yes, of course."

"Well, in that case, you know Ramón Mercader," concluded the man triumphantly.

The painter froze. She searched for Nayeli's eyes as though they were a buoy in the middle of the ocean. The Tehuana was following every word of the interrogation, but she had no idea who any of these people were. Frida had never said anything about a Mercader or a Monard.

"I met Señor Monard in Paris, when I was presenting an exposition of my work there," explained Frida, struggling to remember. She had done her best to block from her mind what had turned out to be a rather sorry experience, a waste of her time, an exposition bringing together the works of various Mexican artists without rhyme or reason. Then she added: "He was hoping I could find him a house here in Coyoacán, somewhere near Trotsky's . . . "

"And were you successful?" asked the detective, taking notes of Frida's statement.

"Quite the opposite. I was too sick and weak to go house hunting for someone I didn't know. But he was able to come to Mexico, thanks to Sylvia—I think they're planning to get married." As she spoke, it suddenly dawned on her: Sylvia Angeloff, the North American Trotskyist whom she had liked so much, had been Leon Trotsky's secretary. Frida could smell the betrayal, and for the first time her anxiety turned into terror. "What did Monard do?" she asked in a wavering voice, although instinct told her what the answer would be.

"He killed Trotsky," replied the detective. "You'll have to come with us. Señora Frida Kahlo, you're under arrest."

The dish of buñuelos slid from Nayeli's hands. The smash was followed by a shower of sugar crystals raining over the floor tiles. The thought of Frida going to jail weakened every muscle in her body, and she could barely stay on her feet.

The painter looked over and hugged her with her eyes. The only human being on earth able to turn her pupils and eyelashes into embraces.

"I'll be back soon" was the last thing she said.

Frida Kahlo wrapped herself in her yellow shawl and, without allowing a hand to be placed upon her, went with the police officers. Inside the car, she started crooning in a low voice, as though singing a lullaby to herself. "Yo no tengo ni madre ni padre que sufran mi pena, huérfano soy." I have no mother or father to suffer my sorrow, an orphan am I. The verses of "El Huerfanito" always calmed her down. Pablo Picasso had taught her the song after he visited Frida's exhibition in Paris and fell at her feet. The very same exhibition where a secret agent had passed himself off as someone else to trick her and get closer to Trotsky during his Mexican exile.

What had been mere impertinence when the police took her from Casa Azul became more violent when they reached the station. Before Frida was fully aware of the situation she was in, she had been shoved into a dark cell. The sparse light entered through a tiny window at the top of one wall. The place reeked of urine and enclosure. When the barred door slammed shut, the painter couldn't help but dissolve into tears. She hadn't even been allowed to bring the medicine that would relieve her aching body.

Her crying left her exhausted. With what little strength she had left, she spread out her shawl on the floor and settled her bones against the wall as best she could. Nayeli, her invisible ballerina, where was she? She needed her more than ever.

Several hours later, one of the police officers came to bring her out of the damp hole. The scared-looking young man was kind enough not to hurry her. Frida's spine, hip, and especially her weak leg had gone numb.

The interview room was much nicer than the cell. There were no damp stains on the wall, and it smelled of freshly brewed coffee. In the middle were a metal table and two chairs. The police chief was sitting in one, and, with an icy smile, he ordered Frida to sit in the other.

"Have some coffee," he said, pointing at a white cup. "It's fresh."

Frida nodded and drank it in one go.

To make the moment last, he told her that Trotsky had arrived at the hospital at death's door and that the man she had met in Paris was actually an NKVD agent who had managed to infiltrate the household on Calle Viena with a puerile excuse and perfect safe-conduct in the form of Sylvia, Trotsky's secretary. He also told her, in great detail, about the work the doctors had carried out on the old man's skull to try to save his life. Uselessly. In vain.

"Did he say anything before he died?" she asked.

The detective showed no surprise at her question. The painter was even stranger than he had been told.

"Those present at the house on Calle Viena claim that he said 'Natalya, I love you.'"

Frida nodded slowly, as though assimilating those four words one by one: *Natalya, I love you.* And her heart broke a little more.

27

Buenos Aires, December 2018

What Lorena Funes and Emilio Pallares had was more intense than a father-daughter relationship. There was admiration, courtesy, and convenience, but without the responsibilities demanded by a blood bond. No affection flowed between them, only money and prestige: two things for which either would have given their life.

The click-clack of her heels on the marble floor of a museum was one of Lorena's favorite sounds. And the Carrara marble at the Museo Pictórico de Buenos Aires was the Stradivarius of floors. Making her way down the main corridor, she decided halfway along to turn into a smaller room on the right. The lights were still off, so she went to the control panel and switched them on to reveal *La Martita* hanging on the main wall. She walked up to it with a slight smile.

"Hello, my beauty. How are you?" she murmured.

She drew a magnifying glass out of her purse and started to inspect the work closely: the shadows between the leaves achieved with different shades of green, the effect of the horse's mane, the shine on the beast's forehead from the oils and the sun reflected in one eye, which situated the work at a specific time of day: dawn.

"It's very good, don't you think?"

She jumped at the sound of Emilio Pallares's voice behind her. She knew she was breaking the rules. No museum in the world allowed visitors to get so close to the works. That was one of the few rules that Lorena Funes did obey. This time, however, she couldn't resist violating it.

"Yes, it's very good," she said as she stepped back over the yellow line marked on the floor. "Your boy Cristo is still the best. The brushwork is impeccable. I would even go so far as to say that the shading is better than Marta Limpour's."

Pallares had never been able to help feeling uncomfortable at his sons' feats. On more than one occasion, Elvira had reproached him for that envious streak that surfaced whenever Ramiro or Cristóbal outperformed him in something.

"You know Ramiro is nosing around *La Martita*, don't you?"

She wasn't the kind of woman to go around betraying people for no reason. And Ramiro was no threat to her, but in this case, she did have a motive. And she decided to do Pallares a favor he hadn't requested, but for which he would soon have to pay. Although she was used to her associate's extravagances, Pallares's reaction surprised her: he tilted his head from one side to the other to release the tension and took a small fragrance bottle from his pocket. With a single glance, Lorena was able to tell that it was rock crystal. The man removed the golden lid and dabbed the perfume on his wrists and behind his ears, with slow, rhythmic movements.

"Palo Santo?" asked Lorena, who was less of an expert when it came to aromas.

"Oh my goodness, please! Do you see me as a hippie or a moonlight fortune teller?" replied Pallares, amused. He enjoyed Lorena's little failings.

Without placing importance on something that wasn't important to him, he accepted the information she provided without question.

"What's my younger son dithering about now?"

"Ramiro never dithers about anything, Emilio. You don't seem to know your son at all. He disguises his certainties with doubts—that's completely different." She turned around and looked at the painting again.

"What does he know?"

"Ramiro? Not much, but it's only a matter of time," replied Lorena, relishing the moment. She liked to highlight Pallares's failings, too. "Who has the original *Martita*?"

"Lorena, my dear, please. You're overstepping. You know there are no names in our business; they don't matter."

The young woman regarded him approvingly. Discretion was a virtue she admired, a mark of class that, in her world, was worth millions of dollars.

"I need you to put me in touch with Martiniano Mendía. As soon as possible." She rushed her words out almost without breathing.

M. M., as Mendía was known in the art world, was a ghost. Many believed he didn't even exist. Very few had access to M. M.'s world, and those who did were part of the mystery. Emilio Pallares was one of the exclusive few.

The man glanced over his shoulder, as if they might be overheard. "Let's go to my office," he said.

They crossed the museum in silence until they arrived at their destination.

"Tea?" asked Pallares as he closed the office door.

"No, thanks, I don't want anything. Well, I do—I've already told you what I want."

"Yes, I heard you," said Pallares as he dropped loose strands of black tea into the silver diffuser he had used for years. "I'm sure you can appreciate, Lorena, that contacting Mendía isn't a matter of a phone number or email that passes from hand to hand like groceries. We're talking about someone . . . Well, I'm not sure I can define it. Let's say *someone special.*"

"I know that old song by heart. And the truth is, I'm not remotely intimidated by how special M. M. might be. I need a meeting with him," she insisted, getting ready to play a card, perhaps the only one she had. "Does he still live in Montevideo?"

The water jug trembled in Pallares's hand. He breathed slowly and finished filling the pot. Then he plunged the diffuser and watched, spellbound, as the water was suddenly tinged golden brown. How had Lorena found out where Martiniano Mendía lived? The possibility that he might be suspected of divulging that information worried him greatly. M. M. wasn't the kind of man who tolerated excuses or denunciations.

"Why do you need a meeting with M. M.?"

An idea had just occurred to him. Sometimes crises can be turned into opportunities, and Lorena, instead of being a hindrance, could become his safe-conduct.

"The only way for you to reach Mendía is through me. So tell me what you have, and I'll take care of it."

"I have a cursed painting," said Lorena, raising an eyebrow.

Pallares smiled. Lorena hadn't used that code word for years. The last time she had, they pocketed a fortune that they were wise enough to invest in what they loved most: art. They shared an armored vault in a European bank, a cooling-off spot for many of the works they received as a form of payment for returning, forging, or recovering works of great value or significance.

"Why do you need Mendía?" asked Pallares. "The two of us have always sorted things out just fine."

"This is different. We're going to need authentications, verifications, studies, analysis. Perhaps a degree of restoration. And an approximate valuation."

"Can I know what it is?"

Lorena stood. She needed to create a special atmosphere for her announcement. She put on her most playful smile, and said, "Diego Rivera."

She didn't need to add a single word or gesture. Nothing. The echo of the Mexican muralist's name rang like thunder in Pallares's ears. He was, of course, aware that the most frequently forged works in Mexico were those by Diego Rivera, José Clemente Orozco, Rufino Tamayo, and Frida Kahlo; indeed, some of his colleagues used to joke that there are more of Frida's paintings in the world than Frida could possibly have painted in a hundred years. But Lorena's word was a huge validation. Although he would never admit it out loud, the Colombian had the most astute eye and the sharpest hunches in the art world.

They sealed the deal with a handshake and Pallares's promise: he would pull the strings to get Martiniano Mendía to take a look at the cursed work.

When Lorena Funes left the museum, she was almost dancing. She had to contain the urge and control her movements. She was happy; she was going to meet Martiniano Mendía, and the distance between her and the summit was no more than the breadth of the Río de la Plata.

She drove to her apartment in Puerto Madero with the car windows down, still smiling. As she parked in the private garage, she took a mental inventory of her treasured whiskeys in their display case. She decided she would open the most expensive one for an intimate celebration. Distracted by her enthusiasm, by the time she realized there was someone behind her, it was too late. A man pushed her into the elevator, pressing a gun to her head.

The barrel of the gun was cold: that was the first thing she felt. The second was anger, such anger.

"Let's go to your apartment," said Rama in a glacial tone, still pointing the gun at her.

Although surprised that it was Rama who was threatening her, Lorena wasn't particularly frightened. Her first thought was that Cristóbal was right: his brother was unpredictable. She slipped her hand into her purse for the keys, her elbow brushing against Ramiro's right arm. In seconds they reached the landing outside her apartment.

"Be careful what you take out of there," cautioned Rama.

"Lower the gun; I'm not going to do anything. I couldn't, even if I wanted to," said Lorena, begging and warning at the same time. That was her style.

Ramiro paid no attention and kept the gun trained on her, even inside the living room. After her initial shock, Lorena decided to take charge of the situation. She had never been one to surrender without a fight.

"Rama, please, I don't understand. Can we talk without you waving that gun around?" she said. Then, with a deep breath, "You have ten seconds to do what I say, or you'll have to kill me. If you let me live, I won't stay quiet, and you'll end up in prison."

Ramiro still didn't lower the gun and gave a cynical laugh.

"I have no doubt that you won't stay quiet, and as for going to prison . . . I don't know. I'm not the one who's had someone killed."

Lorena's legs went weak. She never thought Ramiro would go this far. Had Cristo been talking to him? That was an absurd notion that she immediately disregarded. But he did sound very sure of himself, and he was wielding information of which only two people were aware. And he was still pointing the gun at her.

"I don't know what you're talking about," she replied, trying to buy time.

"Give me Paloma's painting," said Ramiro.

Paloma! So that's the thread he's pulled to find out about the murder, thought Lorena.

"Okay, fine," she said with her hands up. "But let's negotiate—"

"I have nothing to negotiate," interrupted Rama.

As she had done many times before, Lorena Funes chose life. She went to her room, escorted by Ramiro, and opened the closet. The painting was right at the back, rolled up inside a red plastic tube. After making sure everything was in order, Rama put away the gun and left the apartment with the tube under his arm. He had no need to gag Lorena, or tie her up, or to issue further threats. She had much more to lose than he did. Although he had already lost the most important thing.

28

San Francisco, September 1940

A group of fine arts students was waiting for her at the airport, excited and nervous. The wife of the great Mexican muralist, Diego Rivera, had arrived in the country. The reason for her visit, a mystery.

"I started painting purely out of boredom," explained Frida, responding to one of the many questions called out by the young students. "I was bedridden for a year, after the accident that broke my spine, a foot, and other bones. I was sixteen at the time and very much wanted to study medicine. But the crash stymied all that. I was young, like you. I didn't allow the misfortune to become a tragedy. I felt I had the energy to do anything. And without realizing it, I started to paint."

"Are your paintings surrealist?" asked one of the girls.

"I don't know—I'm not entirely sure about that. I do know, they are the sincerest expression of myself. I've only dabbled in painting, with no desire for glory, just the conviction of pleasing myself and being able to make a living from my trade. But there are two positive things I've managed to take from all this: trying as far as possible to always be myself, and the knowledge that even several lifetimes wouldn't be enough to paint as I would like and all I would like."

"Do you paint yourself because you know you're beautiful?" asked a young man in a spotless white shirt.

Frida pondered her answer for a few moments.

"No, I paint myself because I'm always alone."

From the moment Nayeli boarded the plane, by Frida's side, she had barely opened her mouth. Twice only: the first time to eat and the second to vomit into a paper bag that Frida handed her. The journey from Mexico to San Francisco was a nightmare, but she didn't have the heart to ask how a metal tube full of seats could stay in the air without its great weight bringing it down.

The students, goggling at the painter as though she were an eccentric deity shrouded in flounces, necklaces, earrings, and flowers, paid no attention to the skinny, ungainly young woman who had accompanied her. But the driver who was waiting for them noticed that Frida wasn't alone.

"Bienvenidas, señoritas," he greeted them in proficient Spanish, as he removed his felt hat and pressed it to his chest. "Would you like to go to the hotel first, or shall I take you straight to Señor Rivera?"

Frida settled into the back seat and, before replying, took a long slug of cognac from a silver hip flask.

"We're not going to any hotel in this country," she said and looked at Nayeli, who was sliding in next to her. "You know what happened to me last time I was here in Gringolandia? The hotel staff looked down on me, like I was worthless, some kind of inferior being. I'm not going to any hotel."

The driver smiled. His Mexican parents had also frequently found themselves on the receiving end of such looks.

"Very well, Señora Rivera," he replied. "I'll take you to Señor Rivera."

Multiple emotions were bubbling inside Nayeli all at once. The landscape through the window was overwhelming: the buildings taller and grander than anything she had seen in her life, broad streets full of cars, and a sky as clear and blue as the sky over Tehuantepec. But the most disquieting thing was the knot she felt in the middle of her chest, a pressure that almost stopped her breathing. Whenever the driver mentioned Señor Rivera, the knot grew bigger and felt as though it might crush her heart.

When they reached Treasure Island, she felt slightly disappointed. No one had told her it was a piece of artificial land created for an exposition. In her fertile imagination, Treasure Island was a magical place, full of pirates and mermaids searching for gold in hidden corners. Frida's laughter when Nayeli confessed her adventurous expectations made her blush.

The building being prepared to host the Golden Gate International Exposition was wider than it was tall. A crowd of men and women of different ages was milling around it. No one wanted to miss the show.

Two broad-shouldered men wearing identical blue suits strode up to Frida and Nayeli. They were the welcoming committee. They introduced themselves as part of Señor Rivera's security detail. Seeing Frida's astounded face, they explained the fear of an attack by Stalinists or Trotskyists. Rivera was a thorny issue for both sides.

Frida and Nayeli were ushered through a back door, almost the width of the wall. Once inside, Frida had to rest for a few minutes; her leg and back were hurting more than ever, and she had refused to wear the corset that helped her stay straight. She didn't want Diego to see her with her leather and metal supports.

"Señor Rivera is waiting for you in the main hall," said one of the men.

"That sapo gordo never waits for anyone," replied Frida, drying her lips with the back of her hand. "He's used to others waiting for him."

She wasn't wrong. No one knew Diego like she did.

The hall was huge. The only decoration consisted of ten panels arranged in a rectangle twenty-three feet high and seventy-five feet wide. On a scaffold, with a wooden palette in one hand and a thick paintbrush in the other, Diego Rivera was close to finishing the largest mural ever seen.

As if by magic, Frida stood upright, as though her spine had suddenly straightened. She put her hands on her hips and narrowed her eyes. There was something about the mural she didn't like.

"How wonderful, my beautiful dove, Friducha my soulmate!" cried Diego without looking down or pausing as he filled a rounded figure with red paint. He hadn't seen Frida, but he could sense her. "If you're going to get pissed at something, let me come down and give you a hug first."

"I hope you break your skull into ten pieces on the way down from that thing," replied Frida.

Detached from the spectacle, Nayeli couldn't take her eyes off the drawings in the mural: the vivid colors; people she had never seen but who looked real; all around a giant machine with wheels, screws, and cogs that linked the content of each panel.

"Look! It's you, Frida!" exclaimed Nayeli, pointing at the center of the work. "See how lovely you look!"

Frida stomped up to the central panel. She wanted to inspect every brushstroke Diego had devoted to her figure; she wanted to compare them with those of the other women who shared the limelight. Particularly that woman dressed in white, who was the cause of her annoyance.

Diego came down the scaffold steps, fearing that Frida would grab a bucket of paint and ruin everything before her. She was known for her swift and calculated reactions.

"Have a good look, Friducha. See the Tehuana dress I put you in, your favorite. Look at the red and yellow, and the white flounce," said Diego, like a child seeking his mother's approval.

"You didn't put me in anything. I'm not a doll you can dress up as you please," replied the painter, drawing ever closer to the center of the mural. "Who's that sow in the white dress?"

Nayeli preferred not to get involved in the argument. Everything that happened between those two was so public it became private. To interfere in that universe would be to step into the eye of a hurricane. She took a few steps and stood next to Frida, their arms brushing. The painter's skin was hot, a livid energy seeping from every pore.

The woman in white was at the center of the mural, sitting on the ground, behind Frida, with brown hair in a modern style, long shapely legs, and bare feet. In front of her, a fat man wearing blue, also sitting, was holding her hands.

"This is your gringa, your heroine, the one who got you out of Mexico," stated Frida.

"It's Paulette Goddard." Diego nodded.

"Come on, Nayeli. I've seen everything I need to—"

"Stay, Friducha," Diego interrupted her. He didn't want Frida to leave; he had missed her. No one fought with him like she did, and he felt like those arguments and interrogations extended his life by years. "They'll bring in some delicious food soon. There are a lot of Mexicans on this project, and they feed me with flavors from home."

"You see, Nayelita, mi corazón?" Frida continued to address Nayeli. She liked ignoring Diego and leaving him to beg, alone, like a naughty child, because that's what he was: a child who had behaved badly. "That's how this sapo gordo pays his women for going to bed with him. He draws them, collects them, puts them on display for all the world to know about their shenanigans. What an unpleasant man!"

Before leaving, Frida issued an announcement, a warning, and a premonition:

"I'm going to admit myself to the hospital in San Francisco so that Dr. Eloesser can cure my broken spine. When I'm better, I want you to sweep away all those old women scattered like garbage around you." She took a deep breath, smiled, and looked up at the ceiling. Her eyes traveled over it as though, instead of white cement, she could see a blue sky filled with her beloved pink clouds. "I feel in my heart that love is near."

Diego gave a satisfied smile, too. If he had known that Frida's imminent love had nothing to do with him, the smile would have been wiped from his face.

29

Buenos Aires, December 2018

I lost count of the number of times I checked my watch. Four, five, six, maybe more over the course of the hour I waited for Rama to emerge from Lorena's building. That was the name he had given: "Lorena."

It was the gun that frightened me. Just before getting out of the car, he had slipped his hand under the driver's seat and pulled out the small, shiny weapon, then strode off without explanation—not that I had asked for one.

My eyes didn't stray from the door of the building, except to check my watch, until I finally saw him appear. He looked both ways and crossed the street with astonishing calm. A red plastic tube was clamped under his right arm. No sign of the gun. I leaned across the seats and opened the driver's door in a swift movement. A Bonnie helping her Clyde.

I bit my lower lip and desperately searched for a way to break Rama's silence, but I seemed to be finding it ridiculously hard to talk. I gave in with a sigh.

He placed the gun and the red tube beneath his seat, fastened his seat belt, and drove with both hands squeezing the wheel. His knuckles were white. His calm was no more than a façade, betrayed by his hands.

He left the trendy port area at breakneck speed, slowing only to turn onto a street and cross the Recoleta district. Our destination was a boutique hotel opposite the cemetery.

We went to the elevator without stopping at the reception desk. He walked confidently, with me trailing behind. We got out on the fifth floor and entered room 512. The first thing that struck me was the smell, so intense that I had to close my eyes.

"I'll open the window to ventilate it a bit," said Ramiro. "The varnish, oils, and solvents are very strong."

The blast of fresh air blew the tingle from my nose. When I opened my eyes, I found myself in a geography entirely detached from space and time. There was no bed, no nightstands, not even a minibar or a television hanging on the wall. Everything you would expect in a hotel room had been removed.

"It's strange, isn't it? It's my studio, or rather, my nuclear bunker," he explained, laughing.

"Has the zombie apocalypse arrived? Is that why you brought me here?"

"No, not yet. But don't worry anyway, I'm pretty good at killing zombies."

"Ah, that's why you have a gun in your car . . . "

We both stopped laughing at the same time. The moment for humor had passed. Rama sighed—now he had to find the words to explain.

"I got your grandmother's painting back," he said.

It was smart of him to change the focus of my interest, but, like turtles that come out of their winter brumation more active than ever, I wasn't about to relent.

"Why the gun, Rama?"

He sighed again, resigned, and fixed his eyes on me.

"Because we're dealing with dangerous people, people who handle guns, and we need to be on the same level."

"We? What do I have to do with dangerous, armed people?"

"You're the heir, Paloma," he answered.

I was struck silent again. For a woman born in a working-class neighborhood, raised with just enough to live off, the idea of inheriting something other than debts or some kind of useless trinket was unthinkable. The word *heir* made me think of millionaires, noble lineages, silver spoons, people with illustrious surnames. And none of that applied to me.

I stared at the red tube. He handed it to me without hesitating. I opened it and unrolled the painting. There was my grandmother again. I felt calmer. The Nayeli effect was still intact.

"Does this qualify as an inheritance?" I asked, without taking my eyes off the image.

"Perhaps the most important in the art world in recent years," replied Rama.

"I don't get it," I murmured. "I'm telling you, I just don't get it."

Rama stood next to me and gently stroked my hair. He slid his hand to my chin and raised it so that our eyes met. It seemed to me that his green eyes were moist, emotional. And I still didn't understand.

"Paloma, this painting your grandmother left you isn't just any old painting. I think what we have here is an original work by Diego Rivera."

I looked at Ramiro with a mixture of amazement and pity.

"Oh, Rama, please," I said. I couldn't think of anything else to say.

"Paloma, listen, and believe me. I have good reason to think that the painting in your hands is a Diego Rivera. It could be worth millions of dollars, despite that red stain . . . "

"It's a ballerina," I interrupted.

I didn't like him downplaying the red patch that covered part of the painting and felt an overwhelming need to defend the imperfection. He stopped stroking my hair and looked more closely at the painting. I liked the fact that my words held weight.

"You're right, it looks like a ballerina," murmured Rama. "But that doesn't detract from the value of what is drawn beneath it, Paloma. Are you taking in what I'm saying?"

Discomfort again. Annoyance again.

"Okay, enough! I'm tired of you treating me like a silly little girl!" I exclaimed as I rolled up the painting, not entirely carefully. "You're delirious. There's no way this painting is by Diego Rivera. I'm no art expert, but I know who Diego Rivera is, and that man had nothing to do with my grandmother. That's it. Thanks for recovering my memento of Nayeli, but that's as far as it goes. I'm leaving."

As I tried to make for the door, Rama stood in front of it and brought his hands together as if begging.

"Have you forgotten about the murder at the framing store?" he asked in a faint, wavering voice.

"It was a robbery, a coincidence," I assured him, trying more to convince myself than him. "You're writing yourself a crime story where there's absolutely nothing."

"What do you know about your grandmother?" he asked.

"I know everything about my grandmother," I lied. "She was the woman who raised me, who did for me what my own mother didn't."

"Okay, that's great, but that isn't what I want to know," he insisted. "What do you know about her in relation to her country of origin?"

"She was born in Mexico, more specifically in Tehuantepec. She grew up with her family in a rural village. They sold fruits and vegetables they grew themselves. She barely went to school. She fell in love with a village boy and got pregnant. She worked as a cook. She came with her employer and her daughter to Buenos Aires, and, years later, that daughter gave birth to me. That's all."

As he listened to me recite the words I had heard so many times from my grandmother's mouth, Ramiro shook his head. My story, my grandmother's and mother's story, weren't what he wanted, or perhaps it didn't coincide with his fantasies.

"Is that all? We need to know more. That's not enough."

I didn't know whether to laugh, shout, run out, or slap him. The impunity with which he called into question not just my life but also that of my ancestors infuriated me. But as always, I went for the most elegant and least risky response: no reaction at all, followed by escape.

"Okay, fine. Thanks for getting back my painting. That's as far as we go."

He did nothing to stop my leaving. The last thing between us was the slam of the door.

I walked a few blocks around the Recoleta neighborhood. It had always seemed rather charmless to me, as though the souls of the bodies buried in the cemetery had sucked dry the energy of the living. For me, death didn't have the same color, celebration, or intensity it did for Nayeli. I hadn't inherited her reverence for the beyond, but I had inherited a painting.

I squeezed the tube against my chest without slowing my pace. I refused to take Rama's words seriously, but I couldn't erase them from my head. They came and went at the same rhythm as my steps, but none of those thoughts hurt as much as the thorn that Rama had unwittingly plunged into my story. A simple and specific question that stung like alcohol on an open wound: *What do you know about your grandmother?* Nothing. A tiny bit and nothing at all. Just a short list, shreds of a life that Nayeli recited by heart, as though it were someone else's. Someone else she barely knew.

I knew what I had to do. I squeezed the tube even tighter and went down the stairs. I didn't look back. I should have.

30

San Francisco, September 1940

The room in St. Luke's Hospital was small. Everything was white: the walls, the sheets, the linoleum floor, the ceiling.

"Nayeli, I think you'll have to bring me my paints and pencils. It's terrible being surrounded by all this white," complained Frida from her bed. "Everything about it is begging for a bit of color. They've left me wrapped in this cloud; it feels like a provocation."

She had refused to wear the hospital gown, which was also white. With imploring gestures, Frida had persuaded the nurses to let her wear a simple Tehuana dress. That small, broken body, dressed in blue and purple, was the only sign of life in the room. Nayeli soothed her and promised to talk to Diego to arrange some drawing materials.

The doctor, a short man with dark, coarse hair, entered without knocking. One hand clutched a pile of papers and the other held a violin, polished to a shine. Frida's face lit up. As she struggled to sit up against the pillows, she exclaimed: "How wonderful! My friendly quack has come to visit! Look, my Tehuanita. This is Dr. Eloesser, the man who's going to make me as good as new."

The doctor walked up to Nayeli, who regarded him with interest. Dr. Eloesser had the most charming smile she had seen since she set foot in the United States, a country she didn't understand very well.

The doctor solemnly held out his hand and told her he was entirely at her disposal.

"Play us a song, quack, something nice to celebrate this gathering," said Frida. "It's the only way we can celebrate. Those sourpuss nurses took my flask of tequila."

Eloesser perched on the arm of the visitor's chair and rested the violin against his chest. Frida clapped like a little girl, falling still when the first notes filled the room. She closed her eyes and let the chamber music carry her away through the doctor's admirable performance. Nayeli drew near and knelt down, wanting to get as close as she could to the instrument; she was captivated by the music rising from the strings as the man caressed them with a long stick.

"And how is my beloved Mexico, Frida?" he asked as he polished the violin with a cloth from his pocket.

"Mexico is the same as ever, disorganized and going to hell. All it has is the immense beauty of the land and its Indigenous people. Every day the ugliness of the United States steals a piece, and it makes me sad, but people have to eat, and the big fish always eats the little fish."

"Such is life, my dear friend; but this country is big, and it has room for all kinds," replied the doctor.

Frida raised her hand to interrupt him. She always struggled to accept other people's opinions.

"Gringolandia is driven by high society. Those rich bastards I met on my last trip were odious; they hold parties and buy luxury clothes while their countrymen die of hunger in the streets. They have no sensitivity or good taste." She paused. "Anyway, my favorite doctor, I have to admit that here in Gringolandia I have tasted the best cocktails of my life. That's one point in the gringos' favor."

The doctor smiled. He had a hard job ahead of him with this eccentric Mexican. Inside, her body was a debris of crushed and twisted bones that could barely support the flesh and skin. After treating her for years, he had learned that the advances and relapses in her health were almost always related to her emotional ups and downs. Love and passion devastated Frida; they drove her toward the abyss.

"How are things with Diego?" he asked.

"We're divorced, but it isn't too hard. Divorces are easy; it's marriages that are complicated."

Nayeli perched on the edge of Frida's bed. She wanted to follow the conversation closely.

"In my opinion, my dear, the surgery the Mexican doctors are recommending is unnecessary. I think what's troubling you is an emotional crisis, your nerves. You know that Diego loves you very much, and you love him, but he has two great passions: painting and women. You have to give a lot of thought to what you want to do. You can accept facts as they are and get back together with him on his terms, or not. It's one thing or the other," he said in the gentlest tone he could muster.

The three of them sat without speaking for a long time, until the silent tension was interrupted by a booming voice on the other side of the door. Frida rolled her eyes, recognizing those shouts among the thousands of shouts in the universe.

The door was flung open. Diego Rivera's bulk took up almost the entire room; in this tiny space he seemed much bigger than he was. Rivera wasn't alone, a young man with large, round eyes was standing behind him. He was almost as tall as the painter, but much slimmer, with a fragile, elegant appearance.

"Here she is," said Diego, gesturing at the bed. "The one and only Frida Kahlo, the best artist ever to set foot in this world. My dear friend, you'll see when you get to know her; you'll like her a lot. Everything about her is perfect."

At the sight of Frida, Heinz Berggruen was struck dumb, unable to utter a word, despite his deeply rooted manners and his work in public relations. In the end, she was the one to introduce herself, in her own way, without taking her eyes off the man.

"It's hard to say exactly when day ends and night begins, but no one mistakes day for night."

Diego frowned and glanced at Dr. Eloesser. No one understood what Frida was trying to say, but Nayeli was able to interpret her perfectly. She did understand.

31

Buenos Aires, December 2018

Rama was right. He might have assumed my abrupt exit was because of the gun, his mysteriousness, or Nayeli's painting. But no, none of that scared me; none of that sent me running off. He was right about something else, and that was the real reason for my flight. I was escaping the truth, a truth that always caused a silent pain, a truth that Ramiro put into words and condensed into a single question: "*What do you know about your grandmother?*" The explanation I repeated to him, which I had been repeating to myself for years, wasn't enough; it was never enough. They were just the words of a woman who always preferred to stay silent, a woman who chose to define herself in four or five simple, unequivocal lines. What life can be summed up in just a few words? None. But my grandmother did just that and made me an accomplice to her silence and self-definition.

The subway carriage was nearly empty, and I settled myself into one of the seats, leaned my head against the window, and shut my eyes, soothed by the rhythmic rocking of the train, the tinny voice announcing each stop, and the music filtering through the earphones of the boy sitting next to me.

My mother's apartment always smelled of sage, her favorite scent, which she used to hide other odors: the reek of the cigarettes she smoked in secret or the overpowering fragrances worn by the men who passed through her bed.

When she opened the door, the mellow sage crept up my nose. I smiled internally, without changing my expression. Over the years, I realized that my mother was a woman, too, as much of a woman as I was. We were two women whose pasts were marked by desolation. She hid her surprise and didn't ask me how I was or what I was doing ringing her bell without warning; nor did she kiss or hug me. "Paloma," she said. That was all.

She ushered me in, closed the door, and offered me coffee. All at once. I accepted and waited for her on the sofa as I listened to her ranting at the coffee machine in the kitchen.

"What brings you here, then?" she asked, handing me a cup. "It was about time you remembered your mother, eh?"

I let the reproach go without comment and distracted myself by looking at the silk robe she was wearing. It was violet, her favorite color, and it suited her perfectly. I emptied the cup in one gulp. The coffee was lukewarm and watery.

"Tell me about my abuela." I got straight to the point, all too aware that long preambles annoyed her.

She opened her green eyes wide and shrugged twice, as though wanting to shake off my request.

"You knew her better than I did. You always wanted to live with her." Again, I let the reproach go.

"Before me, I mean. I want to know about my grandmother before I was born. The day of the wake at Casa Solanas, you left a necklace with an obsidian pendant on the coffin. Nayeli never told me about that necklace."

"Amulet," corrected my mother. "It was an amulet."

"I never knew, for example, what the amulet protected her from," I pressed on. "There are lots of things I don't know."

My mother had always been an evasive woman, icy and unemotional. But if anyone took the trouble to watch her gestures closely, they would have found some warmth in her. I took the trouble and noticed how the hardness of her perfect skin gradually softened.

"It didn't protect her; it protected me. She hung it around my neck when I was seriously ill with the flu as a child. She was convinced the stone had saved my life. She believed in that sort of thing," she replied. "And I did too, to a degree. That's why I felt it was right to return the amulet to her for her journey to the beyond. You know how serious your grandmother was about death."

"What did she tell you about her life in Mexico? And don't just repeat what you've told me a hundred times."

"Not all lives are interesting, not everyone is the lead in an action movie, Paloma, come on. Or is your life so much more thrilling than the life Nayeli described?"

My mother was able to seesaw adeptly between wounding and healing. A caress, a blow; a kindness, a cruelty. She moved comfortably in both terrains. A moment in one, a minute in the other. And I had learned to ignore the back-and-forth.

She stood up and, right in front of me, performed those ballet steps she always practiced in secret. Long arms raised above her head, toes pointed perfectly, legs moving up and down, and neck stretched out like a swan. The music was always in her mind, only she could hear it. For the first time, I followed her movements. They were gentle, elegant, proud. She had decorated her apartment in a style that made the perfect stage: the color of the walls, the curtains, the rugs, the crystal glasses on the counter, the chandeliers.

All of a sudden, everything struck me as strange. Something was out of place. My mind raced with images of Nayeli's house, the little chalet in Boedo where my mother and I were raised. There was no sophistication between those walls: the furniture was humble and simple; on the main table, a checkered oilcloth with a floral pattern that faded a little more every time it was wiped with bleach; the white walls with no paintings; the single bookshelf filled with ceramic ornaments that my grandmother collected. She never had curtains at the windows.

So where had my mother acquired such good taste? Who had taught her to select upholstery fabric? How had a humble, state-educated young woman become an aristocrat? Where had she learned classical ballet? I had gone to my mother's house wanting to know who Nayeli Cruz was and had been presented with a different question: Who was my mother?

I asked to use her bathroom. I felt confused and slightly dizzy and needed to splash some water on my face. Closing the door, I turned on the faucet, stuck my wrists under the jet of cold water, and took a deep breath. After wetting my cheeks, I dried myself on a fluffy pink towel; it smelled of sage, like everything else.

The door of the wooden cabinet beneath the basin was ajar, and I couldn't help but take a look. Behind her makeup and perfumes, I discovered vast amounts of psychiatric medication. That was another side of my mother.

I heard a gentle tap at the door. I hadn't been all that long, but she was getting anxious. When I opened up, she was standing outside, waiting. She wasn't dancing now. The music in her imagination had stopped. She was holding the red plastic tube I had left on the sofa; it was open and empty. Before she spoke, she gazed at me with that perpetual mystery she conveyed so well.

"Where did you find the painting?" she asked.

Her question gave me an answer to one thing, at least. Nayeli's painting came as no surprise to my mother.

"With her things," I said. I didn't want to explain too much.

"Yes, I had forgotten all about it. I don't think I've seen it since I was a child. For a long time it was hanging on the wall in the Boedo house."

"Why did she keep it?" I asked, playing dumb.

"I don't know. It isn't important. How should I know? Your grandmother was always a bit of a hoarder."

She unrolled the painting on the marble coffee table in the living room. Anger instantly swept over me like a wave, without warning, as it often did.

"I'm sick of you always criticizing her! You can't even leave her in peace now she's dead!" I shouted. "Nayeli took care of me, she fed me, she told me bedtime stories, she wiped my nose and my tears, and she was always in the place you left empty, Mom. I won't allow you to cast aspersions on her."

She fixed her eyes on mine again, and I could see the glimmer of a tear that would never fall. The music started playing in her mind again, and she resumed her dancing.

I looked at the painting of Nayeli, the red stain in the shape of a ballerina.

The same poise, the same elegance.

I rolled up the painting and slipped it into the tube. I was agitated, struggling to breathe. My clashes with my mother always knocked me off-kilter, but this time my grandmother wasn't there to soothe them with a hearty Mexican soup. I left without saying goodbye. She remained in her world, in her imaginary Colón Theater. At that moment I was too flustered to see that my mother, in her deceitful madness, had given me more in that encounter than she had ever given me in her life.

I walked two blocks with my bag over one shoulder, the red tube clasped to my chest. I could have walked for miles without batting an eyelid, I was so disoriented. But I didn't get as far as the third block. A strong arm grabbed me from behind. I wanted to scream. I couldn't. A hard object was jabbing into my ribs; I could only imagine it was a gun. With a gentle pull, the man spun me around, and I was able to see him, or nearly. A scarf covered most of his face. His eyes were hidden behind dark glasses. He delicately relieved me of the red tube. I didn't dare put up a fight. I looked both ways in the hope of finding some kind of help, but there was no one on the sidewalk but the hooded man and me. I didn't bother shouting.

I thought about Ramiro again, and the fact that he was right.

32

San Francisco, September 1940

"Good morning, my beautiful boy!" Frida would cry every time Heinz graced the door of her hospital room. And he would smile, his big, round eyes shining and his cheeks aflame. Like any man in love, he brought gifts for Nayeli, too.

Dr. Eloesser's treatment was starting to show results. A full examination had determined that Frida was suffering from a kidney infection that was worsening her crippled leg. They had to medicate her so that she could rest properly, and she wasn't to drink any alcohol.

"Hey, Nayeli. I want you to help me decorate my hair and paint my lips a nice color," said Frida on the morning of her discharge. "And I want to get rid of these hospital clothes. I need to be Frida Kahlo again."

"But you're always Frida Kahlo." Nayeli found it hard to keep up with the painter's frequent contradictions.

"I'm not, just look at me. I'm nothing without color. My wardrobe is part of me; I am my wardrobe," she explained, with the gravitas of someone giving a speech. "I invented my personality to hide my own self."

Nayeli sat on the edge of the bed and took one of Frida's hands in hers. "Your own self is beautiful, Frida. It was your own self that rescued me," she said tenderly.

Frida had always been an expert in suffering. She howled her pain theatrically, making quite the song and dance. It was emotion that unsettled her. She didn't feel comfortable in that fuzzy borderland between laughter and tears, and she did her best to fall on one side or the other. This time she chose laughter.

"My gentle girl," she said with a strident laugh. "You rescue me when you make your Zapotecan dishes or when you sneak me in a little flask of cognac. Now, rescue your Frida from herself and make her a fully-fledged Tehuana woman again. I don't want to ignore this lust for life, because I've never felt it so strongly before."

In less than an hour, the thin, ungainly woman with dark messy curls and opaque skin became a burst of color. Nayeli selected the brightest of all the skirts Frida had brought in her suitcases: it was sprinkled with flowers embroidered in silk thread, and the stems and leaves were painted in gold. She matched it with a white lace huipil, then laid out on the painter's lap a wooden box filled with necklaces, earrings, and bracelets.

The painter took her time trying on different necklaces of ceramic, acrylic, and wooden beads. When she couldn't decide on one, she wore them all.

"I brought flowers and butterflies for your hair," said Nayeli.

"Use the butterflies," said Frida. "I want my head to seem like it has wings, as though it could take flight and detach from my body."

The final touch was orange lipstick, the shade that suited her best.

"You're stunning," babbled Heinz as he crossed the threshold. The woman in front of him seemed to have stepped out of one of her own canvases.

Frida had plans. She always devised them quietly, without consulting anyone. She formed and reformed her own life, and that of others, in her head. She could spend hours imagining scenarios, walks, sex scenes, whole lives that she shaped in her verdant imagination. Often, what had germinated in her mind would be spewed out through her mouth, and she would be branded a liar. She didn't care. In the end, she alone shaped the stories she wanted to tell.

"We're going to New York, my beautiful boy! The great city of lights and skyscrapers!" she exclaimed, applauding her own idea.

Nayeli and Heinz exchanged an uncertain glance: Heinz, because he didn't know how to react to such a proposal, and Nayeli, because she didn't know what New York was. However, Dr. Eloesser approved the adventure, and even Diego felt that the trip would be the cherry on the cake in Frida's full recovery.

Everything was astir in the apartment on the outskirts of San Francisco that an artist friend and gallery owner had loaned Frida. It was small: two rooms, a living room, and a kitchen that Nayeli could barely squeeze into.

"We won't take much at all, Nayeli, just a couple of outfits we can share. I'm so skinny your size will fit me perfectly!" she exclaimed as she bustled about as though the incision on her back didn't exist. It was momentum that kept her on her feet. "We'll take the necklaces and earrings, though. Those jewels are the envy of the gringas who want to imitate me. And you'll see them; they're like big ugly birds dressed as Tehuanas."

Nayeli couldn't move. She had risen several times during the night to vomit; she could feel a knot in her guts, and her cheeks were burning.

"My God!" exclaimed Frida, touching Nayeli's forehead with a ring-laden hand. "You have a fever, mi amor. I'll call Dr. Eloesser right away; he's a wizard who can cure anything."

Eloesser appeared twenty minutes later, looking impeccable as ever in his doctor's coat.

"This girl has viral gastroenteritis," he declared. "She must rest, drink plenty of fluids, and stay quiet until her fever drops."

"That's impossible, quack," Frida said affectionately. "We're going to New York with Heinz in a few hours."

The doctor shook his head, insisting that Nayeli was in no fit state to travel anywhere.

"Go without me," murmured the girl.

Diego Rivera's entrance through the still-open apartment door put a pause to their conversation. He arrived in parts, as always: first, the sound of his booming voice, then his huge body filling every last corner.

"Well, well, well. What do we have here?" he asked.

His eyes took in the disorder of the room before fixing on Nayeli, who was still slumped on a sofa, a damp white cloth on her brow.

"Ah, Diego, good of you to deign to visit us!" said Frida. "Nayeli has a bad stomach, and the doctor won't let her travel with us to New York. I need you to take care of her."

Nayeli's heart froze, like a dog when it thinks that if it stays very still, it'll be invisible. In the foreground, she heard the gurgling of her blood running through her veins; in the background, the plans Diego and Frida were making regarding her stay in the painter's hands.

After speaking with Diego, Frida announced that he would move into the apartment to take care of Nayeli. The young woman merely nodded.

Frida's departure was imminent. The painter was as nervous as she was jubilant. She sang, she laughed, she talked nonstop about various topics at the same time as she finished packing her things. From the sofa, Nayeli followed her with her eyes, her muscles so weak she could barely move.

"Do I look beautiful?" Frida asked, standing in front of her like a child seeking her mother's approval.

Nayeli didn't have to lie or exaggerate: Frida looked bewitching.

"Truly beautiful, Frida," replied Nayeli. "You look like a rich lady, like the ones we saw at Treasure Island."

Frida wrinkled her nose in disgust.

"Oh, Virgen of Guadalupe, save me from such a fate, please!" she exclaimed, and ran to her bedroom. "I'm going to have to fix that."

Seconds later, she reappeared with a box holding ribbons, flowers, and hair clasps. She didn't need a mirror to fix a hairstyle she was able to achieve from memory.

The final result was striking, like everything about her. They both laughed. They knew that the disguise they had fabricated for Frida's broken body was no more than a trick, and they were well aware that people would point and whisper that the Mexican artist was ridiculous. They didn't care.

Frida reclined on the sofa next to Nayeli. The young woman leaned her head against Frida's chest. The knot in her stomach loosened with the beat of Frida's heart, a gentle, regular gallop. Nayeli closed her eyes and filled her nostrils with the unsettling scent of Shocking de Schiaparelli, Frida's favorite perfume.

"Hey, Tehuanita," she said in a hoarse but tender voice. "Don't let Diego paint you. Being Diego's model is like giving your flesh to his body, not just his art. Never let him do it. I mean it."

33

Buenos Aires, December 2018

Ramiro finally learned what it was to sleep soundly when his brother was arrested. That night, he slipped between the sheets and, for the first time, was able to switch off the light. The monster, his monster, was behind bars.

"*You are not Ramiro Pallares*," his older brother whispered in his ear every night of his childhood.

Cristo could turn into a ghost. He would sneak into the room without a sound, as though he could float.

Every morning, for years, Ramiro ate breakfast with the conviction that he wasn't the person his parents said he was. He wasn't Ramiro Pallares. As the day progressed, that certainty would gradually fade. Until the ghost returned and it started all over again.

He never asked his parents to intervene. He never told them how Cristo used to beat him up under the pretense of teaching him to play soccer, nor the times when Cristo locked him in the pantry for hours. Nor did he ever confess that the time he came home with two broken fingers, claiming he had fallen from his bicycle, he had lied.

Ramiro admired his brother deeply, however. He spent hours hidden behind the furniture watching him paint.

When Cristo picked up his brushes, he was someone else. His gestures became softer, his battle-hardened shoulders relaxed, and he even seemed less muscular than he actually was. The boy who painted wasn't Cristóbal Pallares, thought Rama, echoing the phrase that terrorized his nights.

Over the years, the fear had disappeared and turned to hatred. This wasn't a hatred that flared up uncontrollably; it was calm, gentle, constant. A tiny splinter that he couldn't, and didn't want to, pull out.

Ramiro never visited him in prison. The person he did visit was his mother. Twice a month, he would buy flowers and spend the afternoon sitting next to her grave, drawing. The subject was always the same: Elvira's face. Ramiro was convinced that evoking her features, the shape of her eyes, her mouth, the distance between the ears, the curve of her nose, or the waves of her hair, was the only way not to forget her. And in each sketch, he found her; even if just for a few hours, he felt that, from somewhere, she was dictating the movements of his hands.

He climbed the stairs of the Museo Pictórico slowly, to delay the moment of encountering his father. Although the relationship was rocky, curt, and lacking in any kind of affection, Ramiro still sought paternal acceptance. For his visit, he had worn his best shirt and linen pants and jacket; he knew his father noticed these details.

He crossed the gallery, lingering for a moment in front of *La Martita*. He sighed with a mixture of disapproval and admiration. His brother was still the best.

He knocked twice on the door and, before Pallares gave permission for him to enter the office, walked in. Those small rebellions kept Ramiro in a state of constant tension. His father was that person he just had to annoy. Always.

"I thought you would call before just dropping in. You're lucky I'm not in a meeting," said Pallares.

"I'm a lucky man, yes," replied Ramiro, settling himself into an original bergère armchair. He knew his father broke into a sweat whenever anyone dared go near the eighteenth-century antique.

"What brings you here?"

Emilio Pallares was known for getting straight to the point, believing his time to be worth its weight in gold. Ramiro decided to play the same game.

"Cristóbal won't be able to copy a Diego Rivera. He doesn't have the hand for it."

The silence was short and tense. Ramiro relished every second, sensing his father breaking inside. He pictured a huge crack stretching from his stomach to his head. Although his face remained stony, inside he was laughing like crazy. The satisfaction of small victories.

Before speaking, Emilio gave a short, dry cough.

"I don't know what you're talking about," he said as firmly as he could. "It's time you stopped concerning yourself with your brother."

"Can we talk seriously, or are we going to keep up the charade?" asked Ramiro as he crossed his legs. "I know all about it. And I know that Lorena is right in the middle of it."

It was Emilio Pallares who had introduced his younger son to Lorena Funes; he had harbored the hope of being able to use Ramiro as a bargaining chip. With Cristóbal in prison and out of the game, he needed someone close and easy to manipulate. But he realized too late that his son was neither close nor easy to manipulate. He also realized that, deep down, Lorena was a woman whose judgment could be clouded by a man as handsome as Ramiro.

"My dear son, you've been making the same mistake since you were a child," he said scathingly. "Your arrogance makes you think you know everything, and you don't. Given that you turned your brother in, I'm sure you can appreciate that I don't entirely trust you."

The blow that Ramiro had been expecting for all these years had finally come. For the first time, his father was reproaching him for what he had done at the age of sixteen, and it confirmed his suspicions: his father was behind the theft of the Diego Rivera painting.

"I want to be involved," said Ramiro without flinching. "You don't know the secrets I'm capable of keeping either."

For the first time in years, Emilio Pallares looked at his son with interest. He raised his right eyebrow, as he did when he was weighing up his options.

"I sense a threat in your tone. Am I mistaken?"

Ramiro got up from the bergère chair and paced around the office with his hands on his hips.

"Cristóbal's mark is visible on the lower right-hand corner of *La Martita*. I saw it, and, knowing your eye for detail, I know you've seen it, too." He walked up to the desk, leaned on it with both hands, and drew his face close to his father's. "That same mark is on the recovered Blates, the same mark is hidden in so many paintings, in so many museums."

"Sit down, Rama," Pallares cut in, adopting a more familiar tone in the hope of meeting him halfway. "Let's talk calmly."

"I am calm." Ramiro took a sheet of paper from his pocket and started reading: "Musée Lautaine in Paris, the Museo Internacional in Madrid, the Art Institute of New York, Lopolis Museum, Athens . . . "

"Enough, Ramiro!" Pallares finally exclaimed. "Are you threatening me?"

Ramiro smiled in satisfaction. He folded the paper neatly into four and dropped it on the desk between them. That list could send his father to prison.

Emilio Pallares's head was like an engine turning in a higher gear than it could manage. Where had his son gotten all that information?

"All right, dearest son of mine," he said, recovering his ironic tone, although unable to entirely conceal his terror. "What do you want in return for your silence?"

"To be part of it."

"Nothing else?"

"Nothing else."

The proposal wasn't so absurd. Indeed, hadn't he often fantasized about his younger son being part of the business, too? But his instinct set alarm bells ringing. A young man who issued threats indiscriminately, and even with a certain pleasure, wasn't someone you could trust. Pallares would take Cristóbal's wild outbursts over Ramiro's underhand perversion any day. But for the moment, he had no choice. He nodded, trying to work out how to buy time.

"Very well, son," he said, holding out his hands, palms up. "Welcome to the art family."

Ramiro sat back in the armchair. Talking to his father had never been a pleasurable experience before.

"I accept your welcome. Now let's talk terms."

And there it is! thought Pallares. He was disconcerted by his younger son's spirit. Even as a boy, Rama had known how to avoid other people's messes, until he got bored and started to create his own. He did it silently, craftily, like his mother, Elvira.

She had always wanted her sons to be artists and had put more effort into that plan than she had devoted to anything else.

As children, Ramiro and Cristóbal had both attended classes in drawing, painting, and watercolor. But Elvira didn't account for the fact that their artistic steps were being closely followed by their father, until, one rainy Sunday, Emilio brought out his collection of books on great artists and set the boys a challenge: whoever made the best copy of Rembrandt's *The Night Watch* would win a bicycle.

The afternoon became a nightmare. Cristóbal didn't need to reach a point of extreme concentration to copy a painting. His eyes were perfect machines that could capture other people's techniques and details, and his hands followed with skill. Ramiro worked very differently: his gifts were anchored in the imagination. His drawings came from his head, and he was frustrated by having to appropriate someone else's ideas. But the prize was tempting.

They took nearly eight hours to finish. Cristóbal won the bicycle. His father gave him an extra prize that he knew his older son would find much more satisfying: he allowed him to tear his brother's drawing to pieces.

Elvira, meanwhile, only had eyes for Ramiro, the loser. She noticed the boy's contained tears, his red cheeks burning with fury, and his clenched fists and teeth. The woman knew that this was just the beginning of the nightmare that would lead her sons to disaster.

Things had settled over time, and now Ramiro was the one in a position of power. A power granted by the orange-covered notebooks his mother hadn't gotten around to burning. Elvira, the woman who listened and stayed silent, had documented the crimes committed by her husband for years. The works stolen, duplicated, hidden, and exhibited in museums under false pretenses. She had followed it all painstakingly. Furthermore, she was the one who gave her son Cristóbal the cross-shaped pendant with the idea of using it as a secret signature in all his paintings. She didn't do it out of maternal love, she did it so that her youngest, the weaker son, the punished son, could survive. It was the tool that would allow Ramiro to defeat his brother, if necessary. The proof of his crimes.

"Ramiro, you came to ask me to let you into the business; I accepted your request. I don't understand why now you want to set terms!" exclaimed Pallares, trying to control his fury.

"I didn't come to ask you anything, Dad. I came to explain your two options: either I enter the business, or you go to prison," said Ramiro in a monotone. "You've always been a cautious man who goes for the classiest option. You wouldn't enjoy time behind bars. Cristóbal was able to handle it, but he isn't like you in that regard."

"Your brother was always better than you," said Pallares with the certainty of someone who knows his words can become daggers.

The young man nodded. Perhaps his father was right.

Ramiro's phone rang and made them both jump. Paloma was calling. Ramiro declined the call. Before he could put the phone away, a WhatsApp message flashed up. Paloma wasn't usually so insistent. He read it: *I didn't want to bother you before, but I want you to know that my grandmother's painting has been stolen. A guy on a motorbike. Perhaps you're right and my inheritance is important.*

He took a deep breath and nodded again. Paloma wasn't telling him anything he didn't already know. He was the one who had stolen the painting.

34

San Francisco, September 1940

Dr. Eloesser's medicines and recommendations cured Nayeli. Once she felt well enough to get up, in the solitude of the apartment, her hands were restless. She found her fingertips itching to get cooking: to sink into soft white doughs, to peel fruit and expose its juicy pulp, and to prepare the ingredients for her sauces. Cooking was all she needed, the only thing that calmed her. That was when she could let the textures and flavors take her to Tehuantepec. Her place, her land.

Frida had left some money on the table, green-colored bills Nayeli had never seen before. She had no idea how much they were worth or how much food they would allow her to buy. She wrapped herself in her shawl and ventured out to the streets with a basket. The first block was enough to terrify her. The blare of car engines and horns, people rushing past without seeing her, and the strange clothes made her want to abandon her quest. But her curiosity won. The acrid smell of reused oil made her wrinkle her nose. On a corner, a plump woman with short hair, her apron stained with grease, was serving fried sausages inside strangely pale bread rolls. Her stall was small, crudely built out of painted wood. Nayeli attempted to decipher the letters on the huge poster across the front. Although Frida had taught her to read a little, she didn't understand a word.

"Buenos días, señora. ¿Usted me podría indicar dónde está el mercado?" she asked, raising her voice. She had quickly realized that there were two options in San Francisco: make yourself heard, or just give in.

The woman tilted her head to one side without taking her eyes off the girl. She raised her arm and beckoned a scrawny boy who was sweeping the sidewalk a few feet away. Nayeli didn't need to hear him speak to know that he was Mexican. The shiny black hair, the grin that filled his whole face, and the sparkle in his dark eyes made her feel at home. The woman said something in English, pointing at Nayeli.

"Good morning, señorita," said the boy in Spanish, holding out his hand. "How can we help you?"

"I'm looking for the market."

"Yes, of course. It's your lucky day. There's a good market just across the street. Not a market like we have back home, but it has a lot of things. And there are plenty of Mexicans working there, so the language won't be a problem," he replied with a wink.

The market was small but well stocked. And the boy was right: the vendors calling out the prices and qualities of their wares, boasting the finest fruit and vegetables, were all Mexican. They worked with the passion and understanding of people who know how to make the most of everything that sprouts from the ground. She filled her basket with vegetables, fruit, legumes, rice, and condiments, and bought as well two earthenware pots, a large wooden spoon, and a stone mortar.

After making her purchases, Nayeli returned to the apartment and immersed herself in a kingdom where she reigned without needing a crown: the kitchen. She covered the rice with hot water and waited five minutes before straining it. When the oil was spitting, she started frying the grains and enjoyed seeing the creamy white turn a pale golden color. She stood with her hands on her waist, hips to one side, with her weight on one leg—the same posture Frida used when waiting for her blotting paper to absorb the moisture of her watercolors.

She filled the mortar with tomatoes, onion, and garlic, then ground them hard for some time, her eyes closed. The spicy, sweet aroma brought tears to her eyes. She combined the paste with the fried rice and, using the wooden spoon, defoamed it. Everything turned a perfect coral red. Her mother always said that it isn't enough for dishes to taste good; they have to nourish the eyes and nose as well. Good food involves all the senses, and none should be forgotten.

Diego arrived at dinnertime, always punctual when it came to food. His hungry stomach was a reliable clock. It didn't matter if he was mid-brushstroke, or if the model he was sketching was left alone and naked. Mealtimes were sacred, unpostponable. The smell of the solvents and paint that stained his work overalls blended with the aroma of the rice dish. Rivera's presence smelled of cooking and art.

"Wonderful, Nayeli! You've brought the whole of Mexico into the pan!" he exclaimed as he plunged a piece of bread into the sauce.

The apartment had no dining room, but Nayeli found a way to disguise this absence with abundance. She dragged a small wooden table into the middle of the living room and covered it with one of Frida's knitted blankets, then arranged some fruit in a wooden dish; at either side, she placed two plates with cutlery and two crystal glasses, all that was left behind by the previous tenants. A tall glass served as an improvised vase for some daisies she had pulled from the yard of the house next door.

They started their meal in silence; Diego didn't like to interrupt his acts of pleasure with words, and eating was one of those acts. With each spoonful, he closed his eyes, relishing the flavors colonizing his palate and slipping down his throat to become lost in his body. When the sensation faded, another mouthful revived it.

Nayeli was happy to watch his enjoyment. She alternated her attention between her own barely touched plate and Diego's face. She had never been this close to him before. His towering bulk lost its threatening aspect up close. His eyes weren't as green as they appeared from afar; some specks of yellow gave his gaze a golden effect, like two round leaves dipped in honey. The skin on his face looked different, too: his cheeks and forehead were pale pink, and his thinning hair, ineptly swept across his head, was actually white and soft like the cotton threads that Tehuana women used to weave in the markets.

A few grains of rice had fallen on his belly. Nayeli could count them. That was the strategy she used to calm her nerves: counting grains of rice.

"Nayeli, I'll say it again: you are the very essence of Mexico!" announced Diego after savoring the last spoonful of rice.

A timid "thank you" was all the girl could manage.

Rivera liked listening to the sound of his own voice, even more than he liked to have others listen to it. As his words rang in her ears, the stories became increasingly exaggerated. He had a knack for weaving his tale between reality and fantasy.

"A rice dish like this was my very first meal, the first thing to hit this big old belly," he said, slapping the sides of his bulging stomach. "The first of many. Until the age of three, I ate nothing but this dish—that's why it's my favorite. It tastes of breastmilk."

"Little children don't eat rice," said Nayeli, curious. "The small grains can get stuck and choke them."

"It depends on the child," insisted Diego. He also liked people questioning what he said, because that allowed him to offer his nonsensical arguments and make his stories even more outlandish. "I didn't come into the world alone, you know, I arrived with my twin brother. Carlos María was his name. The poor thing died young; we had barely learned to walk when La Parca came and took him to the other side. It was devastating for everyone, and my mother, poor thing, she became depressed and couldn't raise me. And that's where the rice comes in."

A silence fell. With his spoon, he stirred imaginary rice on his empty plate. Diego was an expert at interrupting his own stories at the most interesting part; like everyone nourished by the imploring of others, he would wait until they urged him to continue.

"So what happened?" asked Nayeli, not realizing that for the first time she had fallen under Rivera's spell.

"My parents sent me to live in my nanny's house. Doña Antonia; she was a good woman who was like a mother to me during my early childhood. She was Tehuana, like you, and she cooked me that rice dish every morning, afternoon, and evening. And I never choked. Not once. And Friducha, too, she makes that same rice for me, you know. It's the food of Tehuana mothers, of course. The best Mexican women, for sure. The only women who don't depend either physically or emotionally on the foreign classes." He looked at Nayeli with admiration and tenderness, a blend that was a mark of his seductive personality. "Never stop dressing the way you dress, or being who you are. Your soul will always be in Oaxaca—don't you forget that."

After dinner, Nayeli washed the two plates, the glasses, and the cutlery. She did it five times, one after the other, and every time she started again, she moved the soapy cloth even more slowly. As her hands splashed in the water, she followed the sound of Diego's movements.

Finally, she heard the creaking of springs. Diego had gone to bed. Before Nayeli could start to wash the plates again, his rhythmic snoring turned into sporadic roars. The girl smiled.

The sofa in the showroom was large and comfortable. At one end, Frida had left the set of linen sheets she took on every journey; according to her, you couldn't trust the gringos with anything related to dreams. But Treasure Island seemed like a dream, and Nayeli hadn't hesitated to accept Diego's invitation. She would be a witness to a historic moment in the art world: Rivera's final brushstroke on the star mural of the Golden Gate International Exposition. That final touch was to add a deep red to the skirt worn by the figure of Frida Kahlo, right in the center of the work. Frida again, always Frida.

"I was never a faithful husband," Diego commented to Nayeli in passing as they devoured bread rolls with peanut butter, provided by the organizers of the exposition. "I've always given in to my whims, my desires. Now that I no longer have her, I decided to take an inventory of myself as a conjugal partner, and the truth is, I don't have much to say for myself."

Nayeli tried to memorize his every word, knowing that Frida would make her repeat the conversation over and over.

"I didn't divorce Frida because I didn't love her; I separated from her because I love her too much and all I do is make her suffer. I insisted so much that she finally agreed. And that victory was my undoing; it brought me nothing but heartache. I just wanted to be free to be with any woman who caught my eye."

"I never heard Frida oppose that," interrupted Nayeli. She felt a strong urge to defend her mentor to anyone who badmouthed her, even if that person was Rivera.

"Of course not. She never opposed it, but she questioned every one of my affairs. She couldn't tolerate me being with anyone she regarded as unworthy or beneath her. She said that humiliated her."

It struck Nayeli that it would be impossible for Diego to find a woman superior to Frida. To her, the painter was the most fabulous creature ever invented. Frida had devised the perfect trap: finding someone better than her was impossible.

More and more people were gathering behind the protective fence that ran along the length of the mural. Men, women, and children who had been invited in the expectation that they would let word spread around the city that the Mexican muralist's wonderfully intense images would liven up the whole exposition.

The front row was composed entirely of women. Tall, short, young, old. All of them were dolled up as though they had been invited to a party. Hats, dresses, skirts, silk blouses, high heels, elaborate hairstyles, and makeup, a lot of makeup.

Nayeli noticed the nudges, the complicit laughter, the fluttering lashes, and whispers that Diego provoked. He moved his hefty form with skill, gesticulated with energy, and pretended to take measurements with his hands of each of the panels of the work. He ran his fingers across each figure. He patted down his messy hair without taking his eyes off some detail, with a look of intense concentration, as though he had detected an imaginary error. Each of the painter's comings and goings unleashed a wave of feminine sighs.

"Have you seen what women are like around me?" Diego asked Nayeli in a very low voice. "I don't understand what they see in me. If only they knew that the more I like a woman, the more I try to hurt her, they'd run away. But they don't know that."

"Or they don't care," remarked Nayeli.

Diego pondered the girl's response for a few seconds. Then he returned to one of the topics to which he was constantly drawn. "My Friducha is the most obvious victim of that unpleasant trait of mine."

A wave of fury flooded over Nayeli. The clarity and apathy with which Rivera accepted responsibility for Frida's pain made her retch. It was she who needed to wound him, to employ the same lethal weapon that he did.

"Frida isn't your little wounded deer any longer, Señor Diego. Frida is one of the women, perhaps the only one, who did run away from you. With her broken dove's wings, she went far away. She flew as best she could, but she flew."

SECOND PART

35

Coyoacán, January 1941

The fleeting time Diego, Frida, and Nayeli spent in the United States left more than one heart broken; the first belonged to young Heinz. He would never forget his days with Frida in New York City.

She didn't love; she devoured. And in the city of lights, Heinz was happy to be devoured.

Then one morning she called time, and the marriage-less honeymoon ended as quickly as it had begun. That was another side of Frida's personality: a torrent of scatterbrained decisions with which she plowed ahead with no thought for the consequences.

She returned to San Francisco revived and with three new overcoats: one for Nayeli and two for herself. When the young woman asked after Heinz, the painter looked at her in bewilderment, as though the poor boy was no more than a bag left behind in a café on the Upper West Side.

"We're going home, my ballerina!" she exclaimed, making no mention of her lover. "We'll spend Christmas at our house. We've had too much of Gringolandia, more than I can stand."

"And Diego?" The question slipped out unwittingly, desperately. Nayeli would have exchanged ten years of her life to go back in time and swallow her question.

Frida smiled and rested her cold, bony hand on the girl's cheek.

"Diego knows how to make himself indispensable. That's his gift."

They didn't mention him again. He became a ghost that, despite its frequent apparitions, everyone preferred to ignore. Until one cold January morning, cozy in the kitchen in Casa Azul, when Frida shared her concerns about the muralist's health. Dr. Ismael Villegas had been clear: Diego was run-down and needed special care.

"Nayeli, come here. Now, this is very important," said Frida as she settled herself in a chair at the kitchen table.

The girl approached, hypnotized, unable to tear her eyes from the wooden box of coloring pencils.

"Sit next to me and don't be so surprised; you look like you've seen a ghost. I have to make a very detailed list of the instructions the doctor gave Diego. And we must both remember what's on it, or that gordo sapo will explode before our very eyes. And now we're going to write it all out."

"I don't know how to write," Nayeli blurted out, although seconds later she qualified her statement. "Well, I suppose I know a bit. My older sister taught me a few letters. Rosa was part of the children's wing of the Campaign Against Illiteracy during the revolution."

Frida's eyes widened, and she brought both hands to her chest. "That's wonderful!" she exclaimed. "I was an ad honorem teacher for a while. Then I found out that my Diego went all around Mexico taking culture to those who needed it most. What a coincidence—we didn't even know each other, and yet we were both part of the same revolution. We were destined for each other. It's beautiful, don't you think?"

The Tehuana nodded; she believed in destiny, too.

"Those voluntary teachers came to my village in Tehuantepec, too. It was before I was born, but my mother told me those bourgeois teachers eventually got tired of working with kids with lice and scabies and returned to their comfortable lives."

This comment made Frida fall silent. That whole epic that she and Diego had boasted about blew up in her face with Nayeli's words, like a piñata at a birthday party. That wasn't her, she thought; she wasn't a jaded bourgeois snob.

"I'll be your belated revolution," she announced. "Come on, don't just sit there like a cactus! Choose a pencil from the box, and we'll write together."

Nayeli picked a red pencil. She had often thought that her favorite color might be red, although she was attracted to violet, too. She hesitated for a few seconds before returning to her first instinct.

"Excellent, good choice. Red is a vital color, the color of the blood that pumps around the heart," said the painter.

For several hours, they concentrated on drawing each of the letters that appeared on the list from Diego's doctor, one by one, in red pencil, on the blank sheet of paper. Initially, the shapes were feathery, uncertain, but as time passed, Nayeli's hand became surer. By the end of the day, they sat back and admired what they had achieved together.

Frida made the girl read the indications aloud. As Nayeli decoded the words and pronounced them proudly and confidently, the painter applauded. Finally, they used a paintbrush to spread paste on the back of the sheet and stuck it to one of the kitchen walls. Frida drew some little skeletons and hearts in the blank spaces. Despite their enthusiasm, both women knew for sure that Diego wouldn't stick to a single point on the list.

The reconciliation between the two artists, including their remarriage, had altered the mechanics between the couple, but some things remained unchanged: Rivera could only find his vital force with a paintbrush in his hand, and Frida still treated him like a big child. Nayeli had often heard people say that women love motherhood. And that every woman does her mothering in whatever way she can.

Frida had set up a modest home for her husband, although she knew that the studio in San Ángel was still his space, where he didn't just paint but also received his lovers. But something had changed in her, and that change had a lot to do with a letter, several pages long, which she treasured and kept under her pillow to reread when her strength faltered.

Diego is basically a sad person. He looks for warmth and a certain air which are always in the exact center of the universe. It's natural to want to return to him, but I wouldn't do it, since what attracts Diego to you is what he doesn't have, and if he doesn't have you tied down completely, he will keep on looking for you and needing you. It seems to me that for you it would be best to be coquettish. Don't let yourself be tied down completely; do something with your own life, for that is what cushions us when the blows and falls come. The blow is not as strong if there is something which allows one to say: I'm here, I'm worth something.

Nayeli never knew what the letter said, but, aware that Frida read and reread it in secret, she knew it must contain some essential advice from Ana Brenner, the woman she had seen just once in San Francisco. The meeting had lasted only a few minutes. With hair so short it barely covered her round head, a prominent nose, and the bluest eyes in the world, Ana Brenner looked like an eccentric young man at first sight.

Straight-legged pants covered her slim legs, and lace ruffles decorated the neckline of her white shirt. Ana's appearance disconcerted and hypnotized Nayeli with equal intensity. The woman who looked like a man murmured incessantly in English, as she held Frida's hands. Sometime later, Nayeli discovered that Ana was Mexican and realized that she had avoided speaking Spanish in front of her so that her secrets would reach only Frida's ears. After their farewell embrace, Ana said one last thing to Frida in Spanish: "*Money is your independence.*"

It was only later that Nayeli understood the significance of these words that echoed through her head her entire life.

The metallic squeaking of Frida's wheelchair distracted Nayeli. She leaned out of the window and saw movement in the studio. There was no doubt about it: Frida was creating. Since they had returned from the United States, her leg was stronger, and she didn't need to be suspended from the harnesses to stretch her spine; what's more, Diego had become her husband again. For those reasons, it had initially seemed strange that she spent hours and hours at her easel trying out sketches, figures, and colors that she claimed to invent. Frida only buried herself in her art when she was overcome by sadness; it had been her mechanism since childhood to help her forget about the pains of her body and soul. Now, a new Frida Kahlo had settled into the body of the wounded dove: a Frida determined to earn money from her work.

Although she was exhausted, Nayeli ran across the house and leaped up the stone steps. There was nothing she liked better than watching Frida paint. Deep down, she was convinced she was witnessing a historic moment. No one had as much faith in the painter's works as Nayeli did. Not even Diego; not even Frida herself.

Frida was sitting in her wheelchair. A blanket woven in greens and golds covered her legs. Her small, chickpea-shaped nose almost brushed the canvas she was painting. In the dying light, she couldn't see all the details, so her only option was to get up close and half close her eyes. Her right hand hovered in the air; the tips of her thumb, index, and middle fingers gripped the brush delicately.

Nayeli held her breath so as not to interrupt her, but it was no good. Frida was as perceptive as an animal in danger, always alert. Without raising her eyes from her work, she smiled.

"Hello, my ballerina. It's nice to have company! I don't like being alone. You can sit next to me if you like."

The girl picked up the small wooden chair from which she usually watched the show, but before she could sit, a painting on the table caught her attention. She didn't recall having seen it before. It was one of the many self-portraits Frida made, but this one was different, special. Frida didn't look like Frida. It was the male version of the most feminine woman Nayeli had ever seen. Ana Brenner flashed through her mind, but she kept her impressions to herself.

Instead of her usual attire, the Frida in the painting was wearing a baggy suit much like the ones Diego sometimes wore. The garments were dark, almost black; a brown shirt, buttoned to the neck, didn't reveal an inch of her chest. All the femininity was removed. Her long tresses were scattered on the floor around her, and in her hands, she held a pair of scissors and a single lock of her hair.

"I look so strange, don't I?" asked Frida. She instinctively knew what would catch Nayeli's attention. "My hair was once that short, do you remember? It was you who helped me shear it off."

Nayeli remembered, but she was still floored by the work.

Frida kept on doing what she always did: giving explanations no one had asked for. She liked to hear herself talk.

"I've often felt I'm loved only for my feminine attributes, which men find exciting and women find eccentric. Both, for different reasons, want my body. When I painted this canvas, I wanted them all to go to hell. I can be like that. When I finished the last brushstroke, I waited a few days until the oil dried and then I covered it with a cloth, so I would never see it again."

"Why did you hide it?" asked the girl curiously. Having gotten over her surprise, she thought the work was beautiful. There was something different in each stroke.

"I hid it because, although I know there's a sadness reflected in each of my paintings, in this one in particular the feeling is overwhelming, and it's too painful."

"And why have you brought it out of hiding now?"

"Because I've accepted that I have no other way out. Sadness is my destiny, and there's an element of freedom in making my peace with that."

The kerosene lamp flickered, and the reflection of the turquoise glass earrings hit Frida's eyes. She was wearing a black tunic—unusual for her, who made color a way of life.

"You aren't wearing any colors today?" asked Nayeli. She was sure the choice of wardrobe wasn't random.

"No, today I'm in mourning. Mourning for what I've lost," she replied with resignation.

Nayeli didn't want to keep digging. Whenever Frida spoke of loss, she was always referring to the children she had never been able to bear. Once Nayeli had heard one of the many doctors who visited Frida talk about something called "miscarriage," and Nayeli swallowed down the questions that usually flowed from her mouth. The heartrending cry her mentor gave when the doctor uttered the mysterious word chilled her to the bone, and she knew this was a forbidden topic. She decided to change the subject.

"Frida, does this painting have a name?"

"No, it doesn't," Frida replied, pensively. "But it isn't going to go alone through life. I'm making it a companion."

They crossed the studio, one in the wheelchair, the other on foot. The yellow light picked out the half-finished painting on the easel. Another self-portrait, but this was the Frida Nayeli knew, the Frida by her side.

As in its twin work, all the painting's strength and its message could be found in the hair: in the first work, through its absence; in the second, through its incontrovertible presence. The hair appeared right in the middle of the canvas: drawn tightly back from the face, with a thick coil wound in a red wool ribbon that swept it upward to shape a high, braided hairpiece.

"What a beautiful hairstyle!" murmured Nayeli. "I used to see a lot of women with their hair like that in Oaxaca."

Frida smiled in satisfaction. "The red ribbon doesn't end. If you look closely, you can't tell when it starts and when it ends. It's like time: infinite. Both paintings should be shown together; they talk to each other. The hair on the floor in the first painting is the same that appears in the second, but neither has a name. That's your job, ballerina. Giving orphans names."

The girl went from one canvas to the other. Back and forth. She took the responsibility of naming Frida's paintings very seriously. Something in her heart told her this was an important task. She took almost twenty minutes to make her decision. She pointed at the first, and in a ceremonial tone announced: "Self-portrait with Cropped Hair."

Frida's powerful laugh jolted the cat Manchitas awake.

"Fabulous, my ballerina, what else could it be? Self-portrait with Cropped Hair. I like it! And the other . . . What shall we call the other one?" she asked eagerly.

"Well . . . Let's see, I think I have an idea," said Nayeli, making Frida beg. She liked it when the painter looked at her with such expectation.

"Tell me, say it now, I'm dying of curiosity!"

"Self-portrait with Braid."

More laughter, and another jump from Manchitas.

"I love it! Of course! Those will be the names: *Self-portrait with Cropped Hair* and *Self-portrait with Braid*," said Frida as she noted down the names with a graphite pencil in her sketchbook.

A door slammed, and a rumbling voice diverted their attention. From the other end of Casa Azul came the unmistakable noise of Diego. There was nothing silent about the painter, who didn't know the meaning of decorum or moderation. His voice was very nearly a shout, his teeth clattered when he chewed, the food thundered down his throat, and, even asleep, he made his presence felt: he snored, moaned, and sang songs with his eyes closed.

"Wonderful, wonderful!" they heard Rivera exclaim, almost breathlessly. Whenever he liked something a lot, he felt the need to repeat it over and over.

Frida stood up with difficulty; since she had remarried Diego, she had tried to hide her physical infirmities from him. She wanted him to see her as strong and healthy, convinced that a sick woman was desirable to no one but doctors.

Diego was in the kitchen, standing in a corner. In one hand he held a sketchbook and in the other a stick of graphite, which danced over the page with astounding skill. When he was drawing, he had eyes for nothing and no one else.

On the yellow table there were three platters laden with fruit and four clay vases filled with colorful flowers. Every day, Frida turned the table into a still life for Diego. She made the most of her morning walks, recommended by the doctor, to gather wildflowers and make bouquets that she sometimes adorned with hair ribbons.

As soon as the sketch was finished, Diego allowed Nayeli to move the flowers aside so that the three of them could use the table to eat. Sweet buns, pastries, and mugs of hot chocolate soon replaced the still life.

"I have a little fantasy buzzing around my head," said Diego, still chewing. Between words, the morsel of food could be seen dancing around his mouth.

"Liar," said Frida, elbows on the table. "You don't have fantasies, you only have plans and whims, and you do them all. Come on then, tell us . . . "

"I want to build a museum, mine and yours. Something just for us and our friends. Something big, monumental. What do you think, Nayeli?"

The girl choked on a piece of apple. Although he had been living in Casa Azul for a while now, whenever Diego addressed her, she was lost for words.

"W-w-well, I d-d-don't know . . . " she stuttered, as both painters looked at her expectantly. "A place where all your paintings would be together?"

Diego raised his arms enthusiastically.

"I hadn't thought of that, but wouldn't it be wonderful? Imagine all the walls covered in my murals . . . "

Frida cut in, banging on the table with the palm of her hand. "If all the walls are going to be covered in your murals, where will my paintings hang?"

All three fell silent. Nayeli stared at her plate. Diego shrugged, like a child whose mother has told him off, and Frida, hands on hips, insisted: "So then . . . Tell me, sapo egoísta, where will I put my paintings? Well, I'll tell you: nowhere near your horrible museum. My paintings are worth money, and I'll only hang them on the walls of people who can damn well pay for them."

Ana Brenner's secret letter had made more of an impression on Frida than even she realized. One of the conditions she had imposed on remarrying Rivera had been clear and nonnegotiable: she would keep the money from her artistic work, and Diego wouldn't be responsible for all the bills at Casa Azul—Frida would pay her fair share.

"Of course, my dove, you're right. My humble museum is no place for your work, and I couldn't even pay five percent of what your every brushstroke is worth," said the painter sincerely, for he genuinely admired his wife's work. "Perhaps I could use it to house my pre-Columbian idols . . . "

Nayeli bit her tongue to keep an idea to herself, until she couldn't hold it in any longer. She wanted to contribute to the discussion.

"Perhaps you could make it into a kind of farm, like the ones in Tehuantepec. Grow your own food, animals in a stable . . . "

Frida broke out in applause. The sound of her clapping, accompanied by the jingle of her gemstone and metal bracelets, interrupted the girl's explanation.

"It's perfect, my little ballerina, just perfect! Nothing would be more exciting than having my own farm with my own vegetables and animals." She turned her body to face Diego. "Sapo gordo, I want that museum."

Diego was exultant. He had never dreamed the idea would be so well received by Frida, albeit with some modifications.

"I already have a place in mind. A large plot in El Pedregal. There's a lot of work to be done."

"And money to be spent," added Frida, who tended to be the more levelheaded of the pair. The dove who knows she needs her feet on the ground when her wings won't make it.

"It's true, Friducha, but I have some savings, and I haven't touched the dollars I was paid in the States."

Frida nodded, and, as she buttered a slice of sweet bun, she weighed up the possibilities. She knew her husband's money wouldn't be enough. Diego was a machine when it came to dreaming big, dreams as big as his murals; no one knew him better than she did, and she was sure he wouldn't go along with the idea of a farm, vegetable garden, and stable. Rivera's mind was too monumental.

"If you say so, sapo," she replied.

An hour later, as she was helping Nayeli clear the table and tidy the kitchen, Frida waited for Diego to retire to his room.

"Hey, ballerina. Early tomorrow morning we're going to see a notary I know. He's a good man; he's already bought two of my best works. I'll tell him to put the house on Insurgentes on the market so we can raise some money."

Nayeli knew nothing about money or the value of properties, but she guessed that Frida was talking about a lot, more than she could ever imagine.

"But Señor Diego said—"

"Pah, who cares what that dimwit says. He knows nothing about money. I learned it all from my mother, who couldn't do anything but count bills. I'll sell what's mine to make the gordo sapo Diego's dream come true—you'll see."

Nayeli rubbed Frida's back, so thin she could count every rib and even the twisted vertebrae of her spine. Nayeli felt a huge admiration for her mentor. Her older sister flashed into her mind, and she gave a pained smile. Rosa and Frida were the only two people in the world who measured loyalty in terms of unwavering devotion.

36

Buenos Aires, January 2019

The tiles in the courtyard at Casa Solanas had just been mopped; a few small puddles, accumulated in the dips, glistened in the sun; the azaleas and jasmines growing in large pots offered a burst of color and fragrance. Although the walls needed a lick of paint, the flaking sections and the damp stains gave the place a homely atmosphere.

Two certainties had brought me to the care home where my grandmother died: one, I was the heir to a valuable artwork, and two, I wanted to get it back. Rama still hadn't responded to my messages. This time I sensed that his silence was because he wanted to get his hands on Nayeli's painting, too, but without me. As at many other times in my life, I knew I was alone, but, far from getting upset, I felt good. Solitude can sometimes be a path toward freedom.

"What do you want from life when you grow up?" my grandmother had asked me one afternoon while we were walking home from school. I remember replying that I wanted a lot of everything. If my grandmother had been alive to ask me again, I would have given the same response, although my desires were very different. I still wanted a lot, but a lot of myself. And, like never before, I needed to know who I was; above all, where I came from and what kind of blood was running through my veins.

I paused in front of one of the large windows overlooking the courtyard of Casa Solanas. The dress I had rescued from the closet at my late grandmother's house fitted me perfectly, as if made to measure. It comforted me to know that we had the same width of hips and chest, the same leg length and waist circumference.

Olive green, in soft, finely woven wool flannel; fitted to just cover the knees; a round neckline with small, heart-shaped mother-of-pearl buttons; elbow-length sleeves and a leather belt in the same color. This was Nayeli's most luxurious dress, the one I had chosen to try to re-create her on my own skin. I wore it in the knowledge that having the right dress would help me come out victorious today.

Gloria was coming down the corridor to the courtyard. It had been only a few months since I last saw her—at my grandmother's tribute—but I noticed that she was walking more slowly, with more of a stoop and less ease, as though time had passed more quickly for her. Her hair, however, was still as impeccable as her nail varnish.

"Hello, Palomita. How lovely to see you! I thought you'd forgotten about us old ladies," she said tenderly, but without missing the opportunity for a gripe.

I gave her a quick embrace and a kiss on either cheek. She watched me closely, with the audacity people tend to have when they've been around for longer than they have left and can't waste time on trivial courtesies or good manners.

"What a lovely outfit, my dear! It's the first time I've seen you dressed up; you're always so scruffy."

I laughed. She wasn't wrong.

"This was Nayeli's dress," I said, with the intention of leading the conversation to where I wanted it. "It's lovely, but the flannel is kind of hot. Shall we sit on the veranda?"

Without a word, she turned and retraced her steps. We sat in a couple of rather battered but comfortable wicker chairs. For nearly twenty minutes, she brought me up to date on the novelties at Casa Solanas. She had barely finished complaining about one thing when she would jump to the next, and she was equally indignant about all of them. I listened patiently, agreeing with everything she said.

"I came to see you, in particular, because you're the only one with a good enough memory to help me." I exaggerated my praise, although it was true. "The day Nayeli died, I remember we spoke for a while in the courtyard and you mentioned a scrapbook of recipes—"

"Yes, of course. I remember perfectly," she interrupted, leaving no doubt that her memory was as sharp as ever. "Your grandmother used to sit at the little table in the nurses' courtyard and write in that red notebook—she would carry it around everywhere."

"It was red?"

"Yes. It was like a fat little book with a red leather cover and gold letters on the front." The stiff corners of her lips suddenly softened, and her eyes became moist.

"I'd like to find it; I need more. I feel like my grandmother can't reach me, that she's slipping away from me."

"I have it."

"That's wonderful, Gloria!" I said—ignoring the fact that she had hidden it from me—and noticed her body relax. "I would love to have it."

"Of course. Come to my room."

Gloria turned away from me, as though my only destiny was to follow her. And follow her I did.

The room was small, and the only sunlight came through one poorly positioned window, lighting up a small section of wall next to the bathroom. Nevertheless, Gloria had managed to make her space quite welcoming.

She asked for my help to move the desk. Behind it was a small door set into the wall, a kind of safe with no padlock or key. We crouched like two excited girls about to open our gifts from Santa. Gloria turned the round bronze handle, and the door opened.

"This is where I keep my private things," she said as she plunged both hands into a hollow only big enough to hold a shoebox. "It's the only place I know the cleaning staff won't stick their noses."

She carefully drew out a bag in a striking bright pink, perhaps a souvenir of some gift received long ago. I helped her stand, and we placed the bag on the bed. She anxiously laid out a number of objects in a neat row and, finally, Nayeli's notebook.

It was just as she had described: a fat notebook with lots of pages, a red leather cover, and two initials printed in gold: *J. K.* Neither of us dared touch it. For a while, we stood in silent homage, as though Nayeli's only resting place was that souvenir found among many others.

"Your grandmother always had that book in her hand; she truly valued it," said Gloria, gazing at it. "When her mind started to slip sometimes, she would leave it around the place. On several occasions I had to rescue it from the kitchen or the courtyard . . . "

"I never saw her with the notebook," I murmured, disconcerted. "I don't understand."

"That's what old ladies are like, Paloma: hoarders. When life starts to slip away before our eyes, we cling to our things. These objects are often a piece of the life that is leaving us, and we hold on tight; we don't want to share it with anyone. It's our right, my dear."

Although I wasn't entirely convinced by her excuse, I decided to accept it. Gloria continued her tale. Her tone was no longer one of gossipy complaint; a note of indulgence had entered her voice.

"The last few months before she died, she was bedridden, as you'll remember. Her bones couldn't support her body; she was very weak. I had left the notebook on her desk. I thought perhaps she would want to have it close, but I was wrong." She paused, picked up the book, and held it against her chest. "Every time I popped into her room to see her, she would twist her head and fix those green eyes on the notebook. The first few times I thought she wanted to hold it, but she shook her head like crazy if I held it out to her. Until one day, by chance, I realized what your grandmother wanted."

"What did she want?" I asked.

"She wanted me to take it, to hide it," replied Gloria. "That afternoon I was with her when Sandra, the nurse, came in—you know, the slim one who's always meddling and never stops talking. I saw Nayeli's eyes. She looked at Sandra, and she looked at the notebook. And then I understood . . . "

"And what happened?"

"I jumped up from my chair—I didn't even know I could get up so quickly—and I grabbed the notebook. I could see the look of relief on your grandmother's face. Without explaining, I turned around and left the room," she said, placing the notebook on my lap. "Since that day, I've kept it in my hidey-hole, until now."

"It was a pact," I said with a smile.

"Yes, a pact of friendship. We old women have friends, too, Palomita."

I couldn't help but hug her. Gloria's body stiffened. She wasn't accustomed to displays of affection and didn't much like it, but she didn't stop me.

I left Gloria's room with my grandmother's notebook at the bottom of my purse. My heart was pounding fast but rhythmically. I was satisfied at having taken a significant step toward my goal of recovering my grandmother's painting; to achieve it, I had to find the truth behind the mysterious and secretive Nayeli.

I walked down the corridor separating the rooms from the main entrance, and that was when I saw her. Eva Garmendia was standing at the foot of the marble staircase. I struggled to hide my shock. She was wearing a dress of olive-green wool flannel, with a round neckline and heart-shaped mother-of-pearl buttons down the front; the sleeves were elbow-length; her waistline marked by a leather belt the same color as the dress. Eva and I were wearing the same dress; they were identical.

37

Coyoacán, April 1944

The walls of Coyoacán market were plastered with handwritten flyers, an invitation promising one of the events of the year:

> This Saturday, at eleven in the morning, the decorative paintings at La Rosita pulque shop, at the corner of Aguayo and Londres, will be unveiled. These murals were created by the "Fridos," pupils of the art teacher of the Secretariat of Public Education, Señora Frida Kahlo. The hosts will lay on a delicious barbecue with ingredients imported directly from Texcoco, washed down with the supreme pulques made by the finest producers of our national nectar. This event will also celebrate the 18th birthday of Frida's esteemed cook, Señorita Nayeli Cruz.

Nayeli was well aware that her mentor was a recognized and beloved figure, but her own sudden fame caused her both excitement and embarrassment.

Frida had promised her a huge birthday cake, with lots of cream, strawberries, chocolate, and eighteen candles. The cake had been commissioned to Doña Lupita, the famous cake maker of Coyoacán, who had been so excited, she had revealed that the painter had requested that Nayeli's cake be made in the shape of a heart.

On the big day, Frida awoke happier than she had felt for a long time. She smiled: her body had relented and offered her a truce for this special day. The nagging pain in her spine was now just a stitch in her left side, and the right femur, which usually seemed to stab like a dagger into her hip with every step, was barely noticeable. She managed to crouch down without issue; she had hidden Nayeli's birthday present under her bed.

She strode down the hallways of Casa Azul singing "Las mañanitas" at the top of her lungs. The aroma of freshly baked bread buns told her the girl was in the kitchen.

"Drop everything you're doing, my ballerina," she said when she saw the bowls in Nayeli's hands, ready to be arranged on the table. "Look, come here. I have a birthday present for you."

Nayeli's face lit up. Although Frida often gave her gifts, the one she was holding out to her seemed very special. It was wrapped in red silk paper, held in place by several ribbons in multiple colors. They sat down in the wooden chairs at the table, then Frida placed the package on the birthday girl's lap. Nayeli closed her eyes and filled her lungs with air.

Her mother had raised her with a custom that, according to her, was inherited from their Tehuantepec ancestors. You had to close your eyes to get rid of any external images and concentrate on those that were hidden in the mind. The aim was to visualize and guess the contents of the package.

But all the visualization in the world couldn't have diminished Nayeli's amazement as she unwrapped the red silk paper to find the most beautiful Tehuana outfit she had seen in her life.

"But . . . It can't be . . . I don't . . . " stammered the girl. "I don't deserve this."

"You deserve it all and more," Frida assured her, helping her spread out the ensemble on the table.

It was gold. The color of the gods, of the sun's rays, of Aztec gold; a bold and lavish color. Not only did the fabric of the skirt shimmer, but so, too, did the huipil and shawl. In a canvas bag, Frida had added some accessories that, in keeping with her style, must be worn with the outfit: two metal brooches in the shape of butterflies and some paper flowers to adorn her hair.

Nayeli could barely contain her joy, but the surprises weren't over yet. Frida got up from her chair and went to the kitchen cabinet. That was where she squirreled away all the souvenirs she bought on her travels. She turned the silver key that was always in the lock and took out two identical notebooks. She sat down next to Nayeli again and placed the notebooks on top of the new outfit. Both had a red leather cover and, in the center, embossed in gold, two letters: *J. K.*

The young woman furrowed her brows with curiosity. Before she could open her mouth to ask, Frida preempted her.

"What you see here are not actually books, although they look like it." She picked up one of the notebooks and flicked through it to reveal the blank pages. "They're personal diaries. A friend gave them to me some time ago. She said she bought them in New York and that they belonged to the poet John Keats. I like to think that's true, but I don't know," she said, and delicately placed one of the books in Nayeli's hands. "This one is for you. I want you to write or draw whatever comes to mind. All the pages are blank, and a blank page is an outrage," she added in a very low voice, as though communicating a very important message. "I'll keep the other one, and I'll fill it with all my ideas."

Nayeli hugged the notebook to her as though it were a small child she had to care for. She was delighted to have a shared project with the painter.

Frida stood up and changed the subject, the intimacy short-lived. "You can wear your new outfit at the unveiling, and you'll be the most opulent Tehuana in all of Mexico. Joselito will be blown away when he sees you," said Frida, with a complicitous wink.

Nayeli's cheeks colored, and all she could do was lower her gaze. Embarrassment flooded through her. Ever since she had first seen Joselito, she couldn't stop thinking about him. The mere idea that Frida had noticed her romantic daydreaming drove her wild with shame.

It all started when Frida had to stop giving in-person drawing classes at the art school. Taking her wheelchair to the school was unthinkable: she didn't want her pupils to see her with wheels for legs, she would say. It was Diego who came up with the solution: if Frida couldn't get to the school, then the school would come to Frida. And so it did. The garden at Casa Azul became a green classroom where the young students drew every plant, tree, fountain, and pet.

"Get your belly down on the ground. Feel the earth. Draw what you see. Don't copy other artists, you are artists, too, and sing as you work. Singing is inspiring," shouted Frida, happy with life. Teaching was one of her favorite things.

Joselito didn't have the talent of his classmates, but no one could question his commitment. He never tired of drawing; he didn't even pause for bread rolls or a glass of milk or juice. For that reason, he was Frida's favorite, because he waged war against obstacles. He was nineteen, but his features—small nose, large eyes with curving lashes, and a slight body—made him seem younger. But what caught Nayeli's attention was his odor: Joselito smelled of roses.

"Very good, Joselito. Ten out of ten!" Frida would exclaim, gazing at her pupils with satisfaction. "I'm the teacher."

Over time, the group of pupils had become a small community of artists that orbited around her. To them, the painter was a divinity. In honor of her mastery, they decided to call themselves the Fridos. There were nine of them, four female and five male students. They had decided to wear a uniform that identified them: dark pants and blue shirts that, as the days went on, acquired stains in a rainbow of colors.

A few yards from Casa Azul, La Rosita pulque shop had become a focus of interest for all Coyoacán. For a month, its outside walls and the sidewalk became the setting for a show that no one wanted to miss. Frida Kahlo, in work overalls with a yellow silk scarf covering her hair, shouted instructions. On days when her leg barely moved, she turned up with a wooden stick she had decorated with ribbons and bells. By her side, Diego Rivera, also in overalls, was responsible for making sure the drawings weren't too big or too small for the walls. He unfolded wax paper sketches on the ground in the middle of the street and used a metal rod to take measurements with his expert eye.

The themes of the mural—rural scenes in which pulque featured strongly—had been chosen, unanimously, when the idea of taking their art to the streets had started to germinate.

"Mexico is inexpressible, severe, rich, wretched, and exuberant. It deserves to be painted," Diego said when the Fridos had asked the corpulent muralist for his advice. And paint it they did.

It fell to Nayeli to bring trays of cold drinks, fruit, and bread rolls, and she took every opportunity to compliment Joselito's brushstrokes, although the boy got embarrassed as soon as he saw her in the doorway of Casa Azul.

The unveiling of the La Rosita murals started on time. Calle Londres was decorated with balloons, papier mâché figures, and flowers. On the corners, girls standing on wooden benches tossed confetti everywhere, so that every guest at the celebration ended up with tiny colored discs in their hair. To begin with, they tried to brush them out, but as time went on, they accepted the extra decoration with resignation, as though it were falling snow.

"Who is that beautiful woman with the long braids?" asked Nayeli.

"That's Concha Michel. She's a communist activist and defender of all our rights," explained Frida. "And what's more, she sings delightful corridos, those ballads that put the rich in their place. Come on, I'll introduce you."

But Diego got there ahead of them. He knelt at the singer's feet, kissed her hand, and begged her to do him the honor of dancing a Yucatecan jarana with him.

"Of course," shouted Frida, walking over to where the mariachis were playing. "It's time for corridos. Let's dance, comrades!"

Concha unstrapped the guitar from her back, positioned it against her chest and, with her long nails, started to strum at inhuman speed. At the same time, she followed the rhythm with her feet. She danced and sang, seemingly able to show off both talents without one detracting from the other. The guests fell at her feet—she was irresistible.

Nayeli had never heard this particular corrido, but the rhythm, lyrics, and melody permeated her every pore. Her golden skirt swayed from side to side, and with the reflection of the sun, she cast luminous rays over anyone who approached. Joselito was dazzled and poured out his fascination into a sketchbook in which he drew a girl in the shape of a sun that eclipsed all around her.

For nearly three hours, the party remained at fever pitch, and no one dared interrupt the celebration. More and more people joined in. For the first time in years, Coyoacán market had to close its doors: none of the stallholders wanted to miss the fun.

At one side of the bar, the assistants who usually worked with Diego on murals for official buildings had set up a wooden stage.

After asking the mariachis to stop playing, Diego stood in the middle of the platform and shouted: "My fellow Mexicans, my friends! Please, come gather around this platform—my Friducha and I would like to say a few words."

Diego took Frida by the hands and pulled her up to the platform, accommodating her gently by his side. The gesture prompted a burst of spontaneous applause from the crowd. Frida crossed her hands over her chest and bowed her head in gratitude.

For the occasion, she had selected a Tehuana outfit with a velvety black background, against which a design of agave leaves stood out in green and yellow, the same colors found in her floral headdress, sitting firmly atop her braided hair. The contrast with Rivera, in a simple brown suit, was as extreme as it was disconcerting. Together, they formed a perfect pair—no one could deny that.

Rivera took a small step forward and shouted in his thunderous voice: "We need another revolution, but one led by artists! Every pulque shop in Mexico should have murals like the ones we see today at La Rosita. People must have spaces where they can express their complaints and their needs." He paused and turned to fix his eyes on Frida, who was listening to him intently. "Take from life all that life gives you, my dove, as long as it is interesting and gives you joy and pleasure. If you really want me to be happy, then nothing could make me happier than knowing that you are enjoying yourself. I don't blame people for loving Frida, because I love her, too. I love her more than anything in the world!"

Once again, applause rang out in the streets of Coyoacán. From the side of the stage, Nayeli watched them, enraptured, her cheeks aflame with a mix of excitement and the pulque Frida had encouraged her to drink. She couldn't recall having ever heard Diego utter such loving words. But Frida's attitude had changed; without putting it into words, her poorly princess posture said something else. With her chin up, shoulders back, and eyes pointed skyward, the painter seemed to exclaim with pride: "Yes, it's true! I deserve it all!"

Now it was Frida's turn. She, too, took a step forward and began. "First of all, I want to say that what we see here is the work of my children, my beloved Fridos." With one hand, she gestured at the group of students listening to her from the front row. Once again, applause and cheering. "I merely provided the impulse they need to become artists, that's all. My painting carries the message of pain; it completes my life. I've lost three babies and many other things that have made my life horrible, and painting has replaced all of that. Many critics have called me a surrealist, but I'm not. My paintings represent the sincerest expression of myself and nothing more. That's why I want my work to go beyond me; I want it to contribute to my people's fight for peace and freedom. And we have taken the first step toward achieving that here today, filling the public walls of our city with images of our country. Here by my side is the best muralist the world has ever seen; my Diego Rivera is bringing palace walls to the people. And from today, every wall in our Mexico will be a palace of colors and customs. That will be our revolution!"

No sooner had Frida finished her speech than a group of men and women, pulque producers, removed the cardboard protecting the paintings on the walls. The surprise was finally unveiled. Frida and Diego stepped down from the platform and joined in the never-ending kisses and congratulations that the Fridos were receiving. Doña Rosita wrote down the huge list of orders in her notebook: every shop in Coyoacán wanted to have Mexican art on their walls.

Nayeli wandered among the guests. A few feet from the bar, she stopped on tiptoe and craned her neck; she wanted to know where Joselito was. She could see him standing next to the door, receiving handshakes, slaps on the back, and kisses on both cheeks. He looked exultant.

Nayeli didn't want to interrupt him; he had the right to enjoy the sweet feeling of being someone once in his life.

She turned around with the idea of going into Casa Azul for a while, when she locked eyes with a girl standing next to a green door, who seemed to attract her like a magnet. Her youth didn't seem to match her appearance, and her sadness jarred with her beauty. She was dressed in black, as though in mourning: a straight, fitted skirt covered her knees, leaving her slim and milky white calves on show; her white gauze blouse was buttoned to the neck, accessorized with nothing but a necklace of tiny pearls. Her smooth hair was so blond it was almost white; she wore it short, just below the ears. Nayeli had the feeling that the young woman needed help. Without hesitating, she approached.

"Good morning, señorita. Are you all right?" she asked.

"No, to be honest, I'm not at all," the girl replied with disconcerting frankness. "Is this Frida Kahlo's house?"

The question surprised Nayeli. There was no one in Coyoacán who didn't know Casa Azul; it was a sanctuary.

"Yes, this is where Frida and Diego live."

The girl raised both eyebrows, as her eyes ran over every corner of the façade; she seemed to want to memorize every last detail.

"Thanks for the information," she said in a childlike voice and with an elegant gesture. "Give Diego my best."

"Yes, of course. Tell me your name and I'll make a point of doing that."

"La Güera. Tell him The Blonde sends her regards," she said with a half smile.

And with the same mysterious and elegant air with which she had arrived, she left. She turned on her low heels and, stepping like a gazelle crossed Calle Londres, plunged into the crowd. Nayeli kept watching her until her blond head disappeared from sight.

38

Montevideo, January 2019

Ramiro and Emilio filled out the customs forms without speaking, as if they were strangers. Both knew that the journey across the Río de la Plata would be a long one. They managed to kill a bit of time in the duty-free store, but it wasn't enough, the boat had only just set sail.

It was Ramiro who broke the silence and offered his father a coffee. Emilio Pallares accepted. They sat in a couple of first-class seats and drank without looking at each other, both pairs of eyes fixed on the tawny river water.

In his head, Emilio replayed every word spoken in the meeting just hours earlier; a rather tense meeting in his office at the Museo Pictórico. The first condition that Ramiro had demanded in exchange for his silence would not be easy to achieve, but he had no option, and fell back on his lifelong strategy: leaving for later the mess his actions would cause. Contrary to what he had imagined, dealing with Lorena Funes had been much easier than calming Cristóbal.

He had arranged to meet them in the museum, afraid of inviting them to his house.

"I brought you here to inform you that neither of you will be involved in the purported Diego Rivera painting."

Lorena's outburst had gone off like a wet firework. "Emilio, you can't cut me out; I was the one who brought you the goddamn work—"

"And where is it now?" he'd interrupted, cynically. Lorena's eyes dropped to the floor. "You don't have it, my dear."

He enjoyed Lorena's efforts not to shout at him.

"It was stolen," she babbled, her eyes begging for mercy. "There was nothing I could do."

"How was the painting stolen, Lorena? You never did tell me about it. I could have helped you recover it. I have my methods," he said, frowning, arms folded across his chest. And she closed her mouth, again. Nevertheless, with a brief glance, she managed to warn Cristo to keep his mouth shut, too.

On the boat, a swift movement from Ramiro jogged Emilio out of his musings.

"I'm going to take a stroll. I need to stretch my legs."

Out of the corner of his eye, he watched his son delve into his backpack for the red tube that had sent them on this trip to Uruguay; he wasn't about to leave the painting in his father's care. He appreciated Ramiro's gesture of no confidence; he, too, felt that the blood bond guaranteed nothing. As he watched his son cross the first-class area and go out to the open deck, his thoughts returned to Cristóbal.

"Who's going to copy the Rivera, then?" Cristóbal had asked.

"You aren't the only one with skills, son."

"But I'm the best."

"Not always. Not at everything."

At that moment he had felt a strange sensation of freedom that, rather than being gratifying, was somewhat unsettling. Emilio Pallares had been around for some time: bursts of happiness were few and far between, and the subsequent falls were always abrupt and painful.

The city of Montevideo welcomed them with sunshine and buildings that seemed to echo bygone times. Ramiro liked the look of it, but he knew he would have to put off his exploration of the historic center until another day. Being in his father's company made him uneasy; he wasn't used to sharing anything with him and had no interest in trying.

The Mendía mansion was just off Rambla República de México—Ramiro decided to take that name as a sign. The wood and iron bars of the automatic gate swung open slowly; security cameras had registered the car's arrival.

On the other side, they were met by a small, perfect wood: leafy, green trees; meticulously arranged plant pots. In the distance, they caught a glimpse of an artificial lake with ducks swimming in it. The path had just been raked and led to a white metal fence. A man wearing a black trench coat emerged from the security booth at the side of the driveway and approached the driver's window. Hanging from his belt was a leather sheath holding a gun.

"I'm dropping off Señores Emilio and Ramiro Pallares. They were invited by Señor Mendía," announced the driver.

"Very good, on you go."

The driver pulled up at the front of the house and got out to open the rear doors. Emilio Pallares gave him a generous tip and bade him farewell with a curt gesture.

"Good morning, my name is Aurelia. Welcome," said the housekeeper.

She guided them to a room with marble floors, walls covered in burgundy tapestries embroidered with gold arabesques, and two huge picture windows that looked out onto a swimming pool with turquoise water. The color scheme was perfect.

As Ramiro's eyes ran ecstatically over the room, lingering on each artwork and antique, Emilio's gaze was more like an information machine.

"The main chandelier is Venetian glass, and the small one in the corner is French. The first is eighteenth century, the second nineteenth," he recited monotonously. He turned around and gestured at the murals mounted on the walls of the hallway. "Those are originals by Soriano Fort and Juderías Caballero, two artists who worked under the patronage of the Marquis of Cerralbo."

Ramiro couldn't help listening to him. The ups and downs of their broken relationship couldn't diminish his admiration for his father's knowledge of art.

One of the carved wooden doors opened slowly; the woman who had welcomed them was no longer alone: Martiniano Mendía came in front of her in a wheelchair. His blue linen pants and light blue shirt seemed to have been made to measure for that weak body that managed to stay upright thanks to the chair's anatomic supports. The wrinkles around his eyes and mouth contrasted with his shiny black hair—not a wisp of gray in sight and combed back with dedication. Around his neck, a silk scarf in tones of red and ochre completed his elegant and simple attire.

Ramiro hid his surprise. His father had never mentioned that the famous M. M. was almost bedridden. Suddenly, he understood the reason behind the mystery surrounding him: never showing his face at the most important auctions in Europe and the United States, nor at the most exclusive events in the art world.

Emilio approached and held out his hand in greeting.

"My dear Martiniano, what an honor to be invited," he said with unusual loquacity. "It's a great pleasure to be in such beautiful surroundings."

Martiniano returned his greeting in silence, as though well accustomed to flattery.

Pallares turned and sent a swift glance in Ramiro's direction. "I'd like to introduce my younger son, Ramiro Pallares," he said, somewhat less effusively.

"Pleasure to meet you, thanks for the invitation," said Ramiro, without moving from the spot.

Mendía looked him up and down, with open curiosity. For a moment, his steel-colored eyes, which always seemed to be wandering somewhere far away, seemed to soften. This tall, athletic boy in front of him reminded him of what he might have been, were it not for that summer's afternoon, years ago, when his horse Imsira reared up and threw him from the saddle to land headfirst on the hard earth of the riding school.

"Do you work in the art world like your father and brother?" he asked with interest. He hadn't heard anything about this second son.

"No, not at all," replied Ramiro, then added with conviction, "We have very different opinions, particularly Cristóbal."

Ramiro found it impossible to refer to Cristóbal as his brother. Mendía noted this detail.

"Ramiro has a talent for drawing, a masterful hand," Pallares cut in. "What he can't do with oils he achieves with graphite, or other materials. His strength is human figures, particularly women."

"Señores, if you're ready, we can move out to the barbecue area for a drink while the meat finishes roasting." Aurelia masterfully cut into the conversation, knowing exactly the right moment to do so. "It's a beautiful day, and perhaps you would enjoy the fresh air."

The three men nodded. Mendía started up his wheelchair and led the way. They went down a long hallway under dim yellowish lights, the kind used in museums at night to avoid any damage to the artworks. Along the way, Ramiro paused to look at some paintings on one of the walls. There were eight small pictures, hung a precise distance apart, each one showing a rose: the famous Pitels roses. Rose number five caught his attention. He peered at it, getting closer than he knew he should, and, after checking that Martiniano was still moving away in his wheelchair, snapped a quick photo with his phone; then he slipped the device back in his pocket and continued walking.

The hallway came out in an outdoor terrace, covered by a white pergola. The table had a simple setting: white cotton tablecloth, round wooden plates, and crystal glasses. Behind it, two professional chefs were manning the grill.

Ramiro moved away a few steps, attracted like a magnet to a piece at the corner of the terrace. He had heard of the mysterious monumental clock, a unique piece made by the French clockmaker Eugène Farcot and the metalworker Ferdinand Barbedienne. The marble pedestal with a clock face, with Roman numerals in relief and two hands, glimmered in the sun, which seemed to caress it side-on. Rising up from the marble was a bronze sculpture of a Penelope looking downward, her diademed head tilted to the left, wavy hair parted down the middle.

"Do you know why they say this clock is mysterious?" asked Mendía. He had noticed the boy's fascination and didn't want to miss an opportunity to talk about one of his favorite topics: his art collection.

Ramiro turned around and regarded him in silence for a few seconds, before replying. "The greatest mystery is whether this is the original, or whether it's the one on display in the Spanish museum."

"No, you're wrong. They say the clock is mysterious because its operating mechanism is concealed and that's what makes this artwork such a special piece," replied Mendía, stroking the marble pedestal, which was all he could reach from his wheelchair. "The surreptitious, the secret, the furtive, the veiled. That's what I look for. That's what I want."

"That's what I have," murmured Ramiro, knowing that his words would be heard and appreciated by Martiniano Mendía.

"That's why I invited you," Mendía replied. "Now I want to see it."

Father and son exchanged a glance—perhaps the first look of complicity they had ever exchanged in their lives. Ramiro opened his bag and took out the red plastic tube.

"Before you take out the painting, I would ask you to please grant me a few minutes." Mendía had a knack for disguising orders as though they were requests.

Whenever Martiniano Mendía encountered a painting, sculpture, or piece of clockwork, he carried out a ritual involving all five senses, an affectation that no one understood, but which everyone allowed without question.

Ramiro put the lid back on the red plastic tube and waited. A look was all Aurelia needed to start the ritual. She touched the buttons on a remote control and the terrace filled with music.

"'An Alpine Symphony' by Richard Strauss," announced Mendía with his eyes closed. "Forty-five minutes of perfection, ascending in tempo."

As the first notes played, Aurelia covered her boss's knees with a gray animal hide. It was the skin of Gala, Señor Mendía's childhood cat. When she had died of old age, the animal's fur helped assuage his grief.

Mendía opened his mouth, and Aurelia carefully inserted a chocolate, made by the Ecuadorian brand Pacari, and finally sprayed a few drops of a specially made bitter orange perfume on her boss's neck.

Emilio Pallares was making a mental note of Mendía's ritual; he was intrigued.

"Now, I have all four senses activated to allow for the missing sense: sight. This part will be your responsibility, Ramiro."

Ramiro opened the tube again and brought out the rolled-up canvas. The only sound to be heard on the terrace was the Strauss.

He had no intention of heightening expectation or adding to Mendía's infamous anxiety, but Ramiro had his rituals, too. He closed his eyes and lifted the canvas to his nose; he filled his lungs with its acidic smell, which only a trained nose could detect. That roll seemed to contain time. In his mind's eye, he saw Paloma; the last time he had sniffed the painting of her Mexican grandmother she had been next to him. He was taken aback by a sudden need, the need to be with Paloma. He concentrated on ridding her from his system—he didn't have the time or the desire to have his heart calling the shots. Like Martiniano, he needed all his senses focused on this moment.

Emilio Pallares was nervous. He had not yet seen the work, and the possibility of looking bad in Mendía's eyes made his blood run cold.

As Ramiro unrolled the canvas with remarkable calm, his father inhaled and exhaled slowly; it was the only way he could control his body, which kept trembling as though he were a gambler playing his last chip at a roulette table.

Without being asked, Aurelia pushed her boss's wheelchair a few inches closer to where Ramiro was holding the canvas from the top corners. Martiniano Mendía's face was inscrutable. The expression lines around his eyes and lips seemed to have been automatically ironed out. Not a single gesture betrayed his emotions.

Emilio was impressed, too. He was no expert on Mexican art, and much less on the muralists, but what he saw here was very different. The figure of that naked girl, her hair, the birthmark on her thigh, the water caressing her legs. The whole thing was fascinating.

"Such passion!" he ventured, with a conviction he had rarely felt.

"Yes, exactly. That's what she was like," murmured Mendía.

Before anyone had time to ask what he meant, the man used his hands to turn his chair himself and go inside.

"You can stay here; the chef is about to serve the meat," said Aurelia, and followed her boss.

The Pallares duo was left alone to ponder. Ramiro rolled up the canvas and slipped it back into the red tube.

"What happened? Why did Mendía behave that way?" demanded Emilio.

Ramiro left his father sitting at the table, his questions still on his lips, and walked a short distance along the path across the garden. Mendía's reaction had raised doubts in his father's mind, but it had given him the certainty he needed. He thought again about Paloma and contained the urge to call her. What would he say? How could he explain the fact that he had been the one to approach her and remove her grandmother's inheritance?

He took his phone from his pocket and opened Instagram, searching for Paloma's account. Her last photo caught his attention. It was the façade of an old mansion, painted white with wooden frames around the doors and windows. Beneath the photo, Paloma had written: *Following Nayeli's footsteps*, and she had added an Argentinean flag and a Mexican flag. He zoomed in on the image. Next to the door was a sign saying *Casa Solanas*; the smaller letters were illegible.

When he raised his head, he saw his father on the terrace, chatting to Aurelia, as the chef served meat from the grill on a wooden platter. The woman smiled when she saw Ramiro approach.

"Señor Mendía asked me to come and get you; he's waiting in his study," she said. "He would like you to bring the painting, please."

The house had an intricate layout of corridors: some sections ran straight, others diagonally; all appeared to lead nowhere. At the end of the widest hallway, a double door opened automatically; on the other side, Mendía was waiting for him, sitting in a leather armchair, specially adapted to hold him upright.

Aurelia led Ramiro to an upholstered chair opposite her boss, then she left the study wordlessly.

For a few minutes, the only sound was the rhythmic hum of the air-conditioning and the birdsong filtering through the window. It was Ramiro who broke the calm to get straight to the point.

"What do you think of the painting I showed you?"

"What's your plan?" Martiniano replied with another question.

"First I want to know whether it's an original work," he ventured.

"You wouldn't be sitting in this study if you didn't already know," said Martiniano.

"I have a degree of certainty," conceded Ramiro. "But I need more information. Not many can separate the wheat from the chaff when it comes to Rivera, and you are one of those few."

"That's true. You'll be aware that there are more paintings attributed to Diego Rivera going around the world than there are genuine paintings by him. That's why the few authentic pieces are so precious." Mendía's tone had changed. "To know whether we are looking at an original Rivera, we have to focus on certain details. Behind that purple curtain, there's an easel; set it up there, and we'll analyze a few points."

Ramiro dusted off the easel, then secured the painting of Paloma's grandmother with special tape, so as not to damage a single inch of the canvas. When finished, he positioned the easel in front of Mendía, at an optimal viewing distance.

"The first good news is that there's no sign of burnt sienna in this painting. Rivera hated burnt sienna, he even said it made him nauseous." They both smiled. Martiniano was enthused. "In 1926, the president of the San Francisco Arts Commission received a painting as a gift from Rivera. It was a portrait of a Mexican woman with a child in her arms. At first glance, it appeared to be rather inferior work; the color palette looked like it had been chosen by an apprentice: a watery lilac, washed-out blues, and a bit of brown. The man was disappointed. He thought the painting was horrible; he didn't even hang it. But then, as the hours passed, something inexplicable happened: he couldn't take his eyes off the work. All of a sudden, the colors seemed to sing. Gradually, he began to notice the perfect saturation. Even the lack of charisma in the woman and her child seemed to change before his eyes. Those hunched features revealed the delicacy of maternal protection. Love, origins, it was all there. He just had to look at it closely."

"I can identify with that," said Ramiro, intrigued. "The first time I saw this naked woman, I didn't like the palette, or the brushstrokes. It all looked rather strange to me. But the more I looked at it . . . "

"You discovered the magic," Mendía finished. "Rivera has that effect."

"So it is a Rivera, then?" insisted Ramiro.

"In my opinion, it's more than that," replied Mendía confidently.

Ramiro caught a glimmer of avarice in the expert's eyes. His face was a situation map that, like a Rivera painting, revealed itself as the minutes ticked by.

"How much more than a Rivera can a painting be?" asked Ramiro, confused.

Martiniano Mendía bit his lip and, with the tip of his tongue, licked away a drop of blood. Pearls of sweat gathered on his forehead and ran down the side of his face without him being able to wipe them away.

"A Frida Kahlo is more than a Rivera," he told a disconcerted Ramiro.

39

Coyoacán, May 1944

Nayeli lifted the mortar down from a shelf, tossed in three tomatoes, an onion, and four cloves of garlic, then used the pestle to grind it all together, a spicy aroma instantly flooding the kitchen.

Nayeli's mind had room for only one image: Diego Rivera. As her hands moved mechanically to form a smooth red paste, her thoughts wandered far, far away.

She poured some oil into the iron pot and lit the stove. When the oil started to sizzle fiercely, she tipped the contents of the mortar into the pot. Her mother always said that sautéing shouldn't take more than five minutes. Nayeli was never sure how to calculate the time, but she had found a strategy that worked for her: she would sing ten rounds of the chorus of "La Tortuga," a song from the isthmus that her father sang as a lullaby when she was little.

Ay, Ay, bigu xi pé scarú
jma pa ñacame guiiñado'
jma pa ñoome ndaani'
zuquii
nanixe' ñahuaa laame yanna dxi!

As she crooned the familiar Zapotec words, she added a generous portion of rice and two cups of water to the pot, and watched with fascination as the colors and aromas merged into a soft, intense soup.

The painter entered the kitchen, hunching to one side and supporting herself against the wall with her hand, her face contorted by the sharp pain from her hip.

"Frida, I've made you a delicious soup," said Nayeli, and ran to help her. She had developed a knack for catching Frida seconds before she fell to the floor. "And don't give me that look . . . you have to eat! You're getting thinner every day!"

"Thin as a skeleton," rejoined the painter, and gave one of her full-bellied laughs. "I'll eat, but only because you ask me to."

Frida's pains had returned. One after another, they settled in like houseguests; guests who had no qualms about penetrating every bone, every drop of blood. The fury that had once driven them away had dissipated. The wheelchair had been discarded somewhere in Casa Azul; Frida was prone to losing or forgetting it in her studio or in the yard. "We don't seem to be able to become friends," she would say, laughing heartily.

Nayeli served the soup in clay bowls, a gift from the Fridos to their teacher. Each one was unique, decorated with a different drawing, and despite their jarring appearance over the table, they were Frida's favorites. To her mind, food tasted better served in her students' small works of art.

"This time I'll have two helpings of soup," announced Frida. "I need energy to finish the piece I'm going to give Diego for our anniversary."

"Better make it three helpings then," said Nayeli enthusiastically. She was worried about Frida's health, even though no one else seemed particularly concerned about it. They all seemed to have accepted her as a sick woman. "Can I see the gift?" She regretted her question when, without even having tried a mouthful, Frida got up to go to her studio.

"Give me a few minutes to arrange my things, and I'll meet you there. I'd be interested to hear your opinion. No one knows that sapo Diego like you do."

Frida's words made such an impression on Nayeli that she forgot to insist on the soup, and she was glad to be left alone in the kitchen. For a moment, she feared that the color of her cheeks would betray her. She had never seen him in that way; she had never thought that she knew Diego, and yet Frida was right: she did know him, very well. At night, the sound of his feet dragging on the floor told her if he was tired; she knew the rhythm of his breathing as he slept; she could describe each of the wrinkles that formed around his eyes when he tasted one of her dishes; she remembered that coffee with sugar gave him heartburn and that she had to warm the milk to body temperature; and she could always tell if he had been with one of his lovers, even more accurately than Frida.

With three slurps of soup, she managed to erase Diego from her mind. Then she went upstairs to the studio and stood watching the painter from the top step. Frida sat as though consumed by sorrow: shoulders slumped, back hunched, and hands clasped tightly together.

"Come here, my ballerina. See how beautiful it is!" Frida invited her, gesturing at a painting that was very different from the others around it.

In the center of a wooden plaque, Frida had drawn and painted her own face and Diego's, united in one same head, split into two halves; a tree trunk joined them from the neck down. The intense reds, the saturated browns, and the pearly whites reflected in Nayeli's eyes.

"Why doesn't the tree have flowers or leaves?" asked Nayeli, surprised. It didn't seem right that an anniversary present should lack flowers.

"Well, because Diego and I haven't had children," replied Frida, smoothing down her skirt with her hands. "I'm dried out inside like that tree trunk. Children won't grow in my body. Motherhood has evaded me. It's been nothing but blood and tears. And collecting dolls—I like dolls so much. They're my frozen daughters that I keep in a box."

On more than one occasion, Nayeli had caught Frida sitting on the floor combing her dolls' hair. She spoke to them sweetly, and, before returning them to their box, she would sing a lullaby in a high, whispery voice. A child's voice.

"It has no flowers, but it does have seashells, and I like that a lot!" said Nayeli, to change the subject. She didn't like the black cloud that enveloped Frida whenever she spoke about the children she couldn't have. "I've never seen a real conch."

"They're very beautiful. To me, conch shells signify deep love—there's nothing deeper than the ocean."

Frida settled into an armchair and launched into a speech, a torrent of words with no logical meaning cascading from her mouth. Nayeli had learned that this babbling was a method of distraction: the more pain, the more words. It was almost impossible to keep up with her—she veered from anecdotes about her teenage years at the Colegio Nacional to her love affairs in the Viveros de Coyoacán park. Eschewing any notion of continuity, she described in great detail the daring clothes worn by Lupe, Diego's ex-wife, and told of the long, tedious days of her first trip to the United States. She never told the same story twice, and, as her spinal column twisted like a dying snake, her tales took on a tragic note: the color of the blood clots following her miscarriages, and the shade of her leg bones when they were exposed in the accident that marked her life. That was when Nayeli would drop whatever she was doing to fetch the doctors' new creation for Frida: a steel corset. It was as heavy as it was menacing: a steel back support that went from her neck to her waist, clamped to her body by leather straps with metal fasteners. Nayeli had learned to carry it in her arms like a baby.

"Here it is," she announced, paying no attention to the painter's wild gestures. Frida's words were getting stuck in her throat. She couldn't continue with her desperate tales. Either she spoke or she breathed. "Easy now. Come on, raise your arms!"

Frida obeyed as best she could. She lifted her arms so that the young woman could put the steel contraption around her body. This pain made her want to die. Not for the first time, she was silently thankful she didn't have a gun nearby at these moments; she wouldn't have thought twice about using it. Both women were sweating, and, as if in imitation, tears ran down their faces. The pain of one and the compassion of the other united them in tides of saltwater springing from their pores.

"That's it. Done. It's on properly," Nayeli soothed her.

The young woman tightened the metal buckles firmly: at the collarbone, between the breasts, at the top of the stomach, halfway down the waist, and at the hips. The leather straps allowed the steel to straighten

Frida's spine and the relief flooded through her as if by magic. Each vertebra settled and released the pressure on the nerve.

"My liquor, ballerina. Let's celebrate!" said Frida, as she always did when she was trapped in the corset and her wounds relented. "Oh, it's worse every time! It'll drive me crazy!"

"Don't say that," Nayeli scolded her as she poured liquor into a small blue crystal glass. "You're not crazy."

"More reason to celebrate!" Frida exclaimed, holding out the glass in her hand. "More liquor for the not-crazy woman!"

The young woman shook her head and returned the bottle to the cupboard.

"More soup and less liquor," she said. "You haven't eaten a thing. I had to tighten the corset one notch tighter—you're getting thinner."

"I wish that was the only problem. Come here, I have to talk to you."

Nayeli sat on the floor, next to Frida's chair. Whenever the painter said "Come here," the girl knew it was the prelude to a story. She liked nothing better than to cross her legs, rest her hands on her knees, and gaze up at this hoarse-voiced minstrel.

"This steel beast that holds me as stiff as a statue has helped a lot, as you know, but it isn't enough. It's like the poor corset has run out of strength, and my pain has returned. Dr. Zimbrón told me my meninges are inflamed and I have to stay still to prevent them from getting worse . . . "

"Meninges?" asked Nayeli. She had never heard the word, and, for a second, she thought it might be one of Frida's inventions.

"It's like a very thin gauze membrane that covers the nervous system. That's what the doctor told me, but I think it's something else. I think it's the devil's drool," she declared.

Nayeli's eyes widened like coins.

"Don't look at me like that!" exclaimed the painter. "Not all Judases are good. Some enter my body at night and leave their saliva inside me to drown my good feelings, but they're no match for me. I know how to keep the balance between good and evil. The quacks say I should have another operation to end this never-ending torment. What do you think?"

"I'm no doctor, I-I don't know," stammered Nayeli.

"What does that matter? You're the only one who considers my trivialities to be important, the only one who takes me seriously. You make me count; you know everything."

Frida's inordinate confidence in her weighed on Nayeli. She could change the subject, as she usually did when her mentor was delirious. All she had to do was point out a new flower in the yard or invent some high jinks the dogs had gotten up to, or even some gossip gleaned from the market aisles would be enough. Frida's attention veered all over the place, like a drunk driver. But Nayeli couldn't. She didn't want to. Having someone else's life in her hands was a big responsibility.

"We should ask Diego his opinion," said Nayeli solemnly.

In response, Frida pulled one of the leather straps on the corset even tighter, and Nayeli knew what she had to do.

40

Buenos Aires, January 2019

I looked her up and down, then lowered my head to check myself. Yes, I was still wearing the dress I had put on that morning, my grandmother's dress.

"It looks perfect on you," said Eva Garmendia. She betrayed no surprise, no emotion. She had always been adept at the social niceties befitting her status as an elegant woman.

"We're wearing exactly the same," I said, pointing at her outfit.

She shrugged, as though it was an everyday occurrence to bump into someone wearing the same dress made in the 1950s.

"Over the years, I realized I wasn't the most imaginative person. When I made blouses, skirts, and dresses, they were all identical. But I was meticulous in my sewing and had a good eye for color and fabrics."

"Did you give this to my grandmother?" I asked.

There was a silence as she considered her answer.

"You could say that."

"It's quite a coincidence that we both chose the same outfit on the same day, isn't it?"

"No, not really," she replied with annoyance. "Let me pass, dear. I'm going to lie down for a while."

"Gloria gave me Nayeli's red notebook," I said in an attempt to keep her there.

Her reaction surprised me: she took a few nimble steps toward me and held out both hands.

"Give me that notebook, Paloma," she said firmly.

I looked at her with a mixture of bemusement and annoyance, instinctively hugging my purse into my body and feeling the hard cover of the notebook against my chest.

"No, Eva, I won't. It's my grandmother's notebook," I replied.

"It's your mother's, Paloma. Stop acting as though Felipa didn't exist and you were Nayeli's only heir."

The certainty of her words hit me like a slap to the face. What she said was so obvious that I was amazed it hadn't occurred to me. For years my grandmother and I had formed a team in which there was room for only two people: her and me. I often wondered whether Nayeli had contributed to the gulf between my mother and me, but I had never wanted or been able to find an answer; I just allowed her to love me, something my mother never knew how to do.

"Eva, please. You know very well that anything related to Nayeli was always part of my world," I said, more to myself than to her. "Don't take away the only part of her I have left—let me grieve in my own way."

With her long fingers and perfectly varnished nails, she tucked her fluffy white hair behind her ears, revealing tiny gold, circular earrings.

"When is Felipa's birthday?"

"November twenty-fourth," I replied, perplexed.

"No, it isn't. That's not her birthday," she retorted triumphantly.

"Oh, Eva, come on—"

"Oh Eva nothing," she cut in. "Your mother was born on December twenty-fourth, but your grandmother always said Felipa shouldn't overshadow the birth of Jesus and decided that her daughter would celebrate a month earlier, for fear of God punishing her. So Paloma, stop asking people not to take things away from you, when the only one deprived of anything has been your mother—your grandmother even took away her birthday."

She took advantage of my distress to sidle past me.

"What's the story, Eva?" I shouted. When she paused in the middle of the hall, I knew I had to insist. "What's the story that's worth more than a painting? You said that when you gave me the key, that the story is the true work of art."

She didn't reply and continued walking, but without the haughtiness she had shown minutes earlier. I couldn't move until I heard her closing the door of her room.

I shut myself in the bathroom at the reception, washed my face, and touched up my lipstick.

Eusebio Miranda's office was a few yards from the main entrance of Casa Solanas. In the early afternoon, after lunch, he always left his door open.

I peered in and knocked twice on the wooden doorframe. Eusebio was sitting at his desk. When he noticed me, he raised his head and smiled, beckoning me in with a jerk of the head.

"Lovely to see you here, Paloma! Have you come to visit your grandmother's friends?"

"Yes, I was with Gloria for a while, and then I bumped into Eva in the lounge," I said, trying to appear casual.

"What a pair! They just can't seem to get along," he remarked with a hint of tenderness, as though talking about a couple of rebellious schoolgirls.

"The reason I've come to see you is that I was looking for the form we filled in with my mother when we brought Nayeli here. Do you keep that documentation?"

Eusebio regarded me with curiosity and nodded. He arranged his cutlery on his plate and walked over to a dresser with shelves crammed with files.

"Let's see, I'll have a look here," he said as he flicked through his archives. "Now then . . . Cruz, Cruz, Cruz . . . Here it is: Nayeli Cruz."

A bundle of pages, some typewritten and others printed, held together with a metal paper clip, comprised the summary of my grandmother's final years. The end of a life stuck in a pink cardboard folder. I felt a prickle of sadness in my chest.

I found what I was looking for in the folder: Nayeli's admission form. I ran my index finger down the sheet, top to bottom, and remembered that winter's afternoon when my mother and I had filled in the empty boxes. I hadn't paid any attention at the time, but now it stood out like a sore thumb. At the top, in my mother's meticulous handwriting: *Felipa Cruz, single, Mexican, born December 24, 1954*. I couldn't read any further. Eva Garmendia was right.

"You'll find Nayeli's entire clinical history in the folder. If you need it, you can take it with you. The only things that have to stay here are the admission form, the visitors list, and the copy of the death certificate," said Eusebio, who was sitting at his desk again, looking at me expectantly.

To hide my unease, I flicked through the pages until I reached the visitors list, where another surprise was awaiting me.

"Eusebio, there must be some mistake here," I said, holding the list out to him across the desk. "It shows lots of visits by my mother to my grandmother, but I know she hardly ever came to see her."

"That's no mistake—I saw Felipa here frequently. Your mother isn't the kind who goes unnoticed," he said with an idiotic smile.

I took the list from his hands and tried to concentrate. Felipa Cruz had visited Casa Solanas three times a week, from the moment Nayeli had been admitted until two days before her death. Her signature confirmed each visit. Beneath each entry with her name, my own name appeared. I could see why we had never crossed paths: my mother seemed to have calculated the perfect time to avoid me, when I was teaching my music classes.

"I'm surprised. Neither of them ever mentioned those visits." I didn't mention that my grandmother had complained during her final days about the fact that my mother didn't visit her.

I placed the visiting list on the desk and dug out the medical history. I ran my index finger down each of the medical indications and diagnoses: arthritis, mild anemia, trouble sleeping, and the cardiac issues that brought about her demise. There was no mention of senile dementia or confusion.

"Eusebio, do you know whether Nayeli ever struggled to remember things?"

"Far from it. I never had a patient of that age with such a good memory. She remembered everything, and I'll tell you what else—she complained if we gave her Jell-O more than once a month. Memory like an elephant, that's what we used to say."

"And did my mother visit her in her room, or did they go out to the courtyard?" Despite holding the proof of subterfuge in my hands, I refused to accept it.

Eusebio pondered this for a moment, stroking his chin, as if it would help jog his memory. "To be honest, Paloma, I don't remember. I tend to spend a lot of time here in my office—I see visitors come and go, but I don't follow them around. I get involved when there's some kind of problem or a rule is broken, but when it came to your mother and grandmother, nothing ever happened that required my presence."

I returned the whole file to him. I didn't need to take anything with me. Eusebio and I said a warm goodbye, and I promised to return—as I did every year—for the Casa Solanas anniversary dinner. I had come with one question and was leaving with several.

I went out into the courtyard. In the corner, as always, Gloria was sitting in her rocking chair under a parasol, reading the newspaper and drinking orange juice. I went over to say goodbye. She fixed her eyes on me; she seemed angry. Putting down the glass and the paper on the little table, she grabbed my hands with a strength that seemed excessive in a woman of more than ninety.

"Listen to what I have to say, Paloma," she said, as though her life depended on this request. "Your mother never visited Nayeli."

I looked at her in surprise.

"Yes, yes, don't look at me like that. I overheard your conversation with Eusebio. You must know by now that nothing gets past me. And I can assure you that the story about the visits is a lie. Felipa did come a lot, that's true, but not to see your grandmother."

"So why did she come?" I asked, with some relief. The possibility of my grandmother having hidden something else from me was unbearable.

Gloria squeezed my hands even harder. "She came to see Eva Garmendia. Felipa was like a daughter to her."

41

San Ángel, May 1944

The San Ángel houses were surrounded by a row of tall cacti planted snugly to form a perfect fence, but there was enough space to peer between the spines and see a little of what was happening inside. The gate was open, and there was no one around to prevent access to the property.

Although the windows were dirty, they gave enough reflection for Nayeli to fix her hair; it had grown past her shoulders by now. She didn't look like a child anymore, and she wasn't one.

Nayeli entered the red house and turned to the right, where the only possible route was up a spiral staircase of smooth cement. She climbed cautiously, partly through fear and partly out of modesty. From the top, she could hear Diego's voice, singing loudly and enthusiastically.

The ceiling was so high that, for a moment, she thought the house must have been designed for a giant. Five papier-mâché Judas figures formed the main decoration; lined up against one of the windows, they seemed to have a life of their own.

Diego was in the middle of the room, atop a wooden stepladder, busily painting a huge canvas. Nayeli wasn't sure how to attract his attention; the only thing she could think of was a cough. A gentle, fake cough.

Diego turned ever so slightly. "Come on in. You're very welcome!" he exclaimed. "Leave that package anywhere you can find a space."

Nayeli looked around for a table or a chair to rest her plate of buñuelos on, but she found nothing empty; everything in Diego's workshop was occupied, everything around him was excessive.

"Señor Diego, I can take the pastries to the dining room, if you like."

"There is no dining room here, my dear. We should be able to eat where we please or wherever hunger strikes us, or where the food is, whichever the case may be. You can leave it on the floor, in some corner," he said, gesturing vaguely around the room, and came down the steps.

At the edge of a table crowded with jars of paint, Nayeli found a small white tablecloth. It seemed a miracle that none of those myriad shades had soiled it. She spread it out on the floor and placed the dish of pastries in the center. Although they had gone cold, they still held their intense perfume of vanilla and cinnamon.

They sat opposite each other on the cement floor, which was cool despite the heat of the day. Diego attacked the little sugary balls as though he hadn't eaten for months.

"These are delicious, Nayeli Cruz!" he said, his mouth crammed full.

The young woman tried to still the trembling in her body. Seldom had anyone ever called her by her full name, and the way it sounded on Diego Rivera's lips made her want to cry.

"We need to talk about Frida," said Nayeli, spitting out each word. This was the real reason why she was here.

"Of course. Mi Friducha hermosa. I could spend hours talking about my precious dove—"

"About Frida's poor health," the young woman interrupted gravely.

Diego looked surprised.

"Frida is getting worse. The steel corset doesn't work anymore, and her doctor has recommended another operation."

"And what do you think?" asked the painter.

Nayeli shuddered. That question seemed to contain the end of her adolescence. Diego and Frida often behaved like two big children, and despite the enormous temptation to take care of both of them, she didn't want to, she couldn't.

"I don't think anything. I just don't want Frida to die," she babbled.

The painter's fury was restrained, very different from Frida's explosive rages.

"I won't hear of such a thing! Frida is eternal—like the sky, like the rain, like the ocean." He sighed hard and abruptly changed the subject. "I have to finish this painting. If you like, you can climb the stairs, cross the bridge, and have a look around. It's worth seeing; don't miss it." His words sounded more like an order than an invitation.

She followed his instructions. Upstairs, the ceilings were as high as in the studio, but the bedrooms were much smaller and rather more spartan. The door to what appeared to be Diego's room was open, and she couldn't resist peeking in. The narrow bed surprised her. How could such a man lie on that mattress without spilling over the sides?

A narrow corridor led her to an orange iron door that opened onto a square roof terrace with a concrete bridge at the far side. Across the bridge was the blue twin building. Nayeli crossed, her heart pounding.

The blue house smelled of women's perfume, something much more cloying than the scent Frida wore. Just before the door, she noticed a shadow flitting from one side to the other inside, like a ghost. Part of her wanted to turn around and retrace her steps, but her curiosity was stronger.

She cautiously peered in through the first door: this was Frida's bedroom; there was no doubt. The bedcover embroidered with leaves, the vase full of colorful paper flowers, the necklaces of gems and pearls draped over the back of a chair, and, on the floor, a purple shawl told of something left behind, forgotten by the painter.

"Don't touch that. It doesn't belong to you."

The voice made Nayeli drop the pillow she had picked up from the bed as though it were a hot ember.

Leaning against the doorframe was La Güera, the blond woman she had met outside Casa Azul on the day the mural at the pulque shop was unveiled. She shone like a princess who had just stepped out of her carriage. Her outfit was very simple, however: a pink fitted dress with a ballooning skirt that came to her knees.

"Sorry. I wanted to make the bed—it was a bit messy," babbled Nayeli, who wasn't good at inventing excuses. "Who are you?"

"You already know. I'm La Güera, one of Diego's pupils," she replied confidently.

"I didn't know Diego was a teacher," said Nayeli, searching for the crack in the lie.

"Nor did I."

La Güera's response left Nayeli silent and helpless; she needed more time to react. The girl turned and made a graceful retreat. Nayeli followed her along a passageway that came out in a light-filled studio. At one side, two easels held canvases with unfinished still lifes. They were Frida's works. In the middle, a table wider than it was long stood empty. What had been on top was now piled on the floor.

Nayeli ran her eyes over the discarded objects, and a wave of rage flooded her. Who was this girl, with the almost-white blond hair, who had dared to move Frida's belongings from their place? She moved swiftly up to the girl, too close, her green Tehuana eyes sparking.

"I want you to put Frida's things back on her table, because that, there, is her table," she demanded threateningly, her fists clenched by her sides.

La Güera raised her eyebrows, her eyes so light they seemed transparent, her lips—painted pale pink—curved upward in a grimace of surprise. She wasn't accustomed to being spoken to in that way.

"I don't know who you are," she said with elegant calm, "but I can assure you that I don't take orders from anyone."

"I'm Nayeli Cruz, Frida's cook," she replied proudly.

"Oh, please!" exclaimed La Güera, fluttering a hand. "I'll pretend this conversation never happened. I refuse to hold a discussion with a domestic employee. You're lucky I'm in a good mood and I'll keep quiet about this little incident. In my family, you would have been out on the street for much less."

Nayeli took a step back, disconcerted. Until that moment, she had believed that being Frida's cook was a merit, a position of importance. But with those few words and a contemptuous gesture, the girl in front of her had demolished both of those assumptions.

She relaxed her fists. She had lost the battle.

* * *

Nayeli returned to Casa Azul. Her feet, which had stepped lightly on the way to San Ángel, were now as heavy as anvils.

On the living room table, she saw the red-cover diary that Frida filled with words and drawings. Guiltily, she opened it and flicked through the pages. Between the hard cover and the first page, Nayeli found a scrap of paper with writing in black pencil. It was Frida's handwriting, no doubt about it. She struggled to decipher the short text. Although her reading and writing lessons were ongoing, the sessions were increasingly sporadic.

Beware of La Güera, Diego, it said. Beneath this warning, Frida had written an address.

Nayeli had to reread each letter several times to be sure of the message. At what point had Frida become aware of Diego's mysterious pupil? Nayeli folded the paper and slipped it into the pocket of her huipil. Something in her chest told her what to do next. Something like a fit of madness, a gut feeling she couldn't ignore.

42

Montevideo, January 2019

Emilio Pallares was furious. He had always known that his son could turn anyone's head; even as a child, he had been able to make the world revolve around him. He was never a friendly or pleasant child, however; nor was he much of a conversationalist, and when he did speak, he seemed to choose the shortest words in the dictionary to say what he had to say as succinctly as possible, as though dying of boredom. But that was enough. Two or three phrases and the rest didn't matter. Elvira used to say that Ramiro was a snake charmer. As far as Emilio was concerned, Ramiro was the snake.

They left Martiniano Mendía's house in silence. And they didn't open their mouths during the entire car journey back to the historic center of Montevideo. Although Pallares was desperate to know what had happened during the private meeting between his son and Mendía, he said nothing; he would rather bite his tongue and swallow bitter saliva than have to beg.

As they walked through Plaza Independencia, the two men were simultaneously captivated by the gateway to the old citadel.

"This monument is stunning, and its history is fascinating!" exclaimed Emilio as he walked up and placed his hands flat on the stones.

Ramiro followed and copied his father, as though he could absorb its history through his pores.

Deep down, very deep down, he admired his father. More than once, he had wondered whether his own interest in art was genuine or just a ruse to get some paternal attention.

"It's a Frida Kahlo," blurted Ramiro.

Emilio drew his hands back from the stones as though they were burning coals. It took a few seconds for the words to sink in. He couldn't respond.

"Mendía told me the painting is more valuable and stranger than anything you could imagine."

"I need something strong. Let's find a bar," was all Emilio said.

They crossed the plaza, this time walking side by side, a million thoughts spinning through their heads, filling them with excitement and trepidation. Ramiro recalled Mendía's exact words and his emotional tears when he had laid the painting across the man's dead legs.

"*It's her. It's her. I have no doubt. All of her passion is here. The fury, the outbursts, the pain. I understand her, only I can understand her.*"

Once inside a bar, the barman poured out the two bottles of beer so slowly it almost drove Emilio Pallares out of his mind. Even the prospect of an ice-cold beer with the perfect head of foam wasn't enough to make him wait patiently.

"Leave it, man. I'll finish pouring. Go on, get on with your job," he said, annoyed, as though the barman hadn't been doing exactly that. Ramiro couldn't help smiling. "All right, enough pussyfooting around. Tell me everything about your meeting with Mendía, and explain what you just said about Frida Kahlo."

"The painting is a unique gem. It's the only artwork in the world that combines two of the best artists in one piece: Frida Kahlo and Diego Rivera."

"I-I don't understand," stammered Emilio.

"It's confusing, but I trust Mendía. He's convinced that the naked figure is Rivera's work and that the red stain is by Frida."

Emilio forgot his gentlemanly manners for a moment; in two gulps, he drained his glass of beer and wiped his mouth with the back of his hand. He was struggling to process his son's words, unable to entirely comprehend the weight of what he had in his hands.

"Okay, son, let's think clearly," he said to calm himself down. "That red stain is just that, a stain. I would even go so far as to say that it makes the whole work defective. Perhaps Rivera spilled a can of paint or, even worse, whoever was taking care of it didn't do a good enough job."

"It isn't a stain, Dad," Ramiro assured him. Both men startled and, at the same time, tried to conceal their reaction. Neither was used to the word *dad* being part of their infrequent conversations. "Mendía is adamant that part of the Rivera painting is covered by Frida's picture, that red image."

Emilio nodded; he had no option but to open his mind to this possibility. Resorting to his vast bank of knowledge, he said, as though thinking aloud: "Frida was a great draftswoman, very figurative. Her intentions can be clearly seen in her work. An apple is an apple, a heart is a heart, animals are animals . . . "

"A ballerina is a ballerina, and a story is a story," interrupted Ramiro, unable to stop thinking about Paloma.

"What are you saying, Ramiro?"

"That the painting is worth nothing without the story."

"Since when have we needed a story in our line of work? This is a monumental piece we have on our hands, and we have to decide what to do with it. I have a plan."

"I'm listening."

"I have no doubt that Mendía will want to buy the original. We can make an exact copy and, with Lorena's help, arrange a press campaign around the discovery—she'll be able to come up with some lie or other." He was pensive for a few seconds. "Perhaps I could have it hanging in a museum."

"And Cristóbal?"

"Well, you know . . . your brother is a phenomenal forger."

"I get it," said Ramiro, bringing the conversation to a close.

The plan in his head was underway, and it was very different from the one his father had just outlined. But, following his mother's example, he pretended to go along with it.

43

Buenos Aires, January 2019

In just two days I managed to move all my belongings to the house in Boedo, that little house where my grandmother had made me so happy. I sold my furniture; I didn't need it. I had decided to sleep, eat, and sit on the furniture my grandmother had scraped and saved to buy. As the outside world retreated, each of her belongings became more important to me. Clothes, saucepans, tablecloths, napkins, towels: all of it, every single thing that had formed part of my grandmother's life was now mine and somehow brought me closer to her.

I had been trying to contact my mother for days; as usual, she didn't answer my calls. She did return one, but in her own way: "I'm busy; we'll talk later." The word *later* was a nebulous period of time measured entirely at her whim.

I knew she was suffering. My mother was the kind of person who hides herself away to disguise her pain. Over time I learned that, for her, what she covered up was always much worse.

The knowledge that she had been visiting Eva Garmendia for years, so frequently it bordered on devotion, left me numb at first; later, confused. The knife of betrayal plunged deep into my mood. She had deceived not just me but Nayeli, too. Perhaps that's why I decided to move sooner; it was my very private way of telling my grandmother: *I'm here. I won't leave your memory alone or abandon your world of geraniums, gardenias, and simple old furniture.*

The red notebook was still in the bottom of the purse I had taken that afternoon to Casa Solanas, when Gloria confessed to having hidden it. Although curiosity is one of my most prominent traits, I didn't want to open or read it. It had become a Pandora's box that I wasn't quite ready to face. In the ring, the boxers who stay standing are those who are able to space out the blows they receive. That's what I was trying to do: space out all these new developments.

"The story is worth more than the painting. The story is the true work of art," Eva had said on the day of my grandmother's send-off. I turned the phrase over and over in my mind. I spent whole afternoons sitting on the patio at Nayeli's house putting the story, or the few pieces I had of it, into order.

I made myself the same aperitif Nayeli used to enjoy: sparkling tonic with a splash of lime and two little plates; one with cubes of cheese and the other with olives. I hadn't even put the tray down on the patio table when someone rang the bell. I was surprised. No one knew I had moved, and Cándida always phoned or shouted over the fence before coming around.

Before opening the door, I looked through the peephole. There was no one there. I unlocked the door and went out into the street.

Some kind of instinct made me look at the outside of the wooden door. My knees went weak, and I felt my heart thumping against my ribs. My grandmother's painting, the very one that had been stolen, was stuck to the door with tape. I stared at it, hypnotized.

Shaking off my fascination, I moved to the middle of the sidewalk. On the other side of the street was Ramiro, looking at me with an expression I couldn't figure out. The warm wind swirled through my hair and exposed my legs. With one hand I tried to flatten down my hair; with the other, hold my skirt. I didn't manage either successfully. My eyes and all my attention were focused on the man who was confidently striding across the street with a smile. That smile that had won me over all those months ago.

"Are you going to ask me in?" he asked, perfectly aware that I couldn't refuse him.

"The painting . . . " I said, gesturing at the door.

He nodded, without taking his eyes off me.

"It's yours. I'm the one who stole it from you that night on the street. I regret that, and now I'm returning it."

I couldn't hide my confusion.

"Let's go in, please. We have a lot to talk about," he said, and carefully unstuck the painting from the door. That small private museum he had set up for me disappeared into the red plastic tube.

I found it strange to see a man like Ramiro walking down the long, flaking hallway that connected the house to the backyard. His linen pants, of such high quality that they only creased in the right places; his light blue shirt with the top few buttons undone; the Rolex on his left wrist; and that scent of someone who has just stepped out of the shower, combined with an unconscious elegance that seemed at odds with the surroundings. But he seemed comfortable, relaxed even, as he settled into one of Nayeli's armchairs and gladly agreed to share my aperitif.

"Explain the bit about your being the one who stole the painting," I said bravely. Emulating my grandmother, I had added a generous glug of tequila to my drink.

"Well, 'stole' is a bit harsh . . . " he babbled, embarrassed.

"Harsher is a guy getting off a motorbike, pointing a gun at you in the street, and taking something that belongs to you," I retorted. As I described the scene, my anger grew.

Ramiro raised his hands, as though surrendering completely. "I'm sorry, really sorry. I didn't want to scare you, but I had no option."

My first impulse was to get out of my seat, send the tray of snacks spinning through the air, and, with a single slap, wipe that wounded-puppy look from his face. But I didn't. In my mind, I drew the image of Nayeli wearing her flowery apron, wielding a large spoon as though conducting an orchestra, and saying: "*Be smart, Palomita. Flying off the handle doesn't help anything. You just have to stay on your toes. The world keeps you on your toes, and that's enough.*" I pushed my fury into a corner and adopted a much more intimidating attitude: calm.

"I don't know whether you had many options before, but you have only one now: the truth," I said in a tone that surprised even me and which I must have inherited from my mother.

That Paloma, who I pulled out of my hat like a magician, had the right effect on Ramiro, who was used to everyone saying yes to him for fear of being expelled from his magnetic orbit. He stared at the floor for a few minutes and suddenly emptied his glass. Magnanimously, I allowed him that time. The truth is never a comfortable place.

He started by running through all that we had experienced together: the first time I showed him my grandmother's painting, the strange excursion to Lorena Funes's apartment, and the moment he made the decision to become a motorbike mugger and take what he called my inheritance from me at gunpoint.

"It was the only thing I could think of, and a lifetime won't be long enough to say I'm sorry. I played it badly, but it worked. I needed to have the painting, and you weren't interested in it being anything more than a postmortem gift from your grandmother."

"That's all it is: a postmortem gift, a souvenir," I said, although I knew perfectly well that it wasn't. I could lie with the best of them.

"You see? You still don't get it. It's as though we're speaking different languages," he said, disappointed.

I felt suddenly saddened. What Ramiro was saying was true: we did speak different languages. Something that was of great significance to me, he regarded as banal.

Although the conversation was slightly stilted, he looked at home in the patio chair. Ramiro's body was visibly relaxed, his legs crossed, and the glass of aperitif held aloft in one hand. The blossoms on the lemon tree released an intoxicating perfume, and the dusk, with its magical light, brought out the shine in his eyes. I looked at him greedily, trying to record him in my memory. Although it was a fleeting image, I felt sure I would preserve it forever.

"Why did you need my grandmother's painting?" I asked with interest.

"To be sure," he said, encouraged by my question. "And now I am."

I didn't open my mouth. Sometimes silence is more effective than questions. I wasn't wrong: Rama kept talking.

"I was in Montevideo, and I showed your painting to one of the most renowned experts in the world," he said, smiling when he saw my amazement. "And he didn't just confirm our suspicion that it's a Diego Rivera. Martiniano Mendía, that's his name, believes that red stain was made by Frida Kahlo . . . "

"It isn't a stain," I cut in.

"No, of course it isn't," he conceded with a wider smile. "It's another painting, even more striking, more passionate . . . more Frida."

"It's a ballerina," I insisted.

"Yes, it is."

We fell silent for a while. We knew we were both mulling over the same question, one that he couldn't bring himself to ask and that I couldn't bring myself to answer. Suddenly, an image came to me. I sprang up from my chair as though nails had suddenly burst through the seat, banging my knee on the edge of the table. I was too excited to care and ran to my bedroom.

I opened the closet where my clothes were still unsorted and retrieved a black plastic bag from the back of a drawer. My nerves made me fumble over the knot I had tied days earlier. After several failed attempts, I eventually ripped the plastic and spread out the contents on my bed. It was the white canvas that, for years, Nayeli had used to protect her artwork. My grandmother's small, careful writing was still there, at the edge.

I don't want anyone to see what's inside me when my body breaks. I want to return to the blue paradise. That's all I want.

At what point in her life had my grandmother decided to write such a request? Was she thinking of me or my mother? At that moment, fulfilling that desire became my only goal.

A shadow jolted me out of my musings. Ramiro was standing next to me, in silence. He, too, was staring at Nayeli's handwritten request.

"The blue paradise," he murmured.

"What could it mean?" I asked aloud.

Ramiro covered his face with both hands, as though trying to stop the emotions from spilling out. He rubbed his eyes, then said, "Paloma, I'm certain of it. The blue paradise is the famous Casa Azul, where Frida Kahlo was raised, lived, and died," he explained, his voice cracking. "Your grandmother—"

I raised a hand and gently placed my fingers on his lips. The moment I was trying to avoid had arrived. The question poured off my lips all at once, as though it had been waiting anxiously on the tip of my tongue. "Could my grandmother have met Frida and Diego? Could she have been part of their lives?"

Ramiro delicately kissed my fingers, which were still on his lips. It was an agreeable prelude to the answer to a question that was more mine than his.

"I'm sure that must have happened, and I also think your grandmother had some kind of connection to Casa Azul." He sat on the bed and pointed at the row of letters. "Her posthumous request is to return there, to a place she describes as paradise. Perhaps she was very happy there."

Suddenly, I felt such a rush of emotion I needed to manifest it. Every part of my body launched itself at Ramiro. I held him; he held me. For the first time in a long time, I felt that relief that only the embrace of certain people can bring, and Ramiro was one of them. The other had been my grandmother, and she was gone. I wanted to cry floods of tears, until his shirt was sodden, as if he had been caught in a storm. In truth, I had a storm inside me, but no tears. I couldn't cry. But I could tremble, and I trembled violently.

Ramiro simply held me, his hands rubbing my back. When my muscles relaxed, he took me by the shoulders and pushed me away from his chest. He looked at me seriously, his brows knitting together.

"Did your grandmother leave you anything else besides the painting?" His pragmatism was returning to the fore.

I smiled and felt like crying again, but this time for the simple reason that I was with him.

"Yes, there were a few other things along with the painting," I said with the enthusiasm of a little girl embarking on a treasure hunt. "I didn't think they were important—they seemed like old junk—but now . . . I don't know."

"Now everything has changed," he finished, and I noticed that the tension that had hung in the air since he entered the house had disappeared. "Show me everything."

We left the bedroom and eagerly crossed to the other side of the house. On one of the sturdy wooden shelves against the living room wall was a wicker basket in which I had placed all the finds. Carefully, I arranged them in a row: the pink velvet box and the empty bottle of Shocking by Schiaparelli; the necklace with bronze coins; the yellow pencil; the blue pencil; the red blouse with geometric embroidery; and the skirt in the same color, with the lace flounce in yellowing white.

The red notebook that Gloria had rescued was still in the bottom of my purse. I hadn't felt able to take it out on my own. But now I wasn't alone.

"What's that?" asked Ramiro when he saw me brandishing the notebook like a trophy.

"A notebook, a kind of personal diary that Nayeli kept," I replied.

"Is there anything interesting that could help us?"

I opened the notebook and flicked quickly through the pages. I wasn't quite as ready as I thought. A recipe for a soup, written in my grandmother's tiny, delicate handwriting was like a light being turned on.

"My grandmother wasn't an artist. She never had any money. The only capital my grandmother had was her ability to cook—she made the best recipes I've ever tasted . . . what if my grandmother was Frida's cook?"

Ramiro nodded in silence.

Before we returned to our seats in the backyard, I poured two large glasses of tonic water with lemon and added a couple of glugs of tequila.

"To your health, Nayeli Cruz!" I exclaimed, looking up at the starry sky, and I opened the red-covered notebook.

44

Coyoacán, July 1944

Joselito responded to Nayeli's summons and came to meet her in Viveros de Coyoacán, wearing a violet silk scarf that Frida had given him for his birthday. As always, he smelled of his mother's rose soap, which he borrowed at bathtime.

Joselito and Nayeli had developed a deeply trusting relationship, founded on their love and admiration for the painter. Both felt that Frida had saved their lives. But although they often talked about Frida and Diego whenever they strolled along the tree-lined paths through the park, what happened between them was entirely personal.

Nayeli ran across the square, her heart pounding. Knowing that Joselito was waiting for her on the other side of the bushes spurred on every last cell in her body. Frida had told her that what she was feeling was love and that she should enjoy it, because eternal loves don't seem to happen like they used to. Whenever she mentioned Joselito, the painter would say: "*Your Diego.*" That was how she judged any feelings toward a man; for her, Diego was the standard, the benchmark against which she measured love.

Joselito's face burst into a grin. Nayeli ran toward him, wearing a yellow skirt with a green huipil that brought out her eyes.

Their young bodies met in an embrace that didn't go unnoticed by the locals walking in the park.

"It's lovely to see you, Nayeli!" said Joselito, delicately tucking back a strand of hair that was brushing the side of her mouth. He almost kissed her but managed to contain himself. "You look beautiful."

She fixed her green eyes on the ground, embarrassed by the growing heat in her body.

"It was a nice surprise to get your call!"

"You're the only one who can help me, the only one I trust." Nayeli took his hand and dragged him over to one of the stone benches positioned around the edge of the park. "Look at this," whispered Nayeli. She showed him the slip of paper she had found in Frida's diary.

Joselito read it with curiosity, unable to understand Nayeli's interest in such a simple note.

"It's an address, isn't it?" the girl asked. He nodded. "All right, I want you to go there with me."

"It isn't too far; we can walk," he replied enthusiastically. "Did Frida write this?"

"Yes."

"Who's La Güera?"

Nayeli stood and took his hand again.

"Let's start walking, and I'll tell you," she said.

Sparing no details, Nayeli told Joselito all about the mysterious girl she had first seen at the unveiling of the pulque shop mural.

They walked slowly, still holding hands. Neither wanted the physical contact to end. Although they were both eager to search for La Güera, they felt an equal need to be close to each other.

"I'm guessing she's from high society. I'm surprised Diego would have an affair with her, though. She's not really his type," Joselito reflected aloud.

"And how would you know if you haven't even seen her?"

"Because of the clothes you described and her contempt when you told her you were a cook. My mother works as a nanny in the house of a wealthy family near Chapultepec. The two rich kids she looks after are made to eat eight courses at lunch, while the lady of the house barely nibbles on a tortilla. My mother says that if that woman needed to go to the kitchen, someone would have to draw her a map."

They both laughed at the image.

"So what do rich women do here in the city?" she asked.

"Nothing. Well, not a lot. They order the domestic staff about and take care of their children and husbands."

"Is Frida from high society?" Nayeli pressed on with her questions. To her, Joselito was a fertile source of information, and what's more, she didn't feel uncouth or ignorant in front of him.

"Frida's a communist," replied the boy firmly.

"And does that mean she's poor?"

"I don't know."

They walked in silence for around twenty minutes, until they reached a mansion that took up almost the entire block.

"Here it is," said Joselito. "So why have we come?"

Nayeli was impressed. She had never seen such an imposing house, either in Coyoacán or in the United States. Spotless white walls; black-painted railings with red roses tangling around them; windows with wooden frames and immaculate stained glass panels.

"We're here to find out who La Güera is and why Frida thinks Diego should be wary of her," replied Nayeli, not entirely believing her own words. Deep down, she sensed that this languid, whiter-than-white girl was dangerous, but not to Diego. La Güera was a threat to Frida.

A police officer was approaching them, moving briskly and with a far-from-friendly expression. "Out of here!" he ordered, waving his arms as though he was trying to scare flies. "This is private property."

Nayeli stepped back fearfully, but Joselito stood his ground, hands on his waist. "Excuse me, but this is a public street, and my girlfriend and I were just strolling and commenting on the beautiful houses in this neighborhood."

The officer and Nayeli looked at him with the same disconcerted expression, but for different reasons: Nayeli hadn't heard him call her his girlfriend before, and the officer couldn't find any logical argument to deny their right to walk through the neighborhood.

He refused to give in, however, and raised his voice. "Very important people live here, and the security of the family depends on me—that's why I'm asking you to move on. You've seen all there is to see."

Nayeli took Joselito's arm and, with a desperate look, begged him not to confront the police officer.

"Let it go," she murmured in his ear.

Behind them, a woman's voice made them jump.

"What's going on here? Clear the street—this isn't a party. Go on, go on!" She marched up to the officer and gestured at him, ignoring Nayeli and Joselito. "And you, go back to the corner—I'll be out in a minute with your tortillas and a beer."

The woman was striking. Nayeli had never seen anyone carry so much extra weight with such grace.

"And who are you?" she asked when the officer had withdrawn to his corner. "I'm María Francisca," she introduced herself.

María Francisca was swathed in yards of white fabric that formed a tunic revealing only her neck and forearms. The turquoise scarf around her head struggled to contain the mane of black curls that escaped from either side.

"Thank you, señora," said Nayeli, "for getting that man off our backs—"

"He's a good worker," interrupted María Francisca. "I don't blame him. Some very important people live in this house, and they're under his care."

"Does La Güera live here?" asked Nayeli, convinced that this amazon of a woman wouldn't lie.

"Which one? A lot of people go by that nickname," she replied.

"Well, she's a very, very blond girl, very skinny, with skin as white as snow," Joselito joined the conversation.

"Ah yes! Of course she lives here! She's my boss's daughter," replied María Francisca. "She's the saddest young thing in the world, poor child. She was born into the wrong family."

"You think so?" said Joselito ironically, gesturing at the mansion.

"Pah, what do you know, kid? These mansions are glass cages. The boss is very strict, and serious," explained María Francisca as she fanned herself with one hand. "He's an important man. He's setting up an agency or something in the United States. The housekeeper told me they want us Mexicans to know all the good and beautiful things the gringos have . . . "

"It isn't all that beautiful," replied Nayeli.

"How would you know?" asked the woman.

"I've been to the United States," Nayeli replied proudly.

María Francisca laughed, not believing a word of it. The Tehuana felt the urge to insist on her story and prove that she wasn't a liar. It was Joselito who got her out of the predicament.

"Señora, do you know whether this blond girl is dangerous—can she cause people harm?"

"Eh, what nonsense! I told you: she's a sad, wretched thing. Her parents are marrying her off to a very important young man, and there she goes, poor thing, getting skinnier and skinnier. They've had to take in the wedding dress three times already—she's all skin and bones. So white, and with those huge eyes, she looks like a ghost."

Joselito and Nayeli exchanged a look of relief. Both had suspected that La Güera was one of Diego's lovers, just one of the many. What marked the difference this time was Frida's unease. The painter never concerned herself with her husband's lovers; she had even made friends with some of them. But the warning written on a scrap of paper in her diary wasn't usual.

"And when is the wedding?" asked Nayeli.

"When the groom returns from his travels. His father is a diplomat, too, and they've gone to Argentina. The fiancé is being prepared to become a powerful man, and when that happens and they marry, that's where they'll go, to Argentina."

"I'd like to meet La Güera," ventured Nayeli.

"Yes, but I'm sure she won't want to see you," replied María Francisca.

"Doesn't she have any friends?"

"As if! Poor thing, she's always so sad and alone," said María Francisca. Then, bringing the conversation to a close, she tucked her hair beneath the headscarf, and added, "Well, I have to get back to the house. I have plenty of jobs to be getting on with."

Nayeli and Joselito said goodbye and thanked her for her kindness. But before leaving, Nayeli wanted to know one last thing.

"What's La Güera's name?"

"Eva Felipa Garmendia."

"Nice name," said the Tehuana.

The young couple made their way home, content at having done their duty. The threatening monster they had constructed in their minds was no more than a sad girl facing her destiny; they decided that this Eva presented no danger to Frida, and promptly forgot all about the matter. A matter that would return years later in the form of a last beacon of hope in one of the roughest seas.

45

Buenos Aires, January 2019

The scorching heat of the Buenos Aires summer didn't bother Lorena Funes. She had experienced worse sun and sweat in her native Colombia. Lorena's mind contained no deeper discomfort than the sensation of millions of dollars sifting through her fingers like sand in the sea. The move Ramiro and his father had played had left her disconsolate for days. All she could do was lie in bed binge-watching her favorite series and eating ice cream under the chill of the air-conditioning.

One of those unsettled nights, as she dozed in the lethargy caused by a few glasses of champagne, a sudden realization struck her. How had it not occurred to her before? The vital piece of information was right before her eyes.

She got up and sped to her computer. There was no time to lose. All her attention was focused on remedying the error.

It took her less than an hour to find the details she needed. She checked her gold watch anxiously; it wasn't even dawn yet. She had no option but to wait for the day to begin.

Lorena had anticipated a dinner or, better still, a lunch, but when the woman at the other end of the line insisted on breakfast, all she could do was accept immediately. Lorena had introduced herself and, in one line, explained the reason for her call. The other woman had been just as succinct: "Brunch at eleven, the Hotel Regidor."

The hotel lobby was still impeccable, despite its age.

"I have a reservation for two people in the bar," said Lorena without meeting the receptionist's eyes.

The woman accompanied her silently to her table and said goodbye with a practiced smile.

The setting was pleasant and had the advantage of not needing air-conditioning in the middle of summer. The thick walls and cool marble gave it a natural freshness. Lorena had arrived a half hour early, a habit she had acquired from Emilio Pallares, which allowed her to choose where to sit at the table in order to assess the confidence, fear, or nerves with which the other party entered the room.

She read the menu unenthusiastically and ordered a bottle of mineral water. She touched up her lipstick and mentally revised her outfit: a white linen sleeveless dress that came just above her knees; flat caramel-colored leather moccasins, which matched her small purse. To prevent the humidity of the port city frizzing up her wavy hair, she had gathered it neatly at the back of her neck. She was just about to refresh her citrusy perfume when a movement at the bar caught her attention. There was no doubt about it. It was Felipa Cruz, the woman she was waiting for.

She had spent hours trawling through the photos on Paloma Cruz's Instagram feed, one by one, needing to know what it was about that attractive but simple girl that had caught Ramiro's eye. Her mother, Felipa, however, was very different, much more serious. She seemed much taller than she actually was. Her long legs and slender arms elevated her, and her erect, ballerina's posture added inches to her height.

Lorena's radar-like eyes noted that the short-sleeved, ankle-length coral dress that Felipa was wearing with supreme elegance was made of natural silk of exquisite quality. But the care taken over her attire contrasted with her messy brown hair, with honey-colored highlights; it looked wet, as though she had just stepped out of the shower. She hadn't even taken a few seconds to tame the strands that fell rebelliously around her face.

Felipa Cruz paused in the middle of the room and looked around for the stranger who had telephoned her. Lorena raised her hand and, at the same time, deployed her most charming smile.

"Felipa, it's a pleasure to meet you! I'm so grateful to you for taking the trouble to accept my invitation," said the Colombian, working her sweet side as best she could. She noticed that her guest smelled of sage, an intense and pleasant aroma that hovered around her.

"I'm going to need some scrambled eggs with ham. And a double coffee, no milk, nice and strong, no sugar," replied Felipa, as though her dining companion was the waitress.

Lorena was puzzled for a few beats, but she composed herself swiftly and waved to summon the waiter. She repeated Felipa's order, adding some fruit and a green tea for herself. Paloma's mother seemed so strange, she decided she would get to the point as soon as possible. She tried not to look at her as she spoke, for fear of being hypnotized by the woman's green eyes.

"As I mentioned on the phone, my job involves recovering and restoring artworks for the State," said Lorena, using her most accepted strategy: peppering her lies with truths. "An international investigation provided us with important information relating to an artwork with connections to your family." She paused to assess Felipa's reaction. The woman was stirring her coffee uninterestedly. Lorena knew she had to move the conversation along if she wanted to snap her out of her boredom. "What I mean to say, Señora Cruz, is that there is a painting worth millions of dollars in your family."

"I don't doubt it." She rested the tiny spoon on the white tablecloth, staining it with coffee. Then she added: "I'm not an expert like you, but I'm not stupid. I'm aware that a Diego Rivera is worth a lot of money."

The Colombian didn't even try to hide her amazement.

"You're aware that your daughter has the painting?"

"There isn't much you can hide from me, so I beg of you, if you want me to stay, tell me something I don't already know. I'm easily bored."

In the past, Lorena had reacted more strongly to much less disparaging responses. This time, however, she swallowed her pride.

She finished her tea in one gulp, the liquid burning her throat, then continued, "Well, I hope it won't bore you to hear that part of my job is to find buyers for exquisite works that have been hidden for years—"

"My understanding is that your job has nothing to do with buyers or sellers," interrupted Felipa, interested for the first time. "When you introduced yourself on the phone, naturally I took the liberty of googling you. According to the official website of the Argentinean government, your job is to recover works for the public domain, as long as you have the agreement of the true owners. It says nothing about buying or selling. Except that you're no more than a dodgy dealer of expensive objects disguised as a public employee."

Lorena's eyes widened like saucers. No one had ever defined her job quite so accurately.

"And would it interest you to have your mother's painting displayed in a national museum for people to enjoy?" asked Lorena, well aware that nothing she had said to Felipa had surprised her.

"That's something you'd have to discuss with my daughter, Paloma. The Rivera painting is hers."

The very mention of that name made Lorena shudder inside. She tried to set her childish jealousy aside and focus on what mattered: money.

"I don't give a damn what your daughter thinks, Señora Cruz," she said, spitting out her words. "The only legitimate opinion is yours."

Felipa frowned and tipped her head to one side. Lorena smiled. Finally, she had hit the target. From now on, she would start to gain points in her favor, she felt sure of it.

"I don't understand," the woman murmured.

"It's very simple," the Colombian explained. "You are Nayeli Cruz's sole heir. That's how Argentinean law works. Everything that belonged to your mother is now yours. Your daughter, Paloma, is a gate-crasher at this party."

This news got Felipa's stomach moving. She shifted in her chair and in three mouthfuls emptied her plate of scrambled eggs. Lorena, practiced at letting other people make decisions, watched her eat. And she waited, with infinite patience, pouring herself another cup of green tea.

Felipa delicately wiped her mouth on the napkin and folded it neatly on the side of the empty plate. "Very well, Señorita Funes." She leaned her elbows on the table, chin resting in her hands, and raised her right eyebrow. "I'm listening. What's your plan?"

46

Coyoacán, August 1949

Frida awoke with a jolt and clambered out of bed. Her long, loose silk nightdress had stuck to her back, thighs, and chest. She was so sweaty anyone would have thought she had just taken a bath. With her heart galloping and her breath agitated, she stood still for a second, allowing her ears to tune in. Her long hair, wavy and uncombed, fell down her back, almost reaching her waist.

"There it is!" she shouted, slapping at the air. "Take that, take that, you devil bug! I've got you! Come on! Come here if you're brave enough, coward!"

The devil bug was so large it occupied half the room. Every blow it received from Frida made it mutate into something different. And it roared with such menacing fury and such intensity that Frida could do nothing but cover her ears with both hands. Now unable to lash out at the devil bug, a feeling of helplessness washed over her like a bucket of cold water.

"Ballerina! Balleriiiinaaa!" she shouted desperately. "Help! I need help!"

Nayeli heard her cries from the garden, but she wasn't alarmed and didn't rush inside. Frida's deliriums had become commonplace. The painter hadn't been the same since her last operation, and she had said as much to Diego, to her doctor in the United States, and to her Mexican surgeons. Everyone agreed that the morphine was taking its toll, but no one found a solution to allow the painter to escape the addiction that was driving her insane.

When Nayeli entered the room, she found Frida completely naked, sitting on the floor with her legs crossed. The attack, which existed only in her luxuriant imagination, was over for now. The scars of her many operations gave Frida's skinny body the look of a prisoner of war. The longest stretched from her neck to her lower back, a straight line that seemed to trace her spinal column; on her right hip, the line was shorter, but it still bore the vivid purple of a wound that needs time to settle. Her torso wasn't much better. The leather straps of her metal corsets left deep marks on the skin over her ribs. Despite the natural salves concocted by a neighbor, which Nayeli applied diligently, the appearance of Frida's skin wasn't improving.

"It's over, Frida. You have to get up," said the girl, helping her stand. "Choose the most beautiful dress you have. Tonight, you have to shine brighter than ever."

"There's time. It's still early," replied Frida. She was exhausted. Her imaginary fights left her drained, as though returning from the war every day. "I need my diary. There are things I need to get out of me onto the page."

As Nayeli looked for the red notebook and the box of pencils and inks, Frida put her silk nightdress back on.

"Here you are," murmured the young woman, placing both items on the bed.

With a knack acquired over the years, Frida arranged a pile of pillows against the headboard and sat with her back as straight as she could get it; she bent her knees and used her thighs to support her diary. In that little book, just a few square inches, she had created a parallel mind for herself, in which she was able to exorcise her ghosts. She opened the wooden box where she kept her pencils and half closed her eyes: choosing a color was never a trivial task for her.

"Green," she murmured and held the pencil in the air for a few seconds.

After filling two whole pages, she read out loud:

"I wish I could do whatever I liked behind the curtain of madness. Then, I'd arrange flowers, all day long, I'd paint pain, love, and tenderness; I would laugh as much as I feel like at the stupidity of others, and they would all say: Poor thing, she's crazy. Above all, I'd laugh at my own stupidity. I would build my own world, which while I lived would be in agreement with all the worlds. The day, or the hour, or the minute that I lived would be mine and everyone else's. My madness would not be an escape from reality."

Nayeli listened to her closely. It wasn't the first time Frida had mentioned madness.

"And what about *your* diary?" asked the painter, more as a complaint than a question. "You should write in it every day so that you don't forget your letters. Hands are sly things, and if you don't train them, they get distracted and you'll lose the skill."

"I don't do it every day, but I do it," replied Nayeli.

"I want to see," insisted Frida.

"I'll show you if you get dressed and come to the kitchen for breakfast."

Her years of negotiating prices in the markets of Tehuantepec and Coyoacán had made Nayeli adept at getting what she wanted in exchange for what she had.

Freshly baked bread rolls, thinly sliced fruit, and strong black coffee formed part of the breakfast Nayeli prepared for Frida every day. The medicines and the sleepless nights had made the painter's stomach a tiny organ that held no more than the minimum required to keep her alive.

"All right, here I am. Now read me something from your diary," she said, taking a seat at the table. She had swapped her silk nightgown for a dark brown tunic that matched her hair.

"Eat," insisted Nayeli.

"Read," retorted Frida.

The two women locked eyes, Nayeli's green piercing Frida's brown. In that exchange of looks they came to an agreement: Frida picked up a bread roll, split it down the middle with a small knife, and buttered one side. At the exact moment she took her first bite, the young woman started to read from her red leather-bound diary, identical to Frida's:

"We spent almost the whole afternoon kissing at the back of Viveros de Coyoacán. It's the perfect place to hide our love. Sometimes his hands bother me, they're so eager and urgent on my body. I feel like he's imagining my clothes will disappear . . . "

The painter opened her mouth and eyes wide, and cried out with a mixture of surprise and laughter.

"Nayeli, my goodness! That's quite something! You have a boyfriend and you didn't even tell me?"

"I'm telling you now," replied Nayeli, embarrassed, not lifting her eyes from the diary.

"Who is this boyfriend?"

"You already know, Frida."

"Joselito?"

The Tehuana gave a slight nod.

"Oh, that's wonderful! I love that boy. He's so good and so talented. Nothing better than an artist, Nayelita."

"Joselito isn't an artist."

"What do you mean? Of course he is! He's a very hardworking artist—he did very good work in my classes. He was always my favorite."

Nayeli didn't want to contradict Frida, but her boyfriend had stopped painting and drawing some time ago. His dreams had been buried beneath his mother's financial troubles. He was the man of the house and had to work from sunup to sundown to put a meal on the table. He switched his brushes and canvases for the tools he used as an employee for one of the railroad companies.

Nayeli kept on nagging about the breakfast; Frida, about the diary. They passed the morning amid tortillas, fruit, and brief readings. The young woman still struggled with some letters and punctuation.

"I can't explain something that comes from instinct," argued Frida. "Sometimes you get a long silence that needs a period, while shorter ones ask for a comma. Let's do an exercise: read your writing aloud, and when you need to take a long pause, take a yellow pencil and draw a little sun; and if it's a short pause, take a blue pencil and draw a little star."

Pleased with her idea, the painter took both pencils from the wooden box and gave them to Nayeli as a gift. The girl's face filled with a smile, and she clutched the furious yellow and the pale blue to her chest. She had never had colored pencils before, and it made her very happy to receive these as her first.

"Take that dopey look off your face. You've got your pencils to practice your handwriting. I'm going to keep a close eye on you, my little ballerina," said Frida in the schoolmarm tone that suited her so well. "Now I'm going to get changed. Diego told me he's coming to visit with a very special surprise."

Frida spent two hours shut away in her room. Assessing every detail of her attire was like gestating an artwork. When she finally entered the living room, Nayeli was spellbound. She couldn't recall Frida ever looking so luminous and dazzling. Even her spine was held straight, without the need for the corset, and her limp was only perceptible to a very experienced eye. She had chosen the finest Tehuana outfit from her collection, the one she had worn at her exposition in Paris, and she looked like she was surrounded by shooting stars. The purple sash tied tightly around her waist was the same color as the velvet ribbons braided into her hair. A couple of bronze clasps in the shape of birds held her braids against her head, forming a stunning headpiece. She had done her makeup, and that was a good sign. For some time, Frida had been saying to anyone who wanted to listen that she was never going to wear makeup again because she wanted to get used to the face of death. Today, however, her assertions disappeared beneath a rosy glow that lifted her cheekbones, and a bright red lipstick.

"How do I look?" she asked, although she knew the answer.

Her pains and illnesses hadn't lessened that endearing vanity in the slightest.

"Fabulous, Frida."

At the very moment the painter announced that she was ready, the door of Casa Azul swung open. Frida and Diego operated perfectly in synch: there was no need for prior warning; they could sense each other like animals in the jungle.

"Frisita, my love, dove of my heart!" called Rivera.

"There's that outrageous fatty," murmured Frida, giving Nayeli a knowing look, and then shouted: "Here I am, sapo espantoso! Come through the garden, I want a bit of sun. I'll meet you there."

It was a lie. Frida wasn't remotely interested in the sun; she just wanted Diego to be able to admire her white dress in all its splendor, to show herself off among the flowering cacti like a Tehuana goddess, like an apparition come down from some paradise invented just for him. More than a tool of seduction, flirtation was a weapon of war for Frida.

She took a deep breath and tilted her head to either side to ease her neck. The morphine had soothed that sneaky, ever-present pain in her back and hips.

As soon as he saw her, he took off his hat and held it against his chest. He smiled with that wide grin that spread across his entire face, and his green, bulging eyes gleamed with emotion. Frida moved him like only a good painting could. Frida was art. And Diego was susceptible to art.

Frida's expression of surprise snapped him out of his hypnosis: her thick eyebrows raised and red mouth half open in a silent exclamation. Diego turned to his right and fixed his eyes on the woman standing beside him. She was also impressed by the figure of Frida Kahlo. She had heard a lot about Frida, and now, just yards away from her, she realized it had all been an understatement.

"Oh, Virgen of Guadalupe! I can't believe my eyes," cried Frida, covering her face with both hands. "Nayeli, Nayeli, come here! Wait till you see the gift my Dieguito brought me!"

The woman released a tinkle of laughter that showed off her perfectly straight white teeth. It flattered her to hear such a fabulous woman describing her as a gift. Frida stretched out her hands to touch her; she wanted to be sure the woman wouldn't vanish as soon as she made contact. The woman allowed herself to be touched with a submissiveness that was unusual in her. She half closed her eyes and felt the cold fingers running over her face as lightly as a butterfly.

"How beautiful you are, María!" murmured Frida.

"No, not at all. Anyone can be beautiful. Genuine attractiveness is something else—it comes from inside—and I'm attractive. And you're attractive."

Diego laughed loudly and broke the spell. He was happy to be together with the two most striking women in Mexico: María Félix and Frida Kahlo. He was a lucky man.

Nayeli had responded to her mentor's call, but she wasn't brave enough to come any closer. She had heard of María Félix countless times, and in the market there was a huge poster of the movie star, a close-up of her perfect face that bewitched anyone who passed the wall—the black, coiffured hair; the thin brows framing her gaze; the almond-shaped eyes; and that air of a tigress that grabbed the whole world's attention.

"You see, my Friducha, see the surprise I've brought you? It's María herself! The beautiful emblem of Mexico, the icon of our great nation!" exclaimed Diego, who could barely contain his joy. "Let's go to the living room or to your studio. Show her the fabulous pictures you paint. I've told La Doña all about you."

The three of them crossed the garden, gabbling nonstop. The women threw out words and exclamations simultaneously, and it was impossible to tell whether they were listening to each other at all, but they seemed happy. Diego followed a few steps behind, his chest puffed out, shoulders back, looking for all the world like the alpha male of the pride.

The strong smell of the paints, solvents, and oils made María wrinkle her perfect nose, and her eyes started streaming with tears.

"Oh, María, I'm sorry!" said Frida as she flung open the windows. "Sometimes I forget that not everyone is accustomed to the smell."

María raised a hand with red-painted nails and slender fingers. A gold ring with a ruby the size of a walnut cast a reddish glimmer onto Frida's white dress. "Don't worry about it, darling," she said, elegantly playing it down, and turned her slender body toward Diego. "I'll have to get used to it—I have many long hours ahead of me posing for the maestro Rivera."

A shot of pain ran down Frida's spine like a bolt of lightning, and her bad leg started to go numb. All her pain flocked back to the place where it felt most at home: her body. The painter leaned on the desk with her right hand. She could only attempt a forced smile, a strange grimace.

"You didn't say anything, Diego. I didn't know you were going to paint Mexico's finest actress," she said in a maternal tone.

"Well, you see, it was a surprise, another surprise. I'll do a huge painting, a magnificent one, so that all of Mexico and the world can admire María's beauty."

After a short tour of the studio, Frida invited María to drink tequila with her in the courtyard next to the fountain. The glamorous movie star accepted, charmed: few things gave her greater pleasure than sharing tequila with another woman.

"I love it when we women can take over a man's space. And in this country, tequila has always been a refuge for men!" she exclaimed, dabbing salt and lime on her tongue.

Frida took advantage of the moment of intimacy. She liked María and didn't want anything to harm her. In her eagerness to mother everyone she met, she warned her: "Be careful, lovely María. Don't let Diego seduce you. I know it's hard not to fall under his spell, but don't fall, don't be deceived . . . "

María Félix fixed her gaze on Frida and winked. She moved her face very close to Frida's. The mixture of her sandalwood perfume and her tequila breath was heavenly. "Don't worry, Frida," she murmured. "No one seduces me. I'm the one who seduces. And no one ever chooses me. I choose."

47

Buenos Aires, January 2019

. . . I let myself go, even though sometimes I feel like the way it makes my skin tingle is almost a sin. Joselito says not, that love isn't a sin and that he loves me. I tell him I love him, too, but I don't really know what it means to love a man, sometimes I feel like I'm lying to him . . .

Decoding my grandmother's notebook was no easy task. Her inexpert handwriting, small and tight, was embellished by yellow suns and blue stars that covered some words and made it even harder to read. It was Ramiro who solved the first mystery.

"The pencils!" he exclaimed with almost childlike enthusiasm.

We left our chairs on the patio and went to look in the basket on the coffee table. Among Nayeli's belongings, we found the two pencils: one blue and the other yellow. Ramiro made two delicate little marks—one with each pencil—at the edge of one page. He looked at me curiously. They were a perfect match, no doubt about it.

"I think the little stars and suns around the letters must be some kind of writing exercise. My grandmother told me she learned to read and write quite late in life," I said confidently.

"These are very good pencils," said Ramiro, scratching the tips with his fingernail. "High-quality pigment. Who do you think this Joselito is? Your grandmother talks about him so fondly—did she ever mention his name?"

His question brought back that thorn in my chest, the one that pricked me whenever some fresh detail about my grandmother came to light. All the things she had concealed from me were more painful than the grief at having lost her. I would have loved to talk to her about that now-distant first love. But no, she had chosen silence.

"Not much. He was my grandfather, but she never spoke about him very lovingly," I murmured.

As I progressed through the pages, my mood changed. The handwriting became much looser, more skilled. No trace remained of the blue and yellow marks. In her later years, my grandmother had become obsessed with lists. Each list had a title, which she underlined shakily: *Courtyard plants at Casa Solanas*, *Condiments in kitchen cupboard*, *Names of nurses on both shifts*. The last list caught my attention. Its title was a name: *Eva Garmendia*. Each of the items was numbered. There were three: *1. pink blanket*, *2. silver cup*, and *3. butterfly clip*.

I didn't want Ramiro to see that part of the diary; I didn't want him to ask about Eva Garmendia. That woman and I had accounts to settle, but I wasn't quite ready for it. We did, however, enjoy looking through the recipes Nayeli had described in detail, and I promised I would cook one for him sometime.

"What are you going to do with the painting?" His voice had lost all empathy: the cold, practical Ramiro I knew had returned.

"What should I do?" I replied with another question, trying to buy time, although deep down I was interested in his opinion. He was the art expert, after all, not me.

He stood up and paced around the patio. Night had fallen. When he moved away from the lights, he became a shadow.

"You have several options. You could sell it to a collector for a seven-figure sum. You could loan it to a local museum, or a foreign one—"

"Or I could hang it on the wall in this house and leave it there," I cut in.

He looked at me and frowned, taking his hands in mine.

"That's no longer possible. It's too late."

"Why?" I asked, half curious, half worried.

"It's my fault. There are people who are aware of the existence of this lost work who would do anything to have it in their possession. We're talking about millions of dollars, Paloma."

I thought about the murdered merchant, the night when I went with Ramiro to retrieve the painting, and the murky reasons that had made him snatch it from me in the middle of the street. I was afraid, but I knew one thing for certain.

"I don't want to get rid of the painting. And I want to know the circumstances in which it was painted. Behind all of that is my grandmother's story, and I need to know."

Ramiro's eyes shone with a strange, almost mischievous glimmer.

"Very well. If you really want to keep the painting, I have a plan."

"I'm all ears."

48

Buenos Aires, January 2019

Emilio Pallares hung up the phone after an almost hour-long conversation. Lorena Funes and Cristóbal were watching him expectantly.

"Mendía wants the painting, no matter what. He's prepared to pay whatever it takes," he said, his gaze flicking from one to the other. "But we don't have the painting."

"But we're going to get it back," said Lorena, sounding unconcerned. "I'm taking care of it, as always."

"For some time now, your methods have been ineffectual and contaminated by your torrid feelings for my younger son," said Emilio Pallares, drinking his untouched tea in one gulp.

"Don't be vulgar! I won't allow it!" shouted Lorena.

"You aren't in a position to allow or forbid anything, Lorena."

"Lower your voice, no one shouts at me. You hear? I've just told you I'm taking care of it, and I never fail."

Cristóbal held his tongue, he didn't need to hear any more to grasp that Lorena was romantically involved with his brother, and he wasn't surprised: Ramiro had snatched away his mother's love—theft was in his nature. But now things were different for Cristóbal; now they needed him.

"When do I start copying the Rivera?" he asked.

Lorena started to fiddle with her gold rings, as was her habit whenever she didn't have a ready answer. Pallares took a deep breath and decided he would have to share the information he and Ramiro had gleaned in Uruguay.

"First, you should know that the painting belonging to Ramiro's little girlfriend is more than we first thought. The red stain is actually the image of a ballerina, and according to Mendía, there's no doubt: it's the work of Frida Kahlo."

"I don't believe it," babbled Lorena.

Cristóbal shrugged. He didn't think faking a Kahlo would be any more complicated than faking a Rivera, and he asked again: "When do I start?"

"That's why I brought you here," said Emilio. "Ramiro has the painting. He's been incommunicado since we returned from Uruguay—he isn't answering my calls, and he isn't in his apartment."

"All right, then, I'll take care of it," said Cristóbal, trying to conceal his excitement.

Neither Lorena nor Pallares dared contradict him. Neither of the two had any better ideas.

49

Coyoacán, May 1953

Casa Azul had become a living hell. Even the dogs were unfriendly: they fought among themselves and attacked visitors—no longer pets, but a wolfpack. The two macaws disappeared one morning, and no one bothered to look for them. Nayeli continued to leave chunks of fruit beneath the tree, but they just rotted as the hours passed. The front door was open at all times, a never-ending procession of people coming and going: Frida's doctors and the nurses who bathed her; her former pupils from the Art School; María Félix, Teresa Proenza, and Machila Armida; a couple of nameless young women who claimed to be the painter's girlfriends; the gardeners and cleaning staff; Alejandro, Frida's childhood sweetheart; and Diego, who, despite spending most of the day in his San Ángel studio, slept at Casa Azul.

From the bed, her living tomb, as she liked to call it, Frida had arranged a carnival parade of professional admirers to spoil and flatter her at all times.

"I hate being alone. The void terrifies me," she remarked, as Nayeli arranged four packages at the foot of the bed. Then, with a bit more enthusiasm: "Open that one with the yellow bow! I love yellow!"

No one knew how, from her sickbed, she had managed to acquire such a well-oiled routine of gifts. Every morning, on the steps outside

Casa Azul, anonymous hands left boxes and baskets full to the brim: fruits, flowers, colored pencils, drawings, hair ribbons, hand-embroidered shawls, earrings, colorful bead necklaces. Everyone seemed intent on adorning the Frida they held in their memories, but no one knew that, behind those blue walls, the woman they were honoring was now very different.

Her long, shiny black hair had become a dull mop of knots that were impossible to untangle; the skin over her bones was yellowed and haggard; her permanently pained expression had turned the laughter lines around her mouth into deep wrinkles; her earlobes, for once unadorned, looked like flaps of cartilage. The only thing left intact were her eyes, which retained their sparkle and still bewitched anyone who had the fortune to fall into her orbit.

Nayeli carefully untied the ribbon. Frida had had the idea of hanging up the ribbons from all these gifts to form a curtain at the bedroom window, as a sign that the gift had been received and was appreciated.

"Another doll," murmured the Tehuana, placing it in the painter's wasted arms.

"Not just any old doll. Take a good look. This one's quite different."

Her fondness for dolls was known throughout Coyoacán. On more than one occasion, her neighbors had seen her scouring the aisles of the market or craft fairs looking for her little daughters; that was what she called them: "my little daughters." She bought them new, used, dirty, clean. Some came with tiny clothes and shoes, others entirely naked. Frida didn't care; her goal was to have them all. She would spend days sprucing them up and sleeping with them on her chest; then she would forget all about them and toss them in a cupboard that had become a cemetery for abandoned dolls. She didn't miss them; she always had new pieces with which to play mother. But she was right: the doll in the box with the yellow bow was different.

"Do you see how elegant the clothes are, Nayeli? This is a luxury doll!" she exclaimed as she caressed the brown woolen hair. "And they're green. Green is such a lovely color! Like leaves in the jungle, exactly the same."

Nayeli drew closer, curious. The doll was simple, made from gabardine fabric stuffed with cotton; the seams looked slightly uneven. But the dress was beautiful: olive-green wool flannel with a round neckline and, down the front, heart-shaped mother-of-pearl buttons; the sleeves reached to the elbows, and it was cinched in at the waist by a leather sash in the same shade of green.

"I want a dress just like this," said Frida with an energy she hadn't shown for a while. "This is the style of woman I want to be. Nothing else. This."

"But you're a Tehuana," replied Nayeli, offended.

"Not anymore. You're the only true Tehuana. Now I want to be an elegant woman, an elegant communist; that's what I want. I'm bored by so many things in life now. I want new things."

The young woman delicately took the doll from her hands, adamant that she would find an identical dress so that Frida could be the woman she wanted to be. She owed her that much.

With the doll pressed against her chest, she crossed the courtyard to the door; she knew Joselito had an hour for lunch before going back to his job in the railroad yard. She was so focused that she didn't notice Diego coming the other way. He, too, had things on his mind. They bumped into each other in the hall, so hard that, were it not for Diego, they both would have fallen on their backs.

"Whoa, honey! Careful!" exclaimed the painter as he grasped her by the arms with his huge, strong hands.

Despite losing her balance, Nayeli managed to keep hold of the doll, but there were other things she wasn't able to do. The body doesn't lie, it can't deceive, it doesn't do what it's told; it's disobedient. The Tehuana's green eyes sank into Diego's. It was a matter of seconds, a particle of time suspended in something that was more than just a glance: it was a secret, forbidden invitation. Nayeli couldn't help getting goose bumps on her skin.

"Sorry," she mumbled.

Diego was watching her, his head tilted to one side, as though seeing her for the first time. The person before him was no longer a girl; a new woman was unveiled before his eyes. Her chocolate-colored hair fell to her shapely shoulders, soft and glowing. But what really caught the painter's attention were the dark eyelashes that framed those green eyes. It was a green he had seen somewhere else, in other circumstances. The green of a happy place.

He had to stop himself from running a finger over the girl's high cheekbones, under those eyes in which he seemed to have gotten lost, baffled by her intoxicating scent.

"Who are you?" he asked, controlling his loud voice.

"Who are *you*?" replied Nayeli.

Both knew they were the same as ever, but at the same time, they were other people.

"I want you to come with me to Chapultepec Park," said Diego.

"I can't. I have to run an errand for Frida."

Frida's name was the incantation needed to snap them out of the daydream. Once again, he was Diego Rivera. Once again, she was Nayeli Cruz. And Nayeli held up the doll in front of the painter's face.

"I need to find a dress identical to this one for Frida. It's what she wants most in life."

Diego burst out laughing.

"My dove always exaggerates. That dress is what she wants most at this precise moment," he said contemplatively.

"What's the difference between a lifetime and a moment?" asked the young woman.

For a man who always had a ready answer, this simple question threw him off-kilter. The woman in front of him was a deep hole, dark and tempting. Clumsy as a teenager, he pulled the doll from her hands and tried to focus on the dress. He had promised to fulfill Frida's every whim. It was the least he could do for her.

"I think I know someone who can help you," he said eventually, taking control of the situation.

He turned on his heel and strode out to Calle Londres. The driver he had hired to take him back and forth between Coyoacán and San Ángel was waiting on the corner, leaning against the hood with a cigarette.

"Take this young lady to the house of Leopoldo Aragón, the Argentinean," ordered Diego, then he looked at Nayeli, who settled herself into the back seat. "Tell his wife you're there on my behalf and give her the doll. She'll know what to do."

As soon as Nayeli stepped out of the car, she felt an immediate relief, and her nausea vanished as if by magic. The walls of the property stretched the entire block, the treetops peaking above like a kind of enclosed forest, a wood for a select few. Nayeli squeezed the doll against her chest and, with her free hand, shook the chain of the bronze bell.

The front door opened in the distance, and a short, plump woman hurried down the driveaway toward her. In moments, she was standing in front of Nayeli with a charming smile.

"Good morning, señora. I'm looking for the Argentinean's wife. I'm here on behalf of Señor Diego Rivera."

The woman's smile froze, a flash of panic crossing her face.

"Oh, my dear! Please, lower your voice!" she whispered. "Please don't say that liar's name in this house . . . "

"Sorry, I didn't—"

The woman cut in. She seemed agitated.

"It's fine. But don't say his name," she said contemplatively. "Follow me. The señora is just finishing her ballet class, and she'll be with you presently."

The garden was much larger, denser, and more beautiful than it looked from outside. Nayeli followed the housekeeper; she took slow steps, trying to make the journey last as long as possible, filling herself with the aromas and the irregular swells of birdsong.

"Come in," said the woman, at the top of the stairs to the front door.

The entrance hall was spacious and cool, with white marble floors and walls to match, but Nayeli couldn't focus on the details. Nor did she notice the classical music playing at high volume; nor did she crouch to stroke the cat that swirled around her ankles. Her astounded eyes could only focus on what was happening in the middle of the room. A young woman, clad entirely in clingy pink cotton, was dancing with her eyes closed. Her slender body and long legs moved in time with the music, almost levitating. Her arms, raised above her head, finished in hands like birds' wings. Her golden, almost white hair fell down her back, the tips caressing her tiny waist. The stunning image of the dancing girl didn't fog Nayeli's memory. It was her—there was no doubt. The floating angel was La Güera Garmendia.

50

Buenos Aires, January 2019

The calm voice at the other end of the line should have warned me. My mother was always issuing orders or throwing out words sharp as knives; but for some reason, her velvety whisper didn't trigger any alarm bells. That was a mistake. The only way to survive as Felipa Cruz's daughter was to be like a fire station, where even the slightest whiff of smoke sent every sense into a state of high alert.

"Hello, Paloma. It's your mother. We need to meet to discuss an important matter. We'll have lunch together."

I couldn't recall ever having received such an invitation before. Perhaps that's why I didn't think anything odd of her friendly tone, and accepted.

Felipa made a reservation at a Peruvian restaurant in the Palermo district. In the taxi, I remembered how Nayeli had hated Peruvian food; she was adamant that Mexican cuisine was much better and that all they did in Peru was try to eclipse Mexico. I smiled. My mother lived for details such as these. With a knot in my stomach and a taste of betrayal in my mouth, I sat at our reserved table in the corner of a courtyard shaded by a handful of trees. My mother arrived late, as usual. Her lack of punctuality wasn't a character flaw, merely one of the many known forms of exhibitionism she employed. She knew she had a body worthy of admiration, and she made a ritual out of it.

"You look lovely. I like your hair that way," she said, as she placed her purse on an empty chair.

I was grateful for the compliment, although I knew it wasn't genuine. I hadn't done anything new with my hair; it was loose, and I hadn't made any particular effort. We made small talk for as long as it took for the waiter to bring our food.

The two plates of ceviche were the starting gun, signaling the moment when the mystery would be revealed.

"No doubt you've been wondering why I invited you." My mother's personality shone clearly through those words, and particularly in her tone of voice: firm, dry, entirely lacking in affection or empathy. I nodded. "I want us to talk about my inheritance."

I gazed down at my plate, slightly disappointed, knowing I wouldn't be able to swallow a mouthful, and turned to my habitual response of playing dumb to buy time.

"I don't know what you're talking about."

"My mother's things, which belong to me by law. I am Nayeli's legitimate heir."

The way she uttered "law" and "legitimate heir" made her sound like a European countess. There are some words that only rich people use, words of privilege.

I nodded again and continued to feign ignorance. "Of course. Whenever it suits you, you can come to the house and take what you like. Abuela put the property in my name, while she was still alive . . . "

"I'm not interested in that shack in Boeda, my dear, please! I have my beautiful apartment. I want the painting," she declared, and took a breath before continuing, "The one you showed me."

My mouth suddenly felt dry. I took a long drink of water, struggling to keep up appearances.

"Why do you want that? It's just an ordinary old picture, not really in keeping with your sophisticated style. But there might be some things in Nayeli's closets that would interest you. I don't know. You'll have to come one day and take a look at your leisure."

As I spoke, my mother's face seemed to harden. For a moment, her eyes glimmered with something that resembled evil, or perhaps just desperation. Felipa always puzzled me.

"I want the painting," she repeated, as though it were a sudden whim.

"So do I," I replied firmly.

"But it's mine. You'll get it when I die. Not before. You're my heir, and I'm Nayeli's. I'm asking nicely . . . "

"And what would happen if you weren't asking nicely?" I preferred to preempt what was coming. I wasn't ready to be threatened by my mother.

Felipa smiled with one side of her mouth and raised an eyebrow.

"We'll go through legal channels, my dear. I'm not a mafioso."

I stabbed a piece of ceviche furiously, as though forking some part of my mother's body. She was right, and it made me livid because she never usually was. But whether she was right or wrong, Felipa behaved the same in all situations: triumphant and fabulous.

We decided on a truce of silence, and each of us savored the Peruvian delicacies as though the other weren't there.

Like a bolt of lightning, I was split down the middle by two certainties: that my mother was aware of the painting's value, and that I had no option but to agree to Ramiro's plan. I pushed my cutlery together on my plate, took another gulp of water, and met her gaze.

"Very well, Mom. You'll get your inheritance."

51

San Ángel, May 1953

La Güera's every movement released an intoxicating waft of palo santo. The moment she noticed that someone had entered the room, she stopped dancing and turned off the music. A pink silk shirt was draped over a chair, and she wrapped it around her body.

Nayeli followed the girl's every move with fascination.

"I'm Eva Garmendia," said La Güera, walking over to Nayeli. "I think I know you from somewhere."

"Yes, we've met. It was years ago in San Ángel," replied the Tehuana. She avoided mentioning Diego Rivera, as the housekeeper had warned her.

"Ah, yes. You're Frida's cook, I remember." Her tone was much friendlier than it had been those few years ago. "What brings you here?"

Nayeli held out the doll delicately, as if it were a real child. La Güera tilted her head to one side and frowned.

"Is this a present for me?" she asked, disconcerted.

"No. It's one of the dolls from Frida's collection, but her clothes are very different, and Frida wants a dress just like this, and perhaps some other similar pieces in her size."

La Güera took a step back, without letting go of the doll.

"Did he send you?"

Nayeli knew she was referring to Diego, the man who couldn't be named.

"Yes, he did."

"Come with me," said La Güera and, without waiting for a response, turned on her heel.

They left the house through a back door and crossed another garden, even larger and more beautiful than the one at the front. At the end of a narrow dirt path, there was a small hut with white walls and a red-tiled roof. La Güera had to shove the door with her shoulder to open it.

"Come in," she said with a smile. "What's your name?"

"Nayeli Cruz." She was still clutching Frida's doll against her chest.

The hut was essentially four walls and a roof. The only furniture was a huge wooden table in the center and three large boxes filled with other smaller boxes.

"This was my workshop," said La Güera, hands on her waist and head held high, like the queen of a palace, "but I gave it up some time ago."

Her expression didn't go unnoticed by the Tehuana, who over the years had gotten used to gauging the weight of words.

"Why did you give it up?" she asked.

"Because I got married and I have to meet expectations."

"Whose expectations?"

La Güera regarded her with annoyance. She wasn't used to being questioned.

"All right, let's get to work," she said, ignoring Nayeli and adopting that lofty tone that suited her so well.

Nayeli placed the doll on the table as La Güera rummaged in a box before pulling out a notebook and a gabardine bag full of drawing charcoal and a sewing kit.

"Let's see," she murmured, scrutinizing the wool flannel garment closely. "This fabric is rather low quality; I can find something much better to achieve an elegant drape. And these buttons are plastic. We'll have to find some that are real mother-of-pearl. And I'll need La Kahlo's measurements."

The Tehuana was surprised. She had never heard anyone refer to Frida as "La Kahlo."

"Her body is more or less the same size as mine. She might be a little shorter . . . Besides, she's very thin from her illness," she replied.

"She's ill? What's wrong with her?" asked La Güera.

"All kinds of things. Her spine won't support her anymore. She's had several operations, and the wounds got infected. And she's also sad. Very sad."

"That's the most serious affliction of all," replied La Güera, wrapping a homemade measuring tape around Nayeli's waist, torso, and hips. "Because there's no cure for sadness."

She spoke as if she were an expert, as though sadness were a tourist attraction she visited regularly.

At the bottom of one of the boxes were some thin sheets of translucent paper that the young woman had hoarded. She spread them out over the table and used a piece of charcoal to sketch a human body.

"This is a fashion sketch, the start of the creative process," explained La Güera, brimming with enthusiasm. "From this sketch, a whole beautiful world opens up. I'll make this design to scale, in real size, and then using the paper, I'll cut the fabric for La Kahlo's dress. What do you think?"

"It's beautiful. You draw very well. Did you learn at San Ángel?" asked Nayeli, although she already knew the answer.

"Yes, I learned all the good stuff at San Ángel," replied La Güera with a sigh.

Eva Garmendia had been born with her destiny marked out, an elite destiny.

"But I was raised to be a wife and mother. We Mexican women are mothers first and foremost; more so than any other women in the world, we are born with that gift," she said, caressing her flat belly. "The best school for a child is the home, and the best teachers, mothers."

"Only rich women can think that way," replied Nayeli, surprised at her own boldness.

"I'm rich, I was born rich. But I would have loved to be a woman who doesn't have any expectations. In my social class, women are divided into three groups: single, married, and widowed. The opportunities each of us has depend on the group we belong to."

"And you are part of the married group?"

"Yes, I'm married. My husband is Argentinean, but he's lived here in Mexico since he was a boy. His father is Argentinean, too, and a very important diplomat. And I'm not complaining—he's a good man and he gives me everything I could possibly want, except the thing I'm passionate about."

"What's that?" asked Nayeli.

"This, here," she replied, tilting her head toward her work. "My dream is to be a fashion designer. To dream up suits, dresses, and hats. To create them on paper and then on fabric, and finally on women's bodies. But it isn't a job for someone of my class."

"Do you have children?"

"Not yet," she replied, and artfully changed the subject. "The sketch is finished now. I think two days of sewing should be enough and La Kahlo will have her dress."

Since they were starting to warm to each other, Nayeli dared to probe a little further.

"Why do you call her La Kahlo? I've never heard anyone else call Frida that."

La Güera folded away the paper patterns and smiled.

"It's such an old story, I almost feel like it was someone else instead of me."

"I want to know—I like stories," insisted Nayeli.

"When I turned eighteen, I thought life would finally open up before my eyes. My parents decided that there was no need for me to go to college. I was fine with that. I didn't want to study or bury my head in books. I just wanted to draw outfits and turn those drawings into reality. Back then, my father often traveled to the United States, and my mother was left in charge of the house." La Güera fell silent for a moment. "She thought it would be good for me to take drawing classes to perfect my technique. A friend of my mother recommended I go to the studio in San Ángel—"

"Why do you never call Diego by his name?" interrupted Nayeli.

"Because that name is cursed. But we're talking about La Kahlo, not that man."

Nayeli nodded and bit her lower lip to remind herself that if she wanted to hear the story she mustn't interrupt.

"So, following the tip from my mother's friend, I went to San Ángel. I spent many afternoons on the top floor of the blue side of the building. Hours and hours. Time slipped through my fingers. Just me and my charcoals, my rolls of fabric, and my papers. I was happy, until Rivera ruined everything." La Güera whispered his name as though scared of being heard.

"What happened?"

"We had arranged to meet outside my usual class time. One Saturday morning, I showed up as he had instructed: hair loose, no makeup, and dressed in white." She gave a slight smile, as though it was a good memory in spite of everything. "When I got there, the studio was all set up. Rivera had cleared the entire first floor and prepared a huge clean, white canvas. I felt important, flattered."

"Perhaps you were," murmured Nayeli.

La Güera shook her head. Time had allowed her to realize that the only things that mattered to Diego Rivera were Diego Rivera and his art. Nothing and no one else.

"We took a long time to find a pose that would allow every part of my body to be portrayed perfectly. Finally, we agreed that I would perch on a stool and stretch out my legs. The hardest thing was keeping my arms raised. He only allowed me to rest when he had finished the sketch. The drawing was perfect. It looked more like a photograph than a drawing. Even my legs and hips looked fuller. He never liked how skinny I was."

She lowered her arms, and her eyes roved around the little studio. Nayeli waited, expectantly.

"Rivera never finished the work."

"Why not?"

"Because my father almost killed him. With his driver and a guard in tow, he went to San Ángel and burst in, shouting. My father yelled that I was a whore, while the guard kicked over the cans of paint, and the driver ripped the canvas from the easel and broke it into pieces. My father dragged me by the arm to the door and, before we left, ordered them to give Rivera a beating. According to him, it was the only way to ensure he didn't come near me again, but the driver was his salvation."

"The driver?" asked Nayeli, enthralled.

"Yes, the driver. He refused to touch Rivera and said that he couldn't lay a finger on Diego, because wounding him meant wounding La Kahlo. And he couldn't do La Kahlo any harm. He explained who Frida was and that it was thanks to her that his family had always had food on the table."

Nayeli stood up in one swift movement. She knew that man.

"Manuel Salinas!" she exclaimed. La Güera nodded. "His daughter Guadalupita was Frida's pupil, one of the girls who worked on the mural at La Rosita pulque shop. Frida used to send the Salinas family a bag of food every month; they were humble folk."

"Yes, and very grateful, too. Don Salinas risked his job out of loyalty to La Kahlo. My father had to back down, but that didn't prevent him from telling Salinas to give Frida a warning."

"Did he threaten her?"

"He threatened Rivera, through her. It was very clear." La Güera frowned and imitated her father's deep voice: "'Listen here, Don Salinas. Tell La Kahlo that if Rivera goes anywhere near my daughter again, I won't leave a bone unbroken.'"

"And what did Diego do?"

La Güera laughed sadly.

"Nothing, as far as I know. But I'm sure Don Salinas passed on the message to Frida, because from that moment on I never heard from him again."

Beware of La Güera, Diego; Nayeli remembered that slip of paper that, years earlier, had led her and Joselito to the Garmendia mansion. They had been mistaken to believe that Diego and the young woman had had an affair. That slip of paper was no less than the warning Don Salinas had brought to Frida's ears.

"And I feel like I owe Frida a lot," she concluded.

"I owe her a lot, too," said Nayeli.

With a tenderness that was unusual in her, La Güera came over and took the Tehuana's hands in hers. Nayeli Cruz's green eyes melted into Eva Garmendia's blue gaze. Their destinies had unquestionably crossed paths.

52

Buenos Aires, January 2019

Before leaving the house, Cristóbal checked the distance on the map on his phone and decided to walk. It was several blocks to his destination, far enough to assuage the fury that was eating away at him. Walking had always been a balm in troubled times. When his mother did nothing but dote on little Ramiro, he walked; when his father got that special gleam in his eye on being presented with one of his younger brother's drawings, he walked; when, as a teenager, the few girls who had caught his attention wangled invitations to the Pallares house just to catch Ramiro's eye, he walked. And later, in prison, pacing in loops like a deranged man around the prison yard had saved him from many a beating.

As night started to fall, Avenida Rivadavia changed its appearance: the commercial hot spot packed with stores of all kinds and shoppers weighed down with bags turned into an alleyway of closed shutters and trash piled on the sidewalks.

His firm stride and the humid heat of summer in the port city overpowered him. The sweat formed damp patches under his arms and on the back of his T-shirt. Over and again, he used the back of his hand to wipe away the droplets running down his forehead, but at no point did he slow his pace. Hatred was driving him forward. He had no interest in

Lorena Funes's plans to recover the Diego Rivera. He was tired of waiting on his father's elegant and diplomatic comings and goings, but above all, he was tired of Lorena.

He had artfully hidden the pain and disgust that engulfed him that afternoon in the museum when his father had let slip that Cristóbal's lover was also sleeping with his brother. He wasn't surprised; he was used to taking second place when it came to Rama. But that was the straw that broke the camel's back, the damning detail that propelled him into action. He went for nights without sleeping, turning the matter over in his mind; deep down, he knew what he had to do. His only fear was returning to prison. Regardless, he was determined to handle this in his own way. Neither Lorena nor his father could fake the work; without him, they were both lost.

The little house he was looking for was lit up by a small lamp hanging from the top of the doorframe. The rest of the block lay in darkness. He hid behind a dumpster opposite the entrance and focused with all his senses. There was no way of telling whether there was anyone at home. The only window overlooking the street had the shutters closed. He breathed deeply to lower his pulse rate and brought a hand to his waistline. The .22-caliber gun was right where he wanted it, between the leather belt and his back. He felt calmer. Nothing was more reassuring than the touch of a loaded weapon against his skin.

He was sure that this was where he would find some answers about a certain Paloma Cruz.

53

Coyoacán, August 1953

"Frida's death is quite near. I think that honors should be given to people while they are still alive to enjoy them, not when they are dead." These were the words with which Clara Lucero announced the start of a marathon task: organizing an exhibition of Frida Kahlo's work in the Galería de Arte Contemporáneo. Frida's first show in Mexico. Her intimate circle, fellow artists, the press, the public, and Diego thought it a great idea and came on board with enthusiasm. But for days, the gallerist's words echoed around Nayeli's head: "*Frida's death is quite near.*"

Although she was getting thinner and thinner, her skin such an odd shade that even she, the mistress of colors, couldn't define it, her hair falling out in clumps, and her pain more excruciating than ever, Frida was undeniably excited about the plan to show her paintings. The first thing she did was to order colored cardboard, pencils, dried flowers, and ribbon; she had decided that the invitations must bear her own unique stamp. No one questioned her, and a tribe of assistants surrounded the bed that she no longer left; they settled her between pillows as though she were a doll, trying to keep her spine straight, and placed a wooden board on her legs so that she could write out the invitations in her perfect, rounded hand:

With friendship and love
born from the heart,
I have the pleasure of inviting you
to my humble exhibition.

In the next paragraph, she added the time and date, then decorated each one with tiny drawings of flowers and skulls.

The morning of the opening, Frida awoke feverish. The pain in her back had kept her up all night, and, although they administered more sedatives than usual, the stabbing pain in her hip wouldn't ease. Casa Azul was a hive of people coming and going; everyone felt it would be imprudent to take Frida to the art gallery in this state, but no one dared say it out loud. As always, Diego was the disruptive element. He strode into the room and, hands on his broad hips, boomed, "My little dove, are you well enough to go to your show? Tell me the truth, now."

"I never lie to you," replied Frida, dulled by her medicines.

"So tell me."

"Of course I'll go. I'm always well enough for everything."

"Say no more, Friducha. I'll take care of it." Diego glanced at Nayeli, who was perched at the end of the bed rinsing cotton cloths in a pot of water. "You, Nayelita, have you got what I asked for?"

"Of course, Diego," replied the cook with a mischievous grin.

She left the pot on the floor and ran to her room to get what Diego had requested. Back in Frida's room within minutes, she found Frida leaning on Diego's chest; she was using her man's robust body to prop herself up.

"What's that, my ballerina?" she asked in a weak voice. Her exhaustion was voracious, the illness eating her up in front of everyone.

Nayeli opened up the package and unfolded a Tehuana outfit, the most beautiful she had seen in her life. Frida's agonized eyes suddenly began to gleam. The skirt was the whitest of silks, embroidered with red and green thread; the band of gemstones emulated the Mexican flag, and the huipil was the blood-red color that Frida adored.

"It's an exclusive design, made just for you. So that you're the most

Tehuana and the most Mexican in all of Mexico!" exclaimed Nayeli. "No one will ever have a gala dress as delicate and luxurious as this. It's what you deserve, the very best."

Nayeli didn't tell her the best part of the story. Frida's joyful clapping as Diego helped her put on the outfit was worth the moral weight of the secret. Eva "La Güera" Garmendia had agreed that her name should remain hidden and insisted that no one should know that it had been her idea to design a special outfit for Frida. She had practiced repeatedly on yards of silks, flannels, and cottons, in the painter's exact size. After the first green dress with mother-of-pearl buttons, Frida had wanted more; Nayeli asked for more, and Eva made more. A perfect, clandestine team had come into operation. That first green dress had become the cornerstone of the hidden friendship between Nayeli and Eva. To seal the pact of silence, La Güera had made three exact copies of the garment: one for her, another for Nayeli, and the third for the painter.

After dressing Frida in her new clothes, Diego also selected the finest jewelry from her collection: a jade necklace, the bird-shaped earrings, and three gold rings he had bought with his first paycheck from the United States. After sprucing her up, he planted his huge, round body in the middle of the Casa Azul courtyard, removed his hat, and acted as the master of ceremonies in Frida's life:

"Ladies and gentlemen, the masterful artist Frida Kahlo will attend the opening of her exhibition. Do what you need to do to get her there."

The ambulance pulled up at the door of the Galería de Arte Contemporáneo. A group of journalists, artists, and guests was waiting for Frida, crowding onto the sidewalk. No one wanted to miss the slightest detail. There had been much speculation around the painter's health, but in Coyoacán it was hard to know what was the truth, what was a lie, and where to find the boundary between the two. A nurse opened the back doors of the vehicle and, helped by Diego, lowered the stretcher carrying Frida. She had been the one to make the decision, some hours earlier: "If I can't stand up, then I'll go lying down," she'd declared. And that is exactly what she did.

Inside, her four-poster bed with its wooden canopy and mirror stood in the center of the room. Nayeli had put on Frida's favorite sheets, in a very light blue linen that made her feel like she was lying in the sky. As the nurses lifted Frida from the stretcher, the Tehuana arranged the pillows and straightened the photos the painter had stuck to the wooden headboard: one of her father and mother, another of her sisters, one of her and Diego walking around San Ángel, and portraits of her top three politicians: Lenin, Stalin, and Mao Tse-Tung.

"There's some perfume in my bag, Nayelita," she said, as soon as she was settled in the bed and Clara Lucero had spread out the Tehuana skirt so that everyone could admire the exquisite embroidery.

Nayeli took the lid off the bottle and sprinkled the fragrance on Frida's chest and neck. With the last few drops, she scented the pillows, too.

"It's finished," she said, holding up the empty bottle of Shocking de Schiaparelli for the painter to see.

"You can keep the bottle—it's beautiful."

When the gallery doors were flung open, the public took turns filing in past the foot of the bed; everyone wanted to greet Frida. She made a brave attempt to do what she wanted more than anything in life: to please.

The constant procession lasted almost two hours, until Clara Lucero shouted for everyone to be quiet. The artist wanted to say a few words. The audience, who usually acted with intellectual and elitist rebellion, responded obediently to the request, and the silence was instantaneous. Frida smiled with her mouth only. Her eyes looked glazed and lost. It was clear that her cheer cost her some effort.

"Many thanks for accepting my invitation. I want you to leave here with a truth from my own lips," she said with a clarity that was surprising, given her state. "I'm not sick. I'm destroyed, but I'm happy to live as long as I can keep painting."

The applause was deafening. Nayeli and Diego exchanged a long, intense look. Both knew what was going to happen in a matter of hours, and Frida knew it, too.

After the art show, she managed to sleep for five hours, without interruption. Recognition of her work was the best pain relief. Before closing her eyes, a cascade of emotions spilled from her mouth. She was excited and happy, and she didn't say a word about the operation she was about to undergo.

The hospital welcomed her, as ever, with open arms. Everyone loved that fragile-looking little woman whose spark and drive to live were hard as steel.

"I will be Frida, peg-legged, the lame woman of the city of coyotes!" she exclaimed moments before entering the operating room.

No one dared oppose her decision to undergo surgery wearing her new Tehuana clothes. She liked them so much she didn't want to take them off. Grudgingly, she agreed to remove her jewelry, with the promise that it would be returned the moment the anesthesia wore off.

"What's wrong with you?" she asked, haughtily. Diego and Nayeli looked at her pityingly from the edge of the stretcher taking her into the operating room. "You look like it's a tragedy. They're going to cut off my foot, so what?"

Neither Diego nor Nayeli could open their mouths, limiting themselves to a forced, but loyal smile. The conversation was cut short by the doctor in charge.

"Very good, Señora Kahlo. I promise we'll do it as quickly as possible, and I'll see to it personally that you don't experience any kind of pain," he said, levelheadedly.

The painter twisted her neck to see him in full. She looked him up and down, flirtatiously.

"I have wings to spare, Doctor. Cut off my foot, and I'll fly."

54

Buenos Aires, January 2019

Ramiro was engrossed in his work. After trying, unsuccessfully, to get him to eat, I decided to slice up some fruit and leave it within his reach. But he took no more than a couple of bites, instead drinking glass after glass of water with lemon and ice. And muscle relaxants every four hours, to ease his back.

Lunch with my mother had been a turning point. I knew there was no going back and that the only way to achieve what I wanted was to climb out of the pit I had dug myself into, just as my grandmother had taught me. I was determined to keep the painting and to return her ashes to the blue paradise. I was going to fulfill Nayeli's final wish.

Ramiro was adamant that Lorena Funes and Emilio Pallares must be behind my mother's sudden obsession with her inheritance. He explained that Martiniano Mendía was so voracious that they would employ whatever devious tricks they could think of to get the painting to Montevideo as soon as possible. Felipa was crucial to their obtaining what they didn't have.

"It's a masterstroke, and absolutely Lorena's style. I know her well," he said.

Ramiro's plan sounded perfect: produce a forgery of the painting, give it to my mother as the genuine piece, which she would then sell to Lorena and Emilio, who, in turn, would take that Trojan horse to Montevideo.

As I followed the movements of Rama's right hand, captivated, I kept replaying our conversation, the one during which we became accomplices as well as lovers.

"Won't this Martiniano Mendía realize the work is a fake?" I'd asked, logically. According to Rama, he was a keen connoisseur of Rivera and Kahlo.

"I'm pretty sure he won't notice. Initially, at any rate, and when he does realize, it'll be too late," he'd replied calmly. "His house in Montevideo is full of artworks of all kinds: sculptures, dinner services, paintings, jewelry. There was something that caught my attention, though, and it supports my theory."

"What was it?" I asked impatiently. Rama's unhurried explanation was driving me crazy.

"One painting in particular, a very small, delicate one, it's called *The Archaic Rose*." He took his phone from his pocket, tapped the screen, and held it out to me. "Look, I took a photo. What do you see?"

"I see a beautiful flower, fragile but lush."

"This little canvas disappeared from the art circuit years ago," explained Rama. "The artist was an Englishwoman called Rose Pitels. The paintings aren't particularly valuable on their own, but in the nineties, there was a big hunt for the Pitels roses, collectors looking for the complete set. No one knew how many there were in total, but anyone who had more than five roses had a small fortune in their possession. Martiniano Mendía has eight roses, but the one I photographed isn't a Pitels, even if it looks like one."

I inspected the photo again.

Ramiro smiled and continued. "In the lower right-hand corner, at the tip of one of the petals, there is a sign, imperceptible to most people, except for me. I couldn't miss it. It's the mark my brother, Cristóbal, adds to all his forgeries. Even the best forgers in the business can succumb to the temptation of putting their own stamp on a work. Mendía must have been so desperate to have the full set of Pitels roses that his expert eye deceived him."

"We all believe what we want to believe," I thought out loud.

"That's right, and Mendía, despite appearances, is as mundane as the next person, and we're going to make him believe what he wants to believe . . . "

"That he's bought an original Rivera-Kahlo," I concluded.

"There's no margin for error here," he said, in the tone of a soldier leaving for war. "First, I'm going to analyze the original painting closely; I have to decode every step and repeat it all meticulously."

I helped him stretch out the work over a display easel and, from that moment on, Ramiro Pallares disappeared. His body was still in the studio, but his mind was somewhere else. It took him twenty-four hours to examine the original. Meanwhile, I had a task even more arduous than forging a Diego Rivera or copying the ceiling of the Sistine Chapel: dealing with my mother.

Ramiro and I needed time, and that was just what Felipa didn't want us to have. She called several times a day, trying out different tones of voice: sweet and sugary, dry and cutting, anxious and childlike, furious and demanding. Sometimes, she used all these approaches in the same call. She wanted her "inheritance," she reiterated. And I wasn't being honest with her, not for the first time, admittedly, but this time with no guilt and perhaps even a touch of satisfaction: "*Mom, I'm not in Buenos Aires. I've come to Salta with some friends—I needed a break, and I have to make the most of the school vacations.*" It was very liberating to no longer be the instrument of her desires. But she didn't believe me, not entirely anyway. Her only response was to murmur a lukewarm "*How convenient*," which at any other time would have caused me to panic. No one would want to arouse Felipa's suspicions.

Ramiro's work was progressing, slowly but surely. I was hypnotized watching the yellowish canvas fill with brushstrokes, so close to the original strokes it made my blood run cold. Meanwhile, I had become an automaton orbiting around that being possessed by the spirit of another age and another country.

One of those nights, exhausted from watching him, I fell asleep without realizing it. I was awoken by Ramiro's damp hand on my forehead.

"Paloma, I think we're nearly there," he murmured, before giving me a swift but gentle kiss on the lips.

I startled, feeling a rush of enthusiasm mixed with nerves and urgency. This must be what thieves feel like when they find the loot. And my grandmother's painting was quite some loot.

Ramiro took me by the hand and led me to the living room. We walked down the hall in short, slow steps, both unconsciously trying to delay the moment when we came face-to-face with the almost-finished forgery. For my part, through fear of noticing imperfections; for him, for fear of my gaze.

When we reached the living room, he released my hand and left me alone to stand in front of the two easels. One held the original, my painting; the other, the fake, my mother's. The cool from the air-conditioning blasted against the heat of my skin. My blood was boiling. It was all I could do not to throw myself on the ground and curl up in fetal position, like a scared child.

The two works were identical. I knew which one was the original only because the fake was still missing Frida's red ballerina. Not even Ramiro's hand on my shoulder could lessen the shock of seeing my grandmother's image in duplicate. Two Nayelis, naked, bending over. Two Nayelis with long, wavy hair. Two Nayelis with magic marks on their thighs. Two erotic Nayelis.

This man waiting for me to comment on his work had magically duplicated my grandmother. I found that possibility almost disturbing and, for a second, I fantasized about the idea of his fabricating a living grandmother identical to the one I had lost. I started to cry. Every part of my body cried at once, in a cascade, and Ramiro's embrace could barely contain the deluge. I didn't have to open my mouth. My reaction gave him all the answer he needed: his forgery was perfect.

"All I need to do now is the red stain," he murmured, his lips against my forehead.

"The ballerina," I corrected.

"The ballerina," he conceded.

We moved apart and held hands again, standing like stone in front of the two Nayelis. Ramiro's hand was freezing. He was afraid, I knew it. To achieve Frida's intensity would take much more than talent. He needed fury, hatred, and pain.

55

Coyoacán, August 1953

Nayeli washed the beans in cold, fresh water, so that not a single speck of dirt remained, then chopped the onion and garlic, her eyes smarting with tears that allowed her to momentarily release her fears: they were operating on Frida. The doctor had sent them home to rest awhile. The operation would take hours, and, when Frida came around from the anesthesia, she wouldn't be allowed visitors.

The aroma of garlic, onion, and tomatoes sizzling in oil calmed her. For Nayeli, cooking was like opening a door to her childhood. When the sauce thickened, she added water, cilantro, salt, and finally the gleaming beans. All she had to do now was wait for them to soften. It was just a matter of time, like everything in life.

She went into Frida's room. The air still held the intense scent of Shocking de Schiaparelli. The beautiful bottle she'd given Nayeli was already stored away in the bottom of the basket where she hoarded her treasured possessions.

The bed was slightly askew, so she shoved it back against the wall, then smoothed out the blue sheets and tucked them in tightly beneath. Her fingers bumped into a hard object, hidden between the mattress and the springs. It was the red diary, from which Frida was never separated. Nayeli sat on the floor with her legs crossed. Although she knew that the diary was a faithful copy of the painter's inner world and that people's inner worlds should be private, she couldn't help but take a peek. Guiltily, but with no regret, she flicked through its pages.

She was shocked by a drawing of a naked woman with a dove's head and wings instead of arms, occupying an entire page. Frida had drawn herself again, but in a much crueler depiction than usual. The spine was replaced by a cracked tube and the right leg was artificial. Nayeli turned the page; she couldn't look at the picture any longer.

She concentrated on Frida's writing, breathing deeply and straightening her back. Reading was still a struggle for Nayeli, and it almost always made her eyes hurt.

I am very worried, but at the same time I feel that it will be a liberation. I hope I will be able, when I am walking, to give all the strength that I have left to Diego. Everything for Diego.

Frida was deceiving everyone, thought Nayeli, except for herself. Although she loved to regale friends and admirers with tales of her sexual adventures, and always kept Alejandro, her first boyfriend, at the tip of her tongue, she still loved Diego. He was her world and the one who turned her insides to lava.

She tried to find some correlation between what Frida felt for Diego and the relationship between her and Joselito. She couldn't find any points in common. Nayeli would exchange Joselito for a journey to Tehuantepec, for example; Frida wouldn't exchange Diego for anything. Diego was her journey, even if that journey almost always failed. But the painter didn't care; love seemed to be a good reason for everything to fail.

She stretched out her legs and leaned back against the bed. The floor was cool, contrasting pleasantly with the suffocating heat of Casa Azul. She squeezed Frida's diary against her chest, still thinking about Joselito, who had recently proposed to her.

"I want you to be my wife and the mother of my children," he'd said, simply summing up both their futures. Nayeli had given the kind of vague response people tend to give to embarrassing questions: she smiled and hugged him. Nothing else. Joselito took it as a yes and from that moment started to work overtime; his goal was to save money for the wedding.

It had been Eva who'd spelled it out in black-and-white. "It's quite simple, Nayeli. When it comes to Joselito, all you have to do is ask yourself whether or not you want to be the one responsible for his heart. The rest doesn't matter."

For months she tried to answer La Güera's question. She hadn't managed until that morning, at the exact moment when Frida entered the operating room to come out with one body part less. She kissed the cover of the red diary and set it down on the pillows. Frida would be happy to find it there waiting for her: she believed that her belongings had lives and feelings of their own.

The aroma of bean soup had flooded the whole house, a sure sign that it was ready. Food is clever like that: it communicates with us through smell before taste.

Diego was in the kitchen standing by the stove, dunking a piece of bread into the pot. He jumped when he saw Nayeli, and lowered his gaze, placed his hands on his chest, and apologized like a naughty child.

Nayeli served the soup in two large bowls and added a glug of olive oil and a sprinkle of paprika to each one.

"Diego, I'm going to marry Joselito," announced Nayeli without hesitation.

"That's great news!" exclaimed Diego, tugging the napkin from his collar and wiping his mouth. "You kept that quiet, Tehuana. Does Frida know yet?"

"No, I'm waiting for the right moment to tell her."

Diego nodded thoughtfully. He knew this young woman was a vital support for Frida, and the possibility of Nayeli leaving Casa Azul would be calamitous to his wife's state of mind.

"I have a wonderful idea. What if you got married and both of you came to live here with Frida? She loves Joselito, and you're like a daughter to her—you know that. There's more than enough room for everyone at Casa Azul."

Before replying, Nayeli took three heaping spoonfuls of soup. It seemed like a good idea, but, like everything that came out of Diego's head, there was always a double intention, and she preferred not to rush her response.

"We'll see, Diego." To change the subject, she stood up and cleared away the empty soup bowls. "Would you like some fruit or a pastry?"

"No, thank you very much. You should rest. I have plans this afternoon in San Ángel. The doctors said they would call here or at the studio as soon as the operation is done."

"That's fine. I'll fill a basket with brushes and sketchbooks so that Frida can entertain herself in the hospital," she said, leaving the painter alone in the kitchen.

Diego lowered his eyes, as he always did when some dark thought crossed his mind. He leaned forward, his head sinking between his shoulders, and sat still, waiting for the storm in his mind to blow over. He was sure that his sense of foreboding was prophetic, a premonition that Frida would never paint again. And for her, not being able to paint was the same as dying.

Nayeli returned with Frida's basket dangling from one shoulder. She tiptoed up to Diego silently, afraid of rousing him from his thoughts too abruptly.

"Thanks," he said, grabbing the basket.

Minutes later, Nayeli heard him closing the front door on his way out. Her hearing sharpened. The only sound was birdsong and, in the distance, the shouts of the traders selling their wares in Coyoacán market. She couldn't recall the last time she had been alone in the house or indeed whether she ever had been.

The heat in Casa Azul was becoming oppressive. There wasn't the slightest breeze. Even the walls and windows were warm. The sun scorched the soil in the garden. She felt a sudden urge to swim naked in the River Tehuantepec, an urge she hadn't felt since childhood.

Nayeli took off her skirt and huipil. Her underwear was soaked with sweat. She removed that, too.

She leaned her forehead against the mirror in her room, hoping that the cool of the glass would sink into her pores. It didn't work.

Her red diary was on the desk, the treasured twin of Frida's diary, and on top of it, the red lipstick that Marivé had given her years earlier. She had never used it, but a sudden curiosity prompted her to try it out. Furtively, as though committing a crime, she colored her lips a blood red. She smiled at the mirror, her large, white teeth gleaming. She liked what she saw.

The sound of water distracted her. Running, splashing water. Refreshing, soothing water. Cleaning, polishing water. She leaned out of the window and fixed her eyes on the fountain in the courtyard: it was full, almost overflowing. With so much coming and going, no one had thought to turn off the faucets. Still naked, she went down the corridor, spreading her nudity through the house.

The stones in the courtyard were scorching, but she didn't mind. The water was calling her like a spell, and walking on burning stones was part of the charm, the price that had to be paid to reach paradise, the sacrifice that had to be made. The rusty metal toad decorating the fountain spat from its mouth a brilliant stream that spattered onto the colorful tile edges. Drops like crystals, water like stars. River Tehuantepec.

Nayeli dipped her fingers into the bubbles and burst them with gentle taps. One after another, until she could no longer resist. She raised one leg and sank it in to the knee. The stream released by the toad became stronger, splashing her body. Her hips, abdomen, breasts, neck, face. She opened her mouth and stuck out her tongue. She needed to feel the cool liquid through her entire body: lips, palate, throat.

In something like a sexual rush, she climbed all the way into the fountain and submerged herself completely. She held her breath until she was about to suffocate. A pleasant suffocation. She reared up suddenly and filled her lungs with air. She was trembling, howling, and laughing at the same time. Her hair became heavy with water, reaching all the way down her back. All she had on was the birthmark on her right thigh. She closed her eyes and lifted her face to the sun, the heat drying her body in seconds. She laughed again and plunged back into the cool water, before emerging like a siren, rubbing every part of her body. Arms, hips, legs, shoulders, knees. She wanted the water to enter her veins. Tehuana blood, the River Tehuantepec.

The basket Nayeli had prepared was missing violet paint, one of Frida's favorites. Diego Rivera never imagined that returning to Casa Azul to fetch it would present him with one of the most striking images of his life. He strode down the entrance hall, but when he reached the courtyard, his body became riveted to the earth floor. He couldn't recall having seen anything like it before.

The Tehuana, naked in the fountain, was spellbinding. Everything around the bathing girl faded away. Gone were the cacti, the fruit trees, the benches; the scene embodied the hills, green vegetation, flowers, and, above all, the sky of Oaxaca, a sky he had seen only once, but which was etched on his memory.

The fountain was a river, the River Tehuantepec. He had no doubt. He recalled the distant sensations of his trip there. He pictured Mexican nymphs, the most beautiful Tehuana women bathing in waters in a shade of brown he could never re-create with his paintbrushes. They didn't get wet; they took nourishment from the water. They were penetrated, irrigated by it; they merged into it. They were river, water, sky, and sun.

For Diego, painting meant leaving proof, some concrete evidence of existence, and whenever something had such an impact on him, he needed to express it on canvas. For the first time in his life, he managed to go unnoticed, suppressing his usual raucousness as he went inside on light feet. He grabbed an unused canvas and looked around him with a touch of desperation: he couldn't find his palette or brushes, nor the tubes of color. He felt like crying. The opportunity to paint Nayeli was slipping through his fingers. He had no choice but to use one of Frida's palettes. He looked closely at the colors already prepared and wrinkled his nose in resignation. There was no time to lose. He glanced through the window: the girl was still in the fountain.

He retraced his steps on tiptoe and arranged his huge body behind one of the columns. From there, he could see the fountain from a distance, but close enough for his purposes. Nayeli was still lost in her own world. She splashed, plunged, laughed. She shook her hair, unleashing a cataract of cool water that wet her even more. She was agitated, her heart racing, her chest rising and falling at an abnormal rhythm. To recover her breath, she bent over, resting one hand on a knee and the other on a thigh. The curve of her back, the perfection of her buttocks, and her dark, glistening skin under the sun provided just the right highlights and shadows to give Diego's expert eye the perfect image.

"You stay right there, Tehuana. I've got you," he murmured as he made a swift sketch on the canvas. The hardest thing to capture was Nayeli's hair. Her locks were usually wavy, but the weight of the water had straightened them out without making them entirely smooth.

Sweat ran down Diego's forehead and cheeks; even his hands were damp. The self-imposed pressure not to miss a single detail of this wonder made him feel like a novice. Not even before the walls of the National Palace had he felt so intimidated.

When the figure was almost finished, he decided he wouldn't draw the surroundings. Just the water and the Tehuana. It didn't need anything else to be perfect.

He stood watching for a few seconds, frozen, unable to move a muscle. The spell had taken over his entire being. Suddenly, a detail caught his attention. Very carefully, he stepped away from the column that was hiding him and raised a hand to his forehead to block out the sun. He had missed a dark mark on one of Nayeli's thighs. It didn't surprise him that the Tehuana should have her own unique stamp.

He returned to his hiding spot and delicately copied the birthmark into his drawing.

Before long, a black cloud, heavy with rain, obscured the sun. Diego looked skyward and cursed. A humid breeze suddenly sprang up, and the birds all took flight at once.

Nayeli sat for a few seconds on the still-warm tiles. She coiled her hair to wring out the water with her hands. With a deep breath, she lifted her legs out of the fountain one by one, padded across the courtyard, and disappeared into the house.

A long thunderclap made Diego jump. The first large drops of the storm started to fall. The dream was over.

56

Coyoacán, June 1954

Whenever Frida fell asleep, befuddled with drugs, Casa Azul became a tomb. She had left more than just her amputated leg in the hospital; she had also left her laughter, her will to live, her good nature, and even her desire to paint. "If I were brave, I would kill her. I cannot stand to see her suffer so," Diego repeated several times a day, but no one paid any heed. Some believed his words came from the heart; others felt he was merely trying to draw attention back to himself. Frida had been hogging the limelight with her screams, tantrums, and desperation.

Nayeli was one of the few who had stayed close. The number of visitors to Casa Azul was dwindling. Many of them were thrown out by Frida herself, who had lost her graceful manners; others simply didn't want to witness the painter's violent outbursts.

"Nayelita, bring me the case with my pretty dolls, and my scissors, too," she asked one day after a siesta.

The Tehuana obeyed, knowing that the effects of the pain-relieving drugs would soon wear off.

"Here you are," she said, placing the case on Frida's lap. The painter could barely sit up in bed. "Careful with the scissors—they're very sharp."

Frida paid no attention and decisively cut a leg off each doll. On some it was the right leg, on others the left. The scene was Dantesque. A shower of lame dolls and a heap of orphaned legs.

"That's how I like my girls: the same as me. It's a pity dolls have no blood; it would be nice to see other people's amputations all over my bed. That's a powerful image, don't you think?"

An acidic liquid climbed from Nayeli's guts to her tongue. She ran downstairs, pushed open the courtyard door, and vomited on the ground, resting her head against the stone wall. She went to the fountain and took a long drink of water. Then, she cried. Frida wasn't Frida anymore.

The two women who cleaned the house had left their jobs, Diego announced one morning. Nayeli and the nurse knew that the poor women had actually fled in terror. Frida had threatened to beat one with the wooden stick that had once helped her walk, and the other was scared that the torrent of curses spewing from the painter's mouth might come true. There were fewer and fewer people around the bed, fewer hearts to share this great intensity.

The only one able to calm the hurricane was Diego. He would lie in bed with her and tell her fantastical, invented stories of his travels through Europe. He spent hours combing her hair with a hard-bristled brush he had bought her at the market, or he would suggest a thousand ideas for drawings in the hope of reviving her former enthusiasm. He was also the only one Frida allowed to make the most important decision: the point on her back where the nurse would stick the needle full of Demerol to send her into that narcotic limbo that relieved the weight of living. Whenever Diego entered the room, Frida would raise her nightdress, twist her body, and lie face down.

"You choose, mi Diego. You'll find somewhere, I'm sure," she would say.

Diego would closely inspect every inch of a back covered in scars, open wounds, new and old puncture marks, and scabs. It was increasingly difficult to find a healthy expanse of skin in which to insert the needle.

"We have to organize our silver wedding, mi sapo. It isn't far off," insisted Frida as the Demerol flooded her body and gave her some temporary respite.

"Of course, mi paloma," Diego agreed every time.

"A party, I want a huge party. We'll invite all of Coyoacán; no one will be left out," she rambled enthusiastically.

Frida wavered between two states when she wasn't asleep. Either she ranted and shouted angrily, or she had some plan occupying her head. Sometimes they were little plans: some soup, a visitor, or the color she wanted to paint her lips; others were larger: parties, trips, and a gold ring for Diego.

"Nayelita, come here, I have to ask you a favor. But you must keep it secret," she said.

Nayeli settled in next to her on the bed and tenderly stroked her forehead. It was cold.

"Tell me what you need. I'll be as silent as the grave," she said.

"Listen carefully. In my studio, in an empty solvent tin, the yellow one, there's money I've been squirreling away. Take it and get me a gold ring for Diego, something beautiful. I want to give him a gift for our silver wedding."

Before Frida fell into a deep sleep, Nayeli swore she would take care of it. She didn't have the faintest idea where to get a gold ring, but she had every intention of keeping her promise.

She went to the workshop where Joselito worked to bring him a basketful of leftovers from lunch, hoping he would know where to buy a ring.

"Joselito, I have to buy a gold ring," said Nayeli.

The boy shrugged and suggested she ask La Güera; she would doubtless know how to acquire something so luxurious.

"Aren't you going to eat, Nayeli? You haven't had a mouthful," he said.

"No, I don't feel like it. Whatever I put in my stomach I just throw up again. I'm very upset about Frida."

"There isn't long to go. We'll get married, and Frida will be a memory."

Nayeli didn't reply. She hadn't told him about Diego's suggestion. She was sure Joselito would never consider the idea of living at Casa Azul.

She hugged him goodbye; she had a long walk to La Güera's house.

As soon as she arrived at the mansion at the edge of San Ángel, Eva opened the door beaming from ear to ear. She was happier than she'd ever been before, and Nayeli's visit finally gave her the opportunity to share her joy with someone.

"Come in, Nayeli, come in. I have some exciting news," she cried, clapping her hands.

They always met in the little hut at the back of the property, where they drank hot chocolate or ate the candy the Tehuana made. That was where Eva designed her dresses and tried them out on Nayeli, who became her fashion model. It was a friendship based on childhood games played late in life between two women who enjoyed rediscovering those little girls they had never been able to be.

"Go on, then! Tell me, Eva, stop being mysterious!" Nayeli pressed her, as voraciously curious as ever.

"I'm going to live in Argentina," announced La Güera triumphantly.

The Tehuana's green eyes filled with an opaque sheen as she struggled not to cry. She didn't know exactly where Argentina was, but she had a sense that it was far away, much farther than Tehuantepec.

La Güera continued, "I'm leaving. You know that my husband works for the government. He told me the diplomatic ties between Mexico and Argentina are very important, and so they're sending him to live in Buenos Aires for a while—that's the capital, you know."

"And is it very far away? Across the ocean?"

"No, there's no ocean, it's in the very south of America. He told me it's a very big country and very beautiful," explained La Güera.

"If you're happy, then I'm happy," said Nayeli with a lump in her throat. "But goodbyes make me sad. I've never liked them."

Eva changed the subject; there would be plenty of time to talk about her trip before she left.

"Anyway, I've stitched together the dress I designed for your outing with Joselito," she said, lifting a purple cotton garment out of a box.

"What outing, Eva?" asked Nayeli, laughing. Eva liked to invent occasions to justify her designs.

"What does it matter? First you get the dress, and then we'll come up with someplace to wear it. Come here. Take off your clothes, and we'll try this beauty for size."

Nayeli draped her skirt and huipil over the table and, taking care not to snap the threads, put on the half-sewn dress. La Güera's expression puzzled her. Nayeli had never seen her so distraught.

"What's going on, Eva?" she asked.

"I don't understand. I took precise measurements," she murmured as she checked the notes she had written on a pad. "Let me see . . . "

She used her tape to take fresh measurements of Nayeli's chest, waist, and hips. They didn't match with her notes. She came up to her and took the Tehuana by the hands. "Nayeli, how long is it since your last period?" she asked gravely.

Nayeli's cheeks flushed, and bile filled her throat. A few years earlier, Frida had explained all about periods and the care she had to take. She had never spoken about the subject with anyone since. Nayeli thought for a few seconds and realized that it had been some time since she had had to cut up her monthly gauze strips.

"Well, I don't really keep track, Eva, but I think it's been a while . . . well, you know," she replied, terrified.

"Have you had sexual relations with Joselito?"

The natural way La Güera asked such intimate questions gave the Tehuana the confidence she needed.

"Yes, but Joselito swore he knew what he was doing and said not to worry."

"All men say that, and that's when we have to worry most," said La Güera, spitting out her words.

"You think I'm pregnant?"

"I do."

Nayeli burst into tears, overwhelmed by a mix of fear, joy, terror, and shame. She looked at her friend in desperation.

"Don't say anything, Eva. Promise me. I'll work out what I'm going to do, but I need your silence," she begged.

"You have my silence. I swear."

The two girls embraced, sealing a pact of friendship, an embrace so tight it took their breath away.

57

Buenos Aires, January 2019

After several hours and countless failed attempts, Ramiro managed to achieve the exact shade of red he needed for the fake ballerina. He was still nervous, though, not entirely sure how to reproduce the precise intensity of that patch of paint. A patch made for one single purpose: to ruin the work.

"Don't worry, Rama," I told him, sinking my fingers into the hair at the back of his neck. "Perhaps we should leave it for a while and let it all soak in. Go for a stroll, relax, and . . . "

Gently, perhaps so as not to offend me, he twisted his head away from my hand and rubbed his eyes.

"I don't know if I can do it. It's very difficult," he explained. "There's no outline, no method. It's just a stain—"

"A ballerina," I interrupted.

He suddenly looked at me as though I had said something new.

"But what if it isn't a ballerina?" he asked, talking to himself more than to me.

"But it is," I insisted.

He went to the built-in bookcase on one of the studio walls, each shelf crammed with art books. Ramiro ran his finger down some of the spines, then selected five and sat on the floor with his legs crossed. I sat beside him.

"These volumes show various examples of Frida Kahlo's work," he said in the gentle but firm tone of a teacher. "You can see that her paintings are figurative. A sun is a sun. Fruits are fruits and human figures are human figures. Frida used objects to re-create themes from her imagination, her dreams, her fantasies. She had the gift of saying a lot in a very simple image—for example, an apple. She didn't just slap down the paint at random. Her work is very planned, very intelligent."

"I don't understand," I murmured.

"I don't think this stain, or ballerina, as you like to call it, is the result of a plan or an artistic strategy. I think it was a splotch of paint first, and then a ballerina."

"So Frida didn't plan to paint a ballerina . . . "

"No. I'm sure of it."

"And that makes your job even harder?" I asked, fearing what his response might be.

"Yes, much harder, because there's no way of knowing what her intention was before she drew it. I can't find the meaning in it."

"None of this has any meaning," I said, defeated.

Ramiro pulled me toward him. We sat for a long while on the floor, leaning against the bookcase, with my head on his shoulder.

I excused myself to go to the bathroom, and when I returned, Ramiro was agitated. He had taken the original painting from the stand and was hurriedly rolling it up.

"Paloma, don't just stand there!" he cried, to my astonishment. "Bring the red tube from the bedroom. Quickly, come on!"

I had no time to figure out what was happening. His words were so urgent I had no choice but to blindly obey.

He grabbed the tube from me and placed a hand on my shoulder.

"What the hell is going on?" I asked, half annoyed, half scared.

"Listen carefully to what I'm about to say. Look at me and don't do anything other than what I tell you."

I gave a slight nod and listened. I decided to trust him.

58

Coyoacán, June 1954

Fury, hatred, and pain had achieved something that nothing and no one else had: they got Frida to stand. She planted her stick firmly on the floor, and, with an energy summoned from the very depths of her being, she prized her body out of the wheelchair. One step, two steps, three steps. The stick stood in for her missing leg, but Frida still had to pause to recover her breath and her balance. She repeated this four times, until she reached her destination.

The old easel Diego kept in his small room at Casa Azul was standing in the middle, between the bed and the wall. Since he had moved his studio to San Ángel, it had remained empty, no more than a wooden skeleton. What had caught Frida's attention and prompted her to enter the room was a painted canvas now resting on that easel, stretched out on a frame. She moved so close that the smell of the paint made her sneeze. She didn't care. She almost wished the vapor were poisoned so that she could drop dead right there on the floor.

The image of Nayeli's body in the water took her breath away. The eroticism, the nudity, the extravagant beauty, the mane of hair, the breasts, the hips—the whole thing was overwhelming. Diego's urgent lines revealed his feelings for that woman, the Tehuana, her Tehuana, her ballerina. She had told her a thousand times. She warned her that letting

Diego paint her didn't just mean giving her body to his art. It meant giving her body to his body. And Nayeli hadn't listened.

Putting her weight on the arm that held the stick, she stretched out her free hand. With her fingertip, she caressed the woman's stomach, Nayeli's stomach. She closed her eyes and let the tears bathe her cheeks, lips, and neck. The images of Nayeli pregnant; the moment when she announced that she and Joselito were having a baby; her hand on the incipient belly, the belly that held a little girl, because Frida was convinced she would give birth to a girl. And now here she was, right before her eyes. Naked with betrayal and lies.

Frida took a step back, two steps, three steps. When she was next to the closet where Diego kept his work overalls, she followed an impulse and opened the door. In the dim light, she managed to make out a silvery can of paint at the bottom. She leaned against the doorframe and gradually slid down. The pressure of her hip against a lower vertebrae sent out a lash of electricity that paralyzed her. She could have called out for help, but she didn't. She resisted the pain, as she had so many times before. Resistance was in her nature.

After taking a few minutes to recover, she stretched out and almost howled with joy when she managed to grab hold of the can.

One step, two steps, three steps, and she was back in front of Nayeli—dishonest, licentious, shameless Nayeli. She used her teeth to rip the plastic lid off the can. The paint was red. Like blood, the uterus, the guts, like betrayal. She drew back her arm and, with a deep sigh of fury and pain and the impetuousness that only an authentic Frida Kahlo could manage, flung the can against the painting.

A stifled cry, a laugh, a crazed guffaw, she watched with fascination as the bulging red drops slipped down the canvas, down the legs of the easel until they hit the floor in little explosions of chaos. She hadn't thrown the can hard enough to hit the painting right in the middle, and the red stain covered only the bottom corner. Nayeli was half covered, half on show. Frida furrowed her brow. "It doesn't work, this painting doesn't work," she murmured.

Her expert eye could always detect the flaws. She had always seen herself as a mechanic who sniffed out which screw was misplaced and jamming, overheating, or simply stopping the machine from working. In this case, the defective part was the red stain that she felt sure was missing something.

One step, two steps, three steps. A deep breath and a moment of rest. The arm holding the stick and the weight of her body had started to cramp up. She didn't care. She was nearly there. Very nearly. She stretched out her free hand and tucked the thumb and index finger against the palm. The three remaining fingers were all she needed. She closed her eyes and forced her memory to rewind through an entire life, to the moment when the ballerina, her invisible friend, had entered through the door Frida's tiny finger had drawn on the window pane. As she shaped the stain with her fingers, she talked to herself: "My imaginary friend was always waiting for me. She was happy, she laughed a lot, and she danced as if she weighed nothing at all. And I followed her and told her my secret problems, and she danced and danced and danced."

It took just minutes for her to achieve what she wanted, accustomed as she was to laying bare her imagination on paper. Without taking her eyes off the ballerina, she wiped her hand on her skirt and smiled, feeling calmer.

One step, two steps, three steps. She collapsed into her wheelchair and, without wasting a second, left Diego's room to shut herself away in her own.

From the kitchen, Nayeli could hear the creak of Frida's wheels. *Time for a bit of oil*, she thought. She plunged a linen cloth into her large pot of oil. Gentle, perfumed, golden, capricious: she liked oil.

As she crossed the house, the red stains on the floor led her to Diego's room, her blood running cold. She went up to the easel and saw it. It was her, no doubt about it. She didn't recall having been naked in any river, but she did remember the pleasure of the fountain, the cool water on her skin. She placed her hands on her belly and knew that her time at Casa Azul had come to an end.

59

Buenos Aires, January 2019

Ramiro would never know what strange impulse made him go out to the balcony overlooking Recoleta cemetery.

By night, the only light in the graveyard was the reflection of the sidewalk opposite. Bars, restaurants, hotels, and two ice cream parlors gave the street a meaning that no one could fail to notice: one side for the living, the other for the dead.

A figure leaning against a trash can at the cemetery gate caught Ramiro's attention. He put on his glasses, and, despite the distance, he was certain: it was his brother, Cristóbal. He would recognize his coarse malevolence anywhere.

He stood watching him, seized by a mixture of anxiety and fury, but also a strange, unexpected affection that had never quite disappeared, despite the knowledge that, behind the social façade of brotherhood, there was nothing between them.

Cristóbal was looking straight at him. Ramiro raised a hand briefly.

He went back into the room, then closed the balcony door and the drapes. The two easels were still there, where he had left them. He knew what he had to do. Ramiro Pallares was good at finding solutions when everything seemed to be falling apart.

The most important things were to get Paloma out of the way and to protect the original painting.

He took it from the easel and rolled it up. Firmly and without a hint of hesitation, he gave Paloma a series of instructions. Surprisingly, although confused, she accepted his every word.

He calculated how long it would take Paloma to leave the building as he peered furtively out of the window. His brother was still in the same place, looking up and smoking a cigarette.

Ramiro went down to the hotel lobby. Through the glass of the revolving door, he watched Cristóbal cross the street and enter the hotel.

"I knew you'd come," said Ramiro.

"I knew you'd be expecting me," replied Cristóbal, taking a sly glance around the low lobby ceiling.

"There are no security cameras, Cristo," said Ramiro. "I don't tend to stay in places that record my image. I didn't learn much from Dad, but that's one thing I did."

"I have a gun," said Cristóbal.

"Let's go up," Ramiro said. "I'm not into public scandals."

Cristóbal smiled sarcastically. "Perhaps you learned more from Dad than you realize."

The short journey in the elevator was silent and tense. Unless Ramiro had miscalculated, Paloma should have been out of the building by now, with the painting under her arm.

"Please come in," said Ramiro with feigned politeness, as he opened the door to his room.

Cristóbal stood in front of the easel. His brother's forgery was astounding; he had managed to re-create the age of the piece perfectly. He drew closer, closed his eyes, and sniffed the pigments.

"Good, very good," he murmured, unable to help himself.

Ramiro's lips trembled slightly. He had waited his entire life to hear such praise from his older brother.

"Now, if you and your whore want a long, trouble-free life, you'd better give me the original," he said, then gestured at the half-finished forgery. "What you've done is very good. Some dumbass will buy it from you."

"I don't have the original anymore, nor does Paloma," lied Ramiro. He raised his hands and shrugged. "When I finish the forgery, you can have it, if you like. It's perfect for you. A fake Rivera and Kahlo for a fake Pallares."

Cristóbal looked at him with curiosity. He didn't know what his brother was getting at, but he knew that Ramiro wasn't prone to hyperbole.

"What do you mean?" he asked cautiously.

Calmly, but with one eye on Cristóbal's gun, he went to the chest of drawers where he kept his pencil sketches. Opening the top drawer, he took out one of his mother's orange-covered notebooks. A white label showed the word *GINA*, the pseudonym with which Elvira signed her writing. As soon as he saw the notebook, Cristóbal wanted to retch.

"Do you remember these notebooks?" asked Ramiro. "Mom was always writing in them. She noted down what she felt and what she saw—"

"And she burned them," Cristóbal cut in.

"Not all of them, Cristo. She didn't burn this one, for example." He sat in the armchair, crossed his legs, and opened the notebook. "I'd like to read you some extracts; it'll be a nice homage."

Ramiro couldn't halt the attack; Cristóbal was far stronger. He could barely put up a fight when his brother overpowered him and tied his wrists with two plastic cable ties.

"I'll give you three minutes to tell me where the original is. This is your last chance before I hurt every bone in your body. And oh boy, it'll hurt."

"Before you rip off the first bone, I recommend you read the marked page in Mom's notebook," asked Ramiro, projecting calm. He knew this was his silver bullet.

Cristóbal hesitated for a moment. He had always wanted to know everything about Elvira but had never had the chance. His mother was a secret.

He crouched to pick up the notebook from the floor. The mystery was in his hands. Ramiro's bones could wait a while.

He buried himself in the words written all those years before, his breathing becoming more agitated and his cheeks glowing red. An unnatural heat was developing in his guts.

"That's not true," he murmured.

He wanted to stop reading, but couldn't, turning the pages desperately. Eventually, Cristóbal sent the notebook flying in the hope that before it fell to the floor it would disintegrate, that none of what was written there would exist. It fell open at the marked page, shameless, obscene. He clasped his head in both hands. He was trembling. He walked to the door and punched it hard, giving a wild, guttural shout as he did. Then he spun around.

This is it, thought Ramiro, almost begging destiny to comply. The can of red paint Ramiro had prepared to complete the forgery was sitting on the floor between the two brothers.

The phone rang. They both looked at it, then Cristóbal picked up the can, turned, and flung it against the canvas. The red spilled over the lower corner of the painting. Ramiro smiled. His brother was the best, no doubt about it.

Cristo looked at the stain with astonishment, as though someone else had done it. Then he felt an overwhelming urge to flee, to escape his mother's revelation in the notebook. He kicked open the door and shot out like a whirlwind, his face contorted and red paint dripping from his fingers. He didn't even notice that the woman standing halfway down the corridor, whom he shoved against the wall, was Paloma; she had followed all of Ramiro's instructions except for one: leave the hotel.

"Paloma, Paloma! It's okay, I'm fine!" cried Ramiro.

The scene in the room was terrifying: there were red stains everywhere, and the coffee table was upturned. Ramiro smiled at me from the armchair, a calm, clear smile that jarred with the chaos around him.

"I'm tied up," he said, trying to move his arms.

I looked for a knife and cut the cable ties.

"And the painting?" he asked. The smile had disappeared now.

"I hid it under the bed in one of the rooms down the hallway, it's unlocked," I replied, dipping the tip of my index finger into one of the pools of red paint. For a moment, I had thought it was blood. "What happened, Rama?"

"Look at the easel, and you'll get it," he replied and ran out to look for my grandmother's painting.

I turned to look, and I understood. The forgery was almost complete.

Ramiro returned with the tube beneath his arm. He stretched out the painting on the other easel. Using his fingers in the wet paint, he copied the ballerina. Gradually, the two paintings started to look identical. While Ramiro made the finishing touches to the work, I set the table upright and used a cloth soaked in solvent to try to get the paint off the floor.

Tossed aside and spattered with paint was a notebook with an orange cover. The handwriting caught my attention: untidy, uneven, urgent. One of the pages had the corner folded down. Ramiro was still painting, as focused as ever. I shut myself in the bathroom with the notebook. Feeling slightly guilty, I began to read.

The difference between my sons is becoming increasingly painful. Although I tried my best to help Cristóbal escape his genes, I couldn't. I decided to carry him, give birth to him, love him. I gave him a father who, although strict, gave him that crucial surname in the art world: Pallares. And yet the beast has nested in his heart. I wasn't able to kill it, soothe it, make it disappear. Sometimes he looks at me distantly, but almost always with hatred, contempt, as though he knows, can imagine.

In Cristóbal's eyes I think I see his father, his real father. The man who hurt me, who forced himself on me, who defeated me, who broke me inside. May God give me the strength to stop the sparks of my rapist igniting in my son. . .

I snapped the notebook shut, unable to read any more. I decided to do the only thing I could for Elvira: respect the privacy of a woman who had done her best with the little she had.

Fury, hatred, and pain. That was what it took to emulate Frida's patch of paint. And Cristóbal was the man able to bring all those emotions to the table.

60

Coyoacán, July 1954

Diego had been standing for several hours facing the living room wall, clutching the gold ring his Friducha had given him hours earlier. He looked like a child in eternal penitence. "La niña Frida is dead," the nurse had told him. And since that moment, he had been begging the saints, in whom he didn't believe, to take him, too.

The news traveled the way all news traveled in Coyoacán, like wildfire. A mantle of sadness settled over Los Viveros, the market, the parks, and every street corner. Some locals hung black ribbons in their windows; others set out the skulls Frida had liked so much. Those who preferred song to tears improvised corrido ballads.

Joselito accompanied Nayeli to the corner of Londres and Allende. The Tehuana knew her orders: Frida had forbidden her to enter, but Nayeli wanted to be near, as near as possible.

The nurse opened the door and came out onto the sidewalk, in need of some fresh air. The atmosphere inside the house was too much to bear. She was sobbing, dabbing her eyes with a gauze cloth. Nayeli approached very slowly. She had been taught to respect other people's tears and, above all, not to interrupt them. Tears, like rivers, had to run freely until they dried up of their own accord. When the woman saw her, she smiled for the first time that day and beckoned Nayeli closer.

"Just look at you, my lovely girl, you're growing a belly already!" she exclaimed. "I assume you've heard . . . "

The Tehuana couldn't speak, and just nodded.

"Want to come in?"

"No, no. Frida's wishes have always been sacred to me, and she didn't want to see me ever again."

"But she can't see you now, Nayelita. Fridita is dead," the woman insisted.

"A person's wishes don't change just because they're dead, but there's something important I need you to do," she said, taking both the nurse's hands in hers. "Frida didn't want people to see her in any old dress, she had chosen a very special outfit."

"Of course, my dear. I'll do anything you ask."

Nayeli gave the nurse her instructions, then the two women said goodbye with a short embrace.

The nurse went to Frida's closet and then shut herself in the bedroom. For a second, she almost thought the painter was still alive. She looked more like a sleeping virgin with her relaxed expression, the shining hair, and hands on her chest. The nurse dressed her in a black velvet skirt and a huipil so white it dazzled. She braided her hair and decorated it with ribbons and flowers and placed a ring on each finger; Frida liked all her rings so much she often wore them all together.

"How beautiful you've made her!" said Diego from the door. "But I want to add one thing."

Rivera had aged ten years in just seven hours. His bulging eyes were black hollows; his hair had become thinner and whiter; and there was no color to his lips, they were just frozen, gray lines. He sat on the bed and fastened a string of jade stones around his wife's neck.

"It's a necklace from Tehuantepec. Green, like Nayeli's eyes."

He couldn't go on. Nor did he need to. It soothed him to know that Frida was leaving as what she was: a woman with the heart of a Tehuana. The nurse left the room so that Diego could say his goodbyes in privacy.

Nayeli was still on the corner, her gaze lost in the stones of the sidewalk. She was counting them until she reached one hundred. That was how Frida had taught her to count past the only numbers she knew. Every walk had been a lesson.

"Hey, Nayeli! Come over here!" called the nurse from the door of Casa Azul.

The young woman went over.

"I did what you asked. Frida looked beautiful in her dark skirt and her special ribbons."

They embraced again, this time for longer, tears dripping onto each other's shoulder. Before she left, Nayeli wanted to know something.

"What were Frida's last words?"

The nurse looked skyward and smiled, as though Frida had given some kind of permission from the beyond.

"I'll never forget them. Her voice was very feeble, but clear. 'I hope the exit is joyful—and I hope never to return.'"

Nayeli memorized those words as though they were a mantra, an amulet. She didn't know that many years later, far away from Coyoacán, that mantra would return to her lips in the end. Her own end.

61

Coyoacán, December 1954

Despite countless attempts, Eva had not become a mother. She used to say that children had evaded her, as though they were little rebels she couldn't pin down, children who refused to come to this world. She handled it with grace and irony, as though she didn't mind too much, showing the decorum and composure expected of her. Only Nayeli knew of her frustration; only she could smell the wounds of a mother-in-waiting. For years, she had heard Frida's heartbroken, animal howls after every miscarriage, every month when her uterus informed her it was business as usual.

Days before Nayeli gave birth, they had made a bet. Eva was convinced it would be a girl, while the Tehuana swore the baby in her belly was male.

"What shall we bet?" asked Eva. "We have to make it worthwhile. There's no point if no one wins and no one loses."

"You're right. Let me choose which of all your beautiful things I'm going to keep," said Nayeli, laughing. She was sure she would have a boy and that he would be called Miguel, like her father.

"I've got it!" exclaimed La Güera, pretending to have just thought of something that she had actually been planning for some time. "If you have a girl, you have to come with me to Argentina."

Nayeli laughed so hard she had to grab hold of her bulging belly.

"My belly went hard, you made me laugh so much, Eva," she said as she leaned back in the armchair in the miniature workshop at the Garmendia mansion.

"It wasn't a joke. It's a proposal, a very serious proposal," said Eva.

The journey she had been planning for so long with her husband, Leopoldo Aragón, was taking shape. The young diplomat had been appointed to Mexico's embassy in Buenos Aires.

"We have a lovely house waiting for us in Argentina, and lots of new things to discover. What will you do here, Nayeli? Have you forgotten that very soon you'll be alone and with a child to raise?"

"I can work, Eva. I've always worked. I'm a cook, and a very good one," she said adamantly. "Besides, I can reach out to Frida's friends; they'll help me."

Eva didn't usually lose her composure. She had been raised to hide what was in her heart, but in front of her friend, she allowed herself the luxury of speaking her mind. She paced from side to side like a caged lioness. She tugged the ribbon out of her hair and waved it in the air. Her very white face flushed, and her eyes sparked.

"And where are Frida's friends, hmm? Let's see, show me, I can't see them. Do you have them hidden somewhere? Did they come to get you so you could say goodbye to her? Have they asked after you and your baby?" As the questions spilled from her mouth, her tone became sharper. "And Diego? Where's Diego? You won't see him again, Nayeli, not him or any of Frida's friends. You're persona non grata at Casa Azul. Think with your head and think of your child."

La Güera was right, and Nayeli knew it. Her words hurt even more than the stabbing pains in her lower stomach and back. She tried to stand, overpowered by a mysterious urge to open her legs. She strained, hands on her knees, and a dark, warm liquid slipped down her legs to the floor. Before she could react, La Güera was by her side.

"Easy, Nayeli, easy. It's coming; it's coming." She helped her get comfortable. "I'll be right back. I'm going to fetch Doña Leonora, she'll know what to do."

La Güera seemed to be gone for an eternity. Nayeli felt a tightening in her very depths that took her breath away, growing more and more intense. She filled her lungs and blew out hard, inhaled again and exhaled again. She felt hot and cold at the same time, trembling hard. She leaned back against the edge of the sofa and slid down until she was sitting on the floor, legs parted. She could feel her child straining to come out, and she knew she had to help, but she didn't know how.

She clamped her eyes and teeth shut and let her mind travel far, far away. The hills, the red and green earth, the flowers, the River Tehuantepec, her house. Her mother, her godmother, her sister. They were close; she could hear them. Another violent pain, stronger this time, but this time telling her what she had to do. With all her strength, she pushed with her lower body. She looked down: her gigantic belly was misshapen. She closed her eyes again; she knew the way now.

The voices of several women were guiding her. Her women, those who had raised her, who had made her the woman she was. Frida's voice rang out above all the others: "*Women are the ones who know about death and birth; they can show you the route.*" Nayeli nodded. She bore down again and cried out.

The moment of relief didn't come in solitude. Just as she was gasping to recover her breath, La Güera reappeared beside her and held her shoulders.

"That's it, Nayelita. Go on, take a deep breath. I'm here," she murmured, her mouth close to her ear.

Doña Leonora's expert hands maneuvered between her legs, until they heard the cry. A sharp, profound, vital cry.

"Very good, very good, my dear! You've done a marvelous job!" said Doña Leonora, bringing the baby up to Nayeli's chest.

Warmth. Skin, bones, blood. A shock of chocolate-colored hair on a perfect head. The scent of herbs. The medicinal herbs of Tehuantepec.

"I won! I won!" exclaimed La Güera, laughing and crying at the same time. "It's a girl, a beautiful girl!"

The new mother rested her mouth against the perfumed crown of her daughter's head. She wanted to laugh; she wanted to cry; she wanted to shout; she wanted to dance. But she did none of those things. She turned her head to lock eyes with her friend Eva Felipa Garmendia.

"This girl is blessed, Nayeli," said Eva, emotionally. "Today is December twenty-fourth, Christmas Eve, the eve of the birth of Jesus."

The Tehuana opened her green eyes wider.

"I hadn't thought of that, Eva. We'll say she was born on November twenty-fourth. I don't want her to compete with the baby Jesus—that isn't right."

"What are you saying? This girl is even more important than the baby Jesus!" exclaimed Eva, chuckling.

Nayeli placed one gentle hand on her daughter's tiny, damp head and stroked her friend's cheek with the other. She had just made a decision.

"Her name will be Felipa, and she'll grow up in Argentina. We Cruz women keep our bets. We're women of our word."

62

Buenos Aires, February 2019

Cándida was waiting for me with a smile and a complaint, as usual. "Did you bring me a nice bottle for my nightcap?"

Not only had I bought her some wine, but also two illustrated poetry books, which I knew she would love. She deserved it: Cándida had duped Cristóbal. Despite her age, infirmities, and a body that rarely did what her brain told it to, she had come out of her ordeal unharmed.

"I played dead, my dear. That great hulk won't get one over on me!" she repeated proudly. "And he made some ugly threats, you know; he went through the whole house, pretty much ransacked the place. He was looking for you, shouting 'Where's Paloma?' And I stayed quiet. He even slapped me, the big coward. But then he found the little notebook with the address in Recoleta and off he went. After everything I've seen in my life, Palomita, I defend myself as best I can. I used to do it with my hands. Now I use my intelligence."

I had invited her to spend a few days at my house, until she was fully recovered from the shock. Although she played it tough, I knew that deep down she must still be afraid. Whenever the doorbell rang, or someone on the TV shouted too loudly, or the neighbor's dog barked, Cándida would jump and rub her skinny arms with her hands.

The police took less than twenty-four hours to find and arrest Cristóbal. The court revoked his parole, and he returned to prison. But Ramiro had been very clear that we must continue with the plan. He was adamant that Cristóbal's arrest wasn't the end of the story, that the brains of the operation wouldn't stop until they had the original painting in their possession, and that we were going to fulfill their fantasy.

The fake painting, inside the red tube, was still on the dining room table in my house, Nayeli's house, guarded by a fruit bowl and a couple of aromatic candles. The real one was safe in a bank security box in my name.

"My dear, are you going to leave that red whatchamacallit on the table for much longer? You have to be tidier—your grandmother didn't raise you to live in squalor," said Cándida every time she went to the kitchen to heat water for her yerba mate.

Her nagging finally prompted me into action. Without overthinking it, gritting my teeth like someone taking a dose of bitter medicine, I picked up the phone and told my mother I was back from my trip and that I had Nayeli's painting for her. I repeated the word *inheritance* twice, knowing she would love to hear it.

I expected her to suggest one of her favorite bars or restaurants, but she didn't. Felipa liked to show that she was unpredictable, surprising, and that I would never be able to second-guess her. She said she hadn't driven for a long time and felt like going out in her car. I couldn't persuade her otherwise.

She waited for me parked on the sidewalk. She didn't want to come into the house that had been Nayeli's; she didn't even get out of the car. The dents in the bodywork revealed her carelessness at the wheel; to her, they were prizes to be shown off; to me, one of the many extravagances she used to disguise her madness.

For the first time, I didn't worry too much about my appearance. Since I was a child, I had always tried to look pretty, neat, clean, and well dressed, all so that my mother would love me. Anything that might deprive me of her acceptance terrified me. But this time I gave up on the impossible: I would never shine in her eyes. Black jeans, a white tank top, red sneakers, and, the only accessory, tied around my neck, a mustard-colored silk scarf that had belonged to Nayeli. I left my hair loose, uncombed.

"Lovely, Paloma! Your skin is glowing; I like that casual look," she said as I sat in the passenger seat.

I hadn't even fastened my seat belt, and Felipa was disconcerting me with praise. I murmured a timid and not-entirely-convinced *Thank you*, and showed her the red tube.

"I brought Abuela's painting. You have to be careful with it. It's very old and delicate. I don't know if you want to frame it or not, but if you do, best take it somewhere good," I said and regretted it. Whenever I lie, I make the mistake of talking too much, giving explanations no one asked for.

"I'll give it some thought," she said, setting off with her chest pressed up against the wheel and her eyes fixed on the street.

What a good liar my mother is, I thought.

She didn't even glance at the tube containing the painting that, as she was perfectly well aware, was worth millions of dollars. The cool calm of her deceit was disturbing.

"We're here," she announced.

"What are we doing here, Mom?" I asked. We had pulled up outside Casa Solanas.

Felipa didn't reply. She took a lipstick from her purse, touched up her mouth, and refreshed her perfume. She got out of the car and, before slamming the door shut, told me to bring the tube with Nayeli's painting. I obeyed, more out of curiosity than submissiveness.

As always, Gloria was sitting at her table under the parasol, occupying her post as guardian. She raised her head from her half-finished crossword, and her jaw dropped at the sight of my mother and me arriving together. I went over to say hello, but Felipa ignored her and, making an exaggerated noise with her heels on the floor, crossed the courtyard to the entrance. I trotted after her, tube clutched to my chest.

When we reached the door of Eva Garmendia's room, my suspicions were confirmed: my mother was a regular here.

She knocked gently three times on the wooden door. "Eva, it's Felipa," she said in an uncharacteristically sweet tone.

Eva opened the door and smiled. They hugged each other long and tight, which filled me with envy. My mother had never held me so urgently. For a second, she seemed to let her body go limp, as though she needed to be held up. Eva was her support.

"Hello, Paloma. Welcome," Eva said without a smile or enthusiasm, although the gleam in her eyes confirmed she wasn't lying. For the first time, I did genuinely feel welcome in her kingdom.

As soon as I entered the room, I realized that Eva had been expecting us. On the glass-topped table, she had arranged a few plates of food: little sandwiches—crusts removed—and butter cookies, as well as a steaming teapot and three cups with saucers and teaspoons.

"Take a seat," she said. "I only have two chairs but we can use the bed."

My mother took one of the chairs, picked up a plate, and scrutinized the sandwiches. She finally went for ham and egg.

"Oh, Eva! These are my favorites!" she exclaimed before taking the first bite.

"I know, my dear," replied Eva with satisfaction.

I perched on the edge of the bed, feeling like someone attending a party where everyone's dancing to a song she doesn't know. I was still clutching the tube against my chest. It was the only thing I could cling to in order to stop myself from feeling so lost.

"Mom, can you explain what we're doing here?" I asked.

Eva smiled as she poured the tea.

"We've come to visit Eva, Paloma," Felipa replied, wiping her mouth with a linen napkin.

"I'm not in the mood for visiting, Mom. I called you to give you what you asked for," I said, my voice rising. My patience was running out by the minute.

Eva returned the teapot to the tray and twisted around to fix her gaze on me.

"You're just like your grandmother," she declared.

"And I'm very proud of that," I replied defensively.

"Rightly so. Nayeli was a wonderful woman."

My mother stood up. She smoothed down her pleated skirt and tugged her linen jacket.

"Now, now, let's stay calm, my dears."

I raised my eyebrows. My mother was incapable of swimming in waters that she herself had muddied. Silence was her habitual escape, but this time she was determined to speak. She gestured at the red tube and said, "Paloma, take out the painting."

I opened the lid and unrolled the painting, alarmed. What was my mother up to? Carefully, I held the canvas from each of the top corners and took a deep breath.

"The history of the Cruz women is contained in that painting," said Eva, without taking her eyes off it.

Questions cascaded into my mind, but my mother's reaction struck me dumb. Felipa raised her arms above her head, her long, slim fingers in a posture so fabulous they seemed like butterfly wings. She kicked off her shoes and stood on tiptoe, stretched out her neck, and raised her chin. She fixed her gaze on her imaginary audience. In her head, the music only she heard began to play, and, with slow spins and tiny steps, she started to dance. For the first time, far from annoying me, her madness made me want to cry.

"She isn't here, Paloma," said Eva gently. "Your mother is dancing far away. It's good to let her take her trip and wait patiently for her to return."

"I'm tired of being patient." I put the painting down on the bed and used the back of my hand to dry my tears.

"That's not like your grandmother. What a pity you didn't inherit her virtues!"

"Who are the Cruz women?" I asked.

Eva came and sat by my side on the bed. She ran her hand down my cheek and let me rest my head on her shoulder. She still smelled of roses, that aroma that had fascinated me when she visited my grandmother during my childhood.

"The Cruz women saved my life, or to put it another way, they gave my life meaning. I rescued your grandmother, and she rescued me. It was in another life, another country, another world."

"In Mexico?" I asked.

"In Mexico," she replied.

As my mother continued dancing in her imaginary theater, Eva started to tell her story, a story in which she was La Güera, a girl born sad and destined for even greater sadness.

"Your grandmother used to be fascinated by my house, my clothes, my perfumes, my makeup. At the same time, I was fascinated by her drive, her courage, her freedom, and her character. All my good points were obscured by my lack of guts, and Nayeli had guts to spare."

I needed to straighten up and look in her eyes. I didn't want to miss a single detail.

"You remind me of your grandmother. She always sat up straight like that to listen to stories; she loved a good story."

I was desolate at those words. It's strange when we discover that we use the gestures and mannerisms of people who are no longer with us. All I could do was smile.

"Your grandmother was a cook for Frida Kahlo," she said, and immediately fell silent. Although I had suspected as much, the confirmation shocked me.

"She never told me," I managed to murmur.

"Nayeli was good at collecting secrets, the best." She smiled tenderly and gestured at the painting. "That painting changed her life. I can't say whether for better or worse, but it changed it. When Frida discovered that Diego had painted her, she was furious . . . "

"Was she jealous of my grandmother?" I asked in surprise.

"No. Frida wasn't that kind of woman, but she was dying, and when death is breathing down our neck, it can change us. It wasn't jealousy, no. Frida felt betrayed. While she was withering like a dry, old branch, Nayeli was blooming, with your mother in her belly. So Frida threw her out."

"She left her without a job?"

"More than that. She didn't allow her to say goodbye. There's no greater punishment, my dear, than not being able to say goodbye to our loved ones."

My mother was still dancing. Every now and then she paused, enjoying the applause in her imagination.

"It's nice to see her happy," said Eva, gazing at my mother.

I didn't respond, but she was right. There's something magical about people who are able to create their own inner world.

"And then what happened?" I asked, resting my hand on her leg. I was afraid she might escape into my mother's world, too. Afraid of being left alone again.

Eva picked up her tale in seconds. Her memory was an elastic band that stretched with ease.

"Frida Kahlo's send-off was monumental, and strange. I was surprised so many people loved her so much."

"Were you there?"

"Of course I was! My husband was invited by people at the Museo Nacional de Bellas Artes, although to be honest, I only went so that I could tell Nayeli all about it. She had asked me to be her eyes. It took place in the museum's entrance hall. The casket holding Frida's body was placed on a black cloth that covered the whole floor, surrounded by bouquets of red roses." She paused and stifled a laugh. "The most scandalous thing back then was the flag that Diego and Siqueiros stretched over the coffin. I still remember the visitors' faces, and I still laugh about it. They covered Frida with a red flag, with the hammer, sickle, and star. A communist send-off."

"And what about my grandmother?" I asked.

I remembered that one of the many things that drove Nayeli to fury was not being invited somewhere. She used to say that her own absence was what caused her the most pain.

"Your grandmother stayed in my house that day. Your grandfather Joselito had been sent to northern Mexico by the railroad company he worked for, and I didn't want her to be left alone," she replied.

I was surprised when she mentioned my grandfather Joselito. Nayeli talked about him very little, hardly at all. To her, we were always "the Cruz women." But I didn't want to interrupt, and Eva kept talking.

"My husband went up to Diego and offered his condolences, and I did the same. For a few seconds I thought he knew who I was. We had met when I was a teenager, but that's another story. He held out his hand; I took it. His skin was cold, like a dead man's. Rivera died along with Frida; there was no blood running through his veins. It was very sad to see him that way. I was glad that Nayeli wasn't there. She had suffered enough from that marriage. Although, well, she still had to suffer a little more."

"What happened?"

"It was a very sad situation. And all because of your grandfather."

I was touched to see that she was angry. Despite the years, her friend's pain still angered her.

"With the greatest respect, Paloma, Joselito was a scoundrel. First, he said his work trip would last a week. After two weeks, he called to tell her he would be another week. After that, he sent a short letter that didn't make any mention of returning. In the last line, he wished Nayeli luck with the birth and sent his love. Your grandmother made me read her the letter ten times, hoping to find some spark of hope in those words. But there was nothing."

"So he didn't come back?" I asked sadly. Although I had never been particularly interested in my grandfather, I felt orphaned and abandoned. I wanted to share the rejection with Nayeli.

Eva fluttered her bony hands with their white gold rings.

"Hardly. We never heard from that worm again. He didn't even get in touch to find out whether it was a boy or a girl."

"That's what men are like, Palomita! Don't you forget it!" exclaimed my mother, raising one of her shapely legs.

I had forgotten she was there, as had Eva. But I liked the fact that she was listening to the tale; this was her story, too. To prevent her from disappearing back into her own invented world, I picked up a topic that would interest her.

"What about Nayeli's painting? How did it come into her possession?" I asked.

Eva stood up and moved her legs with difficulty. The painting was still stretched out on the bed.

“I stole it for her,” she replied matter-of-factly.

My mother loved that reply and burst out laughing. She liked decisive attitudes in other people. I imagine she liked not being the only extravagant one. Eva laughed, too.

“Don’t look at me like that!” she exclaimed, amused. “Who said a woman of my class can’t be a thief once in a while!”

63

Coyoacán, February 1955

Baby gowns, caps, ribbons, flowers, embroidery: La Güera barely stopped, pausing only to nibble on some fruit and cheese. Baby Felipa would have the best layette in all of Mexico, and her godmother would take care of it.

"But Eva, that's more than enough clothes. This little girl will be spoiled!" exclaimed Nayeli, fascinated with the beautiful garments that adorned her daughter like a queen.

"Let's hope so! Felipita will be the most spoiled and the most beautiful. A little Tehuana from head to toe," she replied, tirelessly designing, cutting, and sewing one piece after another. "And I'm going to make you some dresses, too. You only have two skirts and three huipils—"

"And a shawl," interrupted Nayeli.

"And a shawl, yes. Are your clothes still at Casa Azul?" she asked.

Nayeli nodded sadly. The afternoon when Frida threw her out, she had no opportunity to explain herself, or to collect her belongings.

"Yes. My clothes don't matter, but I would like to have the basket with my mementos of Tehuantepec."

Eva tied back her hair and put away the patterns and pieces of fabric that were piling up on her work table.

"Feed the baby. We're going to Casa Azul," she announced so firmly that Nayeli couldn't refuse.

Eva's driver took them to Coyoacán. As they progressed through the narrow, cobbled streets and the aroma of lime trees filled the car, Nayeli felt like crying. That was the moment she realized that Tehuantepec was no longer her home. Her home was the land of coyotes.

Eva stepped out of the car with the airs of a lady. No one enjoyed showing her class as much as she did. Nayeli followed, Felipa in her arms.

The door to Casa Azul was open, as usual. Out of courtesy, La Güera knocked twice and, without waiting for an answer, went in.

"Keep going to the other side of the courtyard," Nayeli told her.

In the hall, they bumped into Doña María, who was in charge of the cleaners. When she saw Nayeli, she broke into a wide, friendly smile and welcomed them in, offering them tea, hot chocolate, bread rolls, and hugs and caresses for little Felipa.

"Thank you very much, señora, but we don't need anything to eat or drink. We've come to collect the belongings of Señorita Cruz."

No one had ever called her "Señorita Cruz" before, but Nayeli liked the fact that her surname was starting to define her. Doña María looked uncomfortable, but she accepted Eva's request and allowed them in.

"Of course." She looked at Nayeli, her smile fading. "You can go to your room and fetch your things."

Casa Azul no longer smelled of Frida. Nor of her tobacco or perfume. Most of the doors were shut, the house no more than a ghost of walls and ceilings.

"These floors are beautiful!" conceded Eva, who had always found Frida Kahlo's aesthetics rather vulgar. "It's very spacious, and there's plenty of light."

"At the back, Eva. That's where my things are," instructed Nayeli.

When they crossed the kitchen, the Tehuana halted suddenly. The pots and pans, the ladles and dishes were no longer in their usual places. It had been completely stripped. There was no trace of the aromas of stews, soups, tortillas. The kitchen was dead.

Nayeli then entered what had been her bedroom. The bed was still unmade, just as she had left it all that time ago. Dust balls had formed in the corners, and the sheen of the wooden desk and closet was dulled by dust. She placed Felipa carefully in Eva's arms. La Güera's face softened, as it did whenever she held that babe, whom she loved as though she had given birth to her.

The basket was still in the same corner. Nayeli emptied it out on the bed. The red Tehuana dress from her childhood, her first coin necklace, the pink velvet box and the empty bottle of Shocking de Schiaparelli perfume that Frida had given her, the yellow and blue pencils she had used to practice punctuation, and her red notebook of memories. Right at the bottom, hooked onto the basket, was her sister's amulet: a leather cord with an obsidian stone dangling from it. She unhooked it and kissed the stone, then went over to her daughter and held it up in front of her eyes.

"This will be for you, my Felipa," she murmured. "It will protect you forever."

Eva smiled, still gazing, entranced by the little girl who seemed to understand every word her mother said.

"Come on, Nayeli! Put your things away while I take the opportunity for a little wander around the house," she announced. "I'll take the baby; she's restless."

The door at the end of the corridor was ajar. Eva glanced over her shoulders to check that Doña María was still busy in the yard. Without thinking twice, she entered. It was a very small room, furnished with a bed and a little table against the wall. In the middle stood a wooden easel. The floor was stained with red paint. *What uncouth people! Ruining such a fabulous floor!* she thought as she circled the easel.

When she saw Nayeli's painting, she understood Frida's anger: there was no denying its eroticism. She carefully propped Felipa up against the bed, rolled up the canvas, and smiled. Her emotionless upbringing had given her an irrefutable pragmatism, and the years of overhearing talk of money had taught her something: Diego and Frida were two of the most valuable artists in Mexico, and time would convert that value into money. This painting would guarantee Nayeli's future; what's more, it would guarantee baby Felipa's as well.

64

Buenos Aires, February 2019

Eva, my mother, and I were like guests at a funeral, the three of us gathered around the bed, contemplating the painted image of Nayeli. A young, beautiful, erotic, and hidden Nayeli.

"And I wasn't wrong in my prediction," continued Eva. "The work became immensely valuable, but Nayeli categorically refused to sell it—she didn't even want to be reminded of its existence. And when she decided something, there was no changing her mind."

My mother and I laughed together; we both knew the truth of Eva's words.

"Why didn't she want to make any money from the painting?" I asked.

"Initially, she said it was because she was too embarrassed to let the world see her naked; then later she claimed that no one would care about a hurried painting made without the consent of the model, and all sorts of other nonsense I can't remember. I think the truth was that your grandmother didn't want to profit from Frida's pain, and that painting is full of the poor woman's pain."

We listened closely to Eva, without taking our eyes off Nayeli.

"Nayeli was always very dignified," she said emotionally. "You had a wonderful mother and grandmother. And I say that in spite of the long period when we weren't on good terms."

"Why not?" I asked, filled with curiosity.

"Because my mother didn't understand my world," replied Felipa. "She couldn't see the theater I danced in, couldn't hear the applause I heard. She didn't appreciate that, although I might have been wearing my school skirt and blouse, in my imagination I was in a leotard and tutu. She wasn't being mean; she just couldn't see it. She thought I was crazy. And I was just a ballerina."

I was shocked to hear my mother's words. It dawned on me that I had never seen a ballerina in her either. Eva Garmendia was the only one who could pull back the veil.

"Invisible ballerinas have to be left where they are," said Eva, "on their stages, with their audience. They're like fairies. You have to believe in them. If you don't believe in fairies, then the fairies die."

"And no one wants fairies to die," concluded Felipa, before issuing a piercing shriek. "This isn't Nayeli's painting!"

My soul plunged to my feet. How could my mother possibly have known that this was a forgery?

Eva sat on the bed and put on the glasses hanging from a chain around her neck. "What are you saying, Felipa? Of course it's her painting!"

My mother's polished nail pointed at the corner of the canvas, at the edge of the red stain.

"Look at this little mark—look at it closely. I spent years looking at the red ballerina, and that little mark was never there!" she declared, still shouting.

It was all I could do to keep my composure. My mother was right: the little mark was the crucifix that Cristóbal added to every work he forged, the shape of his mother's earrings. Ramiro had hidden that detail from me. I should have been angry, but I wasn't. His plan was masterful. He had signed the fake work with his brother's signature, which meant that he and I were in no way connected to it. But now I had another problem to solve: my mother.

"I don't know, Mom. This is the painting I found in Abuela's old filing cabinet . . . "

I felt Eva's eyes stripping me bare. For a moment, I thought she might pounce like a lioness and devour my neck, but she didn't. Instead, she turned her attention to my mother.

"Felipa, my precious, it's been years since you saw this work. Perhaps you've forgotten a detail or you're—"

"I never forget details. I live for the details. I'm almost a detail myself," she said, slowly skirting the bed and coming to stand next to me. "Paloma, honey, I'm going to do what I need to do with this fake, but you have a mission, and you're going to carry it out while I cover for you."

Eva smiled. At the same time, my heart started to beat normally again. My mother, my ally.

"I'm listening, Mom," I said with relief.

She sat on the bed, placed her palms on the picture of her mother, and repeated the phrase Nayeli had written on the canvas that had protected the painting for so many years:

"I don't want anyone to see what's inside me when my body breaks. I want to return to the blue paradise. That's all I want."

I nodded in silence and placed my hands on her shoulders. The decision was made: I would travel to Mexico City, to Frida Kahlo's Casa Azul, to scatter my grandmother's ashes. Perhaps it was the tears, perhaps it was the emotion, but for a moment, I could see my mother dressed in tulle. I could see the ballerina.

Sources

Chapter 1:
Buenos Aires, August 2018

4 *"I hope the exit is joyful"*: Frida Kahlo, *El diario de Frida Kahlo: un íntimo autorretrato*, introducción de Carlos Fuentes (México D.F.: La Vaca Independiente, 2017), 285.

Chapter 15:
Coyoacán, January 1940

77 *"Diego—the beginning"*: Kahlo, *El diario de Frida Kahlo,* 235.

Chapter 26:
Coyoacán, August 1940

148 *"Yo no tengo ni madre ni padre que sufran mi pena"*: "El huerfanito," by Cuarteto Machín, recorded October 29,1931, Victor matrix BRC-70915.

Chapter 28:
San Francisco, September 1940

157 *"No, I paint myself because I'm always alone"*: Hayden Herrera, *Frida: una biografía de Frida Kahlo*, prólogo de Valeria Luiselli, trans. Anjelika Scherp (Madrid: Taurus, 2020), 104.

Chapter 30:
San Francisco, September 1940

167 *"Mexico is the same as ever"*: Frida Kahlo, letter from Frida to Dr. Eloesser, November 1931, in *Frida Kahlo: me pinto a mí misma*, (ed.) Josefina García Hernández (México D.F.: Museo Dolores Olmedo, 2017), 14.

167 *"Gringolandia is driven by high society"*: Frida Kahlo, letter from Frida to Dr. Eloesser, June 1931, in Herrera, *Frida*, 168.

Chapter 34: San Francisco, September 1940

189 *"I was never a faithful husband":* Diego Rivera and Gladys Stevens March, *Diego Rivera: mi arte, mi vida*, trans. H. González Herrero (México, D.F.: Ediciones Herrero, 1963), 175–176.

189 *"I didn't divorce Frida because I didn't love her"*: Diego Rivera and Gladys Stevens March, *Diego Rivera,* 175–176.

190 *"Of course not"*: Diego Rivera and Gladys Stevens March, *Diego Rivera*, 175–176.

190 *"Have you seen what women are like around me?"*: Diego Rivera and Gladys Stevens March, *Diego Rivera*, 224.

Chapter 35: Coyoacán, January 1941

197 *"Diego is basically a sad person"*: Anita Brenner, letter to Frida Kahlo, September 1940, Frida Kahlo Archive, cited in Herrera, *Frida*, 399.

Chapter 37: Coyoacán, April 1944

216 *"We need another revolution"*: Diego Rivera, letter from Diego to Frida, December 1938, in Wolfe D. Beltram, *La Fabulosa vida de Diego Rivera*, trans. Mario Bracamonte (México D.F.: Diana, 1994), 289.

217 *"My paintings represent the sincerest expression"*: Herrera, *Frida*, 350.

Chapter 39: Coyoacán, May 1944

229 *"Ay, bigu xi pé scarú"*: Traditional. "La Tortuga," Isthmus of Tehuantepec, Mexico. "Oh, oh, turtle, so beautiful / but better in a mole sauce / or roasted in the oven. / How delicious if I could eat it today!"

Chapter 46: Coyoacán, August 1949

268 *"I wish I could do whatever I liked"*: Kahlo, *El diario de Frida Kahlo*, 242.

Chapter 53: Coyoacán, August 1953

297 *"Frida's death is quite near"*: Herrera, *Frida*, 533.

298 "*With friendship and love*": Invitation from the personal archive of Arturo Garcia Bustos, in Herrera, *Frida*, 534.

301 *"I have wings to spare"*: Kahlo, *El diario de Frida Kahlo*, 276.

Chapter 55: Coyoacán, August 1953

308 *"I am very worried"*: Kahlo, *El diario de Frida Kahlo*, 277.

Chapter 56: Coyoacán, June 1954

314 *"If I were brave"*: Private interview with Raquel Tibol, in Herrera, *Frida*, 556.

Chapter 58: Coyoacán, June 1954

323 *"My imaginary friend was"*: Kahlo, *El diario de Frida Kahlo*, 246.

Chapter 60: Coyoacán, July 1954

331 *"I hope the exit is joyful"*: Kahlo, *El diario de Frida Kahlo*, 285.

Author's note

Nayeli Cruz never existed. She was a device I dreamed up to allow me to delve into the fascinating world of Tehuanas and the Day of the Dead, to feel the textures and tastes of a land bursting with flavor, to feel for myself the pains and passions that followed a revolution and the people who experienced it. Nevertheless, the story of Frida's cook could not have been told without consulting biographical and historical materials of incalculable value. Books that were the launchpad for me to take the leap, that propelled me forward.

In the name of fiction, many of the stories were modified and adjusted, not just in time but also in form. Here are the materials I used as tickets for this journey: *La fabulosa vida de Diego Rivera* by Bertram D. Wolfe; *Heridas: amores de Diego Rivera* by Martha Zamora; *Diego Rivera: mi arte, mi vida* by Diego Rivera and Gladys Stevens March; *Tu hija Frida: cartas a mamá* (compilation, introductions, and notes by Héctor Jaimes); *Frida Kahlo: me pinto a mí misma* by Josefina García Hernández; *El diario de Frida Kahlo: un íntimo autorretrato* (introduction by Carlos Fuentes); *Frida Kahlo: dolor y pasión* by Andrea Kettenmann; *La tehuana* (issue 49 of the magazine *Artes de México*); *Día de Muertos* (issue 62 of the magazine *Artes de México*); *Frida: una biografía de Frida Kahlo* (prologue by Valeria Luiselli) by Hayden Herrera; *Cocina esencial de México* by Diana Kennedy; *Frida Kahlo: la belleza terrible* by Gérard de Cortanze; *Arte y falsificación en América Latina* by Daniel Schávelzon; *El istmo mexicano: una región inasequible* (coords.: Emilia Velázquez, Eric Léonard, Odile Hoffmann, and M. F. Prévôt-Schapira), and *El Maestro: Revista de Cultura Nacional* (1921–1923).

I visited each of the places I describe, and my every step gave me the sense that many of the stories I tell in this book still pulsate through every Mexican man and woman, because Mexico works its way into your heart and never leaves. It remains there hidden, nesting, and manifests itself in the form of a longing to return. A great longing, always.

Buenos Aires, May 2021

About the Author

FLORENCIA ETCHEVES is an award-winning journalist, writer, and news presenter. She is also the author of several novels, two of which have been made into feature films, *Perdida* (*Lost*) and Netflix's *La Corazonada*. Follow her on Instagram @FloEtcheves.